Labyrinth of Chaos

Labyrinth of Chaos

Brian Wallace

NEW FALCON PUBLICATIONS
TEMPE, ARIZONA, U.S.A.

International Standard Book Number: 1-56184-148-X
Library of Congress Catalog Card Number: 00-104166

First Edition 2000

Cover by John Wagler

The paper used in this publication meets the minimum requirements of the American National Standard for Permanence of Paper for Printed Library Materials Z39.48-1984.

Address all inquiries to:
NEW FALCON PUBLICATIONS
1739 East Broadway Road #1 PMB 277
Tempe, AZ 85282 U.S.A.
(or)
320 East Charleston Blvd. • Suite 204 PMB 286
Las Vegas, NV 89104 U.S.A.
website: http://www.newfalcon.com
email: info@newfalcon.com

DEDICATION

I dedicate this novel to the women I love far beyond the stars:

My mother, Pamela Ann, and my wife, Cherie Marie.

ACKNOWLEDGMENTS

To Ann Knupp, for providing the keys.

To Jack Fitzsimmons and George Coelen, for opening the doors.

To my friends and family, for editing feedback and showing me the way.

To my father, for the love of words and the ideal to question authority and follow my dreams.

Especially, to Todd and Cara, for title development, and Nicholas, for feedback.

To Lupe, Michael, actress Sarah Wallace, Brenda, Billy, and Charlotte, Nadine and Red, Karen and Jean.

To the Marshes, Joglars, Fairlys and Finleys, for love and support.

To Luz Alonso, for French inspirations.

To Laura, Rita, Frank, and all my California pals.

To Kim Novicki for constant love and support.

To Jeff Libby, Jeremy Lieberman, Lindsey Hunt, and Rob Reuter, for astounding humor and friendship.

To Shrayashi Jariwala, for invaluable ideas, friendship, and technical support. My "Secare Mysterorum" girl.

To Waldo Martin for invaluable comments and conversation.

To Cheryl Reicin and staff, for advice.

To Robert Walter, for the use of quotes (from *The Masks Of God: Occidental Mythology,* Penguin Arkana, 1991, copyright 1964 by Joseph Campbell) with the permission of the Joseph Campbell Foundation (www.jcf.org).

To Dave, Kelly, and Constance, graphic artists who paved the way.

To Nicholas Tharcher, for believing in this project.

Special thanks to Jeffrey Brewer and his family, without whom, this book would not have been possible.

In memory of Alex Mathas, Bill Gannon, and Tim Leary.

TABLE OF CONTENTS

CHAPTER I

A fiery red streak shoots out across the late afternoon sky, leaving a tracer trail of alternately fibrillating and soothing retinal images. The images hypnotically give way to undeniably rapturous, euphoric sensations that systematically penetrate every cell, permeate every muscle, and catapult normal waking consciousness into seemingly perpetual reverie—or oneiromantic ocular orgasms, if you will. Images of primarily basic geometric shapes gradually metamorphose into various geodesic, mosaic patterns that assume verisimilitude to ancient Oriental rug designs in brilliant hues of reds, oranges, and yellows. Horizontal, vertical counterpoints of architecture emerge. Vast, ubiquitous walls of stone simultaneously enclose and distance the human soul and precipitate flashes of illuminated pictures of bucolic, pastoral sunsets at the beach out West with children playing and the iridescent glow of the moon after a tumultuous nocturnal rainfall. All of these visual delights and cognitive cocktails emanate from the microscopic, fleeting specks of light that originate from...

Where? a lamp post? a bicycle reflector? a... an ambulance!?! An ambulance—that hopelessly morose reminder that we are, after all, mortal—that life is ephemeral: that this mortal coil is often as fragile as an egg shell; that when your number's up your number's up; that for some, the one with the most toys wins; that when their insurance runs up they go belly up; that for some, no, many, the funny looking white box with flashing red lights careening down the highway is their last transport or one way ticket to the glorious, beatific afterlife—or horror chamber—depending on where one stands with the higher power.

For a moment, our dear friend ponders the existential problem of death. At times like these, when his mind and body were in the throes of near cataclysmic ecstasy, it was of course somewhat a nuisance to be bothered by something as somber and morose as death. Oh well! He reticently decides to call up, or allow to fester—depending on how you look at it—one last memento of the grim reaper before returning to the eternal moment of sentient fulfillment. He introspectively recalls the humorous,

moving poem written by his uncle a few years ago before he succumbed
to the hideous attack of prostate cancer:

Death is knocking and I cannot seem to hear
For the epiphanic memories are difficult to make
disappear

In mind's eye the seductive, seductress siren's song
has conspired with spring's efflorescence, spawning
a blissful neural symphony which renders death's
prospect all the more a despair

I see the sarcophagus smiling, I know the vultures are
near; but how can I relinquish the infinite pleasures
I have held so dear?

I've heard it said a thousand times in about ten thousand
ways: the grave itself is but a covered bridge leading
from light to light through a brief darkness
How poignant and so curt, the problem is I've always
had such an inherently painful reaction to dirt

Worms are fine and I openly invite all birds to an
intestinal plate of spaghetti but as death keeps knocking
louder, I'm going to say, I'm not fucking ready!

So in the end when my funeral bells are tolling I hope
it's not death's but life's virtue you're extolling

A friend in need is a friend indeed but death's
knocking is leaving me tired
You'll never find me on this friend's party list—the
obituary of who's expired

So thank you stars and thank you moon, you know
baby it's you that keeps me floating carefully emotionally
distanced from an otherwise drastic state of blue

To death I leave you nothing except my shit to choke
You always were such a persistent, ubiquitous, and
successful bloke.

His uncle was an eccentric man. A devout, libertarian agnostic aes-
thete who proudly lived his life in full accord with the noble ideals of
humanism, total freedom from organizational restraints (religious, medical, governmental) and undaunted, full-fledged devotion to hedonism of
myriad sorts. Uncle Al Georgianson had received severe shrapnel

wounds in his neck while serving in the Vietnam War. This resulted in such a debilitation and incessant twitching of his head that occasionally he looked like a wind up toy gone awry. Despite his handicap, or maybe because of it, Mr. Georgianson decided he would not allow anything to hamper his resolute drive to absorb the most physical pleasure he possibly could in life.

Despite his anomalies (for which he only allowed limited medical treatment—onetime surgery to remove pieces of metal and reconstruct the neck) he always managed to conjure up enough sexual prowess to thoroughly satisfy most of the innumerable women with whom he slept. Two factors facilitated Al's success with women: one, he frequently acquired an admirable level of confidence and bravado after downing a few martinis, gently quelling any insecurities over his abnormalities and two, it very fortuitously just so happened that most of the women whom he encountered and were responsive to him had decidedly fetishistic inclinations toward his disability.

How carelessly I digress. The locus of consciousness in our spaced-out protagonist returns from its brief visit to thoughts of death and thoughts of his uncle. Only faint glimmers of light and sound remain from the passing ambulance. The original stimulus of his recent reverie of bizarre images and concomitant thoughts gradually completely fades. Perhaps now is an appropriate time to introduce our enigmatic character.

Alan Andrew Agrippa was born in the U.S.A.—in the approximate middle of the twentieth century—in a large, newly prosperous Midwestern city fueled economically by precarious industries such as oil and farming. Alan's home life was relatively stable and healthy. His mother, Christine Elizabeth Agrippa—whose maiden name was Donnel—displayed prominently loving, supportive traits and gladly deferred most of her own occupational opportunities for her dream of being a doting, devoted caregiver and wife. Relatively permissive and open-minded in her approach to raising Alan, she frequently accepted his excuses for misbehaviors and tended to nurture in him an optimistic and slightly anxious perspective on life. Alan was her only child and was very special to her. Prior to his conception, she had almost lost her life during a problematic miscarriage and was told by doctors that she had a condition that would preclude her from ever having children. Therefore, when she conceived Alan she felt that it had been a special blessing from God. Additionally, during her pregnancy she had spoken to a spiritualist in the Bahamas who told her that she would have a son who would do extraordinary things.

Conversely, Alan's father, Karl Agrippa, encapsulated a somewhat conservative, hard-working, and slightly patriarchal mindset that inculcated through religious teachings worries about God, Jesus, and the afterlife. In all fairness it must be mentioned that in addition to a punitive, heavily Biblical approach to discipline, Alan's father consistently displayed an uncanny ability to implement verbal praise and much needed reinforcement in response to Alan's accomplishments. As Alan developed a peculiar artistic disposition into adolescence, he clearly recognized within himself a synthesis of influences notwithstanding the disparate personalities of his parents.

Alan quickly peruses the idyllic setting his brain magically imprints. Attention that had been absorbed in viscerally stimulating lights and images, largely figments of his own mind, softly moves into the actual dimensions of his physical surroundings. Alan is not merely awestruck but actually truly edified by the city of charm. Tree-lined circuitous roads, lush distinguished gardens and parks, and monumental, commanding castles and churches—all testified to man's ability to harmoniously coalesce artifact with nature. Concern for progress and sophistication had begotten a concurrent appreciation for simplicity and elegance in the arts. Alan finds himself enraptured by the city near the river Thames: London, England. London's rich history, in juxtaposition but perfect counterpoint to its modernity, affords Alan an opportunity. He can retrace the origin of human thought in the fields of: visual art, literature, science, politics, religion, architecture, and to Alan—a little known field of study with early correlations with hard science and widespread reverberations throughout time—the field colloquially known as "magic."

Alan feels an overwhelming thirst as beads of sweat trickle effervescently down his brow as well as his back. He quickly seeks a local convenience store and, upon entering, asks politely but pressingly, "Do you have any bottled water?" The store clerk scans fleetingly and suspiciously the ostensibly parched, somewhat erratic image of Alan, smiles reassuringly, and sonorously replies the much anticipated reply of, "Sure, right over there." He quickly adds, "You know, that water comes from the Paris water supply, which is bloody awful." Alan pays very little attention to the clerk's diagnosis of water quality. He hands the clerk 80 pence and rushes out the storefront somehow believing that the satisfaction of his newly purchased beverage will be enhanced by being in the sunlight while he drinks it. For the water of which Alan is imminently to partake is imbued with extraordinarily rare value. Given the esoteric chemical state in which Alan's entire system is functioning, this water will undeniably quench as Niagara's frenetic downpour would satiate a famished desert recluse.

Alan watches carefully as the sun descends beyond Westminster Abbey, with ominous bells heralding the eternal solar accomplishment—dusk—with mirroring, resonant chimes. Alan gurgles, douses, and then besprinkles his physical self with his treasured agua-mysteria as he audibly tunes into the oncoming hoof-beat of a pleasantly anachronistic but entirely realistic horse-drawn carriage. The ebullient voices of the carriage's inhabitants ring musically through his aural canal and seem to trickle down through his entire nervous system in synchronicity with the droplets of water delectably replenishing every relevant cell in his body.

A bit of explanation is in order. Earlier in the day—at approximately 11:00 a.m.—Alan Agrippa had piously ingested a small portion of lysergic acid diethylamide, more commonly known by its three-lettered, DNA mirrored acronym of LSD. He performed this reverent, or irreverent, act while sitting meditatively by the Serpentine Lake at Hyde Park. The effects had been rather slow coming given the large breakfast of lightly cooked eggs, ham, sausage, toast and coffee he had previously consumed.

Alan was extremely well-versed in the psychedelic writings, both scientific and literary, dating back to the 1800s and up to the present. He was formally educated in the liberal arts, with an emphasis in psychology and had always been enthusiastically interested in philosophy, religion, and anything that dealt with the way the human mind works. He had availed himself of the psychedelic works that were, of course, outside the normal curriculum, by starting out with one book and making notations as he went along. Inevitably, he discovered references for future relevant works that proved equally worthwhile to explore. Alan was keenly aware that psychotropic plants and vegetables had been systematically consumed by humankind since literally the beginning of time. It seemed evident that there was a growing symbiosis between the human and plant kingdoms that seemed somehow mystical or magical.

Alan had read that in early Greece, opium was highly valued for its pain-relieving and uplifting properties. The women of Thebes had routinely used nepenthe, probably a mixture of opium with mandrake, henbane, and belladonna in order to inspire and create mirth. Within Homer's Odyssey, mythology exhorts the glories of nepenthe when Zeus's daughter Helen obtains a supply from Polydamna, wife of Thoth and queen of Egypt. Telemachus and Helen commiserated in Sparta with friends by pouring nepenthe into their wine in order to lull pain and forget grief. Pythia, at the Delphic oracle, was more than likely experimenting with variations of cyanide and cannabis to achieve her hidden powers of prophecy. The Eleusinian Mysteries involved a secret potion called, kykeon, which was probably a psychedelic concoction originating from ergot, the same source of LSD.

Alan rhetorically queries himself, "Was not ambrosia, the so-called food of the Gods, a powerful metaphor for psychedelics and their incredible properties? Did not the belief in immortality stem from the hallucinatory state?" The answers to these questions are obvious. Alan simply ruminates for the sheer pleasure of it.

CHAPTER 2

Night graciously falls, providing much needed respite from a day of pushing the nervous system to its capacity. Alan returns by foot to The Kensington Sanctuary hotel for a good night's rest. As he makes his way west, he feels the tendons and muscles in his legs pleasurably straining to reach their destination. Alan always finds it incredibly enjoyable to predominantly walk wherever he travels within a city. The benefits as far as he could tell are two-fold: by walking, one is able to directly experience and absorb all sights and sounds more fully; secondly, by walking he feels he is approaching the drug trip with more health and vitality. By keeping his body in motion, it feels better to him and offsets any unwanted deleterious effects of the drug. After all, he never quite knew exactly what was in the drug of the day. Of course, his policy was to only procure goods from knowledgeable, trustworthy peers. As far as Alan's awareness of the properties of the drugs, according to their respective names, he felt that his knowledge was much more than cursory.

He approaches his hotel and relishes the last few images: a passing cab; a bicycler dutifully pedals by; and skyward—a luminescent moon partially covered by a blanket of cloud. Alan winks at the hotel clerk and takes the stairs up to his room, sauntering in to crash immediately on his bed. No need to set the alarm clock; for he is on vacation. Alan falls asleep, slowly replaying the events and impressions of the day while being acutely conscious of the extraordinarily profuse amount of sweat he had excreted and the peculiar way his heart rate accelerates and continues to beat heavily—seemingly causing momentary palpitations and slight tinges of pain in his chest. These are all entirely expected side effects of the drug for him, which he had grown to accept as a small price to pay for the visionary journey. His eyelids gently close and the curtain softly rises to a theatrical dream production of kaleidoscopic, spiraling patterns and designs of white light and black. He gradually descends into sleep.

Alan Agrippa is an only child. When his uncle Al passed away, he left Alan with several thousand dollars as inheritance. Alan had decided to

17

put his belongings in storage in the states and set off for Europe with a few goals in mind. Partly, it was an opportunity to see a part of the world that he had never experienced first hand; through ancestry, Alan had genetically rich ties (his mother was of Italian/German/Irish descent and his father possessed Scottish, English, and Irish.) Partly, it was the fact that he was bored with life and simply wanted something interesting to do (he had quit his part-time teaching job.) He figured that he might discover a viable opportunity while in Europe, perhaps one that offers some kind of excuse to stay.

The most important aspiration, however, was a resolute commitment to discovering within the various realms of consciousness some answer to the metaphysical dilemmas of: What are we doing here? What is this all about? What is the pervasive, underlying nature of reality and how can one grow to understand it?

Alan perceived that his relentless pursuit of philosophical truth would somehow be more fruitful in countries with rich histories—countries that had spawned some of the great mystics, philosophers, and scientists throughout the ages. In his mind, this night, he dreams of the works and personalities of Jakob Boehme, William Blake, Emanuel Swedenborg, William Wordsworth, Immanuel Kant, Herman Hesse, Thomas Mann, Anaïs Nin, René Descartes, Galileo Galilei, Sigmund Freud, and Carl Jung. All were pioneers of human consciousness, key individuals who met and accepted the challenge of delving within. Many valiantly navigated, through innovative means, the circuitous neurophysiological realms of their own minds in addition to methodically recording exterior, objective data and usually returned with renewed perspective and exceptionally articulate language. While they vouchsafed to the rest of us their revelatory and earth shaking insights, they forever transformed our neural anatomy and enriched our souls beyond human comprehension.

He feels within his dreams this night how very fortunate he is to be breathing the air and walking the streets where the multifarious incarnations of genius had lived. He is in Europe, the birthplace of the Renaissance, which forever transformed the mindscape of man. As his body sleeps, his mind roams through Parisian cafes and Milanese bookstores. He finds himself shaking hands with Einstein while the great genius is elaborating on the special theory of relativity. He surreptitiously drops in on Leonardo da Vinci, who is diligently sketching rough drafts of the airplane. In this state of fanciful depersonalization, Alan pays a visit to Dante Alighieri, who is composing angelic verses for his beloved nymph,

Beatrice. Alan harmoniously concludes his nighttime excursion by eavesdropping Mozart's composition of Mass in C minor. Sleep is sound and lengthy. Alan awakens spontaneously at about 10:00 a.m. refreshed, translucent, and voraciously craving a fresh pot of English coffee. He quietly steps to the window and pulls the curtain back. Springtime's efflorescence is taunting the windows to be left open, allowing the reverberation of bucolic chirps of robins and vibrant scents of daffodils and chrysanthemums to permeate the room. Alan gazes momentarily at the morning sun and relishes its warmth, which is titillating to the face.

He quickly begins to dress. He loads his backpack with essentials: wallet, map, 1 bottle of water, an English pop culture magazine, a few aspirin, and a book titled, *The Mystic And The Schizophrenic—Two Sides Of The Same Coin?* by Michael Wasson. The subtitle is: *Man's Pursuit Of The Divine.* Periodic intellectual stimulation in the form of reading always proves a nice complement to a day of touring. He would keep this book with him and read excerpts whenever he gets the chance. With a remaining item, a notebook, he would jot down interesting ideas that spontaneously occurred to him.

Alan locks the door and descends the steps to the lobby. To the right is a quaint hotel restaurant offering complimentary breakfast, which this morning consists of mainly breads, coffee, and juice. He pours himself a cup of rich, sweet English coffee with a little cream and sugar and nibbles lightly on a cherry danish. It never ceases to fail.

Mornings like this are what Aldous Huxley called "gratuitous grace." Whereas a vigorous night of drinking alcohol often left one sluggish and writhing in pain, the morning following a psychotropic drug trip left one calm, relaxed and actually refreshed. He could not understand why in his country something like LSD, which is recreationally pleasurable and physiologically innocuous, was demonized and rendered illegal while something as potentially aggression-producing, addicting, and physically damaging as alcohol was widely accepted and legal. He had surmised that it must have everything to do with the matriarchal, earth-oriented mindset being squelched by the dominant patriarchal alcohol-loving destructive mindset, well-represented by the power mongers who usurped political office for the past couple of centuries in America.

Please don't get Alan wrong. He firmly believes that there is a lot to be proud of in the way of economic development and the accoutrements of modern civilization as a result of industrialization in the fine country of his, the United States of America. After all, it was a driving individualistic spirit that propelled his ancestors to migrate to uncharted territory and establish profound tenets of personal freedom and goals of prosperity. He commended all of that: free enterprise and an undying spirit of humanism. It's just that he frequently felt that American government and industry had gone a little too much in the direction of testosterone-fueled over-industrialization and pathetic patriarchy. Maybe his country would have been better off borrowing some of that good old fashioned American Indian understanding that the earth shouldn't really be fucked with and that the feminine principle has always been and always will continue to be the more intuitive, rational, and intelligent approach to human endeavor.

After savoring the last morsel of breakfast, he heads for the street. On his way out, the hotel clerk calls out to him: "Mr. Agrippa, you have a message in your box." Alan saunters over to the desk and inquiringly picks up the note, which reads, "Dearest Alan, your mother informed us that you are staying in London for a time and we would very much enjoy seeing you. We shall be eating dinner tonight at The Steak Fritte restaurant at 113 Regent Street in Soho at 8:00 p.m. If you are interested, we would like you to join us. Love, Aunt Mary and Uncle Jim." Alan places the letter down for a moment and contemplates, "Why on earth did I tell Mom where I was staying in London?" "I could have been full-blown tripping; having Buddhist revelations, etc., and sweet Aunt Mary and Uncle Jim could have decided to pop in on me. That would have been fucking brilliant! When I leave London, I'll make it a note to avoid informing Mom and Dad of my future destinations. I need anonymity and the complete discretion to enter or stay immune from any interpersonal interaction that I see fit. I'll never accomplish anything so long as people know exactly where I am." All of a sudden, Alan remembers the passage in the Bible that he quietly contemplates: "For what shall it profit a man if he should gain the whole world but lose his very self?" Through some bizarre logic, Alan rearranges the meaning and thinks: "How can I gain the whole world if I do not first lose myself?" or "How can I gain myself if I do not first lose the whole world?" He smirks at the iconoclastic witticisms swirling around in his mind. He then takes a serious minute to decide what he's going to do about the invitation. He had relegated today a "trip-free day" to give his body and mind an opportunity to recuperate from the energy expended the previous day. A day of reflection after tripping is always treasured. But by evening, there should be no conflict with meeting Aunt Mary and Uncle Jim. A comfortable conversation at some pathetically mundane level won't hurt anything.

Jim had been transferred willingly to London to their division of the engineering company where he had worked for the past 15 or so years. Mary is an eccentric, aspiring visual artist who strove to capture her emotions abstractly on canvas; not so much for the aesthetic appreciation from others—although that would be appreciated—but for the cathartic release. Jim makes good money and Mary mainly spends her time painting, reading, and shopping. Their children are grown and Mary and Jim relish the lives of expatriates embarking upon their golden years with dignity and sophistication in Europe. Uncle Jim is Uncle Al's brother (on Alan's mother's side) and Alan feels obligated to the generous money Al left him. Alan deliberates briefly before deciding wholeheartedly that he will spend dinner with the relatives. Alan slides the note into his backpack and casually descends upon the city.

Alan possesses an approach to touring a foreign city, which would undoubtedly make most tourist agencies cringe. The very concept of a "guided tour" or "group travel package" is interminably inconceivable to him. His unique approach to travel could best be described as disorderly, spontaneous, and arbitrary. In a very loose, chaotic fashion, Alan would arrange in his mind—not on paper—a general idea of what would be interesting places to visit and what would be entertaining things to do. Although often carrying a map, as he is doing in London, he makes it a habit to only consult the map as a last resort; first exploring all subjective, visceral inclinations about where to go. Alan feels that left to his own devices (instinctual, spiritual, cognitive) he can more directly and substantially experience his surroundings. Relying too easily on artificial aids would certainly destroy spontaneity and excitement—the very fabric and essence of the beauty of travel. Who knows? Maybe ancient genetic signals would become awakened. Perhaps enscripted neural encodings from millennia ago would be stimulated in his nervous system. After all, most, if not all of his ancestors had originated in this land whose mystique and ambience he so absorbingly soaks up.

Alan Agrippa, contentedly resolute in his "free-associative" travel approach, gleams as he embarks on his day by penetrating the area of London which to him seems to be a vortex of architectural, cultural genius—the area considered Kensington, containing: Royal Albert Hall; Imperial College; the Natural History Museum; and the Victoria and Albert Museum, among others.

Alan leans back on a park bench and simultaneously gazes in reverence at the magnanimous structures before him. He carefully slides his hand into the pocket of his backpack and with an unconscious saccade, displaces his focus from the Natural History Museum to Victoria and Albert Museum.

He slowly removes his book on mysticism, flips over the cover, and turns to the first paragraph which reads: "When the doors of perception are cleansed, everything will appear to man as it truly is, infinite. This line by the writer, William Blake, is poignant yet elusive. What are these mysterious doors of perception and what exactly is the infinite? These are the types of questions that have plagued philosophers, poets, and even scientists throughout the ages." As Alan reads these introductory lines, his mind softly wanders into a reverie, an interlude of perhaps one to two minutes pondering the eternal philosophical quest which has propelled men and women for millennia. This is juxtaposed to thoughts of the majesty of Gothic architecture and its testament to the ingenuity of humankind.

All of a sudden a grumbling, scathing utterance of barely comprehensible words shatteringly permeates his awareness; the source—a disturbingly disheveled, thoroughly unshaven drunkard staggers up to within five feet—and then two feet—of what Alan proudly considers his personal space. "You know, you have your nose stuck up your ass," the vagrant dribbles out. The pungent smell—something like a combination of freshly burnt possum flesh coated with insect repellent suffused with an undeniable accent of the cheapest vermouth known to man—showers the olfactory senses with an ocean of nausea-stimulating scum.

Alan attempts to synthesize the four intertwining yet seemingly disparate thoughts currently possessing him: first, man's mystical pursuit of the ultimate; second, man's genius in industry; third, the repugnant exudations of the visitor; and fourth, the quizzical statement made by the visitor. Perhaps there is a mathematical formula or model within which Alan can simply plug in the individual thoughts and construct some sort of solution or conclusion. Maybe something simple, like: a+b+c+d=e. The whole can be greater than the sum of the parts. Hypothetically, each thought could be liquidized or transubstantiated into a letter or number and then inserted into the Pythagorean theorem. Then maybe, once formalized, some logical explanation would exist to account for such diverse phenomena all taking place at the exact same moment.

The man assertively but schizophrenically queries Alan, "What part of England are you from, Lancashire or Hampshire?" This sentence is projected surprisingly articulately given a pronounced tremor and nervous intensity in the man's voice. The man continues, "Are you from North England or South England?" Alan dutifully, politely replies, "Neither one," "I'm actually not from England. I'm from the United States." Alan makes his response while curiously taking notice of the anachronistic, almost dignified sounds words like Lancashire or Hampshire make. He finds it impressive whenever he hears one of the myriad words in England that ends with, "shire." Coming from this destitute old man, the words are no less distinguished. In fact, in stark contrast to the pathetic physical appearance of this man, the words ring all the more remarkably aristocratic. Out of the midst of a clearly decrepit, lowly, impoverished, and perhaps mentally ill man, is a brilliant glimmer of consciousness and reason. Ninety percent of what the old man utters might be neologistic hogwash, but somehow out of the haze of profound alcoholic stupor and chronic mental illness is a reasonable, rational discourse, however brief it might have been.

With great volition, Alan blocks off his olfactory perception in a process most everyone is familiar with and that can best be described as partially holding one's breath with the nose and sort of consciously blocking air from getting in. As he stares directly into the man's eyes, Alan further limits his quantity of breaths through his mouth so as to prevent inhaling any of the noxious fumes. Alan tries to understand the complexity of the man's physical and emotional condition.

The man once again posits, "You know, you have your nose stuck up your ass." Alan, despite all efforts to suppress his imminent response, erupts in uncontrollable laughter. This funny, inexplicably cosmic interaction is comedy well-appreciated. Alan diverts eye contact and allows the stranger to wander off.

Alan sits back down and reads on: "Primitive tribes have practiced extraordinary rituals to enter the other world and antiquated orators have proclaimed to have dabbled in this alternate realm. Is Freud's unconscious a primordial cesspool of sea urchin, some of which are friendly pixies while others are horrific monsters? What is this suprasensory reality which provides an occasional swim for adventurous dilettantes but which drowns those less fortunate, whom we call, schizophrenics?"

After solemnly perusing this paragraph, he shuts the book and places it into his backpack. He realizes that time is getting past him, so he heads to Westminster Abbey for a quick tour before returning to the hotel. He enters the vast corridor of—to his knowledge—one of the most stunning examples of Gothic architecture in not just England, but perhaps anywhere in Europe. He gazes in awe at the antiquated tombs and monuments honoring monarchs, literary scholars, and warriors—all received England's highest honors.

   Alan learns that Edward the Confessor was buried behind the altar;
that almost every English king since William the Conqueror had been
crowned here; that the wooden coronation throne contains the Stone of
Scone, removed from Scone, Pertshire, to symbolize England's dominion
over Scotland in 1297. Alan finds these bits of information immensely
interesting. The fact that this magnificent structure serves not only as a
church but as a tomb enclosing some of England's most intriguing characters is intensely moving. Everything in here seems vertical, Alan
muses. Infinite towering columns give way to ornate patterns—seemingly interspersed portals to heaven—counterpoint rhythm of immortal
stone. Alan stands within this national shrine transfixed, mesmerized at
its topographical grandeur and its very spirit, which to him are exemplary of the very essence of England itself.

CHAPTER 3

Alan glances at his watch and realizes that he should start heading back to the hotel to get ready for dinner. He reflects amusingly and appreciatively at the day's events and somewhat begins to look forward to seeing his aunt and uncle. Alan continues the rejuvenated, optimistic perspective on this "post-neural-trip" day and begins to crave earnestly the opportunity to sit down to a perfectly mundane conversation and potentially pleasant interaction with his relatives. The day's main activities for the rest of the city begin to wind down. Taxis unload tired tourists. Shopkeepers close their wooden and ironclad doors. The ubiquitous sounds of car horns and industry gradually lessen. Alan gleefully traverses the scenic, verdant path adjacent to Buckingham Palace and Green Park leading up to his hotel. As he runs up the steps to the front door, he pauses and swiftly turns his head to catch a rapturous setting sun hovering gently and descending peacefully just slightly beyond the trees and rooftops in elegant backdrop to this city of majestic repose.

Alan passes the front desk clerk quickly, asking him, "Are there any messages for me?" the reply: "None, sir." Up more stairs and into his room, Alan drops his backpack on the floor and kicks off his shoes. Fixing himself a glass of water, Alan lies back on the bed and rests for about an hour. He knows this slumber session will restore just about enough energy to get through the night.

At about 7:00 p.m. he arises and showers. The weather is very pleasant in London. Days had been comfortably warm and the nights balmy. Alan pulls on a long sleeve shirt after splashing on his favorite French cologne and sliding on a pair of jeans. After tying his shoes and finger combing his hair with gel, he glances at himself in the mirror and then departs to Soho. As Alan walks rapidly (Alan always walks rapidly—he feels it is excellent for circulation and muscle development) along the sidewalks, a distinctly cool, English North Sea breeze sweeps refreshingly through the streets. A light rain had fallen while he was resting, giving way to a decidedly clean, clear appearance to the city. Climatic conditions and transitions like this always make Alan optimistic. He feels more alive and feels that chords in his body resonate with nature's energy. All of this bodes well for the evening.

Once reaching Regent Street, the Steak Fritte restaurant is relatively easy to find. A large protruding neon sign alerts passers-by to what proves to be one of the more savory restaurants in London. Alan spots Mary and Jim within a few seconds of entering. Mary proudly dons an eccentric artist apparel: a tight fitting, satin textured, oriental designed dress that is grayish blue in color and depicts geisha girls in various poses; a small gray, sequined feather cap. Medium height, gray leather boots complete the picture. Alan is reminded of a vaudeville comedy actress serving appropriate juxtaposition to her staidly, squarely dressed husband Jim. Jim is wearing a plaid button-down shirt with dusty-brown, rayon-polyester, pleated pants. His black, oversized, square-rimmed glasses are fashion-perplexing. Jim's hair is greased straight back in a manner that suggests he had meticulously combed it for hours. Alan smiles warmly, knowing that they are his family.

Alan notices, upon entering, that standing next to Jim and Mary is a beautiful, fashionably dressed young woman about twenty-three or twenty-four years old. With medium length shiny blonde hair and pleasantly pale, creamy skin, she has eyes that shine like shimmering mystic gems of translucent blue. Her lips—plump, voluptuous folds of immaculate flesh—reflect a symmetry unknown in most faces. A delicate, perfectly curved nose sits in harmonic proximity to her mouth. This luscious European nymph has an ethereal nature about her.

After exchanging pleasantries with Jim and Mary, Mary introduces Alan to the mysterious beauty named, Ronia. "Alan, Ronia Vintras is an exchange student taking classes at the local university," Mary speaks excitedly. She continues, "Jim and I felt having Ronia stay with us would serve two purposes: one, to provide a bright, ambitious young lady an opportunity to expand her horizons and; two, to allow us to truly enhance our international experience of being abroad by playing host to a true European!"

Outwardly, Alan smiles. Inwardly, he balks at such a pretentious attempt on the part of an obnoxious American to assimilate the European culture by taking a pawn in an innocent French girl. Mary's comment is forgivable at some level. He knows that she is well-intentioned. "It's very nice to meet you." Alan extends a confident handshake, softly taking Ronia's hand in his for a fleeting exchange of palpable energy through the palms. Handshakes with beautiful women were somehow highly erotic to Alan. He relishes the second or two of touching a beautiful stranger's hand as a magically pleasing moment. With direct focused eye contact, Alan would assess any potential chemistry through this seemingly innocent interaction. If given the liberty to judge potential sparks with Ronia, he would have definitely allotted extremely high marks. Ronia smiles warmly and speaks lightly, "Comment allez vous?" "Trés bien, merci," he answers, hesitantly. "Do you want to speak English?" she asks, coyly. "That would be nice, thank you," he responds. Alan feels a strange warmness permeate inside. "How noble and endearing that she is willing to depart from her native tongue for me," he reflects.

The four finally take a table near a large window overlooking at a short distance the illumination of Picadilly Circus. Alan fails to understand the connection between "Soho," London, and "Soho," New York, but he never really asked. Perhaps he would figure this out. Primarily conscious of Ronia and partially conscious of his embarrassment in the company of two ridiculously dressed, touristy looking people—his aunt and uncle—Alan willingly accepts and defuses the obligatory barrage of queries and expressions of opinion from Jim and Mary: "So Alan, what have you been doing with yourself here in London?" The first shot is delivered with force by Jim. The perfectly honest, heartfelt response to that question, constructed immediately, "Oh well, hedonistically exploring my nervous system and various neurophysiological realms of my brain while taking in the illustrious sights and striving to explore magic," is transmuted, filtered, and delivered in the form of a less shocking, more acceptable answer of, "Well, Jim, I've been educating myself with the rich history of England, touring castles and museums, and thinking about our family line descending from this incredible country." "England's an incredible place, Alan. You're right about that one. Mary and I love to go see Shakespearean plays and take long walks in the parks here. My job is going well and we might even spend the rest of our lives here." Mary chimes in: "Alan, your mother and father were curious to know what your future travel plans are in terms of how long in London—where to next, etc. Do you have an idea of what your plans are at this point?"

"Mary, I don't exactly have real clear plans at this point. Roughly, I plan on touring London for several more days and then head off to the English countryside and surrounding cities; then I will probably venture up through Scotland. It's all very tentative and spontaneous at this point. I will, however, send off postcards periodically to inform Mom and Dad of how things are going." Mary looks dejected. She distinctly feels unsuccessful in her mission of pinpointing Alan's future whereabouts. The waiter approaches and takes their order.

Once the waiter vanishes, Alan swiftly shifts the conversation to Ronia. "Ronia, what part of France are you from?" "The city of Lyon. Do you know where Lyon is located?" "Yes. I have an idea. I know that it is in the southeast region of France. I would imagine that it is quite beautiful there." Ronia fixes her attention on Alan's enthusiastic gestures, words and replies: "Oh, it is. There are quaint trees and hills surrounding my home there. It is obviously more calm and peaceful than a hectic city such as Paris or London. I do love Paris and London, though. For me, a congruence between the luxury of the city and the tranquillity of the country is a necessary prerequisite for enjoying life. By the way, how is my English? It is not too difficult for you to understand, is it?" "Your English is superb and your accent enhances the language with charm." Alan tries desperately not to sound obsequious with his statement. He is being sincere and hopes that it comes across that way.

As he gazes into her hypnotic eyes, he finds himself enraptured by her physical appearance and equally taken with her eloquence. She appears erudite and inquisitive—traits he finds irresistible, especially when combined with physical beauty. While Alan and Ronia converse with one another, Mary and Jim occupy themselves with an appetizer and drinks. They do, however, appear to be listening at least peripherally to the youthful conversation. Alan asks Ronia about which program she is involved in. "I'm studying cultural anthropology at the University of Lyon. I am on a one-year scholarship, which enables me to study here at the University of London. Your aunt and uncle have been gracious enough to allow me to stay with them." This presents an open invitation for Mary to enter the conversation. It is unavoidable. "Ronia has been just like a daughter to us. She is the consummate guest! I never knew how enjoyable it would be to serve as a host family."

Dinner arrives. Alan had ordered roast chicken served with fresh asparagus and carrots. The relative blandness of some of the local fare in London never ceased to amaze him. The most flavorful aspect to his meal was the vibrancy of strawberry in his zinfandel wine. "At least it's healthy," he muses. The four toast to a pleasant gathering among friends. When everyone is done eating, Jim drops the most serious question of the night: "So, Alan, given Al's passing—which was very hard on all of us—I'm aware that it must have been especially difficult for you. With the money that Al has left for you, do you have plans of investing in further education or business opportunities?" It's not that Alan feels extraordinarily guilty about not having so-called "practical" plans for the money. In fact, he feels that the education received from frivolously spending the money touring Europe is probably more valuable than just about any other endeavor. It's not as if it's any of Jim's business what exactly Alan does with the money. Jim is part of his family and these are arguably cogent expectations people seem to have. Nevertheless, Alan feels substantial pressure. He feels compelled to provide some sort of realistic answer.

With all ears anxiously listening—Mary's, Jim's, and Ronia's—Alan carefully constructs and delivers the best response he knows: one that is vague and optimistic; "I will continue to tour Europe for a time while monitoring my bank account in the states. I will evaluate potential employment opportunities here and in the U.S. and subsequently decide what to do with the rest of my life. Could you please pass the cognac?"

It is approximately 10:30 p.m. Everyone has eaten and drank to their hearts content. Conversation has been mediocre, as expected. All in all, Mary and Jim seem pleased with their visit with Alan. Alan is not only pleased but his interest is immensely stimulated through meeting a fairy named, Ronia. Everyone rises from the table slowly and begins to traverse the now darkened corridor that leads to the exit. Jim, having treated the group to dinner, receives many thank-yous. Mary and Jim hug Alan and extend an offer to have him as a guest in their home anytime. Mary offers to cook dinner next time. Alan thanks them once again and politely declines an offer to drive him home, insisting instead on taking a cab.

Jim suavely lights a Cuban cigar and puffs repeatedly, sending wafts of smoke circles into the cool air. Wrapping his arm gently around Mary, they begin to walk east toward their car, briefly leaving Alan alone with Ronia. "I enjoyed meeting you and would be interested in contacting you again. Perhaps we can go out for coffee or something," Alan emits in volume slightly above a whisper. "I would like that very much," she replies. "Here is my number," she states while scribbling on a piece of paper. "It is a personal line at the house." As Ronia turns effervescently to catch up to Jim and Mary, Alan smiles earnestly and says, "Thanks, have a good night." Alan stands for a moment, watches her walk away endearingly, like a fragile angel whose patience with banal Americans is monumental. Alan takes great care in sliding the paper into his wallet. The thought has not occurred to Alan that there is a possibility of genuine companionship while on his European sojourn. After meeting Ronia, the concept starts to take hold.

He looks up at an ebullient, almost ominous moon obscured only by a thin veneer of mist; protectively but deceptively concealing the power of lunar energy. Endless nights sitting on beaches while gazing at a full moon, Alan had pondered the seminally eerie causal connection between the moon and the tides of the earth's oceans. It had been well proven in astronomy that the moon's proximity and gravitational pull on the earth are integral to the vicissitudes of nature. What Alan ponders indefinitely is: Does the pull of the moon have effect on human emotions? Alan had perused psychiatric texts concerning concepts like, "lunacy," and the myths and rumors surrounding such a term. Throughout history, connections between the full moon and wild mood swings had been documented. What is most intriguing to Alan is the potentiality toward exuberance, love, and even genius that the moon might hold for humans. Even if the full moon and meeting Ronia are purely coincidental events, Alan feels this night is auspicious.

Alan hails a cab and returns to his hotel. Back at his room, he reaches for his book and scans to the next paragraph, which resonates: "How do we reconcile what we consider to be rational, objective reality with this other reality that seems equally 'real' to those who have sworn its existence? When a quantum physics theorist with a mystical bent claims to have realized that 'all is one, a whole with inseparable parts,' do we scoff at what we think is obvious flaw in scientific methodology, or do we attempt to strive toward some understanding of the strange phenomenon? We could perhaps employ our own scientific methodology—one that ensures the highest ideals of statistical reliability, validity, and significance. We could take a representative sample of individuals who have claimed to have 'seen the light' or merged themselves with a sense of 'cosmic consciousness' and vigorously test them in order to determine the definitiveness of their claims. We could generalize from our conclusions and predict within the most minute realm of doubt that so-and-so will experience 'eternal bliss, a sense of absolute oneness with others,' on such and such occasion. However, this empirical, scientific approach seems somehow lacking in juxtaposition to the magnitude of such a phenomenon as the one of which we speak." Alan sleeps peacefully this night; his stomach, heart, and the moon above him are all undeniably full.

CHAPTER 4

Alan awakens refreshed and optimistic about the rest of his time in London. Although drugs are not necessarily central to his travel plans, they are certainly much valued accessories, complementing in a sense his main pursuit of exploring mystical questions in the geographical context of Europe. Alan is resolute in his desire to seek out and truly discover metaphysical truths: answers to questions beyond ordinary awareness and understanding. In this sense, drugs are simply tools to unlock certain mysteries: some mysteries perhaps hidden within his own brain and certainly mysteries "out there" in the exterior environment.

Ultimately, Alan would take the knowledge and experience gained and put it into a book showcasing and elucidating for others the mystical path or rainbow and where it led. Through the ingestion of chemicals in congruence with active, discursive perception of people, events, and places, Alan feels that among many other things he will perhaps be able to firmly grasp esoteric notions such as Platonic archetypes or ideals. Alan's understanding of Platonic thought is that we are all in a process of change; of becoming or evolving, which becomes somehow intertwined or immersed in immortal, immutable "forms" or "ideas"—a merging of that which is malleable with that which is static.

During the previous week, Alan had written in his notebook a personal interpretation of a basic tenet within Aristotelian thought. It reads:

> Teleology carries as one of its definitions the following: a belief similar to vitalism; that natural phenomena are determined not only by mechanical causes but by an overall design or purpose in nature. In ancient Greece, Aristotle posited a teleological God that somehow united man and nature in a great cosmological design of beginning and end with purpose. Man possessed a rational intellect that, with the help of his senses, could be directed toward discovering universal truths. Aristotle, however, believed as well in something beyond both logic and empiricism. Aristotle suggested man's importance lies in developing to his fullest potential out of an original form. A form is incorporated in a material substance and

every living creature is a manifestation of form. There also existed a supreme Form, universal and perfect. The fact that man possesses a vastly developed intellect and self-consciousness implies that man participates in divinity; at once separate, a material embodiment striving toward its individual perfection and also one aspect of a multifaceted, ever-recreating essence toward individual being.

"The counterpoint of Plato and Aristotle was as harmonious and transcendent as the music of Mozart," Alan thinks.

He heads to the restroom, relieves himself, and then enters the shower. He dries off and applies sparing amounts of botanical shaving cream to his face before shaving. He proceeds to shave, leaving the faucet off intermittently in order to conserve water. Diligently applying deodorant and cologne, he then runs his fingers through his hair with gel and throws his towel over the shower door.

Alan loads up his backpack and becomes conscious of the fact that he had only brought with him from the states a small supply of acid and "X," LSD and MDMA, respectively. This morning he is not so much in the mood for either one. He decides that it will be most enjoyable to locate and partake of some quality pot. He didn't know how easy this would be in London but if wagering a guess, would bet his chances were pretty good.

The reason Alan had only brought acid and MDMA was simple. While passing through security in airports, it is relatively easy to conceal them with aspirin and other medications. The only drawback Alan can see with this technique is possible contamination of the other supposedly more innocuous substances. Who knows? He might reach for a simple analgesic one day and end up taking one that has drug elements present. "Oh well," he thinks. "I suppose there are worse things in life than inadvertent drug trips." Which reminds him.

He recalls a drug experiment performed by Harvard psychologists back in the '60s in which a subject who desired to learn Spanish was systematically given doses of LSD while focusing on learning Spanish tapes for three consecutive days. Supposedly, when leaving the testing room, she was fluent in Spanish. The only significant side effect she experienced was every time she heard Spanish spoken, she involuntarily slipped into a psychedelic state. Alan goes downstairs to eat a light breakfast—toast, butter, jelly, and coffee—then heads out for another day of adventure.

Alan wants to spend the first part of the day at The London Dungeon. The London Dungeon is a rustic building—located downtown—where, for the price of admission, one can tour rows of mannequins and prop settings depicting medieval torture methods commonly employed throughout Europe only a few hundred years ago. One of the most quizzical observations Alan makes, which defies previous expectations of England, is that England does not attempt to downplay or underemphasize its arguably shady past in the arena of medieval tortures and abuses. On the contrary, England capitalizes on this history by showcasing it as a major tourist attraction. Jack the Ripper is a major celebrity for God's sake.

Alan discreetly scores some grade-A ganja from a Rastafarian at Hyde Park. The pot-induced, sensitized state enhances the extremely bizarre nature of the dungeon. Chillingly expressive countenances that simulate violent screams and writhings make the mannequins haunting representations that bespeak horrors committed really only yesterday and most of the time performed in the name of religion. Whether it was the onset of science contradicting predominant religious views or the vindictive delusion that man has always used to denounce and demonize some underclass or minority group, egregious sins against humankind have been committed.

It started with Socrates who was tried, convicted, and coerced into taking his own life with hemlock—all for guiding youth to question authority and discover philosophical truth. Starting as early as the 1200s, Jews were persecuted. A few hundred years ago, scientists and so-called witches were perceived through supposed beliefs and practices to defy the Judeo-Christian ideals. For this, they were callously put to death, often in excruciatingly painful ways. Thirty years ago, the black race was brutally victimized for the color of their skin. Alan feels that today it is the drug user who serves as scapegoat for society's paranoia and ruthless desire to brutalize.

Walking through these darkened, macabre corridors, lined with gloomy caverns, is walking through horrific scenes from England's past. Alan is shocked at the realization that as organisms evolving on the surface of this luminescent sphere, hurtling through the solar system, we have behaved so barbarically. Within the dungeon, Alan analyzes devilishly ingenious methods of torture: a small cage which encloses a famished rodent on a circumscribed section of soon-to-be devoured flesh; a contraption securing a human with salt-covered exposed toes serving as a delicacy for an aggressively gnawing goat; various decapitation and burning sequences. Alan wonders as his mind hovers slightly above normal level: "Didn't the origin of life itself, albeit pre-biotic molecules, occur some 3.8 billion years ago? Didn't eukaryotic organisms, 'higher organisms,' in a sense, originate about 1.8 billion years ago? The Cambrian explosion occurred 540–500 million years ago. The modern human mind has been in existence for at least 100,000 years. Did something as vastly complex and as intricate as DNA really spend billions of years to evolve into its proudest accomplishment yet—man—so that we could run around irrationally torturing one another?"

Alan sits hopelessly perplexed at the existential conundrum. He learns that in the year 1486, Jacob Sprenger and Heinrich Kramer published the *Malleus Malleficarum*—The Hammer of Witches—published in German, French, Italian, and English several times. This manual substantiated and, in fact, provoked the persecution of "witches." In 1572, witchcraft was declared a capital crime in Lutheran Saxony. In 1600, Giordano Bruno, Italian philosopher and former Dominican monk, was burned at the stake for his advocacy of Copernican theory. In 1632, Galileo published *A Dialogue on the Two Principal Systems of the World.* He was tried by the Inquisition. With 1692, the Salem witch trials took place. In 1885, "hysteria" was treated by surgical removal of the ovaries in Paris; by surgical removal of the clitoris in London and Vienna; and by cauterization of the clitoris in Heidelberg. In 1905, Bernard Sachs, a New York psychiatrist and author of *A Treatise on Nervous Diseases of Children,* recommended the treatment of masturbation in children by cautery to the spine and genitals. In 1925, Adolf Hitler published *Mein Kampf* in which, among other things, he posited the following: "Today I believe that I am acting in accordance with the will of the Almighty Creator; by defending myself against the Jew, I am fighting for the work of the Lord." In 1935, Egas Moniz of Lisbon introduced prefrontal lobotomy into psychiatry.

The list goes on. Alan marvels at the hideous spectrum of human-to-human injustice in this country, England, and all over the world. At times clutching his stomach in states of nausea ad infinitum, Alan desperately seeks to hold on to optimism for the human race. Some of the exhibits in the dungeon are amusing. Most are very disturbing.

It is early afternoon when he exits the building and ventures out to explore other aspects of the city. Cumulous billows of grayish blue clouds float in from the North Sea and blanket the city with mists of rainfall. The cool moisture in the balmy air is refreshing and invigorating. Intoxicating effects of the magic leaf begin to dissipate. Alan quenches his thirst with bottled water and plots his next move. Hunger pangs voice their opinion loudly and Alan obeisantly responds.

Just west by a few blocks, Alan discovers an Italian restaurant with a protruding, inviting red awning, which advertises: "Anna Maria's Trattoria." It appears authentic; encapsulating most attributes of a perfect "hole-in-the-wall" restaurant that probably serves authentic cuisine. It is a small brick building that is dimly lit on the inside and possesses mainly genuine Italian employees and an owner on site.

Alan sits down to a delectable plate of fresh rotelle pasta with zesty meat sauce. Rich, buttery garlic bread fully completes the quelling of hunger pangs and stimulates the onset of epicurean contentment. As Alan sips gingerly on a glass of Cabernet, he peers through the front window, gazes and studies the passers-by. A youthful group of what appear to be British army cadets in full uniform march past followed by a frolicking herd of elementary private school students probably on their way to a field trip. Casually taking in the sights, an attractive Englishwoman with a bright, flowered parasol saunters past pushing a baby carriage. Astute businessmen in expensive Italian suits diligently cling to Wall Street Journals and London Times as they dash to hail cabs. Every multifarious, colorful inhabitant of this bustling city vies for his position within the strata. Each participant in the United Kingdom game of life essentially projects and fulfills his role. Alan surreptitiously reclines in his booth and nurses the red wine. He contemplates the oxymoronic sense of being closely involved, yet isolated and detached from the entire process. He wants so much to immerse himself in the culture but his modus operandi is to primarily observe and analyze: "undeniably a much too scientific, clinical approach," he muses. Another perspective he considers is that he is perhaps striking a judicious, comfortable balance and approach to experiencing the city.

As a bobby steps out momentarily to administer a ticket to a dismayed speeder, Alan feels a tinge of paranoia in the simple sense of the associative connection he had built between cops and drugs. Growing up in the United States, Alan was well apprised of the punitive laws for drug possession and drug dealing. Alan is equally aware of the traditional police personality which seems overly apt to harass and bully the usually passive, otherwise law-abiding "druggie." Further, he is firmly aware that the only risk of taking psychedelic drugs is the, "paranoiac," symptoms which often accompany stress and anxiety. He thinks to himself, "While in the drug state, what could be a worse paranoia-stimulus than the image of a police officer? Perhaps by effectively removing the law enforcement, 'War on Drugs,' among other things we could eradicate the worst known symptom of drugs." It makes sense to him.

The bobby makes his departure and Alan is instantly relieved. Funny Alan should be thinking of stoning, for directly on the sidewalk in front of the building stands a cool looking, dreadlocked Rastafarian who is bee-bopping and grooving to tunes on headphones. Who else could it have been but the Bob Marley resembling, ganja smoking dude who sold him a bag at the park? Alan desperately craves company, so rushes out of his seat and out the door. "Hey man, how's it going? Do you remember me?" Alan shouts while the Rastafarian struggles to remove his headphones. "Oh yeah, how you doin' mon?" They shake hands enthusiastically.

"I'm doing great. Will you come in for a drink?" Alan implores. "Suuuuure. Why noooot!" answers the dread. Alan leads him back to the table and encourages him to order whatever he wants. Alan is buying. "I'll take a Heineken, thanks mon."

"Ma'am, can we please have two Heinekens and two frosty mugs, please?" Alan asks the waitress. "So what's your name, friend?" "Peter, Peter Lesh. What's yours?" "Alan, Alan Agrippa." "So, Alan, what's an American like yourself doin' in the U.K.?" Alan chuckles at the first sentence composed and enunciated by the Rastafarian which does not contain the word "mon" in it. The dread continues:

"Are you some kind of a rock star, mon? I know, I've seen you in Rolling Stone, right?" "I'm actually just your average all-American tourist casually consuming psychedelics and trying to learn about the culture. What about you? What's a Jamaican like yourself doing in the bastion of the Anglocentric universe?" Peter laughs with one of those hearty, selfless, universal utterances that only a true Rasta can emit. "I'm playing reggae and spreadin' da word about love and peace. You know as well as I know det the Anglo nation needs it, mon." Alan smiles in agreement, as the waitress arrives with the beer. "Peter, I think you got the right idea. The whole world needs that message." The two cosmonauts pour the beloved ale effortlessly and toast to the making of friends in jolly ol' England. Peter informs Alan that he and his band will be playing on Saturday at 4 at Kensington Park. Alan is welcome. They finish the beers, shake hands, and thank one another. Alan covers the check and they happily depart in separate directions.

As Alan heads for the west, he runs a memory check on what he knows about the Rastafarian religion or way of life. Aside from the obvious integral role the almighty joint plays in things, Alan is aware that family, community, and a striving for freedom are all hallmarks of the

Rasta way. Additionally, Rastas have an iconographic reverence for the late Ethiopian emperor Haile Selassie.

So far as Alan can surmise, all the world's religions possess a singular demi-god: one hero, usually a man, who is singularly GOD incarnate. For Christians, it is Jesus. For Muslims, it is Muhammad. Buddhists have Buddha. At first blush, it strikes Alan as strange that this intensely spiritual group of Rastas would have chosen a politician—a national leader to be their demigod. Perhaps it is the relative recent development of the religion—back in the 1930s—that makes it necessary to choose a relatively recent persona as opposed to an antiquated, mythological figure. Rastafarians curiously but understandably borrow elements from Christianity.

The Rasta justification for using weed was based on Genesis 1:12 in the Christian Bible: "And the earth brought forth vegetation, plants yielding seed after their kind, and trees bearing fruit, with seed in them, after their kind; and God saw that it was good." It makes sense to Alan. The realization he's having is that the first drug bust, or FDA regulation, in the history of mankind occurred at that once plush, quaint club med— The Garden of Eden. After all, wasn't it chapter 2 verse 16 which read: "And the Lord God commanded the man, saying; From any tree of the garden you may eat freely; but from the tree of the knowledge of good and evil you shall not eat, for the day that you eat from it you shall surely die." Alan had always found the entire Christian bible highly interesting. As far as all time greatest hits in the book department, it definitely ranked up there among the best. Particularly in the first and last books within the bible (Genesis and Revelation) one could find the most sensuous and supernatural stories.

As Alan traverses contemplatively the last three miles to his hotel, he recalls with much amusement the Primacy and Recency effects he once studied in a psychology textbook. The Primacy effect—which Alan creatively correlated with the book of Genesis, held that in a series of stimuli one will find most salient that which comes first. Conversely, the Recency effect held that one will find most salient that which comes last, which in this simplistic analogy is the book of Revelation. Genesis—the phenomenal story of the origin of humankind—magically creates in the curious mind of the reader a sumptuous, paradisiacal realm of the wondrous riches of nature. An idyllic, other-worldly setting of efflorescent foliage and immaculate flesh comes to life; not to mention the proverbial messenger of death—antagonistic element of mystery and danger—the snake. The underground-living, wily, slithering serpent is, of course, mythologically god-like. Out of the pastoral vegetation and infinite harmony of man with God in the garden of Eden comes not only the very first drug bust but also, arguably, the first precept for patriarchy and the first precept for animal abuse. Eve arising from the rib of Adam and man having dominion over all the animals would not exactly fit into today's concept of political correctness.

Alan slows his pace and begins to cogitate over various theories of the symbolization of the story in the book of Genesis. First, there is the literal translation—that what is written in the book is what happened. The original two humans were named, Adam and Eve. They were created by an omniscient and omnipotent god, or omniscient and omnipotent gods, who first created the heavens and earth and then decided there should be basic animals and humans. Man is made in the god's image and has been strategically placed within the plush environs of "sanctity central," the garden of Eden. Man is, in a sense, an extension of God: made in his image and free to experience all the joys of Eden except the fruit from the tree of knowledge of good and evil.

Everyone knows the story. Eve is tempted by the snake to partake of the forbidden fruit, which she does, then graciously shares some with her beloved husband, Adam, and this simple process becomes the "fall of man." Suddenly, the magical fruit awakens the humans' eyes to the "godniscient" notion that they are naked. They are now aware of "good" and "evil" and, to prevent them from further discovering immortality via the tree of life, God banishes them from Eden; eternally compelling women to sustain pain in childbirth and man to toil away his days working the soil for sustenance. "Okay, that's the straightforward, basic version," Alan says to himself. Alan sits down at a red bench surrounded by feeding pigeons that flutter their wings momentarily until he is comfortably seated.

Alan sits quietly, absorbing the warmth of titillating sun rays and brilliant activity on this London street as he devises theory number two on the story of Adam and Eve. As cars whirl by, Alan grabs the idea. The story of Adam and Eve is metaphorical. Adam is a personification or representation of man's left side of his brain: that which according to modern day researchers seems largely responsible for rational, discursive, objective functions. Eve is the embodiment of the thinking, feeling, impulsive right brain. God is the CNS, or central nervous system that attempts to orchestrate a symbiosis and higher functioning of both apparatuses. Genesis 1–3 is basically Physiology 101–103: Adam and Eve simply representing the two hemispheres occasionally in sync but upon reaching conflict, digressing into a state of chaos and turmoil (i.e., nervous breakdown) or—the fall of man.

Alan segues to number three. Adam and Eve serve as an allegory to the Chinese notions of yin and yang. Eve closely correlates with the dark, hidden, mysterious concept of yin as Adam is the bright, positive, masculine side of yang. The universal opposites encapsulated in the Chinese symbol are exemplified in Genesis. Even at the end of chapter 4 it reads, "At the east of the garden of Eden He stationed the cherubim, and the flaming sword which turned every direction to guard the way to the tree of life." Is this not perfectly analogous to the dual lions guarding the path to enlightenment in Chinese philosophy?

Alan twitches in his seat rejoicefully, as if someone should present him an ovation for his astounding insight. The next interpretation is for X-rated audiences only. Luckily there is no censor, at least none that he is aware of. Adam, Eve, and the serpent collectively serve as individual components in the sexual experience. Man's eyes are initially closed. His realm of experience is limited in so far as he has no awareness of nudity in himself or those around him. The serpent (an undeniable phallic symbol) cunningly manipulates the woman into a choice that she makes to taste the fruit. She consumes the forbidden fruit and then persuasively draws Adam into the fold. Alan's ability to improvise and embellish with the story of Adam and Eve makes him feel not only confident in his mental dexterity but also proud that he could perhaps enhance the future of theology and mankind with his theories.

Alan is on the verge of delving into metaphysical musings on transubstantiation of spirit into matter: the idea that the story of Adam and Eve represents man's attempt to explain the origin of humankind from a physico-transcendent-quantum level. Alan suddenly realizes that time is getting past him and he should scurry back to the hotel. He has distinct plans of calling Ronia and asking her out.

CHAPTER 5

Back at the hotel, Alan has a quick dinner and strolls up to his room to use the phone. Frantically searching for Ronia's number in his wallet, he gazes up at his desk to realize he has left the paper next to the lamp. As he lunges to retrieve the note, a loud, repetitive knock reverberates through his door. "Who the hell could this be?" he says to himself. Alan takes three steps up to peer through the peephole and cannot believe his eyes. He swings the door open and gazes in amazement at Ronia. With a surreptitious smile lips pucker and glow in fresh coatings of cherry red lipstick; this ensemble stands in stark contrast to a shiny black leather jacket and slightly faded blue jeans.

"Hey, what's up?" she asks. "Not much," Alan replies. He continues, "You're not gonna believe this but I was just about to call you." "Well, are you going to let me in or what?" "Sure, come on in." Immediately Alan becomes conscious of how staid and unkempt his room probably appears. He feels he can make up for this with exuberant conversation. Ronia beats him to it. "I got your number from your aunt and uncle, of course, and thought, 'Why don't I just look him up?' I knew I was going to be in the area tonight." "Would you be interested in going for a drink?" Alan asks. "Yes," she replies enthusiastically.

"That would be nice." He excuses himself to change into pants and a button down shirt. Upon returning, he discovers her browsing through his book on mysticism.

"This can only be propitious," he muses to himself. He thinks to himself, "She is a cultural anthropology major; the likelihood is strong that we will find rich conversational common ground." Upon noticing that he is watching her, she begins to read aloud from the top paragraph on the bookmarked page as he finger-combs his hair. "Somehow, it seems futile and almost blasphemous to try to pin the 'absolute' under a microscope. When scientists usually approach a theoretical proposition, they methodically follow a systematic series of steps in order to gain a greater understanding of something that is exterior to themselves. Even in physiological explorations we are dealing with specific things that either exist or occur. What happens when the thing the scientist is trying to discover is inextricably bound up with every word, thought, sensation, and even organ he employs? This would call for a radical transformation of what we consider to be ordinary, rational science."

As Ronia concludingly pronounces the word, "science," Alan hovers precariously in an ethereal mental state somewhere between profound admiration for her mental powers and obvious deep understanding for what she is reading: and a simple, visceral appreciation for the spicy, tempting flavor of her strong French accent.

Ordinarily, Alan would have waited to attempt to become intimate with such a delectable, delicate creature for fear of scaring her off, but the intensely attractive concoction of brains and beauty encapsulated in this magical moment are overwhelming. He senses her attraction to him.

Alan draws himself intimately close to her and softly removes the book from her hands, closes it, and sets it aside. With his left hand, he slides his fingers along her waist and allows them to come to rest on the small of her back. The flesh on the palms of his hands is separated from the flesh of her back only by leather and bodies awkwardly intertwined. With his right hand, he proceeds to gently caress the back of her neck as he cautiously but firmly presses his lips to hers, welcomely. As he kisses her succulent lips he fully immerses himself in only the carnal, eternal moment of pleasure in contact with such beauty. For only a moment, they embrace and kiss. Ronia succumbs to the assertive gesture of this strange American as if she has known him for a millennium or as if she at least instinctively knows that he would approach her with utmost care and respect.

Playfully smearing small spots of lipstick on Alan's mouth, Ronia uses her forefinger to gently pull back a strand of Alan's bangs from his forehead. They lightly pull away from one another. Alan suggests that a pub will be fun. He grabs his wallet and throws on a light jacket.

Taking Ronia by the hand, he leads her out the door and down to the street. Realizing that he is now in the intimate company of a young lady, he quickly hails a cab and directs the driver to a place called, Smitty's Pub—a few streets away. While in the cab, Alan asks her, "What brings you to this side of town tonight?" "I had to interview some subjects for the study I am currently doing," she replies. "The professor keeps emphasizing that everything must be statistically sound, so I've got to make sure that the numbers of interviews, subjects, responses, etc. all measure up." Alan inquires about the exact nature of her study. "I'm analyzing the acculturation process of aboriginal Australians to life in the city, the city of London." This sounds extremely esoteric to Alan. He could have feigned enthusiastic interest but his actual interest in the subject is only slight and he wants to be sincere. "That's pretty interesting," he says. "What major conclusions have you drawn, so far?" At this time the driver pulls up in front of the pub. Alan thanks and pays him, leaving a generous tip. Alan is still floating on a cloud after the magic kiss.

They enter the resonantly active pub and locate what appears to be the quietest table. She responds to his question, "Well, the study is ongoing, but so far we have had some expectations met and been quite surprised by some of the findings. It seems that in assimilating the fast-paced, modern culture, many of the natives withdraw and cling tightly to ancient customs and practices while others voluntarily renounce most of their traditions and replace them with elements of their newfound environment." Alan's interest mysteriously grows.

"That's interesting. The so-called primitive, unadulterated in contrast with the so-called modern, industrialized setting is pretty bizarre. Have you ever read, *The Origin of Consciousness in the Breakdown of the Bicameral Mind,* by Julian Jaynes?" he asks her. "No I haven't," she replies. "What is that one about?" "Basically, it's a synopsis of the evolution of the human brain; of modern human consciousness from a primordial, 'bicameral,' state to the integrated, modern state. Jaynes' idea is that the human brain, in so-called primitives, is ruled by two realms, making it quite likely that the individual will listen to a higher voice, or auditory hallucinations which will guide them in their behavior and activities. In this view, the concept of 'God' is a creation from the bicameral mind. As the brain evolved, it gradually developed mechanisms to quell inner voices and subsequently have less experiences of 'God.' After all, most of the world's religions developed at least 2000 years ago—many long before that."

Ronia grabs a passing waitress and orders a Bloody Mary. Alan asks for a scotch and water. "So this Julian Jaynes character felt that modern-day experiences of God were highly unlikely?" Ronia posits. "He would probably say those experiences would most likely occur in schizophrenics and other mentally disorganized—who would be considered to be representations of the bicameral mind frame."

Alan excuses himself and wanders off momentarily to locate a cigarette machine. Alan enjoys an occasional cigarette. After offering one to Ronia, who politely declines, Alan lights up a rich American menthol and inhales deeply. As circles of smoke spiral down the tunnel of his esophagus, Alan savors the taste, then blows a steady stream while casually turning his head to the left. Ronia smiles at this amusingly amateurish, but highly effective gesture to look cool. "Do you like reggae?" Alan asks her. "Yeah, very much." "Well, on Saturday there's going to be a pretty cool gathering. A friend of mine's gonna be rockin. I'd like you to go with me if you want." "I'd love to," she replies in a warm, pleasant tone. Up until this point neither one has made any mention of their moment of passion back at the hotel. It is on both of their minds noticeably but not overwhelmingly. Ronia decides to bring this prevailing emotion to words: "Back at the hotel things got a bit intense. I must say I was not expecting you to kiss me, but I'm glad it happened. Who would have thought dear Mary and Jim would have a nephew who happens to be a wonderful kisser?" Alan strains to suppress his inevitable, uncontrollable blushing. His cheeks flush a raspberry red as he reticently responds, "I must admit, I shock myself. The ambience of the moment; your charm and beauty, all conspired to overcome me. I'm glad it happened, too." He slides his hand elegantly toward hers and then carefully grasps her fingers in his—thus satiating the compulsive, universal need for bodily contact during exchanges of such intimate words. Her fingers are delicate and fragile. He lightly manipulates his fingers between hers, relishing the simple, sentient pleasure of touch. "How precious," he ponders, "that this beautiful, pastoral creature has vouchsafed to me her presence tonight." He speaks up: "I have immensely enjoyed being with you tonight. I better get you home before it gets too late."

As he holds her hand in romantic repose, he leans forward and kisses her gently on her forehead. After motioning for the waitress and paying the check, he leads Ronia out through the front door and onto the sidewalk where he quickly hails a cab.

On the way to Mary and Jim's, Alan makes arrangements with Ronia about what time he will pick her up. When the cab pulls up in front of the house, Alan asks the driver to wait a minute while he walks Ronia to the door. He takes her by the hand and leads her up the sidewalk swiftly and steadily. When they reach the front door of the house, Alan whispers to her, "Goodnight," and kisses her on the cheek. He quickly returns to the cab for he does not want to wake his aunt and uncle. As he opens the door and climbs into the back seat of the cab, he glances back at the house and watches as she safely closes the door behind her. He wonders what future directions this strange union with an enigmatic French girl will take. The one certainty is that his path is irrevocably altered by this unexpected introduction. Alan politely instructs the cabbie on where his hotel is located.

On his way there, Alan attempts to organize in his mind some sort of long term plan for where he wants to travel, what countries he wants to see, and what he can learn in each place. There is still a lot to be seen in England, he figures. He has always heard that the countryside is beautiful. There are castles to be explored and one stop, which seems requisite, is Oxford. Alan desires greatly to see the magnificent halls of Oxford University and the town square where numerous monks were burned for heresy in the 14th and 15th centuries. In addition to Oxford, Alan longs to see the quaint city of William Shakespeare's life and death, Stratford-Upon-Avon. The cab speeds along the darkened, almost deserted streets of London as Alan contemplates the unforeseen. The incipient relationship forming with Ronia was entirely unexpected. At a minimum, it ensures that Alan will prolong his stay in London a little longer.

The cab tumbles up to the front driveway of the hotel and Alan gets out and pays the driver. He scurries to his room while fumbling for his key. Upon entering, he walks over to the book on mysticism and turns to the bookmarked page.

Alan's somewhat alcohol-wearied vision strains to focus intently on the beginning of a paragraph that reads: "In 1934, Carl Jung introduced *Archetypes of the Collective Unconscious* in which, among a myriad of other issues, he sketches a history of the term, 'archetype,' and delineates several implications of this term and its significance to man's interest in the unknown." Alan is feeling extremely tired all of a sudden, so closes the book and kicks off his shoes. He lies back on his bed and gently allows his eyes to close.

When sleep slowly descends, Alan's awareness moves into an odd dimension encompassing fragments of his day's events and fleeting images of Ronia's face juxtaposed with African drummers frantically keeping pace with a passionate, pulsating rhythm. Through a fog of mist, he sees the face of his uncle Al, Alan's parents, Aunt Mary and Uncle Jim, and the physical surroundings of his hometown. All are being overcome violently by a tumultuous, claustrophobic deluge. A child is crying piercingly in a secluded room. Suddenly, a crowd of sports fans which fills a large stadium begins to cheer loudly and them emits thunderous chants of carefully synchronized words of ridicule and laughs. Alan zooms in to get a closer look at whatever sport event is causing such a display. As he flies into the stadium, horror immediately grips his soul as he realizes that he is standing in the middle of the field dressed only in a skimpy, pathetic looking pair of underwear and nothing else, obviously making Alan the shining source of amusement.

Alan is immediately awakened by a thud outside his door. It seems some late night partiers are struggling in and bumping up against the walls as they enter their rooms. Within minutes, Alan is back asleep. The remainder of his dream time is fortunately spent recalling a treasured concert he had attended back in the states. One of England's more delightful purveyors of gloom, The Cure, had sung and played guitar hypnotically, and struck resonant chords within our protagonist. Fortunately he is fully dressed.

Daylight comes quickly. Alan arises not thoroughly refreshed but anxious about an enjoyable day in London. He goes downstairs and has a cup of coffee and toast with honey and butter. With his backpack in tow he traipses over to the subway station and purchases a one way ticket to get him to The Tower of London. As he meanders in the direction of the train stop, he takes notice of a solitary musician heartfully strumming folksy, soulful cover tunes from various artists mainly from the '60s and '70s. The man has an unkempt appearance and plays rather enthusiastically despite the fact that virtually no one is placing coins in his opened case. Alan notices a small pile of mainly small coins sitting near the pick box. He slowly walks up to the guitar player and drops an American dollar in his case. The man looks up and gives a subtle nod to Alan, never missing a chord in his beautiful but strangely more Eastern version of "Give Peace A Chance." Alan hears the distant but rapidly approaching cries of the train's engine. He abruptly stands up to the edge of the track and boards quickly when the doors open.

Upon entering, Alan peruses with great interest the various faces of the train riders. Within each line or crease in the cheeks and every imaginable size and hair color, he sees eclectic appearances and mannerisms that reflect the vagaries of the city he is in. He feels this is a distinct way of getting living, rhythmic pulses of the city at large and how it functions. As the train rapidly departs the depot and heads east, Alan scours the posted map of the subway routes to confirm he is headed in the right direction. Standing between the map and him is a young, demure woman who is more than likely a student. She carries a brown, weathered backpack and keeps her head surreptitiously lowered while the train scurries along. By the centrifugal force of the train's speedy movement and the crowded conditions, the proximity between Alan and this alluring stranger becomes gradually closer. She has curly, dark hazelnut locks and olive skin. Her breasts heave underneath a diaphanous lining of a bronze shirt.

An unexpected bump sends Alan grasping for the handrail. He hovers dangerously close; hopefully unostentatiously roaming with his eyes the sundry curves and fleshly nuances she presents so innocently. Sporadic glances emerge from her mostly hidden eyes. Fleeting visual contact with Alan sends waves of titillating warmth through the channels of his bloodstream. She exudes aromatic offerings encapsulating a pleasantly toxic mixture of mild hormone excretion with sumptuous French perfume.

After several stops, the train comes to rest at Tower Bridge Road. Alan emerges slightly intoxicated from the ride but anxiously anticipating a tour of the Tower of London, as well as an aimless stroll beside the river Thames. Alan buys a ticket for admission to the castle, but before entering, finds a bench to sit on for a moment. He is in the mood for a little philosophy so reaches into his backpack and pulls out his trusty book on mysticism.

Scanning to where he had left off, he begins to read: "Jung proceeds with the following; the term 'archetype' occurs as early as Philo Judaeus, with reference to the Imago Dei (God-Image) in man. It can also be found in Ireneus, who says: 'The creator of the world did not fashion these things directly from himself but copied them from archetypes outside himself.'" Alan reinserts the bookmark and returns the book to his bag. Feeling suddenly inspired, he pulls out his notebook and pen and prepares to transcribe as he allows his thoughts to flow.

Before writing anything down, he takes a deep breath and quietly thanks the higher powers for a perfectly overcast, rainy, and ideally contemplative day. He begins to write:

"Man is currently on the brink; on the edge of a precipitous incline or decline in consciousness or an awareness of himself, his surroundings, and the endlessly chaotic, tumultuous relationship of himself with his environment. Man—some 4.5 billion years ago—began as an infinitesimal amoeba presciently learning to swim (DNA programmed) and to strategically yet mysteriously migrate toward terra firma: an evolution methodically progressing through levels and structures—mere precursors for what man would ultimately become. Arduously penetrating the primordial sludge, selectively adapting morphological/anatomical assets to meet each new challenge. Man arose from very humble beginnings. Life on the surface of this young planet perhaps could have remained simple—unconscious, insentient microorganisms blindly roaming the mossy regions without any use or desire for photosynthetic-oxygen based reality. Ultraviolet protection arose enigmatically in the surreptitious form of an ozone layer shielding and hovering seemingly weightlessly over a blue atmosphere. Amphibious ascension and scaly adaptations propelled aquatic life to assimilate and accommodate with ever-changing demands."

Alan puts the pen down. He closes his eyes briefly to savor the precious, intermittent rays of sunlight peering through the rain clouds. With his ticket in hand, he lifts himself forcefully from the bench and filters in with the crowd that enters the Tower. Alan takes notice of the cavernous moat encircling the impressive building. Tourists endlessly snap pictures and children cry as a foreboding narrator bespeaks the medieval horrors committed here at the castle (all in the name of treason and religious, ideological dissension.)

Alan immediately breaks away from the crowd and proceeds to conduct an individualized tour of the surroundings. Incredibly small, almost claustrophobic corridors showcase relics: priceless jewelry and other regalia from some of England's most infamous kings and queens. On the premises is the small 12th century chapel of St. Peter and Vincula, containing the graves of Ann Boleyn and Catherine Howard, wives of Henry VIII, who were beheaded on Tower Green, near the chapel. Beneath Waterloo Barracks, Alan scans the opulent—and in his mind, sometimes ostentatious—crown jewels that represent regalia from the mid-19th century to 1967. On such a muggy day as this, Alan feels that the moisture extricates and in a sense transubstantiates antiquated scents from the walls of a castle and makes its interior exude with spirits from the past.

While touring one of the on-site towers, Beauchamp, Alan contemplates the terrifying thought of prisoners being held in syncopated, dreary spaces without much of a glimmer of sunlight. While in a self-perceived "enlightened" state, Alan shivers at the horrifying realization that throughout human history man has systematically imprisoned man; that the glorious, autonomous nature of human consciousness existing within each individual skull could be forcibly contained and enclosed within something no more than a small stone box with bars and chains. Alan wonders if perhaps his personal phobia of tight spaces is a result of having had ancestors suffer the abominable dungeon imprisonment. Perhaps through some Lamarckian neural etching, Alan's nervous system would periodically awaken to the ancient fears once propitiated through horrendous, unspeakable tortures against the family tree. He shakes off the morbid musings and shifts his awareness to an aperture at the end of an extended hallway. He gravitates to the sunlight that beckons him as an unpollinated flower beckons a fertile bee. Alan climbs a somewhat circuitous stairwell that leads to the exterior of the castle. He emerges onto what appears to have been a cannon platform. From this strategically elevated site, he can see clearly out over London Bridge and the Thames river. At quite a distance stand a few spires and clocks of the most towering edifices in central London. Alan sits and rests on a stone block.

He reaches into his backpack and removes the small vial containing his now dwindling drug supply. He snaps open the lid and meticulously removes one tab of acid. After placing it carefully on his tongue, he sips casually from his water bottle and semi-consciously constructs the following words:

"What higher, metaphysical truths await me, I shall soon see. For as the ravens hover skyward they foretell the mystery. Hallowed cathedral. Cavernous walls. An echo emerges from a deep, dark chasm as life breathes its energy into the universe. A hush and a whisper softly unfold the very diaphanous fabric of time and space itself. Visual fibrillations titillating, tectonic, retinal, neural plates unfold as galaxies orgasm symphonically. The walls tragically but magically collapse in on themselves giving birth to emergent stellar dust that presciently tells the tale of spiraling eternally rejuvenating existence."

Only minutes have elapsed since Alan ingested the ambrosia. In addition to waves of poetic undulations—sweating beads of bizarre verbiage from his brain—colors and images of vibrancy and structural alchemy pervade his perceptual field. He literally grabs the edge of his seat for this unusual ride. Voluptuous, cumulous clouds float hypnotically above. Various incarnations of amoeba-like figures take interesting shape within the now Rorschach cloud formations. Down below, on the river, sails a steady barge as innumerable passers-by line the sidewalks parallel to the river. Alan sits silently as an influx of words makes a cognitive entrance:

Infinite portals of time rhythmically pulsating and emanating microcosmic fragments of thought collapsing in on space—omnipresent yet transparent.

How I long for the days of purple haze, plummeting into sensual bliss; an interplanetary union resulting in perceptual heights—an undertaking not to be remiss.

An exalting of spirit—an extension of neural heights—an adventurous penetration into the mystery surrounding the pinnacle of pleasure, realizable in a simple yet cosmic kiss.

CHAPTER 6

Cool, treacly droplets of perspiration emanate from all over Alan's body. His heart rate accelerates noticeably. "God, would I make an incredible case study for Ronia," he thinks, rhetorically. He stands up and begins to descend the path, which exits the tower. With the backpack strapped firmly around his shoulder and the sweet tinges of soreness from muscular exertion in his legs, Alan fuses with the bustling droves of tourists.

To calm and balance his now highly stimulated nervous system, he begins to judiciously inhale through his nose and exhale through his mouth and then repeats the process for a series of repetitions. This ancient method of breath control he had learned through the practice of karate always aids in restoring energy and sangfroid during a drug trip. Alan's brain absorbingly imprints the sundry stimuli of the city: the busy refreshment stands; vendors marketing various products; blood red trolleys chugging along with business-clad passengers; lovers embracing passionately while taking in views of seagulls that nibble frantically at bread morsels. The alternately musty and salty scents of the city by the river permeate his olfactory nerves.

Alan wanders by foot up north through the suburbs of Whitechapel and Spitalfields, simultaneously thinking of Ronia and his indefinite plans of leaving London to explore other terrain. He hops on a trolley and pays the ticket handler. This takes him gingerly west through Barbican and Holborn. Alan leans his torso partially outside to feel a breeze as the trolley passes by rustic residences and weathered awnings that represent the homes of London's true residents—hard-working, modest Brits who work their restaurants and other family businesses honorably, struggling to survive.

To Alan, England's economic and social diversity somehow coalesce in central London. In cities like Los Angeles and New York, vast wealth stands in striking contrast to abject poverty. Alan senses a greater harmony and cohesion among London's economically disparate residents. Near King's Cross, Alan hops off and hikes along one of London's

49

busiest streets with everything from beauty shops to pet stores and dance clubs converging with movie stores and hardware stores. Next to stores plying biblical texts are bustling pubs.

With his head still reeling from the drug, he scans the different shops and tries to locate someplace interesting to browse. Next to a tool shop stands a macabre, ethnic store which seems to be largely African, with an array of tribal masks hanging in the window. He approaches cautiously for a closer inspection.

In the storefront window sit myriad assortments of beads, blankets, and packages of tarot cards. Incense burns sumptuously through the doorway as an alluring Nepalese woman motions for Alan to enter. As he always does in such a sensitized state, he hesitates and assesses the situation to determine the level of safety. The place seems eerie, which partly attracts yet simultaneously repels Alan's interest. Curiosity compels Alan to enter. He affectedly saunters through the doorway and consequently catapults his consciousness into a decidedly surreal, mystical zone. Donning all four walls of the shop are various mementos from African countries and Caribbean islands that represent the rich Voodoo religions. Masks, swords, feathers, dolls, and beads in shades of mauve, reds, brown and sundry textures of leather cover the rooms.

"How do you do?" asks the dreamlike chanteuse in a deep monotone voice. Alan notices traces of South American and French accents in the voice. "Very well, thank you," he replies. "You have a very interesting shop."

Whenever Alan speaks during a full-blown acid trip he always—always—wonders if the recipient of his message is aware that he is tripping. He glances into a hanging mirror and notices that his pupils are severely dilated. His cheeks are flushed and his hair is somewhat tousled. He cannot help but notice a beautifully ornate gold-laden frame enclosing the mirror. Small, elf-like figurines are holding hands in a dance around the edge. The top of the frame holds a large joker mask that has an ebullient but mischievous smile. For a moment, Alan uncannily feels a stare directed at him from the joker. "I have traveled all over the world," speaks the woman.

"Everything you see on the walls is something that I have a great interest in." Alan smiles at her while trying to pay attention to barely audible voices emitting from a small room in the back of the shop. Alan wanders back there under the pretense of perusing a box of shrunken heads. A door is open and releases a male and a female voice. Alan peers into the room—as if simply trying to determine if there are further *objets d'art.*

He discovers an enthusiastic man in a turban guiding a female client through a psychic session. They are seated snuggly around a small table with a beautiful crystal ball shining in the center. The man is wearing a tightly fitting black bandanna around his head as he closes his eyes and verbally invokes a saintly spirit to make itself known. The seated woman chants softly a mysterious incantation while Alan trembles with fear.

Alan moves away swiftly and ventures back into the main shop. As soon as he passes a hanging portrait of the 16th century sorcerer, John Dee, Alan hears a glass shatter resoundingly. A reverberating tingle makes its way rapidly up and down Alan's spine as he proudly discovers the source of the noise. He witnesses the shopkeeper leaning over to pick up pieces of a broken ceramic bowl that apparently had fallen with a pile of books that had leaned its way. Alan rushes up to assist the woman. As he leans over and picks up one of the pieces, he inspects its unique design. The acid lens microscope of his perception narrows focus on a gold and burgundy inlaid, flower-pastel lacquer gem that shimmers in ubiquitous candlelight. He hands the piece to the woman, whose silky hair and bronze skin soothe his anxious nerves. "Will you go ahead and move the books over there?" the woman asks, while pointing to a table across the room.

Alan wants to be helpful but doesn't realize he will be put to work. He complies with her directive and then picks up one of the books. Its title is: *From Alchemy to the Symbolists: A Definitive Guide to Mysticism and The Occult.* Alan's mind is on fire. The drug is causing the pages of the book to breathe as he flips through it randomly. The first page he comes to is on the Cabala. It says something about being of Jewish origin and existing as some sort of quest for the secrets of faith. Alan reads something about ignorant people considering only the clothes as the story and not what the clothes actually conceal, which is the true essence. One section speaks of "God wishing to see God." This gives Alan a chill. "This is fairly abstract stuff," Alan thinks. "When God starts to see God and I feel as if I'm communing with God, there's no telling where this could go." Apparently the Cabala is based on sacred texts such as the Torah. A popular book within the Cabala is the Zohar which appeared in the 13th century. Alan learns about "the dream of Golem" in medieval Christian literature; a magician gives life to a "homunculus", or little man. It seems that Golem, an automaton, helps to protect persecuted Jews and the homunculus serves as a sort of housekeeper for the magi-

cian. "Pretty weird shit," Alan thinks. He scans through the book noticing sections on well-known mystics and movements within occultism. It
is all extremely fascinating to him, especially in this drug-enhanced state.
"How much is this book?" Alan calls out to the woman. "It's 10
pounds," she replies. "I'll take it." While Alan hands her the money, he
notices delicate, beautiful veins underneath the skin on her hands. Her
nails are long, finely manicured, and painted purple. He slides the book
in his backpack and gazes at the woman while now almost hoping that
she will recognize his heightened state. She smiles at him and continues
her task of arranging flasks of incense sticks on a shelf behind the
counter.

At this time, Alan hears the two psychic participants' voices much
louder as they emerge from the back room and begin trickling toward the
front. The two appear now quite visibly disheveled, as if their trip to the
outer limits has left them strained. The man is saying goodbye to the
woman, his client, and offering her some consoling words about following her internal guide and about setting a shining example for others.
Being near individuals who strive toward some psychic trance or spirit
world leaves Alan in an ambivalent state. On one hand, he feels that it is
as noble a pursuit as any to try to communicate with the dead or with the
future. On the other hand, Alan experiences intense fear about opening
the soul to such an experience and serious doubt concerning the scientific
success of such endeavors. The man seems to be a charlatan but it fright-
ens Alan, nevertheless. The woman writes the man a check, swings her
purse over her shoulder, and says goodbye as she walks out of the store.
"Sir, would you like to have your palms read?" the man asks Alan. Alan
thinks: "No thanks, I'm afraid my bloodline's operating in hyperspace
right now," but actually declines respectfully by saying,

"No thank you. I would rather not know if something catastrophic is
going to imminently befall me." The man laughs and in a strong English
accent retorts,

"There is safety in astrological knowledge, my friend, and the stars
never lie." Alan responds, "There is safety in psychedelic knowledge, my
friend, and to spiritualize with the dead freaks me out." Alan watches the
man step behind the counter and put his arm around the woman. He
thanks them for the book and promptly leaves.

Alan is hungry, so he stops in a deli and orders a sandwich. He sits on
a stool by the window and proceeds to chastise himself for not interact-
ing more substantively with the two mysterious shopkeepers. There are
many things Alan does not know much about. He has always held in

question the veracity of certain paranormal experiences such as the invoking of spirits or telekinesis. Alan maintains a highly skeptical, cynical perspective on these matters despite his bent toward mysticism.

The major reason he is traveling is to learn more about the unknown; to gain knowledge about those things he is unfamiliar with. He tortures himself for not engaging in conversation with the woman and casting aside preconceptions of the man. "Why is it?" he asks himself, did he so quickly judge those individuals and curtail further involvement with them? A cornucopia of ideas is there for the mining and all he can think about as he eats his sandwich is how he has fucking blown it.

Psychotomimetic effects from the drug are gradually waning. Traces of psychotropic effects will remain until he sleeps but they are gradually dissipating. The lights appear very unpleasantly bright so Alan takes his sandwich outside, walks across the street to a park and assumes a comfortable lotus position on the grass. The strange African masks he has seen in the voodoo shop have left lasting images in his mind. The enigmatic couple operating the shop seemed to have been carefully designed and placed characters created to intrigue and propel him toward further questioning and philosophical pursuit. "What role does such a spiritual hodgepodge of a shop play in the greater scheme of things?" he wonders. "What exactly does the seeker of truth gain by visiting a so-called psychic or palm reader? Does the crystal ball truly foretell events or does the participant simply project her own guesses onto the situation?"

Alan reaches into his bag and removes a cigarette, which he solemnly lights and takes a deep drag on. The rich, smooth caress of smoke stimulates his taste buds. His eyes feel watery and are slightly burning as the lysergic acid periodically returns for encore effects. As a soft wind passes swiftly through the trees, Alan listens intently to the chatter of leaves and the creaking and swaying of branches. Various robins and cardinals flutter through the sky as Alan sits back very still and simply relishes the symphony of chemicals in his system.

While taking another drag, he pulls out his original book on mysticism and begins to read where he thinks he has left off: "The term, 'archetype' occurs as early as Philo Judaeus, with reference to the Imago Dei (God-image) in man. It can also be found in Ireneus, who says: 'The creator of the world did not fashion these things directly from himself but copied them from archetypes outside himself.' In the Corpus Hermeticum, God is called the archetypal light. Jung lists a few other examples and then proceeds to discuss the importance of archetypes in providing man meaning for that which would otherwise be incomprehensible. Religions have traditionally imbued their subjects with dogmatic symbols upon which to base their beliefs and implant their trust."

Alan shuts the book and puts it back into his bag. He longs to call Ronia and feels almost well-composed enough to communicate. After one last puff on the cigarette, he crams it into the dirt and throws the butt away in a trash can. He locates a pay phone and dials her number, praying that his aunt and uncle will not answer the call. He covers the speaker with his hand in case he needs to disguise his voice. Sure enough, Aunt Mary answers: "Hello!" "Hi, may I speak to Ronia?" Alan strains to mutter human but unidentifiable words in the midst of his other-worldly state of mind. "Yes, just a minute please," Mary replies, apparently not recognizing his voice.

While Mary is apparently searching for Ronia, Alan wonders if he effectively disguised his voice. He can hear Ronia making her way to the phone. "Hello, this is Ronia," float the heavenly words into Alan's aural canal. Ronia's French accent meets caressingly with Alan's somewhat ringing mind. "Ronia, I had to call you—not to sound frantic or anything but I have some interesting ideas that I want to discuss with you. They might pertain to your studies," he adds, to offer further enticement. "Please meet me at Carlton's Pub near your house. Do you know the one?" "Yes, I think so," she responds in a reticent but mildly receptive manner. "What time do you want to meet?" Alan states that thirty minutes would be perfect. "Alright, I'll see you then," she concludes.

CHAPTER 7

Alan picks himself up and dusts off his pants with his hands. A light, cool breeze sweeps through as he heads to the subway. He drops a token in the slot and locates the appropriate train. When he arrives at the destination, he exits the train and hikes vigorously up two flights of stairs to the street. Quickly running his fingers through his hair, he hopes that his exhaustion is not too evident in his outward appearance.

He arrives at the pub first, saunters up to the bar and slides onto a stool. He methodically composes in his mind a series of topics and a general modus operandi for broaching and maintaining conversation with her. She arrives only ten minutes late and glides through the entrance with her hair fashionably braided and slim, curvy hips swaying smoothly. The distaff signals in several places at the bar awaken and compel their hosts to gawk not inconspicuously. Alan's pulse quickens. He smiles as their eyes meet across the room. When she gets to the bar, Alan has already ordered two drinks.

As he hands his cash to the bartender, within his periphery he notices with not much alarm but mainly amusement a young man assertively engaging Ronia in conversation. Alan has heard some truly pathetic pick-up lines and has probably used a few but the ones he is currently listening to are some of the worst. The only difference is the distinct English accent, which if this had been America, might have actually created some competition for Alan. "I haven't seen you here before, lassie." "What's a pretty looking dame like you doin here?"

Ronia successfully ignores and politely rebuffs all advances as she leans over to kiss Alan on the cheek. She exercises deft politeness and the utmost of grace in declining attention from men at the bar. "I hope this is what you want," Alan offers, as he hands her a red wine. "This is great," she graciously responds. He steps to a table and borrows a chair for her to sit down. She sits and begins to gaze imploringly into his eyes. Her anticipation for hearing the so-called revelatory ideas is immense.

"You look beautiful tonight. I'm very glad you could come out," he speaks softly. He continues a little more audibly: "I've had a pretty interesting day today and wanted to share it with you." "I'm glad I came out, too. I was working on a paper but needed a break and was anxious to hear your stories," she enthuses. Alan fights hard the seemingly irresistible urge to slide everything off the bar, violently rip off her clothes, and with their bodies naked and serpentinely intertwined, make extended passionate love. "You look like a little boy at an amusement park," she whispers in a barely sonorous voice. "I feel like I've been at an amusement park," he replies playfully. "I've had an incredible time today. Are you ready to hear my story?" he asks. "Just a minute," she says as she reaches into her purse and removes a lighter and cigarette. She elegantly places the filter between her lips and lights the tip. "Okay, I'm ready," she hums.

"Well, I started out at the Tower of London—which I must say is one of the most historically and architecturally impressive places I've ever seen. After touring the mysterious, darkened corridors and feeling as if I had stepped far back into time, I studied the royal relics and the contraptions where prisoners were held. I then ascended to the top floor from which I could view London in all its grandeur: from arguably the best vantage point around."

Alan had deliberated over how and when he would introduce her to his interest in psychedelics. He could have cautiously brought it up in the context of anthropological theories and correlations of sorts. Instead he opts for the brazenly forthright choice of simply confessing it. "While sitting next to the remnants of a cannon—which I'm sure had fired infinite rounds of ammunition in its time, I ingested about 200 micrograms of LSD, which fired off some of the more bizarre, tantalizing neural connections I have ever experienced."

He waits for her reaction. He then continues to speak while her face carefully transforms from complacent anticipation to a surprising look of eagerness and almost enrapture. "It took about thirty minutes for the effects to take hold dramatically; and then, well, it got pretty crazy. I felt at times that I was one with the elements—somehow depersonalized from my individual existence, yet unified with life around me. At other times, faces of passers-by would transmogrify into contorted, animatedly expressive countenances reflective or reminiscent of extraterrestrial life. I would then identify with the—at times—pleasantly painful tension in my muscles, particularly in my legs as I walked. Adrenaline ran frantically through my veins and my heart pounded alternately loudly and docilely."

He knows he is rambling but his craving for conversation is intense. He tries to slow himself down and recollect his thoughts. She listens intently. "I relished the view of London from where I sat and truly felt that in my heightened state I was perceiving it in a way that no one had ever done. Of course we all have subjective experiences and no two people see things exactly the same."

Ronia smiles warmly and continues to look interested, despite Alan's concern that he is either unable to sufficiently articulate his magnificent experience or that Ronia actually couldn't care less about this sort of self-indulgent, chemically induced voyage. She inhales one last puff of the cigarette and asks the bartender for another drink.

She thinks she will attempt to somehow narrow down or quantify his revelations. "Did you feel as if you were transcending reality or actually experiencing objective reality a little deeper?" "Both," he quickly answers. "Now, at any point during this trip, did you become distressed, disturbed, or panicked in any way?" "At times, I was slightly uneasy and it is a little peculiar to entertain stories of decapitations and burnings while in the sensitized state; but other than that, it wasn't until later at the voodoo shop that things got a bit spooky. You didn't let me finish. I was getting to that part." "Okay, please continue—so sorry to interrupt," she says, sarcastically. "All right," he begins with feigned seriousness. "So after the castle, I basically wandered around a bit before coming to a mysterious-looking, very interesting shop containing various religious and occult paraphernalia and a few enigmatic people. The drug effects are still noticeable at this point." "You're telling me," she quips. They both laugh.

Alan pauses for a sip of beer. "I entered very cautiously and scanned the mementos and artifacts which mainly represent some of the darker, more ominous dimensions. A beautifully frightening lady attended the shop while her male friend was conducting a psychic session or seance in the back with another woman. In a strange way I felt that I had been in this place before or that there was some higher reason for me being there. I studied the store meticulously and came across some interesting things. Here, take a look at this."

He reaches into his bag and pulls out the book he purchased at the shop. He hands it to her as she starts a second glass of wine. She arbitrarily opens to page 100 which has the name "Rosenkreuz" printed at the top. She scans the first couple of paragraphs, which tell the story of the man who—having been born into a penniless home in Germany—very early in life becomes interested in touring the "Holy Land" in which he can learn about various subjects ranging from Arabic to physics. "Christian Rosenkreuz"—for whom Ronia cannot determine the reality of (mythic or actual)—was a Rosicrucian written about in the *Fama Fraternitatis*, the basic text of Rosicrucianism.

She looks around briefly, wondering what people must think of her reading this book at the bar. Alan is sitting and passively enjoying watching Ronia study the pages. Her eyes are luminescent as she begins to read aloud: "The Fama Fraternitatis refers to the Trigoneum Igneum, the triangle formed by the heavenly Aries, Leo, and Sagittarius in 1603, which was supposedly the fortuitous, promising start of a brand new period." "Alan, this is pretty cool stuff," she proclaims with exuberance. "This is pretty wild. This page goes on to tell of a spirited journey Christian embarks upon in which he seeks knowledge from various wise sources and travels to a castle in which he undergoes a series of tests. He is then magically initiated and wakens to a new spiritual life. That sounds uncannily like what you have been through today."

Alan is appreciative of her enthusiasm but somewhat bemused at the prospect of yet another significant dimension to his day. He wonders at the perplexing prospect that his individual existence—in particular, his spiritual goal of traveling to Europe—is maybe just the recreation of an age-old, perpetuating myth. "How bizarre," he thinks. Ronia quickly examines several more of the pages which contain names such as: Abulafia, Bacon, Boullan, Cagliostro, Crowley, Della Porta, Fabre d'Olivet, Flamel, Fulcanelli, Guenon, Gurdjieff, and many, many others.

"I've been in the process of trying to figure out where I'm going from here," Alan asserts. "I feel satiated from my stay in London although I'm sure one could live here interminably and never really see or do everything. I've been thinking of renting a car and touring the English countryside; places such as Oxford, Stratford, and Warwick seem to be essential stops. I think I may start making arrangements to leave pretty soon." "That sounds like a good plan," Ronia replies, reticently. "However, I would be sad to see you leave."

Alan feels the overwhelming urge to envelop the silky folds of her lips in his mouth and tenderly caress Ronia's hair. The light in the bar is slowly dimming and Alan selectively tunes out the noise of voices as he leans in her direction and delicately places a kiss on her mouth. Alan tastes the sweet combination of saliva, smoke, and barley from the beer—all of which bathe her tongue in a mixture that is dangerously tempting.

Not wanting to let go and sensing that Ronia doesn't either, Alan cradles the back of her head with his hand as their mouths fuse in sensuous delight. He savors her fragrant, womanly aroma and relishes the heavenly soft touch of her skin. Her breath is spicy, almost honey-tinged energy that he absorbs in ecstasy.

Alan's pulse quickens. He stands up from the stool and gently but firmly takes Ronia's hand. He settles the tab and proceeds to lead Ronia to the exit. It has begun to rain as a dense, charcoal mist envelops the street. Under the barely penetrating lights and faintly visible towering spires, Alan can make out the outline and color of an approaching cab. He steps out into the street and calls out loudly for it to stop.

With his arm wrapped lightly around Ronia's waist, he motions for her to enter the cab and then follows her inside. He directs the driver to take them to Alan's hotel. On the ride there, Alan cradles Ronia's delicate frame and treasures the intimacy between their bodies. The cab barrels along the circuitous streets that Alan had grown to know and love. An indelible imprint of the respective sights and sounds emanating from these London streets has been formed from within Alan's mind.

As the car progresses further toward what might soon become an erotic destination, he gazes out the window. Through the fog and rain are fragments of images that seem to bind with neural receptors. With this beautiful creature in his arms, he philosophizes that his mind has evolved in unison and congruence with the daily evolutions of the city.

The cab comes to an almost screeching halt in front of the hotel. Alan pays the driver and politely but commandingly leads Ronia up to his room. Pausing momentarily at the door to kiss her, Alan thanks the higher powers for such a fortuitous night.

Smoothly unlocking and pushing back the door, he resolutely lifts her up and carries her to the bed. He lays her down gently on the bed cover and begins to drop effervescent kisses that start at her forehead and systematically but freely move down, stopping only long enough to linger at her lips, neck, chest and stomach. Then he successfully pushes aside pieces of clothing with his lips and teeth. He straddles her slender body with his legs and supports his weight by leaning to the side and extending his elbows to the mattress. Warmth and fragrance exude from her body as he softly caresses various portions of her skin with only his lips. Stopping at her chest, left revealed by the unfastening of only a few buttons, Alan holds his mouth and cheek against her long enough to feel the throbbing, pulsating rhythm of her heart. Sensing an imminent explosion of pleasure from Ronia's titillated, pheromonally oozing body, Alan brushes his mouth lightly down to her freshly exposed navel in which he gradually deposits his tongue.

She emits emotionally fueled whispers and moans of pleasure as Alan stimulates with the tip of his tongue the microscopic walls and concave surface of that mysterious anatomical feature which serves as natal lifeline to us all. With an infinitesimal trail of saliva he traces a line from her navel to her vulva, stopping only momentarily to unbuckle and slide off her pants. He feels rapture as his head hovers between her creamy white muscular thighs.

With both of her hands she grasps the headboard behind her as Alan slides his tongue along the vaginal folds. He firmly extends his hands to the inside of her thighs as he orally makes contact with her now steaming, highly erect clitoris. Sporadically, Ronia's thighs close in around Alan's cheeks as the muscles in her buttocks pleasurably tighten in response to his stimulations. He slowly, alternately strokes the labial contours and sensory hot spots in rhythm with the subtle cues her body is giving him. He taunts her patiently as her anticipation grows in proportion to the fluids accumulating on and around his tongue.

As the swollen tissues throb against Alan's mouth, he repetitively tantalizes and manipulates her organ into a resounding crescendo of orgasm. Hopelessly involuntary pulses of energy, muscular contraction and release, and spasmodic vibrations accent her screams and sighs of pleasure. She gleefully succumbs to the powers of nature, highlighted within the throes of ecstasy. Alan cheerfully tastes the sundry offerings of honeysuckle—ambrosia that gentles the motion of his tongue while he maintains contact inside her.

She pauses to rest and revel in the coital ambience and appetizer as Alan removes his pants and manually tickles her thighs and buttocks. She then reaches down with both her hands, grabs Alan's arms and pulls him on top of her so that his gushing, erect shaft merges flush with her bristling mound. Reaching down to hold the tip of his penis between her fingers, she places it up against her crevice, allowing him to plunge into the moist, warm folds. Inch by inch he penetrates her depths until the base of his vulva is flush against hers, pleasantly intermingling the pubic strands in a primordial dance. He slides the rest of the garment from her body and presses his chest against hers. Her skin is soft and translucent like silk and her bones as delicate as an angel's. With smooth motion he repeatedly plumbs her sentient walls while perceptively responding to her ecstatic moans with according movements. As he melts inside her, he softly kisses her cheek and whispers to her that she is beautiful. Her hips willfully swing back and forth in harmony and rhythmic synchronicity with his as they both gladly fall further into bliss.

Both drift into a state of deep sleep. Their bodies are intertwined. Ronia awakens periodically to find herself disoriented in this strange room, but is quickly relieved to find Alan next to her. She had not known him long but as she idles in a state of alternate sleep and slumber, she rests in the knowledge that this young man is a strong, compassionate spirit capable of great love and caring. As penetrating rays of moonlight fall upon his bare chest, she studies with great admiration the well-defined biceps and pectorals that protrude through the sheets. She surreptitiously pulls back the sheet covering his lower torso to reveal a mostly solid, detailed abdomen. When he turns to his side she notices his V-shaped, svelte back flanked by sinewy triceps. He breathes evenly and strongly, appearing godlike to her. She runs her fingers softly through his brown, wavy hair.

As she glances around his room, with its scattered array of personal items belonging to this interesting American, she contemplates the dual nature of her feelings toward him and the situation she is entering with him. In one respect, she feels awkward giving herself sexually to this man so soon, sharing intimate moments with one she has known for a relatively short period of time. "What does he really think of me?" she wonders. "All of this happened so fast. Is there something fortuitous happening here? Is this just a one-night fling?"

She ponders these questions only briefly before her mind is swamped and all concerns quelled by an overwhelming sense that something not just physical but actually spiritual or transcendental is occurring. In the presence of this sleeping peaceful man, Ronia is overtaken by the realization that Alan Agrippa is someone she enjoys being with. Her mother had told her when she was very young that she would meet someone who would satisfy her intellectually, physically, and spiritually. Ronia's mother had also told her that she deserved to be with someone who would satisfy her every desire and that this would definitely happen for her one day. As she lies here in this bed with Alan, a phenomenal warmth and fulfillment evolves, a promise of things to come but also the undeniable satisfaction that if this is all there is, it has certainly been enough. Her eyes begin to feel heavy. Alan's hand slides comfortably around her waist as she descends lightly into sleep.

CHAPTER 8

Saturday has arrived very quickly. Alan arises with thoughts of the reggae concert at which he will see his friend Peter and hopefully chill out to some pretty cool tunes. Ronia awakens with plans of getting some research work done during the day before meeting up with Alan later. They agree that he will pick her up at 3:30. He mentions the obvious to her: that dress is casual. He had forgotten to ask if she would want to get stoned. For that matter, he had not asked about her full opinions regarding numerous philosophical subjects, including the drug issue. He would probably bring it up when he picks her up.

Today, Alan's focus returns to philosophy. He has, in addition to having partaken of delightful, stimulating conversation with her, run the gamut of carnal pleasures to the point that he craves to dive back into the intellectual stimulation and insight of his books. Having done so much touring, he decides to stay mainly by the hotel for the afternoon. His plan is to read the book he purchased at the voodoo shop and do a little writing, ample activities that will not expend physical energy he wants to save for the night's recreation.

Before leaving the room, Alan cracks open his original book on mysticism and begins to read where he had left off: "When Brother Klaus has his religious experience filtered through an image of the Trinity, Jung says, 'This example demonstrates the use of the dogmatic symbol: it formulates a tremendous and dangerously decisive psychic experience, fittingly called, an 'experience of the Divine,' in a way that is tolerable to our human understanding, without either limiting the scope of the experience or doing damage to its overwhelming significance.' Another piot, Angelus Silesius, experienced a dramatic inner conflict without these safeguards and became 'insane.'"

Alan shuts the book and grabs his other book, the pad of paper, and heads down to the lobby with Ronia. He hails a cab for her and they say goodbye. He walks into the dining area and prepares himself a large cup of coffee. As he sits down on one of the large plush leather couches in the lobby, he hears German voices coming from what appear to be business travelers who are checking into the hotel. The lobby area where Alan sits is off to the side and away from the check-in desk. Ornate tapestries in burgundy and pink hang on the wall. Quaint antique tables and lamps fill the floor space.

The past week has magically brought Alan psychedelic revelations and romantic moments. With a sense of peace and contentment, Alan slips into a contemplative state of reverie and then a spontaneous urge to communicate something to someone. He opens the pad of paper, takes a sip of coffee and writes:

Dear Mom and Dad,

I'm having an enjoyable, enriching time in London. The weather has been pleasantly cloudy with sporadic rain and intermittent sunshine. I have toured the magnificent Buckingham Palace and the spirit-filled Tower of London. I'm sure that by the time you receive this letter you will be made aware by Mary and Jim that I have been seeing their boarder, Ronia. She is a delightfully interesting French student who shares my passion of foreign travel and the study of psychology. We are going to a concert tonight. Am having a great time. Hope everyone is doing well.

Love,
Alan

He slides the letter into his notebook with plans of mailing it whenever he gets a chance. The sudden caffeine high opens up neural channels and excites new thought. Alan places the tip of his pen on a new page and begins to write:

"Today I feel refreshed from recent experience exploring various pleasures of the mind and body. Whether or not up until this point I have achieved divine insight or metaphysical truth—well, I am not sure. I have been thinking lately about the enigmatic nature of consciousness itself, though, and its various implications. Are we placed upon this planet by some mysterious force or extraterrestrial entity that uses DNA as its vehicle for life propulsion? Is the process of life an ever-recurring, ad-infinitum, with no beginning and no end? Has the earth spawned us into individual incarnations or materializations only to absolve our particular essences into some higher realm of collective consciousness at the end of our individual chronological lives? Has spirit through some mysterious aberration of physics spontaneously donned a material—our bodies and nervous systems—simply to allow the universe to experience and become aware of itself?"

Alan wonders, "What is that song by The Grateful Dead? 'You Are The Eyes Of The World'?"—the chorus that Alan had hummed at the one and only DEAD concert he had attended before Jerry Garcia died and the band more or less disbanded. Alan had certainly reached what he felt was a sense of oneness and collective consciousness with the fans that filled the stadium. "Had the band been sent by extraterrestrials to vouchsafe to the crowd some semblance of understanding about the cosmos?"

Alan thinks back to that night out in the desert when an incredible fusion of lights and sounds had transported him with the help of a joint to an ethereal, cosmic place where certain cult-like movements—as in this case with the Deadheads—had evolved on the planet to educate and transmogrify a sleeping mindset to one of brilliant radiance and compassion.

An almost perfect enlightenment, what Jung called, "individuation," is something that Alan felt he had successfully achieved through his pursuits of martial arts, philosophy, and Zen Buddhistic practices such as meditation and the cultivation of love toward others. What had happened to Alan the night of the Dead concert represents one of those fleeting moments where Alan no longer identified simply with his concept of self, but actually felt that his consciousness was scattered into pieces which merged with all of those around him. The synchronous hums, chants, and cheers resounding through the stadium that night had been moving and powerful. He was certain that, at least for a moment, he had merged with something higher than himself.

"Excuse me, sir," a maid calls out to Alan as she runs a vacuum cleaner astride the couch. He gazes into her eyes—ominous strobes of hazelnut and cream—he thinks, as he ventures to guess the possible interstellar connections that he has with this woman. Alan remembers the metaphor promulgated by Joseph Campbell that consciousness appearing on the scene in various incantations is comparable to a light fixture containing many bulbs. As each light bulb is alternately illuminated or darkened, so is each manifestation of so-called "consciousness." Although each bulb is a separate expression of the light, they are all funneling energy or electricity from the same source. So it is with consciousness, according to Joseph Campbell.

Alan watches as the olive-complected maid dutifully completes her chores. He considers that he is sitting there philosophizing while she is busy cleaning. "How different the two activities," he muses. "But how similar she and I are in that we are both human and share the same feelings and experience." Their eyes make contact and they smile briefly at one another. Two Arabic men pass by the couch and walk over to one of the tapestries. They deliberate over it in a language incomprehensible to Alan.

Alan begins to write a little bit more: "The powers of the human mind have evolved over thousands and thousands of years, delving into various modes of communication and systematically creating new technologies to meet the needs of the time. Art has undergone drastic changes yet preserved some of its original essence and its value lies not so much in the technological innovations which have rendered it more complex but actually in the primal, subjective impact it has had in the viewer." Alan ponders the newfound craze over the Internet and its heavily touted capacity to bring about global change and freedom of information. He is aware of modern theorists who proclaim that the Internet is finally the culmination and realization of Marshal McCluhan's "global village."

As Alan glances around him at a sample of the international flavor of a city like London, he wonders if there will be a unified language or mode of communication understood by all. According to the Judeo-Christian bible, God had scattered the languages at the Tower of Babel, compelling humankind to have divisions in their languages. Alan questions what the Vedas or the Koran have to say about this.

He places the notepad and pen into his backpack. He sips his coffee, which is now lukewarm, and he begins to think about Ronia. Basically, he calls up her image in his mind and cogitates over the picture as if it is a gift sent from heaven. This beautiful, intelligent woman had shared with him one glorious night in which they had reached transcendent spiritual and physical highs. Alan is looking forward to going to the concert with her. He meditates until about 2:30 and then goes upstairs to get dressed for the show. He throws on a pair of jeans and a black loose-fitting cotton shirt he had purchased in Mexico.

Ready at 3, he decides to take the letter to a post office and mail it before going to pick up Ronia. Remembering that Peter had told him the concert would be at Kensington Park, Alan figures that he will pick Ronia up at 3:30 with not a lot of time to visit with Jim and Mary as the show is starting at 4. Alan grabs his wallet, shuts and locks the door, and glides out the hotel with the letter in hand but forgets to ask the desk clerk the location of a post office. As he begins his return to the lobby, he is abruptly bumped by a stoutly built, bespectacled gentleman in a long overcoat and top hat. "Pardon me," remarks Alan. "I wasn't watching where I was going." "That's quite alright young man. You obviously have a lot on your mind," replies the man, mysteriously, but affably. "I was actually wondering where a post office might be," Alan implores.

"I'm heading that way myself," speaks the gentleman in a distinguished English accent as he reaches into his coat pocket and carefully lights a pipe. Alan begins to walk beside the gentleman as they are fortunately heading in the direction of the subway stop where Alan needs to go. They walk at a moderate pace as the sun shines brightly down upon the street. "Why did you perceive that I have a lot on my mind?" Alan queries. "Your countenance suggests a serious, exploratory mind, more than likely interested in some of the more esoteric philosophical systems," the gentleman knowingly commands.

The man is both articulate and amazingly perceptive. "That's truly amazing," Alan offers. "I'm actually here in London developing ideas which would certainly fit within your category of 'esoteric' philosophical systems: mysticism to be more exact." "Heard any good jokes lately?" the man asks. Alan pauses and thinks of the only joke he can remember at the moment. "Okay," Alan declares. "What did the Zen Buddhist say to the man at the hot dog stand?" "I don't know," answers the man as they stroll up to the post office. "I'll take one with everything." "Ha, ha, ha—a regular Hermann Hesse you are!" exclaims the man, jovially. "Hermann Hesse—author of *Siddhartha,* correct?" Alan questions the wise, friendly man. The gentleman speaks up:

"Hermann Hesse was the raconteur; accomplished writer of *Magister Ludi* (The Glass Bead Game) *Steppenwolf, Narziss* and *Goldmund, Demian, and The Journey to the East*, as well." "I really must be going. I've enjoyed talking to you," Alan hastily responds.

The gentleman smiles and waves graciously as Alan scampers off to mail the letter and get to his destination. The subway is sparse with people. Alan grins at the serendipitous meeting with the stately, erudite stranger. Alan wonders, as he so often does, how saddening it is that with some of the more interesting people we come across in life, we only encounter them briefly and we'll probably never see them again.

The subway train rushes up to the depot. Alan boards and quickly assesses the map to confirm his stop. He arrives to pick up Ronia at about 3:40. Mary answers the door, somewhat to Alan's chagrin. He hates to be late to concerts and knows that Mary will be anxious to speak to him, in light of the time he has been spending with Ronia. "Hello, Alan. How are you, sweetie?" They kiss and hug. "So you and Ronia have a big night ahead?" "Yep, we sure do and we're running a little late at this point. Is she about ready?" Alan fails in his attempt to not sound rude. Ronia stands smiling behind Mary in the hallway.

"Sorry we can't stay," he adds. "We'd like to linger and visit; we'll chat again, okay?" "I know, Alan. You two go and have a great time." "Love you, Aunt Mary. Please say hello to Jim for me." Ronia says goodbye to Mary and steps through the doorway to leave with Alan. "Hi, Alan," she warmly greets him. When the door closes they kiss lightly on the lips. They walk a couple of blocks and hail a cab.

Showing up at the park shortly after 4, they join the crowd that is congregating around the stage that is playing host to a rockin' ambient act. Ronia and Alan, who are hand-in-hand and bristling with energy, merge with the crowd. Alan grabs a leaflet that advertises the festival's lineup and showcases the names of the band members. He scans for Peter Lesh and finds it under the amusing title of Moksha Revellers. It says they will appear at 5:30. The park is blanketed with myriad rockers, partiers, and hippie revisionists basically hanging out and soaking up the Rasta vibes. The percussion-backboned African cadences from the stage are hypnotizing and entertaining the crowd while inculcating messages of hope and freedom.

The anthem of "legalize" is already in full swing—much to his pleasure and amusement—as he notices bemused, indifferent bobbies stationed in certain locations with the virtually useless task of keeping an inherently peaceful crowd in line. Ronia is beautiful, as usual, and quite hip with a yellow and orange tie-dye shirt and braided hair. She is wearing leather sandals, which accent shapely, muscular hips and legs that are wonderfully covered in ragged-out blue jeans. Alan smiles brightly as he holds her hand.

He casually broaches the subject of mind-manifesting chemicals: "I was thinking about getting some pot and figured I would ask you if you would like some and generally what your elaborative thoughts are—on the subject of psychotropic recreation—that is. "Well," she begins, as her face illumines. "The answer to your first question is sure; we are at a reggae concert so, naturally, pot would be fun. I'd love some. In response to the second question, I would have to say that humans have been modifying their consciousness with various psychedelics throughout time and probably always will. I am certainly not one to stand in the way of evolution." Alan beams in recognition of her not mere approval but actual adamant acceptance and biological endorsement. She goes on:

"I would add that, among the illicit drugs, I'm much more accepting of LSD, pot, and designers like X, chemicals that basically promote intelligence, self-exploration, and interpersonal comfort. I would probably be much less apt to recommend ones like heroin, crack, and PCP. I look around me and see most people killing themselves with alcohol and cigarette abuse. Basically, moderation is a good approach to most everything in life." Alan appreciates her candor and beautifully clinical, almost poetic summation of the transporters to altered states.

They walk casually through the crowd while observing the grand splendor and diversity of the human race. Men with shaved heads and pierced noses walk beside young smooth skinned women in saffron flowing robes swaying in unison to the beat. There is a nice mixture of brown, black, and white skinned people; many are English and some are from all over the world. The pleasantly international styles and fashions are refreshing to Alan. He particularly likes the barefooted, cut-off jeans that look so reminiscent of the '60s revolution.

Then there are the cybers. One svelte, attractive brunette woman in her early thirties wears a tight-fitting diaphanous purple long-sleeved shirt which covers a tantalizing flower-patterned black bra. Matching purple triangle earrings dangle in perfect juxtaposition to shiny black tight-fitting leather pants and a matching backpack. Prominently dilated pupils, framed by tortoise shell horn-rimmed glasses, complement a profusely sweating face.

Alan notices various booths set up to market environmentally conscious and social-change oriented wares. He leads Ronia over to a refreshment stand and buys two beers. "I think I see my friend Peter over there by the bandstand," Alan exclaims.

They make their way through the crowd and stumble up to Peter, who is drinking a beer and mingling with other band members. "Peter!" Alan calls out, wishing for more than a second that he is—himself—a member of a groovy reggae band. "Alan, me mon, so glad to see you," Peter responds in a pleasantly gruff, matured voice nurtured by years of Jamaica's finest weed and rum. "Who is da pretty lady?" he asks. "Her name is Ronia. Ronia, this is Peter. Peter, Ronia," Alan answers.

"Hello, it's very nice to meet you," Ronia politely states as she extends her hand to shake Peter's. Peter wraps his arm around Alan's neck in a friendly, loving manner. While looking at Ronia, Peter exuberantly but halfway incoherently articulates:

"Your man Alan, here, is a young American genius who wants to save—but first learn a little about—the world. I hope you guys enjoy the show; we're gonna be on soon. Here's a joint to take you to the other side. Peace, my friends." Alan and Ronia thank him for the joint and wave to him. Just as they turn around to find a place to light up, Peter comes dashing back up to them, pleading: "Hey kids, Hey kids. I almost forgot. Tonight, after the show, we are all meeting at a club called, Backstreets, on Sussex Gardens Road. Please come. It'll be a blast. Take care and enjoy the show, my friends."

Alan watches Peter depart to head backstage and thinks with some amusement how curious and enchanting the opportunity is of knowing this dreadfully entertaining chap. Ronia smiles at Alan and then motions toward a wooded spot located just left of the stage—which will be a perfect location to lie back and smoke a joint. Although it is readily apparent to anyone with common sense that many in the crowd have partaken of intoxicating substances, it is not obvious that people are actually doing drugs at the show. So they steal away to the bushes for a taste of the sweetleaf. The opening band has left the stage and roadies are performing their work to get ready for the next act—which will be Peter's band, The Moksha Revellers.

Alan places the finely prepared joint in his lips, reverently ignites the lighter, and lights the tip with such confidence and zeal that Ronia smirks at her own relative inexperience with this particular hallucinatory ritual. Alan slowly but deeply inhales the aromatic holy smoke and then hands the joint to Ronia. She thinks she'll be cute so she playfully simulates a peculiar smoking behavior she has seen on an international MTV rap video. She cups her hands in a spherical shape around the joint and strikes a most hilarious, affected homeboy pose. She then takes a mild drag and with the joint clasped precariously between her thumb and fore-finger, offers the next toke to Alan. He spews out a convulsive bout of laughter at her histrionics and then quickly sucks up another hit. They alternately smoke the pot until the paper has burned down almost far enough to burn the finger. As Alan flicks the remnant to the ground, in grand hopes that some bugs will be affected by a surprise gift of con-sumed microscopic marijuana particles, something happens. A mysteri-ous mosquito-like bug flies directly into his right cheek and delivers a harsh sting. As Alan brushes the remains of bug carcass particles from his face he yells out: "I'm sitting here trying to enjoy the paradisiacal realms of sound and vision and this uninvited guest comes zooming in for a vicious blood suck. My cheek fucking stings!" "Your cheek is red and pink in the spot were you were stung. I'm so sorry, Alan," Ronia pleads.

CHAPTER 9

An announcer comes out on stage to introduce Peter's band. Uproarious cheers erupt from the crowd. As the tie-dyed and dreadlocked musicians take the stage and grab their instruments, the mental effects of the pot become quite bizarre. Alan feels the overwhelming sense that the world is vibrating and rotating in a randomly sequenced, uncontrollable rhythm about ten times faster than normal. Ronia is overcome with the powerful sensation of a displaced, newly located point of reference or locus of consciousness. She feels she can control this at will and places her frame of reference wherever she fancies. They stagger up to within about twenty rows of the stage. There are not exactly rows in this set up. It is basically lawn seating or standing depending on what people want to do. Ronia and Alan stand together holding hands and begin to fashion some sense of reality of simply watching a band in concert.

Peter and his Moksha Revellers hold forth with an electrifying performance that infuses elements of hip-hop, metal, and acid rock into a predominantly reggae set. Alan takes this as Peter's creative way of showcasing the sense of universality among seemingly different styles or forms of art. Ronia smiles ebulliently as she taps her foot in rhythm with the passionate, international beats. The crowd swoons to the tunes as Alan visualizes the show as nothing less than a moving, stunning typification of the idea he had touched upon in his first meeting with Peter: that the Anglo-Caucasian materialistic mindset definitely needs at least a little touch of soul and spiritualism from the dark-skinned, often more mystical set. Perhaps it is his mood; or maybe it is the chemically induced perspective. Or, better yet, it is due to being in a state that might be love.

Whatever the reason, Alan conceptualizes this marvelous show as a re-unification of two disparate sides: the two hemispheres of the brain if you will. Europe, with its scientific, industrial accomplishments, had utilized the infinite resources of the rational, discursive, mechanistic realm. Materialistically, more underdeveloped regions like Africa and India had been more fertile ground for some of the earth-conscious, intu-

70

itive, mystical movements. The spiritual reggae harmonies are bathing the European mental landscape like fresh drops of water that sprout springtime efflorescence from virgin seeds—or so, at least, is how Alan's mind is perceiving things at this moment.

He turns to Ronia and plots a soft kiss on her cheek. In her marijuana radiance she exudes an angelic, pristine, yet sensuous energy that catapults Alan into a momentarily powerful, but controllable lust. He passes over his hormones in favor of the platonic, visceral intercourse between his brain, her brain and this idyllic London park with its varietal goings on, the drug in their systems, and the spicy, resounding symphony of music.

The sun is completely down. Scattered lights that flicker from the stage are complemented by sundry lighters and matches in the crowd. The band has played about ten or twelve songs before Peter gravitates to the microphone to speak:

"Ladies and Gentleman, Brothers and Sisters. We are gathered here today to celebrate love, peace, and to thank the mighty Creator for all things good. This next one goes out to two special people, my dear friends, Alan and Ronia." The other members of the band—except two female backup singers—exit the stage as Peter grabs an acoustic guitar and slides up to a solitary stool and microphone on the sole illuminated spot on the stage. He sits down, pulls out a guitar pick, and glides into a poetic, riveting version of "Satisfy My Soul" by Bob Marley. The song sends shivers up Alan's spine and Ronia gushes with pride.

The London night air is cool and breezy. As the show progresses, the majority of the crowd stands or dances transfixed by the music while the rest mingle and wander from booth to booth trying to discover things to occupy themselves. Peter breaks into a frenzy of rocking and balladic numbers that feed the well-behaved potheads, acid eaters, and reggae lovers a much needed musical banquet. He consequently realizes his goal of becoming in a sense a leader or shaman for the peaceful, mystical way. After a few encores and the rest of the bands have played, the concert reaches its conclusion at around 11:00 p.m. Alan's mind feels slightly hazy and tingling.

Ronia motions for Alan to lie back on the ground while the crowd slowly disperses around them. They find a pretty clean spot and recline on the earth. Ronia lays her hand on Alan's lap and he begins to gently stroke her hair. They watch as roadies move in to disassemble the stage equipment. The eclectic, interesting fans seem satiated—somehow, spiritually fulfilled—as they embark upon conversations regarding the music they had heard and how this show compares to others. Alan and Ronia listen to the voices with great interest and, of course, heightened perception. As Alan cradles Ronia's head on his lap, he thinks of her as a treasure that has been vouchsafed to him from gracious gods somewhere up there in the vast expanse of night; celestial, starry spheres ages and ages away.

"How did we come to be here?" Alan wonders, as he leans over and kisses Ronia's lips relishingly. His mind spirals: "Atoms give rise to biological processes. Advance of molecules that come together so beautifully to allow two organisms the perfect joy—bliss of falling enraptured—minds and souls intermingling magically; of hopelessly and gleefully falling in love. Out of infinite space and time with seeming purposelessness but of such profundity; on a blue planet among billions of planets in solar systems and galaxies framing multitudes of stars, particles had arisen forming two nervous systems with billions of neurons and neural connections bonding and creating a microscopic model or blueprint of the universe itself."

Alan gazes into Ronia's eyes—two crystalline orbs—spherical geometry of perfection and the archetype or prototype for all that is life-giving. The shape of the mother's womb mirrors the earth itself. "Yes," Alan thinks. This planet is magical and this—he gazes at everything around him, contemplating its phenomenality—is magical. On this night, the infinite array of stars shines more brilliantly than Alan could ever remember. His individual sense of self has peacefully dissolved. It has transubstantiated into Ronia's and she has long sense merged with the cosmos around her.

Alan cradles her head with one arm. With his other hand, he reaches into his backpack and pulls out the original book on mysticism. He begins to read where he had left off: "Aldous Huxley discoursed on the glories of psychedelic mind expansion in his book, *The Doors of Perception.* Obviously borrowing Blake's terminology, we cannot help but think of Blake's 'doors of perception' as analogous to Jung's 'dogmatic symbols.' Jung says, 'For what comes of the door is, surprisingly enough, a boundless expanse full of unprecedented uncertainty with apparently no inside and no outside, no above and no below, no here and no there, no mine and no thine, no good and no bad. It is the world of water, where all life floats in suspension; where the realm of the sympathetic system, the soul of everything living, begins; where I am indivisibility this and that; where I experience the other in myself and the other-than-myself experiences me.'"

Alan knows that he and Ronia need to be going but he feels a creative impulse that compels him to write. He slides the book back into the bag and removes a pen and his pad of paper. With the rapturous image of Ronia and the angelic touch of her skin soothingly impressing the caverns on his mind, he steadies his pen at the top of the page and heartfully composes the following poem:

Angelic eyes: a symphonic counterpoint of hue; a universe within encapsulating interpenetrating but divergent shades of blue.

Phosphorescent, incandescent, shimmering mystic gems, resplendent with the glory and grandeur of Gothic cathedral hymns.

Hypnotic and possessing, an orchestration of perfect enchantment and delight.

Brilliant radiance shining forth, a visual immanence of immaculate light.

Fortuitous and prophesiacal, a hint of things to come, a microcosm of immortal truth with cosmic depths to be plumbed.

As with Pandora's box and Houdini's cage, an eternal search begins for enigmatic keys to unfurl a higher evolutionary stage.

Geodesic and mosaic patterns—panoramic vistas gently open up, to a deoxyribonucleic concoction served in a porcelain, diamond cup.

To partake of the fruits of infinity, a mesmerization into aesthetic arrest.

To succumb to the pleasures of beauty, a raptured suspension of every last mortal whisper and breath.

Angels sing, children cry, and man will risk his very life to glimpse the wisdom—to glean the insight—the embodiment of paradisiacal charm, magic, and illumination in Ronia's eyes.

Alan sets the pen down and silently reads in its entirety the poem he has just composed for this dear, sweet creature resting with him. He feels that it is an apt expression of the transmogrifying effect she is having on him. He has been pleasurably stroking her cheek and hair with his fingers and the entire tranquil idyll is something he fears to disrupt. At the same time, he craves interaction with others and wants terribly to have more social stimulation before leaving London. So he awakens Ronia and tells her they should run to get a cab that will take them to the club Peter had mentioned.

Alan and Ronia make their way through the partially trash-strewn, well-trampled lawns of the park which is now displaying a dwindling population. When they get to the street, Alan hails a cab and instructs the driver to take them to "Backstreets" on Sussex Gardens Road. The driver does not appear to speak or understand a lot of English, so Alan has to repeat the words "Backstreets" and "Sussex Gardens Road" several times

until the driver shows some acknowledgment in the form of an indefinite
head shake. They end up about four blocks from Backstreets.

Alan asks a local where exactly it's located. The compulsory walk
turns into an unexpected gift in the form of relishing the cool night air for
a few moments longer before entering a smoke filled building. As they
walk along another cobblestone path, Alan begins to see a large neon lit
sign with the letters spelling, "Backstreets." The sign is about twelve feet
tall—a vertical French 19th century style—in the unmistakable shape of
a phallus.

As Ronia and Alan get closer to the building, he can make out the
fading white paint markings signifying that this had once been a bath
house. At the front door there stands a plaque on the left commemorating
the building as a historical site. Alan reads something about the fact that
this building had been a favorite haunt of Oscar Wilde. A portly and
affable bouncer working the door promptly cards Alan and Ronia as they
enter. The place is bustling with activity as it seems the entire neighborhood has gathered in the joint.

Alan and Ronia fight their way through the bar and search thoroughly
for their dreadlocked friend. There are several rows adjoining a main
restaurant area. The interior style of the place is a contrast of various
Victorian influences: opulent, crystalline chandeliers, old time pianos
and black and white star photos intermingle with gargoyles and Gothic
columns. "Very interesting place," Alan mentions as they peruse each
room until they glance upstairs surrounding the dance floor and spot a
large table with various dreads and model types carousing and cavorting.
Alan stares until he spots a smiling, adamantly drinking Peter simultaneously placing an order with a waitress and reciprocating her flirtations.

A throbbing techno-beat emanates from the sound system below as
Alan and Ronia climb the spiraling staircase to the balcony. On the way
to the table, Alan stops off at another bar and purchases a bottle of champagne, grabs a couple of glasses, and then cheerfully carries it all to
Peter's table. Alan walks right up to Peter and joyfully smacks the bottle
down in front of him. As Peter's face lights up and he stands to give Alan
a friendly embrace, others at the table scramble to make room for the two
youthful Caucasians. "Alan, my man, I hope you enjoyed the show."
"Peter, it was wonderful. You guys rocked!" Ronia interjects: "The show
was a blast. Thanks for your dedication to Alan and me. That was cool."
"You are welcome, my friends. I'd like for you both to meet my family.
These are my spiritual brothers and sisters. This is: Phillip, Tonya,
Maurice, Sera, and Elija. Over there is Michael, Olympia, Candice, and

Perry." Alan smiles and waves at everyone, knowing perfectly well that he would not remember their names but wanting to be cordial, nevertheless. Ronia smiles as well as they take their seats with the group.

Everyone resumes their conversations as Alan pulls his chair up to Peter and thanks him for the pot. "Did you see the heavens unfold, my friend?" Peter queries Alan. "The eye of the universe itself unraveled in all its glorious splendor in front of me, no less," Alan dramatically replies. "I might add," Alan proceeds, "that your indelibly hypnotic grooves catapulted us both to some pretty incredible dimensions. A true sense of love and vibration with the harmonies of the Earth was aroused. Truly groovy stuff!" Somebody passes around cigars. Alan politely accepts one and quickly lights up, only after first offering one to Ronia, which she respectfully declines.

The group sitting at the table is decidedly eclectic in their appearance but remarkably homogenous in their attitudes. Conservative, Anglo-looking businessmen sit next to black, fashionably dressed women in long flowing island wear. Dreadlocked Rastafarian men in stylish, colorful sarongs sit next to myriad ethnic women, mostly model types who sport stunning designer dresses that are casual, but definitely expensive. Alcohol is plentifully served as Peter pours champagne for Alan, Ronia, and the woman seated next to Peter, whose name is Olympia. They toast to joy and friendship and then savor their drinks. Although separate conversations are in full swing, Alan can peripherally hear bits and pieces of information suggesting that the interests and primary orientations among those seated are along the lines of conservationism—at least in theory—social conscientiousness, and intellectual-backed, strategically construed, unbridled, unrepentant hedonism. This hedonism involves conscious self-indulgence with various psychoactives, sexual freedom and comfort in diversity, and enough material wealth to translate to the value of living fairly leisurely. In other words, this is exactly the sort of group Alan enjoys hanging out with.

Olympia and Peter are quite cozy in that they are holding hands and smooching between drinks. Alan surmises this arrangement can fall anywhere on the spectrum between marriage and one-night stand. Olympia has dark skin, long black hair, and thin features. "Probably Mediterranean," Alan thinks. She has honey brown, piercing yet soothing eyes. She speaks elegant English and seems to enjoy gazing at Ronia. From the table where everyone sits, a full view of the dance floor, strobe light, and restaurant is provided. Invigorated drones are dancing to a disco beat down below, which alternates between American pop and Euro-alternative.

Peter broaches conversation with the source of his girlfriend's attention: "Ronia, dear Alan has told me his uniquely interesting plans for coming to England. What brings a wondrous person like yourself?" "I'm studying anthropology at the university. I'm a foreign exchange student staying with Alan's aunt and uncle."

Fluttering lights from the rotating strobe light keep everyone visually stimulated as the conversation turns toward Olympia. "Olympia, what do you do here in London to keep yourself busy?" Alan speaks rather loudly. She smiles as she responds, seemingly glad to be brought into conversation: "I'm a full time model for an agency here and my avocation is photography." "What type of photography are you mainly interested in?" Alan presses. "I enjoy taking pictures of various things which interest me but black and white photos of impressive architecture is my particular focus," she politely and intelligently responds. "What styles do you enjoy the most?" Ronia interjects.

"Among many, I seem to favor Roman Domestic," Olympia answers. She continues, "Byzantine and Spanish Romanesque; one of my favorite photographs is one taken of the magnificent Hogia Sophia in Istanbul. It is an awesome Byzantine structure, breathtakingly massive and ornate." Alan savors intermittent puffs from his cigar and succulent sips of the champagne.

Partly from his knowledge that Gothic originated in France, Ronia's homeland, and that mentioning this style will likely fall upon her mind with some interest, and partly from the fact that Gothic is one of the few styles Alan is truly familiar with and interested in, he offers to the group: "I personally enjoy the French and English Gothic styles. Here in England the Gloucester Cathedral is impressive with its appealing fan vaults. I have seen pictures of it and plan on seeing it soon."

"Did you know?" Olympia asks: "that Gloucester is the first example of that type of vault in England?" "No, that's pretty interesting," Alan replies. Trying to convey to the group the mystical effect Gothic architecture has had on him and attempting to compensate for his lack of technical knowledge on the subject, Alan proffers: "To me, walking into the vast, awe-inspiring corridors of a Gothic church evokes something larger and more profound than anything man knows. It seems to hint at the infinite." "It is in a sense man's representation of the infinite," Olympia clarifies. Throughout the conversation, Peter seems to enjoy a laid-back passive, observatory position in the group. Ronia exhibits and feels jealousy of the passionate conversation taking place between Alan and Olympia. At one level Ronia can truly appreciate the aesthetic nature of Olympia. At another level it pleases Ronia to see Alan engaging in intelligent discourse with another woman and the inherent challenge this presents to Ronia in maintaining his interest. Olympia is running her fingers along Peter's neck. "Peter darling, you are so quiet. You brought such pleasure to us with your music that I feel your energy has been spent for the evening," she speaks endearingly, as she continues to stroke the nape of his neck and leans to kiss him. "I'm having a wonderful time," Ronia whispers to Alan.

A waiter appears. "How's everyone doing, mates? Can I get anyone a drink?" The champagne is nearly finished. "I'll take a scotch and water," says Ronia. Alan politely motions for Olympia to order. She asks for a beer. Alan and Peter order glasses of Cabernet.

"My friiiiiends," Peter proclaims—his words amusingly slur. "I would like to take this opportunity to recognize the surreal, fantastical work of Antonio Gaudi, a man who truly revolutionized abstract expressionism through stone. And he managed to piss off more than a few people too. You gotta respect the man," he concludes with his glass raised high. Everyone laughs. Peter recalls the bizarre style of Gaudi pictured in art books about Barcelona. This is a place Alan needs to go.

Ronia decides to extend the name dropping by mentioning the most famous American architect: "I enjoy the refined, rectilinear approach of Frank Lloyd Wright, myself," she reports. "Who else integrated so beautifully artifact with nature?" she asks rhetorically. Everyone seems to agree—Frank Lloyd Wright was a genius. The drinks come quickly. The four have become oblivious to the frenetic club activity around them. Their insulated meeting of the minds is enjoyable but they feel they are rudely neglecting the others.

So Peter begins to walk around and mingle with the rest of the table. Olympia excuses herself to the restroom and Alan and Ronia depart to dance. They figure their drinks will be waiting for them when they get back. As they glide onto the dance floor they are swept away by the gyrating, pulsating beat of tribal techno. Any need for conversation is absolved as the two lovers shed their inhibitions and succumb to the rhythm of dance. After spending about fifteen minutes grooving on the dance floor, they return to the table. On the way there, Alan takes her by the arm and leads her to a secluded area on the ground floor behind a column. "What do you think? Are you having a good time?" he asks. "Yes, but I wouldn't mind leaving soon. I'm kind of getting tired," she replies. He responds: "Okay, let's go back and finish our drinks, say goodbye, and then we'll take off. Alright?" "Okay, that will be great." They saunter back to the table to find only a few remaining. Peter and Olympia have paid for all the drinks and will not allow Alan to reimburse them. "How was the dancing, guys?" Peter asks. "It was pretty cool. I've had quite a mixture of tunes tonight," replies Alan. "Variety is the spice of life, my friend."

Peter's words ring profoundly in Alan's mind. Resonant chords herald the synthesis of nuances, a syncretism of eclectic people and media which clinch today as a hallmark or step on the path toward understanding, which Alan continues to pursue resolutely as well as entertainingly. "Peter, we've thoroughly enjoyed ourselves. Thanks for everything." "Oh man, do you really need to be going? The party is still goin' man." "Let me know how I can contact you, Peter. I'd like to stay in touch." They exchange numbers. Peter explains to Alan that he is staying with Olympia while in London until the band moves on.

Alan and Ronia finish about half their drinks, say goodbye to Olympia and the few remaining and then make their way to the door. Alan notices Peter running up to him and placing a bag of pot in Alan's backpack. "It's for the road, mon. When you write your infamous book on the meanings of life, I want you to put something in there about me. I know you're gonna do it, mon. You've got what it takes." Alan imprints these words indelibly on his mind. They are kind, thoughtful words but most of all, they emerge from a man whom Alan perceives to be highly spiritual and developed in interesting dimensions of esoterica.

Unscientific generalizations notwithstanding, Alan feels that the average black Jamaican probably has an intuitive grasp of the mystical. Peter is a shining example. "The hip, humorous, knowledgeable, talented and sultry Olympia is perfect for Peter," Alan thinks. Alan and Ronia emerge from the club and stand quizzically underneath the neon phallus. Limping slowly down the sidewalk is an elderly gentleman with gray whiskers and a dusty, disheveled brown overcoat. He winks at Ronia as he passes.

Alan thinks of Uncle Al—Al's bold approach to life and unwavering commitment to enjoying his time on this planet. Alan ponders the beautiful, interesting women Al must have known in various parts of the world. Most of all, Alan thinks of his gratitude toward Al for thinking of Alan in his will and leaving the money which Alan is now converting into the invaluable experiences of travel, self-exploration, philosophic exploration, and the joy of being with a woman.

"Ronia, where would you like to go? We can head back to my place or I can take you back home. Whatever you want to do is fine." "Um, I'd like to walk for a bit in the cool wind and then decide," she responds. Alan takes her hand and they begin to walk toward Paddington Station. A brisk north wind tousles her hair like willowy strands of silk. The very early morning moon casts luminescent rays upon the streets as distant sounds of car motors are the only audible remnants of the previous day aside from the delicate footsteps and soft breath of Ronia.

The two stroll along the boulevard in a contemplative state pleasantly recalling the delightful, elegant moments of their day together. After walking about half a mile they come upon a well-lit bench on the sidewalk, and Alan suggests that they stop for a moment. They sit down, begin to relax, and Alan reaches into his bag and removes the paper upon which he has composed the poem for her.

"Earlier today, I composed this poem for you. I would like you to have this." He holds out the poem and she eagerly and with great surprise takes it from him. She carefully unfolds the paper and begins to read it. Alan sits quietly and nervously awaits her response.

As she slowly scans the poem from top to bottom her face begins to lightly blush and a peacefulness seems to envelop her. She pauses when she has finished reading it and looks away momentarily. She then looks back directly into Alan's eyes. "Thank you for the poem," she whispers. "No one has ever written me a poem before. It is beautiful." She leans over and wraps both her arms around him and kisses him softly on the cheek. A comforting warmth permeates him. He had wanted so much to move her emotionally and had tried to put onto paper what he could have never articulated through speech. He hoped that he had touched her in some meaningful way.

She folds the poem and places it in her purse and then asks him if they can go to his place. They walk to the nearest intersection and wait about ten minutes until a cab approaches and they get in. When they arrive at the room, Alan kisses her goodnight and they soon fall asleep in each other's arms.

CHAPTER 10

They awaken around eleven in the morning. Ronia gets up and goes directly to the phone to call Mary. "Hi Mary, this is Ronia. I just wanted to call to tell you that I'm alright. I slept over at a friend's last night. I'm going to be doing some work at the library today and will probably talk to you all a little bit later. Bye." She hangs up the phone after having successfully avoided mentioning that she was with Alan. She had not really discussed with Alan how much he wanted his aunt and uncle to know about their relationship. He is in a blissed-out state of slumber. She climbs back into bed and rests her head on his shoulder. She sees that his eyes are open and she begins to whisper: "Good morning, here comes the sun." She hums the chorus to "Here Comes the Sun" in a mock English accent. It is simultaneously humorous and pretty. Alan smiles and turns to kiss her on the forehead.

"Did I tell you how beautiful you are without makeup?" he asks. She smiles back at him and winces bashfully. He begins to stroke her hair caressingly and methodically initiates a conversation which would forever alter their futures: "I plan on leaving London soon and, understanding that for the time being you have significant commitments here, would like for you to join up with me on some of my future travels—if you would like that, and could arrange it." "It would be an invaluable study on the nature of man and womankind and I think we would make amazing travel partners," he adds. He quickly shuts up, so as not to "oversell" the deal if he has not done so already.

Some of his close friends back home are fond of describing relationship dynamics in practical, mundane business terminology like: "closing the deal," "royalties," "breach of contract," "canvassing." Although certainly not wanting to "capitalize" or "finagle" anything on Ronia, he does sincerely wish for her to be with him and "consolidating" this plan will require a persuasive, tactful approach not unlike a well-designed business proposal. The sun's penetrating rays have blanketed the sheets and their near-naked bodies. Ronia's face is almost non-expressive as Alan continues to stroke and massage the back of her head. He pauses long enough for her to ponder solely the rather significant, if not paramount suggestion he had just put forth. Seconds turn into days and minutes turn into millennia as his heart hovers precariously on the pendulum of her emotions. With the tip of her tongue she lightly moistens her lips before breaking the silence with:

"Well, aren't we dropping some bombshells bright and early this sunny morning? One minute we're lying here with our minds pleasantly empty of all thought except the glories of slumber, and the next minute you casually mention that you'll soon be leaving and would like me to meet up with you. Are all Americans this impulsive and unpredictable?"

"Actually, I'm probably a little worse than most on that mark," he replies, adding, "I'd like you to think about it. My plan is to rent a car and visit Stratford-Upon-Avon, Oxford, Warwick, Manchester, Liverpool, Gloucestershire, and a few others. Not necessarily in this order. I then would like to go on to Scotland and Wales. From there it may be on to Ireland and the mainland of Europe, in which I plan to travel by Euro-Rail throughout the land." "Will you have hotel reservations in advance?" she asks. "No," he responds. "I plan on picking out bed and breakfasts along the way which suit my fancy." "Suit my fancy" was something he never would have said in the states. It just seemed like the English thing to say.

"I'm looking forward to getting used to driving in the right-hand seat and operating the stick with my left hand," his voice resounds through the room. "You see, I'm right-handed of course, but I feel I am up to the challenge." "Alan, I've got to be getting ready. Do you have a t-shirt I can borrow? I'm going to take a shower and then run. I've got some work to do at the library close by. I promise I'll think about what you said today. You are quite an adventurer and I would certainly love to travel with you but I do have school commitments. Can we talk later?" she pleads. "You're not leaving this minute, are you?" she asks. "No, no," he retorts. What time can I see you later?" he asks.

"I'm heading back home after I study. You can pick me up there at eight. Maybe we'll get some food and talk," Ronia explains in an objective, organized manner, as if attempting to distance herself from Alan and from her own emotions.

"Obviously, I should not have dropped the bombshell in such a haphazard manner," he thinks. "I very well may have fucked up the whole plan." She is already in the bathroom getting ready. Alan arises optimistically, perhaps unrealistically, thinking that he has successfully planted a seed of thought, which will flourish in her mind and ensure that everything will work out in his favor. He stretches his sinewy limbs and creaking joints as his senses adapt to the room. Ronia is quick in getting ready. Alan hands her a baggy cotton shirt to wear with her jeans. He watches her brush her hair with a small comb she keeps in her purse. As she pulls her hair back into a ponytail, Alan becomes aware of a serious expression on her face; her countenance—one that he has not seen before—reveals an introspective, intellectual mind that is exemplified through an intensity that mirrors her scholastic endeavors. As he gazes at her reflection only momentarily appearing in the mirror and his mind, he is simply captivated that the mysterious DNA process had evolved such an immaculate incarnation and wondrous coalescence of physical beauty and mental vigor. He walks over to her and whispers into her ear: "Be safe today. I'll talk to you tonight." She smiles, grabs her purse, and exits the room.

Alan walks over to the desk in his room and peruses the various items he has strewn all over the top until he comes across his map of England. He sits at the chair and with a quick Gestalt overview scans the lines, letters, figures, columns, and geographical layout of the countryside depicted in a few pastel colors on the map. He views the various diverging and converging branches or neural highways yet to be explored within his own brain—a cognitive map so to speak—at once geographical coordinates and soon to be axons, dendrites, and synapses; roads to the internal frontier, territories heretofore uncharted. For he is about to immerse himself in the neural delicatessen of the glorious English countryside.

He reaches for his original book on mysticism and begins to read: "This reference to the sympathetic nervous system is interesting. According to physiologists, the sympathetic nervous system is that part of the autonomic nervous system whose nerves originate in the lumbar and thoracic regions of the spinal cord and that is especially concerned with mediating responses to alarm, as by speeding the heart rate, dilating the pupils, and raising blood pressure, etc. If there is a significant correlation between stimulation of the sympathetic nervous system and mystical experiences this would account for why paranoia is a frequent side effect accompanying psychotropic states."

Alan closes the book and begins calling rental agencies. Much to his dismay, insurance is about 100% of the cost of actually renting the car. He checks on mid- to small-sized sporty models with a stick shift. Being very tentative on plans, he simply gets information and tells them that he will call them back later. He hangs up the phone, throws on some clothes, and walks to the lobby. He then enters the sparsely inhabited dining room and sits down to a plate of breads, cheese, jelly, and coffee. The imminence of his departure to the countryside has generated some excitement in him. The rich, biting English coffee leaves him pleasantly jittery. With his food on the table he gets up from his seat and ventures over to the gift shop, where he purchases some stationery and a pen. He returns to his table and begins to write a letter to his parents:

> Dear Mom and Dad,
>
> Hope everyone is doing well. Am having a wonderful time here. Have struck up a very enjoyable relationship with Ronia, who is Mary and Jim's border. She is an erudite and charming person whom I am lucky enough to have met. I have seen many beautiful sights here in London and am looking forward to exploring the rest of the country soon. I'll write again when I get a chance. Take care. Will talk soon.
>
> Love,
> Alan

He seals and addresses the envelope, and slides it into his pocket. When he finishes breakfast, he arises and walks back to his room to slide out of his clothes and into the shower.

As the warm droplets splash on his face he closes his eyes tightly and begins to creatively visualize what he will soon be seeing: verdant rolling hills touched only by an occasional sheep grazing; placid, circuitous streams that interweave through mountainous, tree-lined slopes; palatial, regal castles nestled within gargantuan acreage. He washes completely, steps out of the shower, and grabs a towel. As he dries himself off he steps to the bathroom, reaches into his backpack, and removes the bag of pot Peter had given him.

With a towel wrapped around his face he sits down and rolls a paper with Jamaica's finest, which emits rich, sweetly aromatic signals that this will certainly be a great smoke. Staring at himself in the mirror, he lights the special stogy. After inhaling deeply, he holds the smoke within his lungs for as long as he can and then blows a steady stream into his reflection in the mirror. It is stimulating for him to watch the smoke circle and collide toward the mirror and then scatter into dissipative particles throughout the bathroom. The flavor is part hickory and part pine with dashes of sugar coated mint leaves and a hint of chocolate. Perception is immediately enhanced with the room appearing pellucid and undulating. Disorientation sets in quickly, compelling Alan to float toward the bed upon which he immediately falls—as if into a billowing cushion of cloud and then layers and layers of silk. The bed seems to be flipping over as he all of a sudden realizes: "Shit, I left the joint on the bathroom sink."

He miraculously arises from the bed and staggers toward the bathroom. As he takes each progressive step, the room successively expands into multifarious, distant dimensions. The hallway has in a sense become a seafaring vessel stricken with turbulent waters on the hull and constantly shifting objects on the mass. Alan's eyes and brain become the oars and sail of a captain-abandoned ship and the longitudinally-challenged compass was thrown overboard sometime around when Alan stepped out of the shower. Somehow, Alan maneuvers himself to the bathroom sink and grabs the joint. He carries it back into the bedroom, takes another deep drag, then snuffs the end and falls back upon the bed. He closes his eyes and happens upon swirling, kaleidoscopic images flaming in a seemingly endless dance of pure, undiluted, absolutely perfect chaos. A smooth, melting warmth permeates his body as titillating sunshine bathes his naked skin.

Alan revels in this bliss for about an hour—or was it a lifetime?—and then lifts his now immensely relaxed frame effortlessly from the bed. He drops the towel and reaches for a pair of underwear, slides it on, and then proceeds to throw on a shirt and pair of jeans. He grabs his black shoes and briefly runs his fingers through his hair. Loading up his backpack with essentials, Alan then descends gingerly upon the street. With any afternoon destination completely unknown, he simply wanders aimlessly with the sole intention of taking in a few more impressions of the city before his departure. The weather cannot be better: sunny, cool, and pretty clear with a northerly wind that invigorates. Myriad automobiles, including the occasional red trolley, shuffle in droves past Alan as he strolls whimsically down the sidewalk.

Alan cheerfully recalls Thomas Mann's contemplative protagonist, Hans Castorp, in the seminal novel, *Magic Mountain*. Hans Castorp—in his spiritual journey toward a more enlightened, mystical consciousness—was fond of taking regular moments to stop and organize significant events which he had experienced in order to better analyze, assimilate, and understand them. Alan takes this opportunity to reflect upon his experiences in London in a similar way. He calls up pictures in his mind of the interesting places, people, and interactions he has had the pleasure of experiencing and would never have experienced had he not come to London.

Alan thinks of the uniquely sophisticated accent and mannerisms of the English: their intelligence, kindness, and veritable sense of adventure. He considers the comforting feeling of community that Londoners foster in their everyday activities. From the genuine smiles and laughs, to the proper pronunciations of their words and firm handshakes, Londoners cannot help but engender a defining element of compassion that is extended at the most unexpected times. Alan would soon be experiencing a more relaxed and nonchalant approach to living. The English countryside seems to evoke a different side of the spirit and history of the people; the hope is for a more direct, up-front assessment of the psychology of the people. Additionally, Alan considers one more fine point directly pertaining to the pursuit of mysticism and the transpersonal dimensions: that the countryside of England, Scotland, and Ireland had somehow conceived and cultivated the quintessential mystical mindset as manifested in such oddities as Stonehenge and the fairy faith.

As he walks beside Lincoln's Inn Fields on Holborn Street, he philosophizes about man's evolution from primordial Neanderthal beginnings to present day developments in science and high technology. He gazes into storefront windows as he walks on and ponders the various products and services that man has created and chosen to market and he asks himself: "Has any of it really amounted to anything as important as mystic peace and awareness?" Perhaps some of these items have enhanced the process and search. If DNA always has a plan or design, then maybe there's a reason for industrialization and byproducts like smog. Hadn't he read somewhere, he wonders, that something as seemingly noxious and deplorable as industrial waste actually must have a purpose for being present? It is a strange theory, Alan concedes.

All in all, he feels that the creation and proliferation of multitudinous goods and services presents equivocal benefits, at best. Ostensibly, man is gaining his wants and not merely meeting his needs. Further, it seems that man satiates even the most superfluous desires and extravagances, but where had this really taken humankind? Alan wonders. He slides over to recline upon a small hill in front of an office building. "Is man really any happier than he was a thousand years ago?" Alan queries as he focuses on the spectrum of military-style office workers, hurriedly paced shoppers, and steady stream of high performance motor cars busily racing off to some supposedly important destination.

The frantic pace of the local business district touches Alan's soul in a remarkable way. With his awareness heightened only to the busy goings on of a bustling, metropolitan city, he sucks up and savors this last heavy dose; for he is resolute in soon departing for at least a couple of weeks to places completely away from a city this size.

He walks onto the grounds of St. Paul's Cathedral where, outside a fence, provisions of food have been set up for a line of homeless men and women. In the line there are tattered, dirty clothes being worn and shoes on some of the people while others are barefooted. Soot and matted hair cover the heads and faces of many of them. Alan gazes into their eyes with a profound sense of sorrow and sympathy. He has seen great wealth in the city, and now he is face to face with the most materially and perhaps emotionally destitute. The poorest of the poor were likely mentally ill and victims of unspeakable abuse. Capitalism had brought not only a thriving economy but actual opulence in this great country aligning the North Sea. In its wake it had also left a portion of the population isolated and hunger-stricken.

Alan sees a gregarious priest supervising the buffet table and he appears to be making sure that everyone is getting fed. The priest has a cleanly shaven head and wears silver wire rim glasses. He has a muscular build and a modest, self-effacing expression. His majestically lined face possesses strong, almost simian features: a prominent chin with high, well-defined cheekbones and a full beard. He wears a traditional frock and stands with an authoritative but friendly posture. Smiling and with his hand extended, Alan approaches the man and introduces himself: "Hello, my name is Alan. I just wanted to tell you that I think you're doing an admirable job." They shake hands firmly. "Why, thank you," the priest replies. The priest instructs an assistant to take over responsibilities temporarily.

"I'm about to take a break young man. Would you like to walk with me a bit?" the priest asks Alan. "Sure, I'd actually like to see parts of this glorious church, if I may," Alan replies. They begin to walk at a slow pace toward the front entrance to the church. "What brings you here my friend?" the priest genially asks. Alan responds: "I'm basically just wandering around today and arbitrarily chose this street. I noticed the beautiful church and then walked up and saw the work you all are doing." "What's your name?" "Brother Rivett, James Rivett," the priest replies. "Son, are you in search of spiritual guidance or simply worldly conversation?" the priest queries pregnantly. Alan retorts: "My interests lie in the realm of spirituality within this world but I am not necessarily in search of any sort of guidance, although I sincerely appreciate your inquiring." "What type of priest or should I say, of what order do you belong?" Brother Rivett smiles and speaks in a soft manner: "I am a Jesuit priest, part of a group of individuals in residence fulfilling certain obligations to the church. I began the food bank program to serve a specific need within our community. This is one of many responsibilities we have to fulfill our calling from God." Brother Rivett turns the questioning back to Alan:

"What sort of spirituality are you interested in, my friend?" Alan answers, "I am interested in understanding more about the interconnectedness and love that exist among and between all earthly organisms; the unifying field of consciousness or force that seems to move us from behind the scenes." Brother Rivett smiles and attempts to elucidate what Alan has just said: "You mean, of course, the Holy Spirit as it manifests itself from God to Jesus and down through the clergy and then to man." The priest's simplistic, hierarchic summation in its highly limiting, constricting, and predictably authoritarian manner is at least slightly disturbing to Alan.

In Alan's opinion, the altruism exhibited on the part of the priest toward the homeless population is both moving and admirable. As Alan now stands with this man—as they are both about to enter the church—he only wishes that the good acts are being performed outside the realm of a strictly organized, bureaucratic system; mostly from the heart.

"Father," Alan utters—as he can not even believe that he is saying the word—with all do respect, "I tend to take a more flexible, syncretistic—more mystical perspective of things." The priest opens the door and they begin to walk into the corridor of the church. Alan continues: "I believe the church serves an invaluable role in healing communities as is so clearly evidenced by the remarkable work you are doing for the homeless. It's just that I have always had a challenge with hierarchic concepts such as The Trinity, or the implied necessity of going through a church or another human (i.e., priest or preacher) to achieve communion with God, or salvation."

Alan suddenly recalls the business terms used in relation to women and it occurs to him that there is one that pertains aptly to what he is trying to tell the priest: "cutting out the middleman." Alan can see the clear reaction of concern on the priest's face. Brother Rivett speaks up: "Young man, what is your name?" "Alan, sir," Alan responds. The priest goes on: "Alan, you remind me of an individual who created and stirred up quite a controversy in his time; a highly interesting man by the name of Pierre Teilhard de Chardin. De Chardin conceived that God was omnipresent in the created world; that we have a responsibility to cultivate an active participation in the divine in our everyday lives. Chardin wrote, *Hymn Of The Universe,* among others." Alan's interest perks up. The priest continues as they stroll down one of the baroque hallways: "Teilhard de Chardin wrote through immensely poetic language of God's representation through human lives; his various incarnations, so to speak." Alan listens intently as the priest seems to show an open-mindedness to idiosyncratic approaches to religion. Alan interjects: "I have only heard a little bit about de Chardin before speaking to you. It seems to me that he is a precursor for modern day thinkers like Fritjof Capra, who wrote *The Tao of Physics* and *The Turning Point.* Are you aware of these books?" Brother Rivett replies: "I have heard of the writer but am largely unfamiliar with his works." Alan elaborates: "Capra is a theoretical physicist who has managed to articulate very poignantly the significant ties between modern day physics and antiquated doctrines of mysticism. It's very fascinating work."

Alan senses that his newfound friend needs to return to the food line. Alan gazes around briefly at the palatial, breathtaking environs of gold chalices, white drapes, and towering, monstrous organ pipes. "I suggest we start walking back," Alan offers. He continues: "I appreciate your generosity in spending this time talking with me. I hope I was not disrespectful. I just wanted to stimulate some interesting discussion." "Not at all," says Brother Rivett, as he leads Alan back to the front door. "You are a young, inquisitive man who will surely find his own way." As they push open the very old wooden door, wonderful disconnected rays of sunlight drip in. Alan and the priest descend the steps to the sidewalk and the priest quietly resumes his humanitarian role at the food line. As Alan departs to go find himself something to eat, he smiles and waves to his friend.

He then reaches into his backpack and pulls out his map of London. He locates the British museum, which seems to be in an area that would also have some restaurants. Alan finds his way to a subway stop and boards a train to the necessary stop. He emerges to another busy London street on which, next to the University of London, he quickly spots The British Museum. Among its vast, encyclopedic collection, Alan had heard that one of the most interesting pieces it contains is the Rosetta Stone. The only thing that Alan really knows about the Rosetta Stone is that it is some interesting tablet or block containing ancient hieroglyphic text and that was found somewhere in or near Egypt.

Before reaching the museum, Alan locates a Chinese restaurant. He goes in and finds a table near the windows in front. He sits down and orders garlic pork for his entree, and water to drink. He sets his backpack down on the chair next to him and observes the business of the place. People are milling about and cavorting like it's some kind of a party. Behind him sits a boisterous group of six people, probably students. Alan turns around to see one of them, who is wearing a university sweatshirt and the others who are dressed pretty casually in mainly t-shirts and jeans. Scattered books and a couple of backpacks cover the table. There are four women and two men. Two of the women are smoking cigarettes and most at the table have cups of coffee in front of them.

As Alan waits for his meal, he sips on his water and cannot help but begin promptly eavesdropping as one of the women, who has her hair pulled back in a ponytail and legs crossed in almost a lotus position, begins to discourse in a delightful English accent: "Susan is telling me that conservatives are trying desperately to save Charles Darwin's house in Downe. I cannot believe that it's even a struggle. Darwin wrote *On The Origin of Species and the Descent of Man* in this home. He was arguably the most important scientist of the 19th century. Why does anyone think that this is not important?" One of the young men speaks up in a less prominent accent: "Yeah, I hear a well-known American evolutionary biologist is assisting an eminent scholar here to save it. I hope they do. Darwin was certainly a very important man." Alan continues to listen with great interest; for he had not been reading the paper too much while in London. The waiter shows up with the meal, asking if Alan needs anything else. "No thank you," Alan responds. Another of the women speaks up:

"Darwin is one of the great scientists of all time; along the lines of Galileo, Copernicus, Newton, etc. He is as representative of the greatness of England at least as much as Sir Isaac Newton!" Alan feels strange about interjecting into their conversation but is very interested in participating. He sets his fork down between bites and turns to contribute: "Hey, I couldn't help but to overhear your conversation. I was wondering if any of you know that over in the states right now they're still debating within some school districts about how or even whether or not evolutionism and creationism can be taught in the classroom. There's still a hell of a lot of controversy. A lot of the bibliolatrous conservatives have been terribly successful in keeping evolutionism out of the classroom." One of the men announces: "I've heard something about that, mate. I don't think it's very Christian-like to keep students away from scientific theories in their science classes. Perhaps it's because he's English and everyone in the states knows us English are all crazy anyway." Laughter erupts. The other man asks: "Hey, what's your name, mate?"

"Alan, Alan Agrippa." "You guys are students at U. of London?" Alan asks.

"Yeah, we meet here each week to do homework, or discuss issues, or fuck around with a ouija board or something," comments the student with the sweatshirt. He continues: "So Alan, what are you doing in London today?" Alan answers: "I'm going to tour the British Museum within which I'm looking forward to checking out the Rosetta Stone." "Ah, the Rosetta Stone," comments one of the women, who continues to say: "I once did a report on the Rosetta Stone. It contains three styles of language: hieroglyphic, demotic, and Greek. When Napoleon sailed to counteract British strength in Egypt, his people discovered the stone at the Fort of St. Julian at Rosetta, a town near the western section of the Nile. When the French surrendered, the stone was forfeited to the British along with many other treasures making up the Egyptian Collection in the British Museum." One of her friends speaks up:

"A French Orientalist interpreted the demotic text based on equating the Greek Ptolemaic titles with their Egyptian parallels." The former of the two women continues: "The Jesuit scholar, Athonasius Kirchen, attempted to unravel the complex hieroglyphic, only to further complicate things by failing to consider the phonetic nature of the script. The English physicist, Thomas Young, took a shot at it and the French scholar Champollion further championed the task by limning out a more thorough interpretation of the hieroglyphic text." Alan responds: "You are all very knowledgeable and generous with the info. I'm now totally intrigued about seeing the stone and exploring the rest of the museum." As he proceeds to finish his meal, his newfound acquaintances resume a more mundane conversation.

The restaurant still buzzes with the bristling activity of voices and clanging glasses. Alan whips out a credit card and hands it to the waiter with the bill. As he waits for the waiter to return, he reaches into his backpack and removes the original book on mysticism.

Picking up where he has left off, he begins to read: "Dr. Timothy Leary, formerly a tenured professor of psychology at Harvard University, and humorously referred to as 'Johnny Acidseed' by William S. Burroughs, was a well known proponent for the use of psychedelic substances such as mescaline, psilocybin, but particularly lysergic acid

(LSD–25). Vehemently lauding LSD as a propellant for the expansion of unlimited neural pathways, and a facilitator for the exploration of the vast realms of your own nervous system, Leary led an entire generation to the mystical tune of, 'Turn on, Tune in, and Drop Out.' Other writers and psychologists joined in the campaign, some of whom are the following: Alan Watts, Ken Kesey, Allen Ginsberg, Aldous Huxley, Richard Alpert, a.k.a. Ram Dass, and Robert Anton Wilson. This was popular mysticism at its best in the roaring '60s revolution, a theory supported by Ph.D. psychologists! Just pop one hit of acid on the West Coast and accomplish in terms of spiritual progression what took the Buddhist monk years to attain." Alan smiles in amusement, shuts the book, and places it back into his backpack. The waiter returns with his card imprint to be signed. Alan signs his name and leaves a generous tip.

As he gets up from the table, Alan waves to his friends who genially wave back and then he heads out the door. The wind is blowing swiftly and the sun is shining incandescently. Alan crosses the street cautiously, and in the direction of the museum, observes a steady, slow stream of visitors pouring in. A bevy of pigeons flutters and clambers the air into the cerulean sky. On the exterior of the main entrance to the museum stand towering concrete walls which enclose an impressive collection of art. The walls are tinted charcoal gray from the ongoing effects of time and pollution.

When Alan reaches the door he pays admission and eagerly enters. Mainly tourists and students fill the corridors of the spacious rooms. Alan adapts a typically whimsical approach with only two major things in mind: the Rosetta Stone and the Elgin Marbles from the Parthenon. Alan learns that the museum contains most of the frieze of the Parthenon and the remains of the East Pediment. As he enters what is called the Large Elgin Room, he begins to read a little about the Parthenon. He discovers that the frieze is the section of the sculpture which ran along the top of the outer wall and continued above the columns of the porches at each end. This section contained festal and ceremonial scenes which encapsulate most of the community. The event portrayed was part of the great Panathenaic festival held every four years, which involved a procession that carried a sacred robe (the peplos) to drape the wooden image of Athena. Alan gazes in awe at the intricately depicted scenes on stone, actual stone from the Parthenon in Greece. He studies carefully the stunningly detailed representations of musicians, elders, and chariots. The West Frieze portrays horsemen and attendants preparing for the Panathenaic procession. Alan turns left to observe the North Frieze. A boy is clearly depicted arranging his master's tunic while a horseman adjusts a wreath. An effect of lively horses in motion is magically created. To the right of the door leading into the Ephesus Room stands a slab that portrays the leading horseman of the cavalcade. To the left of the slab stand the first depictions of chariots Alan has seen. With great interest, he spots four-horsed chariots with charioteers in long, flowing robes. Scanning more of the pieces, Alan sees elderly citizens carrying olive branches and walking cheerfully beside lyre and flute players. Boys carrying trays of offerings, and leading unknowing sheep to slaughter, create hypnotic images that propel Alan's consciousness to a time and place of another world. He envisions beautifully sculpted bodies and rigorously exercised minds that emerge in a setting unparalleled in its natural aesthetics and architectural genius: Athens, Greece.

As Alan progresses to study pieces that depict Poseidon, Apollo, Artemis, Aphrodite, Eros, and Olympus itself, he contemplates the convergence of man's perception of the supernatural (i.e., gods), with the evolution of a rational, logical intellect. In a country with such diversity and richness in its pantheism, there emerged hallmarks of man's intellect: discursive thinking, logical reasoning, and scientific methodology. Just as astrology had been the crucial underpinning of modern day cosmological insights, so had a belief in gods given rise to the modern day powers of disputation and logic. Alan further peruses the East Frieze and South Frieze, quickly moving through the Room of The Metopes, in which graphic stone reliefs showcase aggressive battles between Lapith people and centaurs. The amalgamation of animal with man anatomy as depicted in the centaur has always seemed very strange to Alan. He theorizes that this peculiar image of the lower body of a horse attached to a man's torso represents bizarrely the peculiar evolution of man from a more animalistic form.

Alan familiarizes himself with another common theory which is written about in the museum: that the fight between the Lupiths, a people living in the mountainous districts of Thessaly, and centaurs exemplifies the ongoing struggle between civilization and barbarism. The images are dramatic and surreal. The fact that pieces of the slabs had been destroyed only intensifies the theme conveyed and powerfully reminds the viewer of the sometimes violent history of the Parthenon. Earthquakes, wars, and looting had left their indelible marks on almost every piece in the collection. Alan is amazed that even part of the Parthenon remains standing in Greece. He decides at this time that he will definitely have to travel to Athens to inspect what remains.

Alan exits the Elgin Collection and rests on a bench in the hallway before beginning his search for the Rosetta Stone. Time has stood still while he has immersed himself in the magic of Greece. He checks his watch and discovers that it is close to 3:30. "Okay," he thinks. "I've got time to go out and smoke a cigar and then I'll come back in and explore the Rosetta Stone until the museum closes at 6." He reaches into his backpack and pulls out a cigar and lighter. Standing up slowly, he finds his way to a large glass door that leads to a shady courtyard outside. Alan steps into a sunny spot and sets his bag down. He kneels beside an angelic sculpture which generates a light waterfall through an olive branch. After carefully placing the cigar into his mouth, he lights the end and takes a long drag. He allows the smoke to circulate within his closed mouth and gradually seep its intoxicating nicotine into his pores. He blows the smoke out and sits contemplatively as an occasional tourist passes him in the doorway.

CHAPTER II

At about the halfway point of the cigar, Alan looks up and notices a long-haired skate punk-looking adolescent boy meandering up to him. "Hey, you got a light?" the kid asks. "Sure, here you go," Alan replies as he lifts his lighter to the end of the kid's cigarette. The kid is wearing a white t-shirt bearing the logo, "Indie Fortune 500" and he has on baggy jeans with a dangling chain and high top basketball sneakers. His hair is brown, shoulder length and bangs sway periodically in front of his eyes. "You're from the states, aren't you," the kid asks. "Yeah, how'dya know?" Alan replies. The boy answers, "I could tell by the way you talk. Thanks for the light." "What's your name?" Alan asks him, as the kid stands there puffing on his cigarette. "Jonathan, Jonathan Fields," replies the youth.

"What's yours?" he retorts. "Alan, Alan Agrippa," Alan responds, attempting to speak in the same intonation as Jonathan has. "What kind of music do you like?" Alan asks him. Jonathan responds: "I like rap with a message, stuff like Public Enemy." It figures, Alan thinks. He comes all the way to England and meets a young white kid who loves Afro-centric American music. Alan's decidedly Anglo-centric interest in bands like New Order, The Smiths, and Depeche Mode will probably not go over too well, he thinks. The grass is always greener on the other side of the ocean, he muses. He intrepidly speaks up anyway: "I like Depeche Mode. They're from good ole' Basildon, aren't they?" Jonathan grimaces and replies consolingly, "We've all got our cross to bear, mate." Alan laughs heartily at his own expense.

"I'm trying to figure out a way to the secret collection of erotic works that the museum holds," Jonathan suggests. "Erotic works?" Alan queries. Jonathan continues: "Yeah, there is a collection of works that has either been banned or at least hidden from public view—books about sex and stuff." Alan questions him further: "Well, how does one get access to such books?" "If I knew the answer to that question, would I be out here with you?" Jonathan quips, amusingly. The two friends finish their smokes. "Come with me, let's figure this one out," Alan commands. Jonathan happily complies.

They walk back into the main building and Jonathan follows Alan up to an information booth. A studious looking librarian is sitting at the desk. She is wearing thick-rimmed black glasses and has her hair pulled up in a conservative style. Alan isn't sure exactly how to bring up the request. He implements as tactful an approach as he can muster up: "Excuse me, ma'am, my assistant and I would like to inquire about a selection of books which has been deemed inaccessible to the general public. Could you be of some assistance please?" She seems slightly endeared by Alan's politeness but also a bit curious. She asks him to clarify what type of books he is looking for: "Sir, in what category would the books you are referring to fall?" Alan ponders what would be a professional way of answering her. "Ma'am, we are interested in procuring those works which fall into the erotic and sexological categories," he strains toward professionalism. The woman's pupils appear to dilate as she ponders Alan's statement. She clears her throat and responds. "Well then sir, you must be referring to The Arch Room, which houses the incunabula."

"Incunabula! That word has an interesting ring to it," Alan thinks. "What exactly are the incunabula?" Alan asks in a manner not so much revealing his ignorance as much as flattering and showing deference to the woman's wisdom. She replies proudly, authoritatively: "The incunabula are books printed mainly before 1500 and are kept in private stock for very valid reasons, of course." Alan presses on: "What valid reasons?" Instead of answering that question, she refers them to the principal keeper of books who at this time is on a break. There is a note on his door indicating he will be back in thirty minutes.

Alan turns to Jonathan as they stand by the supervisor's door. "So, Jonathan, what books in particular are you looking for? Do you know the names or titles?" "Well," Jonathan begins. *"Nymphomania* by Bienville would be a good start. Then something like *The World of Sex* by Henry Miller and just about anything by de Sade." Alan smirks. This kid is obviously well-versed in the pornographic cornucopia of literature. The two sedition-seeking men make small talk until the keeper of the books returns. He is an astute, middle-aged gentleman, bespectacled and balding. His naturally tonsured scalp shines luminescently, reflecting light from the ceiling lamps. He wears a brown, dusty sports coat with dark brown patches that cover the elbows. At first, he pretends not to notice Alan and Jonathan as he enters his office. Leaving his door open, he sets his briefcase down and slowly shuffles some papers on his desk and then sits down in a large swivel chair. Alan and Jonathan peer eagerly into the office. After loudly clearing his throat, the gentleman spins around in his chair until he is facing them. "May I help you, gentlemen?" Alan speaks up: "Yes sir, my colleague and I would like to request access to your private collection of esoterica, or should I say erotica literature. I have traveled very far and would most appreciate your kindly assistance in this matter." The gentleman's piercing eyes appear to be probing Alan's inner nature and true motives. Alan and Jonathan wait patiently for the response.

They watch and listen intently as the man, who had previously picked up a pencil from his desk, twirls it lightly between his fingers, gently sets it back down and then straightens his glasses before speaking: "And what, may I ask, is the extent of your studies?" Alan glances at Jonathan, clears his throat, and then before speaking, thinks to himself: "Oh, basically the unrepentant, frivolously perverse interest in that which is forbidden, particularly if it is sexual." This, of course, is transmuted into the following proclamation: "Sir, we are on a most professional, academic endeavor to uncover and categorize within scientific parameters the various works through history (of arguable ill repute) which have possibly had a deleterious effect on society. We understand that many of the works in this private collection were quite controversial in their time." The bookkeeper replies authoritatively: "Gentlemen, I sincerely hope that you do not find my cautious approach to be offensive. You understand, in my position I must demonstrate extreme discretion despite my personal belief in the dissemination of open information to the masses. The private collection has, of course, a long history of being kept secret in order to either protect people's minds from the books or to protect the books from people's minds. A prevalent belief in the past was that the potential for volatility was high with regard to the correlation between people and these books. Although objective evidence for the destruction of minds has not been clearly established, in my opinion, there has been a significant, measurable risk to these books falling into the wrong hands. Theft and vandalism are the abominations of which I speak."

The man pauses, as if to decide the fate of a potential viewing. "I feel confident that you two are upstanding and respectable. Please follow me." The gentleman escorts Alan and Jonathan to a corporate-board-room-looking, glass-walled room. It contains a long, rectangular mahogany table; leather bound reference books line bookcases on both sides of the room. "Please take a seat. I shall be back shortly." The gentleman excuses himself. Alan and Jonathan sit reticently, not sure if they are about to be arrested or awarded for apparently cracking the cryptic seal of the forbidden books. About fifteen minutes later, the man returns with a lengthy computer readout. He sets it in front of the two young men and politely requests that they scan the list and circle those titles which they are interested in seeing.

Alan sits with a pen in hand as Jonathan peers over his shoulder and they begin to peruse the licentious list. With occasional verbal cues from Jonathan and with the headmaster-looking gentleman looking over them guardedly, Alan circles titles such as: *Kalogynomia, Or The Laws of Female Beauty* by T. Bell; *Plague of Lust, Being A History of Venereal Disease in Classical Antiquity* by Julius Rosenbaum; *Memoirs of a Woman of Pleasure,* more commonly known as *Fanny Hill,* by John Cleland; *The Romance of Lust* by William S. Potter. Alan quickly locates *Nymphomania* and *The World of Sex,* the two lively titles Jonathan had requested. To satisfy the de Sade criteria, Alan proudly circles the title, *Justine.*

After getting Jonathan's approval—for he is, in fact, smiling brightly—Alan hands the list back to the bookkeeper. The gentleman dutifully exits the room and returns shortly, pushing a cart filled with the chosen books wrapped in protective covers.

As he lays them out on the table one by one, Alan and Jonathan perk to attention. "I am going to be in the next room. I'm sure that you will handle the books with care." The gentleman quietly departs after politely vouchsafing the titillating texts. Alan fancies himself a proud corrupter of youth as he suddenly notices a gleam in Jonathan's eyes. Alan has a feigned, altruistic notion that a good healthy dose of erotica will be a perfect catalyst to propel Jonathan into the world of truly great literature. Not all of the works are literary genius but many of them are challenging and intellectually stimulating, as well as emotionally stirring.

The two young men begin to pore over the words which exude a spicy, rambunctious sexuality that emerged from jolly ole' Europe. Alan takes notice of interesting expressions like: "a rod for a proud lady," "bawdy," "vulgarly," "lecherously," "ready to be whored out in the public streets," "sex swastika," "manufacturing machine." Jonathan takes a fantasy tour: group sex; anal intercourse; two women; sex outdoors; using various objects; and epicurean enhancements, like licking savory foods from body orifices. When one of the pioneers of perversity comes across something exceptionally lewd or humorous, he readily brings it to the attention of the other. Whenever they see the bookkeeper pass by or look in, they affect the best approximation of professional demeanor they can, which, of course, is the exact opposite of how they are truly behaving.

As Alan smoothly turns the pages and holds these books in his hands, he approaches the task with an almost reverence. His attitude and feeling about handling these books falls along the lines of deep respect toward the authors for systematically expanding the sexual, psychological horizons of the readers and concomitantly lessening the moral restraints and hypocritical underpinnings that the church and state had exerted over society. As Alan scans the cornucopia of erotica, he develops a sincere appreciation for the pioneers and liberators of the human spirit.

"Hey Alan, which one is your favorite?" "Out of the ones we've looked at here, the classic Sade work, *Justine,* is pretty impressive; from the standpoint of its eloquent and no-holds-barred language and the undeniably unrivaled infamy of its author. From the standpoint of interesting, bizarre sounding titles, I think that *Kalogynomia* by T. Bell takes the cake. What about you, Jon, which one is your favorite?" *"Nymphomania,* definitely. If I could get my girlfriend to do some of this stuff, then I'd be a very happy man, my friend." "My girlfriend and I plan on writing the sequel," is Alan's reply, which is immediately met with jovial laughter from Jonathan.

"Jonathan, this has really been a blast but I'm afraid I've got to run. I've got to see the Rosetta Stone before I leave today and time is running out. Here—he hands him one of the books—you should continue to hang out here as long as you want. Just tell the superintendent dude when you leave." "Alan, it's been real, man." The two shake hands. Alan gets up from the table and swiftly passes through the exit and out onto the main floor. He looks back at Jonathan, who is sitting in the reading room peacefully, intensely absorbed in the amazing, fantasy realms of the stories. This time, Alan does not question whether he will see this guy again. He just preserves the moment in his mind.

CHAPTER 12

An attendant at the information booth instructs Alan on how to find the Rosetta Stone. He thanks her and goes on his way. He becomes regretful that he does not have more time. For as he makes his way through the hallways of the museum, he notices that it contains a wide array of Renaissance and Post-Renaissance works among those of many other time periods, all showcasing many pivotal works of the eminent artists of the time. Alan winds his way through the circuitous route leading to the Egyptian Sculpture Gallery, that contains the Rosetta Stone. There, in a soft glow of light, hanging in all its grandeur, is the Rosetta Stone.

The enigmatic slab of black basalt stands three feet, nine inches in height and two feet, four and a half inches in width and eleven inches in thickness. He reads that its weight has been calculated at just under three-fourths of a ton. A large section on the left-hand upper corner is missing as are smaller sections on the upper and lower right sides. The top of the stone is rumored to have been rounded and it contains the winged disc of Horus of Edfu with pendant uraei, wearing the crowns of upper Egypt and lower Egypt and each carries a shen ring and ceremonial fan. Below the winged disc would have probably been an image of the king in the midst of gods and goddesses.

Alan scans the text in its two forms of Egyptian—hieroglyphics and demotic—and then the Greek. He learns that, based on an analysis of the only cartouche—the oval figure enclosing characters that represent the name of the sovereign—it was fairly well determined that what was written was the name, Ptolemy. The inscription on the Rosetta Stone represents the decree passed by a council of priests assembled at Memphis on the first anniversary of the coronation of Ptolemy V Epiphanes, king of all Egypt. The date of the coronation was 27 March 196 B.C. The text focuses on the honors bestowed upon Ptolemy V by the temples of Egypt in return for the services rendered by him to Egypt. Priestly privileges are elaborated upon.

Alan stands transfixed, allowing his mind to absorb and imprint the mysterious, antiquated stone. He muses over the interesting attempt on the part of man to document in writing—events that are felt to be significant. Throughout time and often in the midst of tumultuous wars and climatic chaos man is compelled to put into text that which is often perceived as divinely inspired or decreed. The Rosetta Stone, in its powerful, ominous black physical form and its cryptic trinary nature of script, is a shining example. Lights begin to flicker. Security personnel begins to lock doors. A voice rings out from an intercom that the museum is now closing. Alan takes one last picture in his mind and then he turns to leave. A steady flow of visitors streams out the exit. Alan steps outside and takes a deep breath of fresh air. His soul feels enriched and full from the day's events. He looks forward to picking up Ronia and hearing what she has to say about any potential for plans together.

He crosses the street and walks two blocks up to a pay phone on the side of a coffee shop. Alan thinks it will be a good thing to call Peter and say goodbye. He unzips his bag and digs around for Peter's number, locates it and then puts a coin in the slot and dials the number. Olympia answers the phone in her usual sultry, casual style. "Hi, Olympia, this is Alan. Can you please tell me, is Peter in?" "Yes he is, dawling. Tell me, how are you and your elegant girlfriend doing?" "Very well, thanks. We thoroughly enjoyed hanging out with you guys the other night."

"Alan, hold on just one minute and I'll get Peter." With his left hand lightly plugging up his left ear in order to screen out the noise of traffic, he wraps his right hand tightly around the receiver and presses it to his ear. "Hello," Peter answers, in that unmistakable Jamaican accent. "Peter, my friend, this is Alan. I was calling to let you know that my travel will soon be taking me elsewhere. You're pretty cool and I'd like to stay in touch." "Where are you goin', mon? Where's the next stop?"

"I'm heading into the English countryside and then making my way over to Scotland," Alan replies. "Alan, my band and I are going to be tourin' for a while. Maybe we'll all hook up. Olympia will know my schedule. While you're in Europe, call occasionally to get a report about where I am." "Will do. Take care, my friend. We've had some good times. Let's have some more." "Adios, Alan." "Adios, Peter." Alan sets the phone down and smiles. He walks a couple of blocks to the subway, purchases a token, and then boards the train to take him to Ronia. When he arrives at Mary's and Jim's, Jim answers the door. "Hello, Alan, come on in."

"Hi, Uncle Jim, how are you doing?" "I'm doing fine. Mary and Ronia are out back in the garden. Would you like to join me for a smoke?" "Sure," Alan replies. They walk back to Jim's library, a beautiful, warm enclosure possessing hardwood floors that are blanketed with an ornate, burgundy Oriental rug. A large polished oak table sits in the middle of the room, and long rows of bookcases—containing a vast selection of engineering and technical books—line two walls. Alan admires the thick-leathered binding on myriad editions as Jim offers him a choice of Cuban's finest: four chestnut colored, colorfully wrapped cigars that brim with a rich aroma. Alan takes one and offers his sincere thanks.

Jim lights the tip of a cigar as Alan begins to speak: "I'm going to be leaving really soon to see the rest of the country and then on to the rest of Europe." "That sounds like a great plan, Alan. I'm sorry we have not gotten to spend much time together but you're a young, adventurous man and we wouldn't want to stop you." Alan begins to hear the voices of the two women walking down the hallway. Mary and Ronia enter the room casually conversing.

"Hello, Aunt Mary." Alan rises and kisses his aunt's cheek. "Hi Alan, dear." Alan smiles at Ronia and hugs her gently. "Hi Alan." "Ladies, please come in and sit down," says Jim. Alan speaks up: "Mary, I have some news that I just shared with Jim. I'm leaving London soon to explore the rest of the country. I love you guys very much and wish that we had all gotten a chance to spend more time together. Who knows? I might end up back in London." Mary seems surprised and a little dejected at the news; she carries a frown but listens attentively and strives to understand. Jim interjects lightheartedly: "Alan, be sure to get to Stratford and Oxford; both are very interesting cities." "I plan on it," Alan replies. "Alan, honey, if I can get your mother on the phone, will you come and talk to her?" "Yes, I'll talk to them." While Alan continues to puff on the cigar, his eyes remain fixed on Ronia—who, wearing slick black jeans with a black, long-sleeved shirt, looks stunning. Mary calls out from the kitchen: "Alan, I have your mother on the phone." Alan puts the cigar out and rushes into the kitchen. "Hi Mom, how are you?"

"We're all fine here, Alan. What have you been up to?" "Well, I have seen most of the wonderful sites of London and met some pretty interesting people on the way. The weather's been pretty nice and I've basically been having a blast." "Where are you going from here?" Alan's mother has obviously picked up on the news that he is leaving. "I'm going to tour the countryside and then go to Scotland. I've written you a postcard that should have gone out today." "Alan, please give us an idea of where you are along the way, okay?" "Sure, Mom." "Take care and let everyone know I love them, okay?" "I will, Alan. I love you." "I love you too, Mom." Alan sets the phone down and thanks Mary for the call. "Mary and Jim, Ronia and I should probably get going tonight." "Alright, you guys take care and have lots of fun."

Mary leads the group to the front door after Jim extinguishes his cigar. Ronia and Alan step out into the street and hail a cab. When they get in, they instruct the driver to take them to a great Italian restaurant. They end up about twenty miles away. Alan should have known better. They step out of the car and enter the restaurant optimistically. The two order simply mildly satisfying plates of pasta and a bottle of tasteful burgundy wine. "How did your project go today?" Alan queries. "Very nicely," she answers. "I got a lot of work done. Although, I must say, my mind is frequently elsewhere, if you know what I mean." By the animated, enthusiastic tone in her voice, Alan gushes with a contentment and an almost prescience that Ronia's forthcoming remarks and disclosures seem remarkably promising.

"Alan, I want you to know that the time we have spent together has been truly joyful for me. I haven't known you really that long but I feel that you're a special person to me—unique in your intelligence, wit, and perspective." Alan gulps. "Further, I would like to say that once I have finished up this current research project and get a break from classes, I would like to meet up with you to share some adventure." Intense satisfaction permeates Alan's soul. He immediately sets his glass of wine down, leans over, and kisses her softly on her lips.

As the candlelight flickers playfully on the side of their table, Alan catches Ronia's image in the glow and sits back transfixed. He is striving to preserve the image in his mind's eye in a strange attempt to ensure that her promise will come true. As they finish their meals, Alan suggests that they go to a dance club to hear some cool music. He is in the mood for techno, ambient, and tribal sounds that will catapult them to another dimension. Far surpassing Alan's wildest dreams, Ronia's words have innervated him in the most positive way. He now glows with energy and wants to express it on a dance floor in a most stimulating club. Fortunately, Ronia is in a similar mood. They firmly clasp hands. Alan generously tips the waiter.

Chapter 13

They glide out the restaurant and walk seven blocks until locating the marquee to a happening club. They penetrate the darkened, smoke-filled entrance and emerge onto the electrifying interior landscape of what is undeniably a cool London scene. A baseball capped, close cropped, blue-jean and t-shirt wearing American DJ is spinning and orchestrating technically savvy, hypnotic vibes. Throbbing, repetitive, pulsating textures of sound skillfully weave fragments of hip hop, house, and trance rhythms that jolt Ronia and Alan onto the dance floor and into synchronous gyrations with the crowd. Seriousness has gleefully departed and given way to combustible partying that transports the lovers into a sanctuary of unbridled, passionate dance.

As beads of sweat begin to pour, Alan motions for Ronia to walk with him to the bar. He gazes around with great amusement at the youthful, spirited crowd that dons immensely interesting collections of mostly seventies and eighties styles. Baggy and bell-bottomed jeans give way to pop culture icon jerseys and gypsy, braided hair. Alan approaches the bar and orders two martinis with extra olives. Ronia glides next to him while she slowly sways to the groovy music. They sip on the drinks and enthusiastically absorb the amusing sights and sounds of hip London.

Occasionally, Alan strokes Ronia's hair and kisses her on the cheek. Her beauty draws him like a moth to a flame or a bee to honey. As he scopes the array of youthful, pubescently attractive females in the club, he recognizes a more mature, alluring aspect to Ronia's aesthetics. Hers is a beauty slightly older, and to Alan, one that is slightly more evolved. Fresh from the latter stages of youth and gently into the onset of womanhood, Ronia emanates an attractiveness which to Alan seems perfect—an ideal.

Ronia suggests that they go back to Alan's hotel. He gleefully obliges. As they ride the shuttling subway back to the hotel, Alan comes face to face with the stunning realization that this is probably going to be his last night in the city. As resolutely impulsive and capricious as he had long ago decided to be on this trip, he thinks that it is only fitting that he leave on practically the verge of the moment.

When they arrive at the room, Alan shuts the door behind them and begins to hold her closely. The warmth and delicate, fragile nature of her body provides Alan a sort of comfort. The two stand firmly embraced for several minutes, until Ronia begins to caress his lower back with both her hands. Her hands gently move inside his shirt and along his buttocks. With her lips, she begins to lightly kiss his throat and upper chest as her hands continue to caress him from behind. Alan strains to remain still, despite the tantalizing pulses of pleasure enveloping him. Ronia removes her hands from his back and begins to systematically unbutton his shirt with her fingers while the palms of her hands rub his chest and stomach. Her left hand slowly makes its way from his lower abdomen down to the shaft of his penis as her lips edge closer to meet his. She rubs the erect shaft until it hardens and slightly moistens at the end.

Alan has restrained from reciprocating until now. With highly dexterous fingers, he quickly removes her shirt and plunges his tongue into her cleavage: voluptuous mounds of silky, elegant flesh bursting forth from within the lacy confines of a black flowered bra. Disconnecting the latch, he slowly pulls the cups away from her now erect, plump nipples. Alternating between caressing with his hands and manipulating and sucking with his tongue, he loses himself in her chest while she draws him to climax with her hand. Droplets of semen trickle along the interior of his leg and on her wrist. She lifts one of her fluid-dipped fingers to her mouth and licks softly as he slips his right forefinger inside her panties and aside her clitoris. Gradually massaging the supple, tender, sentient folds into a vortex of energy and pleasure, he lifts her with his other arm.

He carries her to the bed and lays her down. Cool night air blows in from spontaneous rainfall and proves a refreshing complement to the fusion of their bodies. Waiting for Ronia to succumb to multiple orgasm, Alan climbs on top and gently slides inside her. Quickly navigating and strategically maneuvering their bodies to an optimum position, he then allows her to gain physical control over him and initiate a highly sentient rocking motion which will soon bring him to another stage of bliss.

Their bodies are now fully, lusciously intertwined. Ronia develops a steady, rhythmic motion as her smoothly toned legs slide like feathers across Alan's thighs. He playfully grabs a lock of her hair and tugs lightly as her warm, moist vagina involuntarily contracts and alternately releases tension, before exploding into a carousel of cum. Warm droplets effervescently, almost elegantly land along Alan's inner thighs as he admires the impressive visage of Ronia with her muscular arms and beautiful breasts above him. She breathes and moans heavily, as she strives for continuous orgasm through balletically pivoting her hips and extending her legs.

As they both tire, and begin to revel in the afterglow of sex, Alan holds her close and listens intently as she whispers words of praise for the pleasure he has brought her. As she gently massages the contours of his chest, she delicately fingers the sparse strands of hair scattered in a manner she considers perfect upon his chest. With their bodies now lying side by side, Alan carefully fondles the smooth curve of her hips, as he leans and kisses her succulently on the lips. "That was amazing," she says. "It was pretty wonderful," he responds. Ronia gets up and walks over to the table to grab a cigarette. She lights the end and takes a deep drag. "Will you get me a cigar?" Alan requests. "Sure, here you are, lover," she speaks playfully. The cigar she hands him is freshly lit from the top of her cigarette. Alan puffs briefly and smiles at her shapely silhouette, that reveals slightly tousled hair from the breeze. The curtains sway as Ronia returns fully naked to the bed. She gazes at him with hypnotic optical spheres and utters solemnly: "Are you leaving tomorrow?" Alan pauses before answering directly: "Yes, more than likely. I'm going to rent a car and begin my trek through England. I would love for you to come with me from the start but I understand your obligations and pursuits here." Ronia takes another puff from her dangling cigarette and then sets it in the ashtray next to the bed. "Alan, I would love to hook up with you in Wales or perhaps Scotland." "I plan on calling you fairly regularly to let you know where I'm going to be and what I'm up to. I would love for you to hook up with me in Wales, Scotland, or even sometime while I'm still in England," he reiterates, adding, "It all depends on your schedule." He runs his ring finger along the curve in the small of her back. She looks good enough to eat, he thinks.

Sleep descends upon them shortly after Alan finishes his cigar. Ronia falls asleep snugly in his arms with her head resting on his chest. Their dreams are less than serene; both are troubled—Alan's being plagued with inescapable worries, concerns, and excitements about his imminent trip and Ronia's being consumed with thoughts of sorrow and loneliness about Alan leaving.

Luminous morning rays cast their warmth upon the lover's cheeks, awakening the two lovers almost simultaneously. Alan turns his head and kisses her on the cheek. Upon awakening, Ronia starts to quietly cry. Tears uncontrollably fill her eyes as she begins to realize that Alan will soon be gone. He can hear her slight whimpers that emerge from beneath the sheets, as she attempts to conceal her emotion.

As Alan lies practically motionless next to her on the bed, he quietly does battle with himself over two disparate, powerfully conflicting emotions. One is the deep, almost all-consuming desire to stay with this woman for all eternity, no matter where she is. Secondly, he feels the irresistible, driving urge to travel at any cost in order to see other parts of the world and experience their grandeur. It had been clearly decided in his mind long before this moment that as long as his money lasts, travel will serve as the guidepost on the interesting course toward his unknown destiny. They stand and silently embrace for about twenty minutes, before Ronia peers up, gazes into his eyes, and smiles. They kiss briefly, before she gets dressed and turns to leave.

He watches as this beautiful angel vanishes through the narrow English doorway. As the door closes tightly and he listens to her departing footsteps gradually fade, a flood of emotion wells from within him and soon pervades his every pore. Alan begins to fall back on the bed, but suddenly staggers over to the desk chair, upon which he immediately slumps. A profusion of tears rains down like waterfalls over his cheeks and down to his chest. He sobs, uncontrollably, as he catches a waft of Ronia's fragrance left on his body, which only exacerbates the torture of having told her goodbye. He wipes a remnant of her scent left on his chest and raises his fingers to his nose. He inhales deeply, as if this will materialize her and somehow reconcile the quagmire of emotions in his soul. As he slowly regains his strength, he lugs his body cumbersomely to the shower and begins to run very warm water that immerses his physical self.

After finishing his shower, he dries off. With the towel wrapped around his waist, he steps to the phone to call a rental car agency. After setting up arrangements for the car, he begins to pack, loading up his suitcase and backpack. As he gets dressed and carries his belongings through the hallway, he attempts to locate the whereabouts of the rental car agency on his map.

Upon checking out of the hotel, Alan heads to the subway, abruptly boards the appropriate train, and arrives at the rental car agency within the hour. As he expected, the process of renting the car is time consuming and hassle-full. He pays the customary charges and hops into a small, Japanese-built economy car that is specially constructed for European roads. In particular, the steering wheel is on the right-hand side and the stick is on the left. Anxious to learn how to handle the roundabouts, he throws his bags in the back, puts the key in the ignition, and revs the engine before bolting away. The first couple of hours are harrowing to say the least. A lot of unintentional stops and starts send repetitive jolts that send him forward and back. Several times the engine stalls and the car swerves as Alan struggles to adjust his coordinates. Friendly honks from fellow cars in adjoining lanes hold him in check.

He locks his eyes on an upcoming lane as he approaches his first roundabout and feels his adrenaline rush. He maneuvers the vehicle tactfully around the curve while making sure that he has the right of way and can predict the actions of oncoming cars. The engine revs and Alan accelerates quickly before completing the circle safely in unison with traffic. As he continues in his lane, he takes a deep breath and smiles in pride at his accomplishment. He pauses by somewhat familiar landmarks and gradually the scenery changes into more distant, unfamiliar territory.

As he drives out of London, he begins to enter largely industrial-based smaller cities on the outskirts. Monstrous smokestacks line mammoth factories. Seemingly endless rows of provincial apartments are superimposed with clotheslines and junked cars. Alan watches as the working-class takes their lunch break or picks up their children from school. Solemn, almost non-expressive countenances reveal personalities that seem less concerned with the styles of the city, opting instead for functional, inexpensive clothes in dark matted shades of tan, brown, and charcoal gray.

As Alan drives further and further away from London, he wonders if he will ever return. With an extremely loose travel agenda, Alan heads northwest, toward the Stratford and Warwick areas. He glances down at the map and notices that in the southern region there is a place called Hampshire, as in the Hampshires of the United States. He presumes that there must have been a physical resemblance in the geography of the two places and muses that it is interesting that early colonists drew from their hometown vernaculars when settling the U.S. Looking at the map, he notices the town Wiltshire and immediately realizes it as the origin of "Wilshire" Boulevard in Los Angeles.

Occasionally, an intractable European quickly passes on very narrow roads despite Alan's average speed of about eighty miles per hour. Noticeable signs of industry begin to fade as Alan enters vast expanses of lush, verdant hills and valleys as foggy mists appear to blanket most of rural England. This creates a haunting, yet almost comforting feel. Alan rolls down the windows in the car so as to more directly soak up the air and moisture from the land. He drives for a few hours through High Wycombe, Thame, Bicester, and then into Warwick.

As he segues into town, he follows signs that direct him to parking for Warwick castle. He takes notice of the exquisite stone buildings that comprise the village of Warwick. Up until now, Alan has not gotten a true feel of old England. However, Warwick, in its perfectly quaint, antiquated milieu, has preserved a small town medieval decor and rich cultural heritage. Festivals highlighting significant historical dates are organized in Warwick to give people a taste of yesteryear.

Alan parks his car on the outside of the castle, grabs his bag, and begins the winding, tree-lined stone path leading toward the moat. Other than a nondescript camera shop and simple refreshment stand, the view of the castle and its surrounding land is similar to how it must have been in medieval times.

Before entering through the monumental wooden gates, he sits down in the grass and pulls out his original book on mysticism. Turning to where he—or was it Ronia—had left off, he begins to read: "Instant cosmic consciousness! Dr. Leary had actually begun his stint with what appears to be serious scientific research using LSD in therapy sessions to foster interpersonal comfort and psychological growth. The 'Harvard Squares,' as Leary refers to them, were appalled that they had a mad scientist on staff who was actually altering his own brain chemistry on campus. Leary was booted, so he took his show on the road."

Alan sets the book down and gazes out over the expanse of awe-inspiring stone magnificence of Warwick. As Alan's eyes scan each carefully laid block of stone, he entertains the question of whether or not those who built this impressive structure knew the centuries it would endure. In his mind, he cogitates over the interesting path of psychedelicists like Timothy Leary and the pioneering research they had done within the dimension of the human brain. Concurrently, Alan muses over the lascivious and sometimes torturous goings-on within this castle. Alan stands up and enters through the gates and heavy walls.

While penetrating dark, cavernous walkways with low ceilings and cool moist air, he moves through the crowd and tries to imagine that he has literally stepped back into time. He imagines vagaries of life in the feudal system: the interesting relationship of vassal to lord and its striking parallels to slavery in the Deep South of the United States. Alan envisions fierce battles with incoming enemies violently penetrating the palisade and then raping and killing the castle's inhabitants. He weaves in and out of the innumerable rooms and witnesses, among other things, another dungeon in all its despicable inhuman grandeur.

An aperture along the wall in one of the rooms reveals a breathtaking view of a pastoral, inspiring stream that flows circuitously through pines and oaks. Many of the rooms exhibit stunning artwork that majestically captures the colorful personalities of England's aristocracy. Vivid Renaissance impressionistic paintings depicting a variety of regal biographical renderings and picturesque landscapes reveal the intimate connections the artists of the time had with their physical and interpersonal connections. The artwork as well the architecture of this magical time had fortunately survived into perpetuity and are here for all to see.

Alan winds his way carefully through a hallway that leads to a balcony which overlooks the serpent—like stream down below. Rapid crystalline blue waters and voluptuous white boulders protrude through the surface. Lively tourists picnic by the stream as medieval—garbed tour guides on horseback gallop around proclaiming Old English greetings and storytelling narrations.

Alan focuses his attention at the breathtaking arrangement of clouds that hover high above. The comforting sounds of the rushing water soothe as he takes notice of a towering oak and a figure of a man sitting peaceably against its trunk. The man cuts a studious visage in a dark tan jacket, safari hat, and glasses with a cord attached and wrapped around his neck. The face of the man appears unshaven and a prominent goatee protrudes with authority. Several books lay stacked in miscellany while the man scribbles diligently on a notepad.

Alan descends the stairs and walks over to the man. Although the man is clearly deep in thought, Alan abruptly but politely introduces himself: "Excuse me, my name is Alan, Alan Agrippa. I'm sorry but I'm very interested in discovering what it is you're working on." The gentleman responds: "I do not mind at all. My name is Rupert Allport and in answer to your question, I'm conducting a study on the fairy faith in Celtic countries. What brings you to England, young man?" The middle-aged man reveals a scholarly, distinguished English accent and through a concentrated, intense look in his eyes, exudes an extraordinarily erudite demeanor.

"I'm touring the English countryside at this time after an extended stay in London. I'm actually interested in an area of study which perhaps shares commonalities with yours, my friend; namely, mysticism. What can you tell me about the fairy faith?"

Mr. Allport fingers his pockets and locates two cigars, which he lifts into the air, and then extends one to Alan. "Would you like a cigar, young man?" "Sure." The two men light up. "Well, for starters, I can tell you that we are sitting on very magical land right now. England, Scotland, Wales, and Ireland have a rich history of belief in various beings possessing names like: leprechauns, carrigans, Sidhe, Gentry, lutins, and, of course, fairies—just to name a few. I can tell you that it's not just simple, uneducated country-folk who believe in these beings. Many higher echelon, very well-educated professionals equally believe in the validity and reality of these beings."

"That's very interesting," Alan replies. He continues: "I don't really know much about the belief in fairies. I suppose I've held the prejudice that it was once a common, perhaps necessary function of the human brain that has long since been rendered obsolete; transcended in a sense. However, being open-minded to the transpersonal realm of mysticism, I'm always willing to give any idea a chance. So you've been interviewing people and recording data?" Mr Allport puffs on his cigar and replies energetically: "Yes, I've been traveling around getting personal testimonies about the interesting things people have seen. My position is to be objective and pretty much detached although I would love to see one myself." Alan smiles and happily concurs. "I'd love to see one, too. Will you share with me some stories about some of the experiences these people have had?"

"Sure, Alan. I'd love to. I once spoke to a minister who told me that a girl in his town came up to him and described little people kicking and dancing. The minister said that he knew she was describing fairies, for he had seen them many times himself. There is another story of a boy visiting a Tylweth Teg King. The boy was ten years old at the time and had been whipped—physically abused by his schoolmaster for not learning his lessons well enough. One day, he runs away from school and goes to a river. Little folk come up and sit beside him. He explains to them his difficulties, to which they reply that he can stay with them if he likes. They then take him to a secret cave where the Tylweth Teg were playing games. The boy begins to play with the king's son. After playing for a short time the boy picks up a golden ball and returns to his mother. What he thinks is an elapse of two weeks is confirmed to have actually been two years. The boy often tries to find his way back but is never successful. He finally returns to school and becomes an accomplished scholar. Alan, are you with me? I hope I haven't bored you with my stories." "On the contrary," Alan replies. "I'm very much amused. Please tell me two more."

"Okay. There was once a gentleman who told me that he used to see fairies or manifestations thereof who would rise up from lakes and proceed to dance merrily around. Their amazing attractiveness would lure young men to follow them back into the water where they would marry. If a husband ever wanted to return, he would have to leave his fairy wife behind. These fairies were as big as other people and they traveled by horse. Here's another. A man I met told me a story about a priest. We'll call him David. Father David was out swimming one day and accidentally drowned. Onlookers called for the priest's brother. We'll call him Peter. Peter was also a priest. Father Peter said a prayer to revive his brother. He whistled in between reciting lines from his breviary. Miraculously, Father David's spirit appeared. When asked where he had been, Father David replied casually that he had been at a hurtling match with the gentry. Father David's spirit returned to his body and resumes functioning as a priest for a good amount of time. Many people were around to substantiate this story."

"Rupert, please tell me, if you will, what various forms these creatures take." "Well, Alan, from what I've learned you have a few types: the leprechaun has a hat and stays around natural springs. His job is usually shoemaking. Pookas tend to be black-featured. They usually ride horseback. The gentry are a big race who usually appear white. These are just to mention a few."

Alan smiles at Rupert and thanks him heartfully for the stories. Looking up at the sky, Alan visually envelopes the spectacular cumulous configurations that swirl like tornadoes. The almost constant overcast climate in England seems strangely appropriate for the evolution of fairies, Alan thinks. He hypothesizes and muses entertainingly that as the three great bodies of water—The Irish Sea, the North Sea, and the English Channel—swept their refreshing, rejuvenating winds into counterpoint over the glorious land of Great Britain, the channels of perception and potentialities of visionary experience were magically stimulated and awakened. Ordinary belief and reliance upon reason were simply transcended and what emerged was what is modernly referred to as "the supernatural." In the short time Alan has spent roaming the grounds of the castle, he fortunately has had a delicious taste: a representative sample of England's diverse array of flora, fauna, and mythology which distinguish the idiosyncratic English mind. Various shrubby plants like the white hawthorne, the briar, the holly, and the honeysuckle enrich the landscape. Among native herbaceous plants are the cowslip, hyacinth, primrose, blueball, and foxglove.

Alan notices with some amusement the ubiquitous mistletoe which he, as a child, used to sell from door to door. Rabbits and squirrels move gingerly through the leaves and brush as Alan spots a myriad of colored cuckoos, finches, wren, blackbirds, robins and nightingales. He extinguishes his cigar and looks up just in time to catch a pheasant frolicking high aloft in the treetops.

"So Alan, your interest is in mysticism. Are you familiar with the remarkable work of Evelyn Underhill?" "Yes, I am. A little bit at least. I know she published in the mid-50s. Her seminal work was called *Mysticism*, wasn't it?" "Yes it was," replies Rupert. He continues: "Its extended title was *A Study in the Nature and Development of Man's Spiritual Consciousness.* It is a delightfully bold, incisive discourse on the various systems of mystical thought and their chief proponents or metaphysicians, if you will, who systematically peeled back the nuances or layers of human consciousness to reveal absolute truth. Very heady stuff. If I remember correctly, it weaves a highly interesting thread starting with the likes of Philo, the Alexandrian Jew, to St. Paul, Plotinus, St. Augustine, St. Francis of Assisi, and then on to Dante, Meister Eckhart, St. Ignatius Loyola, and many, many others. I highly recommend it. Alan, just look around you. The majesty that is the nature and history of this land is mysticism itself. It takes those of us like you and me to methodically study these minimally charted realms and construct some sort of cartography. Heaven is all around us yet modern man does not have the eyes to see. It is true that intellectual rigor and scientific rationalism have enabled man to realize the most remarkable accomplishments. Interstellar voyages and medical breakthroughs have exemplified the greatest of left-brain processes—shining hallmarks of man's vastly developed intelligence. We see it in our ingenious conversion and utilization of fossil fuels, and we see it in the riveting displays of architecture in our metropolitan cities. However, I ask you my friend, what has been sacrificed in the process of these strides? When the seas and air are poisoned from the chemical pollution, have we truly gained? When chemical wars and spills have killed masses, what have we truly gained? When modern day neuroses and psychoses arise from the pressures of overproduction and consumption, has the gain been worth it? These are questions, my friend, that need to be asked."

"I agree, Rupert. You've touched on some immensely important issues. I often wonder what the balance is between harmonious concern for nature with the desire for progress and increasing standards of living. Material prosperity in congruence with conservationism is a lofty ideal, but I choose to maintain hope. Back to fairies. Do you feel that the theory of ever-present Jungian archetypes or some other explanation can explain the belief in the little creatures?" "Well, Alan, there are many theories and I choose to explore them all. One is the idea that within each generation there are perhaps vestigial beliefs which bespeak a race previously existent. In this case, it would imply that a dwarf-like race had preceded more modern types of and heights of humans. This, however, is largely unproven theory. There is no clear evidence that such a race existed. Then there is the somewhat hazy Jungian concept of primordial archetypes of the little green men variety that—for whatever reason— have always been floating around. Then, of course, we have the revelatory physiological insight of Dr. Julian Jaynes, who posited..." Alan interrupts: "that certain visions or auditions in the evolution of the human brain were necessary steps, so to speak." "Precisely, young man," Rupert announces proudly. "I'm so glad you're aware of Julian Jaynes, Rupert. It's rare that I meet someone familiar with his work," Alan beams. An equestrian rides up to announce that there will be a mock jousting event held shortly—in about ten minutes. Mr. Allport rises and folds up his belongings.

CHAPTER 14

The two men then begin to walk toward the 15th century castle with its inspiring ancient towers looming overhead. In the interior courtyard, there stands a line of medieval dressed men and women who appear ready for battle. Knights in shining armor cavort with voluptuously breasted women whose long flowing curls dangle protectively atop their shoulders. A large silver chalice majestically displayed in the center of a burgundy silk-covered table serves as the prize or trophy for a jousting victor. Surrounding the field stands an extended row of multi-colored flags with various symbols, the meanings of which Alan hasn't the slightest clue. As two jousters line up their horses for battle, Alan and Rupert merge with the spectators, who all look on with enthusiastic interest. The riders, mostly tall, burly men with unshaven faces, straddle their horses' saddles and carry with them sturdy silver helmets and swords, that in their glistening steel look almost too realistic. At a distance of approximately twenty yards, the two men are facing one another with intensity and they begin to lop at each other briefly before moving into a smooth gallop with lances cocked and raised intimidatingly. A flurry of adrenaline engulfs the crowd as the two horsemen race toward one another.

Although a reenactment of violent combat, what emerges is a spectacular, beautiful display of strength, tact, elegance, and showmanship exceptional in its grandeur and decidedly unrivaled in its crowd-pleasing success. Dramatic "oohs," and "aahs," from the crowd precede an initial miss between the jousters as the riders circle the field and resume their positions toward one another. The horses puff loudly and scrape their hoofs in the grass before accelerating quickly, surging forward with their riders in battle repose. The expressions on the men's faces, only partially visible through their masks, reveal an at least feigned intensity that hints at the medieval clashes that divided man against man and nation against nation. One of the jousters is struck and immediately falls to the ground. The riderless horse wanders away as the fallen knight writhes in dramatic agony and rolls briefly in the grass. The victorious opponent runs a victory lap as fair maidens rush to the assistance of the fallen rider. Vociferous cheers erupt from the crowd to reward the performance. Alan turns to look at the spot where he has been standing with Rupert. For a moment, he thinks he sees a fairie beyond the maple with the drooping branches. From within the mist which rises out of the river, a fleeting apparition floats mysteriously. By the time Alan alerts Rupert, the image has vanished. As the crowd begins to disperse, Alan shakes hands with Rupert Allport and thanks him once again for the enjoyable conversation. "Young man, here's one of my cards. Feel free to contact me with any sudden insights or simply for conversation. Good luck on your voyage." Alan takes the card which reads:

RUPERT ALLPORT
WRITER
RESEARCHER
PHILOSOPHER

He places it in his wallet and waves goodbye to the scholar. "What a serendipitous stop on my sojourn," Alan muses. He walks back to his car and turns momentarily to take in one last look at the castle. A thick fog blankets the grounds. Grayish stone in the walls could barely be made out. Alan takes one last deep breath before climbing into the car.

Tonight, Alan arbitrarily chooses a quaint bed and breakfast on a highway in the outskirts of Warwick. He takes his bags in with him as he checks in with the caretaker, a congenial woman in her sixties, who projects a decidedly maternal role over her guests. Alan is endeared to her quickly as she explains what time breakfast will be served and then affably offers him a cup of tea. He accepts a cup of hot tea before thanking her and then retiring for the evening.

It is a windy and rainy night that is both comforting and slightly unnerving—in the sense that Alan is feeling soothed in the isolation of the countryside but also strangely isolated in the realization that Ronia is far away. The windows rattle periodically and the wind howls chillingly. A certain peacefulness pervades his sleep and allows him to overcome his solitude. He has attained an ostensible comfort in traveling as a solitary soul in a country not his own. As the wind howls, an arousing shiver winds its way through Alan's spine. The auspicious accidental meeting with Mr. Allport has confirmed in Alan's mind that it is indeed a privilege to be a member of the human race. The intellectually uplifting conversation with Mr. Allport earlier in the day was an awesome representation of the mystically powerful union among all humans. A warmth permeates Alan's soul and this spirits him off into deep sleep.

He awakens at around eight in the morning to infinitesimal drops of sunlight on his cheek and, from the kitchen—the rich, aromatic waft of coffee and friendly clanging of dishes. He throws on a pair of jeans and a t-shirt, waltzes into the breakfast room and promptly takes a seat. Seated at the table is a family from Australia that is colorful to say the least. The father is a heavyset, introspective man who delicately and concentratingly sips a cup of hot tea. The woman is pleasant, red-haired and quite vocal. Their two children, polite and expressive youngsters, sit quietly eating their breakfasts.

"Good morning," Alan offers to the room, before forthrightly introducing himself to the Australians. "G'Day. Are you from the United States, mate?" the Aussie gentleman asks. "Yes," Alan responds. "Could you please pass the coffee?" he asks one of the kids. "And you are all from Australia, I presume?" "Yes, we are," the man answers. "My wife and I have taken a couple of months off from our jobs so that we may tour parts of Europe and then the United States." Alan notices with great curiosity that none of the Australians are drinking coffee. However, they all have cups of pure cream from which they daintily sip at their perfect leisure. As Alan carefully monitors the nominal amount of cream he pours in his own coffee, he wonders how the human body can handle a full cup of pure cream on a daily basis. Although pretty buxom, every member of the family appears quite vital and ebullient.

"Where in the U.S. do you all plan to visit?" Alan asks. The man elaborates: "We will go to Disneyland in Southern California and tour Hollywood, Universal Studios, and the rest of Los Angeles. From there we will drive up the west coast and into Utah, Arizona, and maybe Colorado. Then we will fly across the country to New York." The caretaker brings a traditional English breakfast to Alan. She remains quiet and withdrawn in a seeming attempt to allow the visitors a chance to mingle on their own. Her husband occupies himself by doing lawn work, traipsing back and forth through the kitchen door only periodically. "Those are some jobs that allow you two to take so much time off." "We typically get at least a month off each year but both of us have accumulated additional weeks."

"A whole month; that's amazing. In the U.S., we are likely to get two weeks off each year, if we're lucky." Alan continues, "I think you will enjoy Los Angeles. You'll have perfect weather, the beach, mountains and beautiful European flora. Santa Monica, Beverly Hills, and West

Hollywood are some of my favorite haunts." The pleasantly corpulent woman interjects: "I'm a little bit leery of traveling to L.A. You know; with earthquakes, shootings, and riots—not to mention fires—it seems to be a place filled with chaos." For a second, Alan bounces around in his head a nifty little jingle for probably a brand of cereal, or detergent, or something, called, "Chaos:"

Chaos, chaos, chaos is the spice of life
if you're in the mood for order and fortune
chaos will bring you strife
Security is a superstition
and nature an equal opportunity destroyer
so if you want safety and serenity don't
look to the church, state, or your employer

The bubbly, buxom beauty continues: "I'm not sure why someone would want to live in L.A." Alan responds matter-of-factly: "Well, I think behind the illusory, ominous veneer or shadow that media like CNN paint over L.A., there actually just may be a highly interesting, culturally stimulating, and aesthetically pleasing environment. From L.A., one has access to beautiful Santa Barbara, tranquil San Diego, and up north are the world renown, monumentally stunning Yosemite and Sequoia."

The woman becomes somewhat defensive and then retaliatory: "I just think that—although a nice place to visit—the United States has its problems. Just think of violence in American film. It's no wonder that young black children in L.A. are shooting one another. There are many movies that I will absolutely not let my children see," she adds protectively. "I suppose no place is perfect," Alan quips, sarcastically, as he nibbles on some ham and eggs. "There is no question that America glorifies violence and denigrates sexuality—the opposite of what they should be doing. However, one would be ill-advised to form a prominent opinion of a country on the highly biased, sensationalistic sort of medium that many world news networks are. For instance, do you own a kangaroo? Are you friends with Crocodile Dundee? Do you see my point?" The woman's husband, who had been assiduously forging through breakfast, glances up in a wrinkled but concentrated expression that speaks of part agitation and part amusement. The woman rolls her eyes and emits a muffled giggle, then quickly resumes sipping her cream.

When Alan finishes his meal, he politely thanks the host. After wishing the Australians an enjoyable sojourn, he returns promptly to his room. Alan flips open the map and spots Stratford at a close southeast turn from Warwick. Peering through the bedroom window, Alan beholds a spectacular cerulean sky with scattered clouds but plenty of sunshine. He decides to shower, get dressed and load up his bags to get ready to leave.

Upon exiting the room and paying the caretaker about thirteen pounds, the price of the room, he heads to the car to begin the excursion to Stratford. It is around ten when he drives into town. He is instantly captivated by the magically sunlit, serendipitously-placed city by the river with its tranquil Elizabethan and Victorian homes and shops and the anachronistic winding cobblestone paths and roads. History had thoughtfully stood still and presciently shunned the future. Alan reverently drives through the birthplace of the genius mind that created such eminent works as *King Lear, The Merchant of Venice, Othello, Hamlet,* and *Romeo and Juliet.*

Alan parks the car in front of a red post office that is skillfully decorated in an old town style that deftly conceals its modern usage. He begins to walk along a stone sidewalk that lines numerous small decorative storefronts offering sales on everything from impressionistic art to ice cream. He walks past New Place, a large house and garden that Shakespeare had moved his family into when he left London and the stage. It is colorful and warm but simple, belying, or at least not revealing, anything symbolic of Shakespeare's greatness. Alan briefly strolls along well-maintained grass that is dotted with crimson and lavender flowers as he beholds the soothing waters of the Avon River.

He ventures over to the home where Shakespeare was born: a one-story wooden gabled structure that appears to have been preserved and protected in its heritage. Within Trinity Church, which is surrounded with an antiquated, almost spooky cemetery, Alan wanders aimlessly until he stumbles upon the graves of Shakespeare and his wife, Anne Hathaway. The 16th century is captured beautifully in and around the church, a quaint sanctuary with an intricate altar that presents honorifically, probably the most poignant representation of the true essence of the time. Mysterious, ominous warnings in the form of poems or benedictions have been placed clearly on top of the graves of the wealthy, including Shakespeare's: warnings that clearly delineate interestingly stern, posthumous forms of punishment that will befall those foolish enough to disrupt the bones of the departed. Alan ponders the superstitious paranoias that were alive and well in this time period, even among the well-educated like Shakespeare. That corporeal existence was simply one aspect of an immortal soul which would rest peacefully only if the bones remained intact, was a conviction held strongly and evidenced by the solid, sturdy arrangement of multiple layers of stone. Alan could only make out some of the words of warning written in Old English upon Shakespeare's memorial, but if eloquence in the language had any tangible effect on the future of the soul, then Shakespeare certainly gained blessed immortality.

Alan leisurely strolls around Stratford watching the droves of tourists who shuffle throughout probably one of the most thoroughly trodden cities in all of England. The wind is brisk and Alan is accompanied in his walk by the constant music of birds chirping in the trees and along the wooden rooftops of the buildings. He meanders until he comes to a theater in renovation. Out in front is a banner advertising the future performance of "Richard II." Alan sits down on a bench in front of the entrance. The crowd has trickled in different directions, providing Alan an only occasionally disrupted solitude in which he contemplates the place and organizes his thoughts.

Out of his backpack he pulls a pen and paper. As he considers the physical environment and tries to imagine the effects it had on the developing mind of one of the world's greatest writers, he places the tip of the pen on paper and begins to allow his words to flow:

Dearest Ronia,

It is only days since we breathed the same air and felt with the same skin. As I am optimistic about my travels I am equally forlorn at your absence. These past several weeks have had a strange pull on the fabric of my emotions in a way that I sense I will never be the same. When I am with you, the world envelops me in a cocoon of peacefulness and warmth that scintillates every nerve in my body and elevates my soul to beyond the stars and into infinity. Your harmoniously precious voice and saintly gestures are movements that possess my inner being and subsume every conscious and subconscious frame of reference I have. Willingly, I succumb to this inundating, overwhelming capture of my spirit. It is both soothing and edifying and I am forever transubstantiated in its wake. Eons will pass and take with them mountains, valleys, oceans, and glaciers. Multitudes of generations have existed on the surface of this chaotic, hypnotic, spectacular orb. Each generation to come is equally one cog in the gargantuan machinery of infinity. The stars shine brilliantly and twinkle in unison with every heartbeat we feel. As the periodic eclipse temporarily quells the luminescence, so is the human life softly extinguished. In the palatial, immeasurable landscape of time, my years, months, and days are simply fractions of infinitesimal fragments. Within this tiny spectrum I have known you only a very short time. I guess what I'm trying to say you devilish, angelic beauty, is that I love you and I always will..

Yours Truly,
Alan

He quickly puts the pen down and begins to fold the letter up. He stuffs it into an envelope and rushes it over to the post office. He buys a stamp, licks it and carefully sticks it on the corner of the envelope before dropping the letter in the mailbox. Hungry for lunch and for any distraction from the fact that he has just poured his heart out to Ronia, he is simultaneously thankful that he has quickly mailed the letter; for had he not done it so quickly, he probably would not have done it at all.

After locating a seafood restaurant, he saunters in and orders fish and chips and an ice water. He reaches into his backpack and pulls out the second book on mysticism, the one he purchased in the London voodoo shop. He scans through the book until he arbitrarily stops on page 145. Sabbatai Donnolo is the name listed at the top of the page.

Alan begins to read as he periodically looks up to see passers-by stroll on the sidewalk: "Donnolo perceived himself as heir to knowledge, or gnosis, magically vouchsafed to certain initiates. In 930, he uncovered the *Sefer Yetsira* or 'Book of Creation,' which promulgated the classical Cabala. With the Cabala, the Sefer Yetsira communicates in a language that is both ontological and cosmological. Sefer Yetsira coalesces mythology with monotheism and brilliantly illustrates the four elements of earth, air, fire, and water." Alan closes the book and places it back in the backpack. He motions for the waiter to come over and then orders an espresso as he finishes his meal. As the caffeine playfully tampers with his neurons, he quickly pays the bill and eagerly reenters the world of Shakespeare simply by stepping out into the street. He strolls around town briefly before returning to his car. Alan starts the ignition and drives only about a hundred or so feet before stopping in front of a small bed and breakfast—that looks like a gingerbread house—just off the road next to a garden. He discovers there is a vacancy, so pays for the room and moves his luggage inside. Once inside, he gingerly lights up a joint, kicks off his shoes and slowly reclines on the bed.

Time has been slipping past him, with his awareness of this change only semi-conscious. The leaves have started to change color. Cool winds were replacing humid nights. Fall was approaching or had already arrived. It is as difficult for Alan to tell the exact date as it is for someone who is out of school or out of work. A psychological reality test would undoubtedly reveal a person grossly, but happily out-of-touch. He gazes at the ceiling with its textured, alternately raised and indented surface which is now—as a result of cannabis visions—rhythmically oscillating, almost breathing. Alan envisions the white paint dripping from the ceiling and spilling upon the floor. The style of his room is a bland, non-descript, almost functional convergence of conservative, conventional furniture and art in various patterns of fuchsia and mauve. An emerald green painted bronze Victorian lamp, in the shape of vines with flower petals, looms pleasantly and ominously on a table near the window.

Alan slips into a state of consciousness vaguely resembling meditation or day dreaming but nothingness or sheer reverie are not the main agenda. For as he lies there peacefully, semi-contemplatively focused on absolutely nothing in particular but one thing, he feels he has success-fully stumbled on something interesting. His aforementioned mental preoccupations of taking in the bizarre design of the room converge with a ponderance of the Eastern notions of what can be called: satori, moksha, or nirvana. Atman blends with Brahma; Conscious merges with the unconscious; Knower shakes hands, smiles, and gradually becomes the known. The antipodes of his consciousness are alit as a lighthouse flickers its solitary spot of brilliance beyond and within a deep ocean fog. The one thing is the precious, gratuitous pleasure seething in his skull—the spontaneous, pervasive sensation of his brain percolating—almost drenching with pleasure.

Thought has become for Alan a mere plaything, something to be toyed with and manipulated at alternately whimsical and serious moments. The art of simply feeling good and idly rejoicing in the immense pleasure of being alive had become long forgotten. As the neural cannabis canals are dilating and vibrating through Alan's physical self, mental expansion and acrobatic transcendence flip flop any semblance of perception of self into scintillating, vibratory fragments that shower across the entire atomic landscape of the room. Alan laughs at the concept of Alan laughing; for the expectation or bias that there ever was or ever would be simply an "Alan" in the infinite portals of time and space is truly comical. That he—whoever "he" was—had ever fooled himself into believing that such an entity as a personality or self actually existed was ludicrous. The mere accidental collaboration or collection of elements of neural strands and arrangements of energy particles that arbitrarily led to a man named Alan

Agrippa to be in England at that particular time, is a curiosity that Alan relishes for at least twenty minutes of actual time—whatever that is. At a distantly close point sometime in the early evening, Alan drifts off into sleep.

The next day, Alan arises and showers. He gets dressed quickly and saunters out to the dining room. A dapper dressed Parisian named Paul is diligently debating with the vociferous caretaker over some political topic which Alan can only make out has something to do with the English Channel Tunnel resuming passenger services on Wednesday. Alan peers through his groggy, early morning haze and serendipitously discovers the coffeepot on the edge of the breakfast table. "Good morning, sir," the Parisian offers. "Good morning, how are you?" Alan returns.

Alan looks around the room only after several sips of coffee have elevated his senses. At the table is an elderly white-bearded gentleman with a long, very gray queue and dressed in a lush white and black fur coat. He is sipping his tea assiduously while reading the paper. Seated next to him is an attractive nubile woman with dark amber hair and pale, translucent skin. Their intimate proximity suggests to Alan something different than a father and daughter relationship, despite the obvious fact that the man is at least two and a half times her age.

"How do you do?" Alan asks them. "Fine. Are you an American?" the man queries in a pronounced Texas drawl. "Yes Sir," Alan responds as he sips his rich coffee that tastes like some variation of Mocha; an Italian roast, Alan guesses. The young woman smiles demurely and then leans to kiss her man—an action that quickly reveals the paramour she is. "You know, that's John Cole Davis," the person seated next to Alan whispers in a slightly reverential tone. "The famous country western singer," she adds. Alan turns to see the informant of this newfound bit of trivia: a beautiful dark-skinned Indian woman with voluptuous hazelnut eyes, long wavy black hair, and well-defined cheekbones and nose. Her smile is ebullient and warm; her voice bespeaks a midwestern United States accent spoken both articulately and with pleasant, mellifluous cadence. "God, I can't believe this," Alan gasps. "I'm sitting here in rural England, half a world away from home, and I find myself surrounded by Americans. What brings you to England?" he asks the woman. "I'm a student back home and my friends and I are backpacking through Europe. I had to come see Shakespeare, right?" "It would truly have been a shame to have missed this stop," he replies. "Alicia, will you please pass the jelly?" the Frenchman pleads as he gazes in the direction of the

Eastern nymph. "Sure, which do you want, the orange marmalade or the grape?" "The grape." Alan notices a prolonged, endearing stare that Paul, the Frenchman, projects her way. She hands Paul the jelly. "My name is Alan Agrippa." Alan extends his hand and shakes hers lightly.

"Alicia, Alicia Arnaut. It's nice to meet you." "Nice to meet you," he replies.

"Alicia darling, who is your friend?" Paul implores. "Alan, this is Paul. Paul, this is Alan." Alicia smiles as the two men shake hands. The country-western singer and his youthful friend are eating their breakfast heartily as one of the caretaker's children runs up eagerly to receive an autograph. The relaxing singer graciously obliges and the boy's mother turns and smiles. "Alicia, I think Paul takes a special liking in you," Alan whispers forthrightly as Paul is distracted by something the country star has said. "Alan, Paul is gay. I met him the other day and we discussed some of the men we had seen whom we found to be absolutely beautiful." "Whoops." Alan blushes a healthy, ruddy complexion.

"So, Alan, what are you doing here in England?" Alicia asks. "Well, it's funny you should ask. Every time someone asks me that question I consider all possible responses because there are many that are equally sincere but not just one that in and of itself succinctly and effectively encapsulates exactly what I'm doing. I know that's long-winded but essentially I'm exploring the flora, fauna, geography, mindscape, and intrigue of Europe while developing ideas on philosophy and such that will hopefully go into a book someday. Will you pass the coffee, please?" "Wow, Mr. Agrippa. You sound like quite a busy man." "It's not as busy as it sounds. It's actually more of a capricious approach if you could say I'm using any approach at all."

"Alicia is a pretty name by the way. It has a musical, highly palatable sound to it." "Thank you. I'm part of the first generation in my family to be a natural born American. My parents experimented with derivations of the name 'Ali' and felt that an Americanized name sounded just as good. So where are you going from here?" "That's a good question. Probably Oxford, although that will be backtracking toward London, from whence I came." "It's been a pleasure to meet you, Alicia." "The pleasure is all mine, Alan." Alan says goodbye to everyone and then rises from the table to leave. He returns to his room, gathers his belongings, and loads up the car. Going back into his room, he pulls out his phone card from his wallet and dials Ronia's number. After three rings, the recorder picks up. Alan does not leave a message.

Grayish white shades of clouds float high above as Alan maneuvers the car out onto the winding highway. His destination is Oxford, which, in his mind, evokes primarily the prestige and aura of Oxford University, the heir apparent capital of cognoscenti in Europe. The billowing, voluptuous skyscape is only intermittently interrupted by ambitious, burnt orange rays of sunlight as supercharged Volvos and Audis race by. Alan ponders the landscape and its vicissitudes. The pristine land that had once bred beliefs in fairies and mysterious constructs like Stonehenge has now given rise to modern automotive technology and unrivaled institutes of higher learning. Again, the contrasts baffle and amuse him. Through a light screen of smoke up ahead on the left side of the road stands an eighteen-wheeler in a jackknife position. Alan approaches rapidly and notices the blinking red lights of a police car. To the left of the truck sits a demolished Volkswagen that lies on its side in the grass. Two limp bodies lay contorted in diverging proximity from the car. One of the back wheels on the car is still spinning. Alan slows to inspect the wreckage. A larger, dark blue car had apparently flipped over with the passengers thrown at some distance. He can see blood dripping from the neck of one of the victims who prostrates in agony upon the ground. The Volkswagen has two passengers still trapped in their seat belts in the front seats. The windshield is shattered. A tattered cigarette pack and soft drink can are crushed on the dashboard. To Alan, the passengers seem unconscious and perhaps even dead. An ambulance rushes to the scene but for the few moments before it arrives, there is an eerie, seemingly eternal silence and stillness that surrounds the scene. The lush, verdant, and temporarily foggy environs had begotten a horrible destruction of life and property. The cause of the accident is unclear to Alan but he is only consumed with the thankfulness that he had not been involved. As he drives on, he sees another ambulance approaching with sirens blaring. He hopes that lives will be saved.

He builds up speed as the thought of the crash lingers. Notions of the ephemeral, unpredictable nature of life and death weigh heavily on his soul. He begins to think of his grandparents back home, whose almost daily routine in their retirement years is attending the funerals of close friends and relatives. As the engine roars and hums, he devises a more conscious approach to driving, for he is falling into a deep contemplation of the teary-eyed, mournful countenance of his grandfather in reaction to news of another friend passing. Alan keeps his eyes on the road and wonders momentarily when and where he will be and what circumstances will surround his own death. Periodic signs start to indicate the distance to Oxford. Alan pulls over at a rest stop and buys a soft drink. He pulls out his notebook and pen and sits down at a table. A light, cool breeze caresses his cheek as he places the tip of the pen on the paper and begins to write:

"Within the billions of galaxies and trillions of stars hung majestically in the parapet of heaven are millions of planets with interesting, viable arrays of chemicals and climatic conditions predisposed toward life as we know it on this planet. Is the divine drama unfolding throughout eternity playing itself out in similar ways on other spheres and orbs? The vast constellations of celestial bodies covering and infusing the universe are multifaceted yet synchronous. Therefore, why does each brain on the planet simply occupy itself with a circumscribed, narrowed version of the world? Are the biological, survival skills required of each one of us so extensive that we must ignore the much more grand, magnificent realm around us? Are the dimensions of mind merely microcosms of the astronomical dimensions of space?"

Alan thinks of Aldous Huxley's concept of Mind-At-Large, the universal consciousness that ties all of us together. The strands of rivers, highways, and oceans connecting the various continents are mirrors or reflections of the neural strands connecting the geographical interior sections of the human brain. As various cultures and ethnicity clash over their differences and have difficulties understanding each other, so is the brain often at odds with itself. The conscious mind is always trying to understand the unconscious or subconscious. Neuroses and psychoses are entanglements and knots of anatomical space as earthquakes, black holes, and typhoons are tumults in the exogenous zones. Alan shoves the pen and paper back into the backpack. He goes to the restroom, then exits the store and gets back into his car. Thoughts of Ronia enter his head throughout the day.

CHAPTER 15

He glides into Oxford with plenty of time to tour the university. He parks near the front entrance: a prominent stone arch opening up into a deep corridor, which spills out into a sunny courtyard. In the front lawn stands a directory outlining the alphabetized listing of the various academic departments on campus. Alan walks around trying to locate which building houses philosophy, which one is home to physics, and the hallowed halls of psychology. Swarming in his mind are considerations of the scientific breakthroughs and revelations that emerged from this intellectual vanguard. Poets, philosophers, mathematicians, and physicists through the centuries had illuminated the classrooms and lecture halls. The conception and gestation of cognitive excellence had started here and then precipitated a proliferation throughout the rest of the world. Haunting, awe-inspiring chills spiral up and down Alan's spine. He moves from the west exit to a street that leads to the town's square. Charcoal, blackened wooden iron-lined doors bespeak the atrocities of the fifteenth and fourteenth centuries when burnings of priests and scientists—for their thoughts—became commonplace. Alan ponders the witch-hunts and The Inquisition, with body counts surpassing those of innumerable wars. Thoughtful, visionary, and probably highly eccentric individuals had been put to the stake and viciously slaughtered in public view. He stops at an antique store that has two beautiful stone gargoyles perched on a mantle high above the door. They are the traditional, pseudo-smirking, pseudo-frowning, hands-in-hands critters properly winged but not quite anxious to fly: simply perched, if you will, at the mysterious threshold of the Medieval era.

Alan walks in and browses through an intriguing collection of Elizabethan, Renaissance and early twentieth century art. Titillating, opulent tapestries that depict kings, queens, and their subjects in regal repose line the walls. A crystal chandelier with dangling glass droplets and beads of gold hangs delicately from the ceiling. A narrow, circuitous path is cut along satin upholstered chairs and mahogany tables. Bronze lamps from the nineteen twenties sit next to opium pipes from the mid-nineteenth century. Buddha and Shiva sculptures manufactured from ivory and plaster of Paris wear shining pearl droplets and necklaces from antiquated Parisian jewelry stores. A tinge of spicy incense roams the air. Alan notices two bookends—sculptures of Atlas—one in white and the other in black. He carries them to the storekeeper, haggles over the price by fifteen percent, and then makes the purchase. He arranges for them to be sent to Ronia and ensures that they are properly wrapped before thanking the merchant. Alan walks over to a watercolor reproduction of a painting by William Blake, which depicts angels in flight. He muses at the irony. In Blake, such beautiful visual artistry had been almost completely overlooked because of his dominant genius of poetry that had propelled him to the forefront. The genius and insanity of Blake seemed dichotomous but related shades within the human experience. A pristine, nubile state of childhood that merged with the strained, sometimes cataclysmic nature of hallucination, encapsulated the amalgamated mind of William Blake.

The store's ambience showcases the distinctive milieu of many different places in diverse parts of the world. The vigorous walking Alan has been doing as he tours seems to be elevating oxygen doses to his brain. His senses are heightened just in the nick of time to imprint the marvelous artifacts in the store. "Sir, may I help you with anything else?" the storekeeper asks. Her hair, pulled up beautifully in a bun, releases only a few delicate strands that fall whimsically upon her neck and shoulders. Her skin is cloudy alabaster and her eyes a shimmering, hypnotic green. Faintly distinguishable lines under her eyes reveal devoted years of admiring beautiful things.

Alan smiles and asks: "Do you possess any mementos of historical significance concerning the university and any of its lectures, or..." "Actually, we do have a few things which we keep under lock. We can show them, although they are of a different price range than most of our other objects, as I'm sure you can imagine." Alan presses on: "What exactly do you have?" "Well, in our collection, we have photographs of Albert Einstein, Niels Bohr, Thomas Mann, and Carl Jung. In the category of lectures, we have copies of manuscripts containing lectures given by notables such as: Edison, Darwin, Freud..." "What do you have by Freud?" Alan queries excitably. "I think we have one he did on the interpretation of dreams. It was done after his infamous trip to America." "Oh yeah," Alan responds. "I remember he was somewhat disillusioned by America at first, only growing to respect it as he spent more time there accepting honorary degrees and such. I also heard it took some time for his stomach to get used to American food."

"Follow me and I'll show you what we have." Alan watches the woman carefully as she leads him to a back room and opens a prominent black iron door. Engraved in gold antique letters upon the door is the name SATORI BANK. She pulls out a set of cumbersome keys from her pocket and locates a small silver key, with which she proceeds to open one of about fifteen large drawers in the small room. A fluorescent image of a diamond is portrayed on a black velvet canvas above the drawers. To the right is a glass-topped tray of ornately arranged and glimmeringly sharpened daggers in various sizes. Out of the drawer she pulls a large black binder tied together with gold colored string. Within two envelopes inside the binder, are off-white, partially weathered, almost coffee-stained copies of the manuscript of which she spoke. Large clear laminated covers protect them from harmful tactile or environmental effects.

Alan's pupils dilate as she adjusts the lighting in the room. His focus intensifies as he casts his vision upon the treasured text. Luckily, someone has successfully translated much of the German into English; but Alan cannot determine how much of the lecture Freud had given in German and how much in English. He scours the page and happens upon terms which have now become common parlance in psychology and in mainstream culture: subconscious, displacement, transference, hysteria.

Alan asks the woman her name. "Linda," she replies. "Linda Schaufhausen." "Linda, do you understand German?" "A little bit. My parents spoke it at home and I picked up a little bit." "Can you tell me? How much do we lose in English translations of German and French texts?" "Well, I suppose that's like asking what does one lose in multiple translations from language to language in texts like the Christian bible. I suppose one loses some of the original flavor and vitality but not necessarily enough to really shake one's faith." "The Gospel According to Freud," Alan muses. He thinks to himself that Germans and Austrians on the whole are probably quite proud of their founding father of psychology.

Lisa approaches her task of showing the papers with an almost reverence. As she folds up the materials, Alan thanks her for her personal attention. He gazes at her luminescent figure that is illuminated only partially by the solitary lamp in the room. From the foothills of the mountain of Freudian theory and ideation, Alan contemplates quantum mechanical theories. What would they have to say about the sexual tension, in this intimate room, with this alluring woman?

They slowly depart the room. Lisa closes the huge door and then turns the handle, a gold, circular design that is shaped like the captain's wheel of a ship. The monetary price of the Freudian papers is in the high five figures—a veritable bargain, Alan figures, but so clearly beyond his reach. It has been an immensely enriching experience; to directly view the papers in the wondrous context of Oxford, with his newfound German friend, is an unparalleled adventure that makes Alan feel privileged, almost blessed. Value, worth, and quality are, of course, relative terms. In Alan's free-floating but intensely perceiving travels, he has already begun to realize that the quality of experience is an intrinsic, indescribable, ephemeral—yet enduring reaction or impression—that goes far beyond the concepts of wealth or ownership, or success.

Lisa walks with Alan carefully through the store and shows him a photograph of Oscar Wilde at a celebration commemorating *The Importance of Being Earnest*. The brighter lights in the main show room bring out a vibrant auburn in Lisa's hair. She speaks exuberantly of the myriad ways in which spending her time selling objects of such sentimental substance is her soul's mission and that it has brought her great happiness. Alan listens to her respectfully and enjoys the release of his empathy, which her words have unfurled. While sharing in the happiness of which she speaks, he is simultaneously mildly vexed that he has not found a similar fulfillment in his life. She walks as if a celestial force carries her, with concern that no movement is made too sharply or abruptly. Her beautiful red flowing sarong matches her silken lips which bear a matching color of lipstick. "I want to thank you for showing me around. You are knowledgeable and your store is wonderful." "I enjoyed meeting you, Alan."

Alan steps out onto the sidewalk and traipses around the town square while trying to imagine himself there in the fourteenth century. Treacly, cool drops of rain begin to fall. Tourists rush to find shelter in stores, restaurants and churches surrounding the square. Alan slides into a charmingly landscaped bed and breakfast. Brilliant red roses symmetrically line the front flower bed astride the doorway as they swell happily to greet and bathe in the oncoming shower. With very little actual effort, Alan attempts to protect himself from the rain, which is only refreshing and delightfully innervating to his skin. With his hair and clothes tousled and damp, he slides through the corridor leading up to the front desk, whereupon arriving he promptly requests information about vacancies and prices. They have one vacancy and the price is a bit steep. Alan takes the room anyway. Before going to his room he meanders over to the bar, orders a Cabernet and waits for the rain to subside. Seated at the bar to Alan's left is an elderly couple sipping martinis and smiling at one another lovingly. To Alan's right sits a beautiful black woman whose well-defined cheekbones and thin, strong stature make her slightly ominous and strikingly alluring. Alan turns and introduces himself. "Hello, my name is Alan. What is your name?" "It's Carla. Nice to meet you." They shake hands. Her hair is closely cropped and highlighted with blonde streaks. Her eyes are two fantastically dilated pupils surrounded by hazelnut and irises that burn holes in Alan's mind.

"Staying in from the rain, I presume," she coyly offers. "Yeah," Alan responds as he cradles the wineglass so that it refracts multiple lights from the bar into an amusing prism. "I've got to move my car in a minute but for now I've got a great excuse to savor Australia's finest." The bartender had recommended an Australian Cabernet which Alan determined to be delectable. "Can I buy you one?" Alan beseeches Carla. "No thanks, I've got a vodka tonic coming. So let me guess. You're a college student over here between semesters." Alan detects a hybrid accent that he guesses is a cross between English and South African. "Not quite," he begins to answer. "I've already graduated but I am sort of a student; I guess a student of life, if you will." "Oh, a student of life. I suppose that's the best kind of student to be. What have you learned so far that you can share?" "Wow, that's a tough question, but a highly amusing one. I've learned that there are many different types of people, places, and ways of life that seem to keep this interesting planet in motion. I've learned that DNA has evolved a bizarre mixture of forces, desires, and impulses which drive humankind toward equally productive and destructive behaviors. I've learned that love is a phenomenally exciting, worthwhile goal that seems to make the whole fucked up thing seem worth it at times. I've also learned that somehow it seems as if our goal as self-reflective, conscious beings is to question and explore in detail the very fabric and underpinning of the universe in which we not only live but which is—in itself—ourselves. I've also learned that making friends is an enjoyable experience: But what do I know? I'm just a student, right? Hopefully, this isn't a Ph.D. discourse."

Carla laughs and conveys her acceptance of his summation with a toast: "You're a man who seems to be full of ideas. Have you studied the early philosophers such as Aristotle and Plato?" "Yeah, to some extent. Plato's archetypal forms or ideas and Socrates' devotion to reason ring synchronous chords with Aristotle's subsequent push into the tangible, concrete world of direct perception. Who are some of your favorite philosophers?" She sips her drink and then answers: "I like or should say have a personal fondness for the scientific revolutionists who boldly took on the religious zeitgeist. People like Copernicus—who seemed to be the first to suggest that the earth moved—were pioneers. Kepler propelled scientific philosophy forward with mathematics. Galileo, Descartes, and Bacon all pushed for the rigorous, critical methodology and empiricism which are the hallmarks of modern day science. You asked for philosophers and I give you scientists. Oh well!" "That's quite alright. They're certainly philosophers by my book. What I find pretty interesting is the early partnership between astrology and astronomy. Today, reasonable people scoff at the grocery newsstand reputation of astrological graphing. People do not seem to realize that Pythagorean, Babylonian, and Ptolemaic threads ran along astrological and astronomical lines commensurately. The two fields seemed mutually inclusive, almost inseparable at times." "You're right, Alan. Platonists discoursed on the significant effects certain planetary alignments had on peoples' behaviors. Aristotelian physics had its dip in the astrological ink as well."

As Alan orders another wine, a young handsome white male approaches the bar and kisses Carla on the cheek. She introduces the two men. "Alan, this is David. David, Alan." "Hey, it's nice to meet you." "Nice to meet you." They shake hands. David orders a Guinness and pulls up a barstool. "Carla, I've got the invitations printed up and they're ready to go. Did you mention to Sarah and Matt the time?" "Yes, I think so but you listed it on the end, right?"

"Yes." "So where are you from, David?" Alan queries. "I'm from Belgium. How about yourself? Let me guess—the United States." David's tone is pleasantly, surprisingly not condescending. "Yeah, I'm an American. What do you do here, David?" "I'm studying political science at the university. I'm in the graduate program." Carla pulls her chair closer. "Alan, David and I are going to be having a party tomorrow night. We'd love for you to join us. There are going to hopefully be thirty to forty people there. You're really welcome to join us." "Yeah, that sounds like fun. Where is it going to be?" David pulls out some paper and borrows a pen from the bartender. He sketches for Alan some rough directions. Carla adds, "People should be showing up around eight or eight thirty. We'll have plenty to drink and eat." "Sounds great," Alan replies. "I'll see you guys then. Thanks."

The rain has subsided. It has left copious amounts of water all along the ground within Oxford Square. Alan makes sure he still has his keys with him and then he rushes out to move his car. The freshly fallen rain has fortuitously cleansed his path of most tourists. A peaceful silence permeates the air as visitors have filtered into the restaurants and hotels and nestled up to their tables for warm English meals. On the way to the car, Alan stops off at a convenience store to buy a pack of cigars. Still wearing his backpack, he reaches in for some matches and stops to light up. One inhalation of the Cuban tobacco proves soothing and energizing. As he sits complacently at a park bench, he allows the tobacco to circulate in his mouth and through his nasal passage several times. He then reaches back into his backpack and grabs the original book on mysticism.

Picking up where he had left off, he begins to read: "A Swiss psychiatrist named Stanislav Grof conducted research using LSD with subjects under differing experimental conditions. The results were shocking. Not only were the 'cosmic consciousness' and 'Mystical union' motifs prevalent, but some of the subjects supposedly experienced 'plant identification' feelings, in which they sensed they were experiencing the psychic equivalent of what a plant feels. These were published results."

The sky overhead is doing strange things. A ruptured portion of a thick cumulous formation splits further into fragments of grayish white which float in separate directions. The sun reemerges only long enough to frame a syncopated, burnt-orange horizon. Alan locates his car and drives it back to the hotel. Upon entering his room he notices the usual quaint Victorian decor: big fluffy pillows in flowered pastel designs cover a luxurious queen-sized bed with a pine frame and posts. The spacious bathroom has a large whirlpool tub. Alan flicks the cigar butt out the window. Although realizing that cigars are easily biodegradable, he hesitates each time he throws one on the ground. Tossing his bags on the floor next to the bed, Alan then sits on the chair next to the phone. He locates his phone card and places a call to Ronia's. The phone rings a few times before Ronia answers. "Hello, this is Ronia." "Ronia, this is Alan. How are you doing?" "I'm doing okay. I can't believe it's you. How are you?" "I'm doing great. I'm in Oxford right now and I plan on traveling up into Scotland soon. How's school? How's everything going?" "Everything's fine sweetie, except that I miss you terribly. How has your trip been so far?" "It's been good. Did you get my letter?"

"No, I haven't yet. I'm glad you wrote me a letter, though. I'm sure I'll get it soon." "It's wonderful to hear your voice, Ronia. Although I've met a few people along the way, at times it can get kinda' lonely. I did meet two interesting people today. They actually invited me to a party for tomorrow night." "Wow, that's pretty cool." "Ronia, I saw Shakespeare's grave in Stratford. Can you imagine?"

"That's awesome." "I also met this highly intriguing man who pontificated on theories of fairies and forest creatures. Isn't that bizarre?" "Yeah! Have you done any writing, Alan?" "A little bit, here and there. I'll come up with ideas and jot them down in my notepad. How are the studies coming along?" "Great. I'm nearing the end on the important stuff and things are coming along pretty nicely."

"When can you come out? Have you given it much thought?" Alan pleads. "If I can arrange things as I hope, then perhaps in about a month I can break away."

"That's cool. We'll stay in touch closely so it will all work out. How are the aunt and uncle?" "They're fine. I'll tell them that you're doing well. Alan, do you know what I miss more than tripping with you?" "What?" "Feeling your strong body up against me and you kissing my cheek." "Hugs, and drugs, right?" "Right," she proclaims while chuckling. "Ronia, I guess I'll let you go. I just needed to hear your voice." "Alan, thanks for calling. It means the world. Take care of yourself and we'll talk soon." "Talk soon!" he answers and then hangs up the phone. His heart is full.

Alan awakens early and skips breakfast. He just grabs a cup of coffee as he heads to his car. Alan drives due south to a place called Henley-on-Thames: a beautiful, serene area where solace can be achieved simply by pulling up to the nearest wooden bridge and simply laying out on the grass and doing nothing. Alan discovers a shaded spot where a barely trodden hiking path leads to an embankment. This provides the audible joy of tuning in or allowing one's ears to tune in to the hypnotic torrent of raging river rapids.

He pulls out the second book on mysticism and arbitrarily chooses page two hundred, which covers an excerpt from a biography of Sophia: "The famous Gnostic text *Pistis Sophia* is a source for the story of the 'Virgin of the Light.' Sophia judges the soul's capacity, or lack thereof, for reincarnation. Sophia is often described as the 'wife of God.'" Alan scans a few more pages before landing on one referring to the Operative Mason's Lodge: "The journeyman traveled from place to place and presented himself to a lodge in which caretakers served almost as parents."

Alan reads on about the importance of a traveler succeeding at the dual purposes of discovering the world and discovering his very self. He sets the book down momentarily and feels a sharp tinge up and down his spine. He glances around at fallen leaves that lie scattered in diverse piles, providing ample play for squirrels and rabbits that scamper about like melodramatic characters in a great cosmic play. A towering birch looms with its foreboding branches that stretch in multifaceted directions, superimposing an incredibly kaleidoscopic web over the sun.

In front of Alan lies the twisting Thames with rushing waters that carry branches and leaves from other trees and whose vacillating depth and temperatures have spawned various fish life—which subsequently feed off the river bottoms. River bottoms had generated endless layers of microbiotic-organismic substance. The air is cool, very brisk and comes in alternating strong and weak waves. Alan shivers at times, but is calmed and collected, almost solemn as he warms himself by running his fingers through his hair. He contemplates deeply this poignant page on the Operative Mason's Lodge and its implications and elucidations on the mysterious two-fold ritualistic journey. The theme or the symbol of the journeyman—who must go outside of himself to learn about himself or go inside himself to learn about the outside—strikes a hauntingly resonant chord in Alan. He had set out from the very beginning on a mystical, albeit frivolous—in many ways—quest. The power of coincidence and the seeming causality among ostensibly disparate events are things Alan has now had some familiarity with.

However, at this moment he is truly taken aback at the sheer marvel of ending up on this page which so clearly describes what is happening to him. As a deer—a young white-tailed doe—dashes off into a thicket in the distance, Alan sits quietly with the book in his hand and his mind in a million places, but simultaneously in what seems to be a unified dimension. He deliberates for a moment but then reclines beside the tree trunk and reaches a level of contentment and an uncanny sense that his newfound discovery—that there are parallels or relationships among things—is an integral part of a greater whole of understanding that he will ultimately realize. He also figures that even if this doesn't happen, there is certainly enough to be said for the simplicity of listening to the delicate sound of bird chirps and the natural melody of a rapid flowing stream after a strong rain.

In this solitude and in this natural environment, Alan feels that he has successfully cast aside any allure of the glow of city lights and frantic stimulation of the city; he has in effect given his nervous system an opportunity to rejuvenate. Individuals choose different paths, he muses. Like a flame to a moth, for some the city offers an unbridled captivation of all attention-neurons and draws them into its energy and intensity. For others, the relative quietude and placid, pastoral country is the proper milieu for life-sustaining, life glorifying possibilities. For Alan, he isn't quite sure what is the ideal. What he does know is that some approximation of elements from both environments seems the most pleasing to him. Despite the overactivity of Alan's mind and the unlikely surroundings, he drifts off into sleep.

At least a couple of hours elapse that consist of alternate uninterrupted sleep and light slumber. As he lies there by the tree, he dreams of emerald cascades and Arabic palaces. He sees fairies and elves frolicking on lily pads in tiny whirlpools on a lake. Hovering above them is some unidentified flying object—a flying saucer of some sort, telekinetically transporting tablets with inscriptions or on closer inspection what appear to be owner's manuals for how to operate the human brain. Hurtling through the rest of the sky are golden boomerangs. Off in the distance are majestic snow-peaked mountains and an enormous lake, upon which float twenty ducks, a combination of brilliant-hued mallards and regal hens. Suddenly, the sensation of eminent drowning befalls Alan. He awakens spontaneously to the fresh dripping of cool, gooey sap from the side of the tree trunk. Alan touches the sap on his cheek and places his finger to his nose so that he can smell the fragrance of what he considers to be arborous seminal fluid. From the little bit Alan recollects of his dreams, the significance or meaning is a complete mystery.

He stands up abruptly and dusts himself off. He hikes for at least an hour along the trail, which winds through sights and sounds best described in a poem. He composes while walking along and stopping intermittently to write. With his pen and paper in hand and his mind in the clouds, he composes the following poem:

Autumn's incandescent, shimmering leaves exude a warmth and gleam foretelling and remembering ages away.

Kaleidoscopic images retract sunlit rays casting oranges, greens, and browns into retinal bliss.

Haunting shadows intermittently loom—a juxtaposition of immaculate light and dark mirroring the two great universal antonyms.

Audible perceptions decode into fragmentary "chirps" of a robin and "whispers" of October's wind.

A calming, reflecting cognitive concoction blending neural wavelengths with nature's patterns—a synthesis once again uniting man with his surroundings.

A chemical cooperation emerges compelling man to endure, and propel himself onward as DNA's plan mysteriously unveils itself before him and from within him.

Olfactory titillations are marvelously spawned from nature's aromatic offerings concealed furtively from all sight yet simultaneously omnipresent.

Hemlock revelations occur—anachronistic vestiges belying an earlier, glacial period or ruminations of a doomed philosopher's very last beverage transporting him eternally into the great unknown.

Crickets harmoniously prophesize the forthcoming dusk with secret songs bespeaking the language of the forest sung for millennia by an ever-recurring panoply of earth beings.

If all the world's a stage are other planetary productions being played out elsewhere in the universe or is the only galactic-commissioned theater production here on our strange Mother Earth?

It's gradually segueing to curtain call and nature's enigmatic and effervescent creatures are taking their night's last bow.

Solitude is comforting as the deep, thick chasm of night envelopes the soul as a seemingly membranous, spirit-filled cocoon silently caresses every living being.

The great cosmic abyss calls sporadically inviting and sometimes demanding one of its sons and daughters to return home.

Those who remain seem hell-bent or purgatory-fixed on sentient illusions or mere vibrations symphonically conducted by a force of nature unbeknownst to man.

Into the unfathomable; the nameless; the order and structure within apparent chaos lies the key to understanding, the philosopher's gold at the end of the mystical rainbow.

Beyond all sight and all sound; Beyond all touch and taste; lies the realm where colors can be tasted, where flavors can be seen, and where thoughts can be touched.

A map should not be mistaken for a territory and a pointing finger should not be mistaken for the moon; but when one gazes upon the works of nature he experiences not only himself but a representation of God's plan itself, and not a moment too soon.

CHAPTER 16

Alan places the pen and paperback into his bag. Putting into words the phenomenal effect the environment is having on his mental state has taken precedence. Direct awareness of the steps he is taking on the trail and the strategic movements of his legs has been bypassed. As he gradually begins to think less and less about how to describe the physical surroundings, his focus shifts to the rapid pace he has achieved in walking. Somehow his body has achieved a rhythm and quickness which enable him to hug the contours of the trail and place each step firmly, securely on the ground as he brushes past lush, fertile varieties of willows, pines, birches, and ferns.

His olfactory nerves are hooked tightly to the vibrant aromatic offerings from the plants and trees around him. A soft, northerly wind pleasantly tousles Alan's hair. Despite every effort to the contrary, he cannot completely stop thinking about Ronia. As he makes his way into a small clearing, Alan spots a scenic pond upon which there gingerly float five ducks—three mallards and two hens—that are alternately flapping their wings and ducking their heads under the surface, ostensibly in search of fish. Alan glances up at the sky in time to see a soaring hawk cut a majestic image in the cerulean backdrop.

He reaches into his backpack and removes a sandwich and bottled water he had packed. As he eats lunch, he retraces in his mind the odd series of events which led to his meeting Ronia and the almost unbelievably serious turn their relationship has taken. He thinks of the great freedom his bank account has been allowing him; to be sitting here contemplating the nature of a relationship he has been able to form only because he has had these very resources to travel. He realizes his fortunate state of affairs and wants to give thanks to a higher power for it. Vying equally strongly for his attention is the idea that essentially man spends most of his time on this planet struggling to survive and save for some indefinable and often ethereal future; as opposed to achieving a level of peacefulness and contemplation in which he can focus on life's pleasures and riches.

While Alan continues to eat his lunch heartily, the afternoon gently passes on. He begins to march back up the path to the car. As he drives back into town, he wonders what the party being hosted by Carla and David will be like. He also wonders how many people will show up and what kind of scene it will be.

Arriving back at the inn, Alan goes to his room and showers, then puts on a pair of jeans and a button-down long sleeve shirt. Adrenaline climbs steadily through his veins as he returns to the car in great anticipation of the party. As he exits the hotel, he notices that the lobby is pretty vacant and the bar holds only a couple of patrons, who appear relaxed. The entire city feels strangely solemn and peaceful.

Alan follows the directions closely and winds through scenic and precipitous inclines to a slightly wooded area that has several rows of houses, each house being separated from the other by about twenty yards of pleasantly arranged trees and plants. Extending from one of the homes is a long, winding driveway, at the end of which stands an amusing bird-house designed mailbox that is very colorful and is covered with bal-loons. Alan drives up slowly and confirms the address. The house is a white, two-story colonial with a large porch, swinging hammock, and slightly worn, but pleasantly arranged white and blue shutters.

Six large columns line the front of the home. A golden Labrador retriever, perched on an Oriental rug on the porch, lets out sporadic barks and howls that seem to beckon each guest. On the way to the home, Alan had not been cognizant of where in relation to downtown the house is situated. As he briefly turns around before entering the home, he casts his eyes on a placid and moving view of the city, with its perfectly placed twinkling lights and portentously arranged luminescent moon which hovers high above in the midst of grayish blue clouds. The dog growls in a sort of moaning, loving agreement with Alan's surmising of the view. Alan leans down and strokes the dog's head and then knocks formidably on the front door. He can hear several voices on the inside.

Carla answers the door. "Alan, I'm so glad you could make it." They hug casually. She is wearing a shapely red satin dress with fashionable black boots. Her hair is let down and she religiously nurses a glass of white wine. Alan finds her breathtaking. "Alan, what can I get you to drink?" "A beer would be great. Thanks." "Alan, this is Nathan. Nathan, Alan." The person to whom she introduces him is an affable, punk-look-ing Englishman who appears to be in his early twenties. His hair is bleached blond and carefully spiked. He is wearing a black leather bomber jacket with shining metal buttons and tattered blue jeans.

Nathan's countenance coalesces an expressive mixture of melancholy and intense amusement.

"So Nathan, how's the party coming along?" "Pretty cool, mate. As you can see, there are lots of ravishing felines roaming the halls and you'll find plenty to eat ánd drink, as well." Alan smirks and then glances around to confirm everything Nathan has just posited. Carla returns with a beer. "Alan, David is here somewhere and I'm sure that you will find many interesting people to talk with." "Alan, this is Katie, Katie, Alan," Nathan interjects. Katie is a tall brunette with rapturous hazelnut eyes and delicious ivory skin. Her frame, which is pleasantly thin but well endowed, sports tight black pants and a halter top that fits like second skin. She locks eye contact with Alan and immediately engages him in conversation as Carla politely excuses herself. "So, Alan, when the hydrogen fuel supply runs out in about five billion years, what do you think is going to happen to the earth as we know it?" "It's very nice to meet you, too," Alan responds jokingly, and then without missing a beat replies: "Unaware of what's going on around us, I suppose a rather large fiery explosion will either cause the sun to burn itself out and thus render the earth uninhabitable or it will simply fry the earth; i.e., make it a highly unpleasant place to live—for beings such as us at least." She continues: "But after about five hundred million years the sun's helium will run up. Things could get pretty nasty then, too." "You're right, but I suppose when the sun becomes—what is it, a white dwarf—like all those other stars the carbon, oxygen, and other chemicals rearranging themselves through the universe, then life will simply have to take on different proportions. No problem, right?" Alan continues as Nathan's curious look of amusement increases slightly:

"The billions and billions of stars throughout the universe do mirror the billions of neurons in the human brain; do they not?" Alan adds. "The synapse as the imploding of stars, right?" comes a mysterious voice from the stairwell. Alan looks up to see David rapidly descend the stairs in an amazing feat of acrobatics that matches his phenomenal auditory prowess. "David, how are you doing?" Alan asks while shaking his hand. "Great, how are you? I see you've procured ample company in your short time here. Hello Katie, sweetie." David kisses Katie on the cheek. She smiles demurely and then grabs David's arm, says she wants to talk to Alan later, and then leads her new dance partner over to the stereo.

Nathan leads Alan into the kitchen, through a long hallway, and into an entertainment/recreation room that has various couples in intimate corners and sporadic passers-through; everyone is either drinking, eating, or smoking in an obvious state of delight. Alan and Nathan walk over to a patio door that leads out to a poolside barbecue. Two large dogs— brown shepherds, it appears—are clambering on the other side of the doors. Alan grabs a plate of food.

"So, Nathan, are you in a band?" "As a matter of fact, I am. We're called the Bullock Testers; and that's 'testers' not 'tasters.' It's a play off 'Never Mind the Bullocks' and the term 'Battery tester.' I play the drums and I'm really fucking brilliant if I don't mind saying so myself. Do you like punk?" "The Clash is cool. Generation X is pretty groovy. I'm actually more an ambient and techno man myself. Industrial rolls my marbles, too."

Many people begin to fill the kitchen adjacent to the patio door. Alan looks on with amusement as several bottles of Cabernet and Chablis are popped open. All of a sudden, Carla appears. "Nathan, if you would excuse us, I'd like to show Alan around and introduce him to some of the folks." Carla takes Alan by the hand and leads him through the large kitchen. He notices mainly men and women in their twenties and thirties with preppy looking athletic types flanking svelte, cutting edge fashion models. Gaudy looking transvestites cavort with frumpish professorial types. "So, Carla, please tell me once again, whose house is this?" "Alan, do you see the tall, thin man with dark skin over there? He's wearing a tan coat." "Yes, I see him." "That's Jimmy Orlovsky. Now do you see the shorter guy with the funny looking hat on and the wire rim glasses? That's William Patterson. Now, I don't see Jason right now, but these three guys rent the home. They are good friends with David, whom I have gone to school with for some time. They like to throw wine parties where everyone can try various brands and styles of wine. How's your beer by the way?" "It's wonderful." "Here, let me get you another."

She steps over to the refrigerator and pulls one out for him. "Susan, will you please come over here? I'd like you to meet a friend of mine. This is Alan. Alan, what is your last name again?" "Agrippa." "Alan Agrippa, meet Susan Macpherson." "Hello, it's nice to meet you." "Nice to meet you, too." "Susan is working on her Ph.D. in psychology. She's been working on an interesting study about the effects of classical music on the brain. Susan, will you please tell Alan about it?"

Susan, of medium height, with tempting curly brown hair, has eyes of aqua blue and artistically sculpted cheekbones. She ingratiatingly replies to the question: "Well, we've been testing the endorphin levels in the brain and trying to determine the extent to which interesting forms of stimuli such as classical music can affect the levels of these chemicals.

Our premise is that various forms of exercise, diet, electrical stimulation, climate, drugs, and music orchestrate differing nuances of endorphins in the brain."

As this erudite woman articulates passionately about her subject, all Alan can think about is the ridiculous "Partnership For A Drug Free America" commercial back home that depicted an egg in a frying pan and the words: "This is your brain on drugs." Alan's twist would be based on the work of this lady and be something like: "This is your brain on Bach."

"I'm a little bit familiar with the actions of the neurotransmitter chemicals like serotonin and norepinephrine; that antidepressants block the re-uptake and allow a higher level of those chemicals to accumulate. The action of adrenaline surely has to be taken into consideration, doesn't it?" "It's actually another name for epinephrine—adrenaline that is," Susan demurely confirms. Carla enthusiastically interrupts: "Guys, in about twenty minutes a lot of us are meeting in the master bedroom for a little smoke and hopefully some equally sumptuous conversation. You guys are not only welcome but highly encouraged to attend or show up." Everyone thanks her as she quickly departs.

Alan walks over to one of the windows and gazes out at the radiant stars and ever-changing moon. A rather large wooden humidor with an interesting looking mandala depicted on top is sitting on the kitchen counter. Above it reads a note, "Help yourselves." Alan complies happily with the directive by picking up one of the cigars and lighting it before taking several puffs. He can tell right away that the medium-tinted tobacco is good quality Cuban.

He steps back over to the sliding glass door and saunters out to the patio. A cool, northerly wind blows softly over the backyard. Several people circle the pool and are casually mingling, drinking, and absorbing the pristine view of the city. The leaves in the surrounding trees bristle in unison with the intermittent winds. The comfortably cool temperature is gradually metamorphosing into what will probably be a chilly morning. A few people say hello to Alan as they return inside. Alan takes mental notes of the comparisons and contrasts between European and American fashions. Imported magazines had always molded Alan's perceptions of how people in Europe dress. What is interesting in reality—as exemplified by this sample of young Europeans at the party—is how popular American-made blue jeans and casual button down shirts are, whereas in America it was easy to imagine the likes of Armani, Oscar De La Renta, and Versace to be popular.

Twenty minutes have easily elapsed before Alan decides to go back inside and find the master bedroom. He stops off at the kitchen and pours himself a glass of Chardonnay before wandering through the house. He assumes the master bedroom is upstairs so he climbs the steps, which are lined with several prints depicting everything from a half naked American model to impressionistic landscapes by Monet. At the top of the stairs, Alan passes by an attractive couple that is alternately kissing and smoking cigarettes. "Maximus Oral Stimulation," Alan muses to himself. He peeks into various rooms, locating small bedrooms, closets, and restrooms before finding a closed door that conceals rambunctious voices on the inside. He does not knock despite, or because of the fact that he might walk in on perhaps a couple making love.

As he walks in he discovers an enormous king-sized water bed with posters all over the walls depicting: Jimi Hendrix, Led Zeppelin, various English punk bands, Pamela Anderson Lee, a photo of the Scottish Highlands and sundry memorabilia commemorating primarily soccer, or in England what they call "football." Manchester's team is featured prominently as well as some American organizations.

"Alan, come sit down. We've got a game of cards going and pretty soon John is going to get the Ouija board out," Carla announces in an affable way. Alan notices a purple and pink bong in the center of a table. The base of the bong—by the mouthpiece—is shaped in the form of a joker's head. He finds this amusing. "Mate, will you have a go of it?" are the polite words offered from a tousled, grunge-looking twenty-something with mousy brown hair and a Nirvana t-shirt. "Sure, why not?" Alan replies, as he marvels that the kid is so perceptive. A guy who wears a large straw hat over a turban takes a deep inhalation before passing the bong to Alan. "I just refilled it mate. It's all fresh," are his polite words as he hands it to Alan. Alan adjusts the position of the bong and then carefully places his lips around the mouthpiece as he lights the pot with the lighter. Jovial gurgling of water is the only ostensible sound as Alan sucks the rich smoke into his mouth and feels its traveling waves spiral their way down his throat. After holding the smoke in for about forty seconds, he exhales slowly through his nose as he passes the bong to a voluptuous redhead sitting next to him. "Hi, my name is Jennifer. How's the hemp?" Alan chuckles at her amusing use of alliteration. If only the anti-drug crusades could be so witty. "It's quite nice. Please have a go of it."

Alan hands her the lighter. The chap in the Nirvana shirt scampers up to Alan. "Are you an American?" "Yes, I am. Have you been to America?" Alan asks. "No, I'm dying to go. I'd like to go to some concerts in the states. I'd like to see how the American crowds relate." Alan is never the same stickler for words that he is in a so-called normal state of mind. Otherwise, he would have questioned the use of the word, "relate." "The concerts in America are pretty cool," replies Alan. He elaborates: "I've seen some pretty cool shows. A few notables are: Cocteau Twins at Universal Amphitheater; The The at the same venue. Bryan Ferry at the Pantages Theater; Dead Can Dance at the Wilshire Ebell; Peter Murphy at the Wiltern; and of course, David Bowie in Raleigh, North Carolina and San Francisco. Do you notice a pattern here my friend?" "I sure do," replied the hipster. "They're all British, you bloke." "You're right. What can I say? I have an affinity for European bands. I don't know why. To turn this around buddy, tell me the American bands you've seen in Europe."

"Alright, let's see. R.E.M., The Pixies—rest in peace, NIN, Nirvana, Pearl Jam." Just at this moment, Carla rushes in. "Hey dudes, what's up? Hi Jenny, can I have a puff?" she asks before kissing her on the cheek. Carla takes a light puff. "Alan, I see you've met Timmy. Timmy's an incredible artist. He's done some beautiful renditions of architecture in France and Switzerland." Timmy blushes as Carla punctuates her explanation with the cough of a virgin smoker's first bong hit. "Carla, honey take it easy," exclaims Timmy.

"Leave your baby pink lungs alone as we rogue smokers smoke away." "Young dear Timmy, believe me; my lungs are not baby pink and I certainly do not need moral preaching from such a 'rogue' as yourself." They all laugh. Alan notices that Jennifer is very quiet. Timmy tries to pry her out of her shell. "What's the matter Jenny, cat got your tongue?" "Oh Timmy," Carla exhorts. "What's the matter? I was only trying to see…" "Jenny's cat Oscar died yesterday." "Jenny, I'm sorry. Will you help me get my foot out of my mouth?" Timmy puts his arm around her and gives her a hug. Jennifer speaks up: "That's okay Timmy, I'm going to be alright. You didn't know."

"Cats are very wonderful. I know how you must feel," Alan offers. Alan is taken aback by the way Jennifer looks. Naturally reddish brown hair frames a slightly freckled light skinned face with emerald verdant eyes and majestically designed brows. A healthy, fleshy frame is covered delicately with a cashmere pullover sweater and snuggly fitting jeans. An indefinable, almost ethereal glow seems to exude from her and seems to permeate those around her. Shallow, tepid souls could be replenished and edified in her presence. Alan is sure of this.

The four pass around the bong three more times before some guys named John and Kevin enter the room wistfully with a Ouija board in hand. The card players begin to wrap things up and collect their respective earnings. A space is cleared in the middle of the room. Somebody sets the Ouija board down and most in the room sit down around it. The current pot smokers' spatial orientation is perhaps not the most amenable to finding appropriate places to sit, but they do their best. It seems that John is the elevated spokesperson for the imminent spiritualism.

"Okay, everybody, we are gathered here today to explore the psychotic; I mean the psychic realm," John stutters in a decidedly drunken English fashion. A few chuckles can be heard around the room. "Will somebody please dim the lights?" Two young women dash to various corners of the room to light some rainbow colored candles. Alan's head is spinning at this point. His body feels warm all over and his visual field is bordering on topsy-turvy as he's thoroughly enjoying almost every step of the way. The only problem he is having is that he feels he is already communing with the spirit realm. "What in the hell will the seance bring?" he wonders.

"Okay, we must take a ritualistic puff of the magic leaf before we proceed," John mutters again, eliciting jubilant laughter. A requisite "passing of the pipe" promptly follows. Each person except for two in the corner of the room takes a toke at the bong. The two in the corner are not participating. They are two dweebish-looking cyber types preoccupied with an intense and highly sober game of chess.

There is a knock at the door. "Who's there?" shouts John. "Make thy intentions known," he blurts, in a quasi-medieval tone. "It is I, David. May I enter?" David opens the door and peeks his head into the room. "What is the special password my friend? Speak now or forever hold thy peace." Alan wonders what odd combination of American legal movies and medieval folklore went into John's hilarious dialect. "Um, Musicolous. That is the word. Musicolous," David quizzically announces. "Musica what? What the fuck does that mean?" inquires John in utter disbelief, if not horror. David obliges: "Musicolous: 'Growing on or around mosses as in certain lichens grown within swamps.' Is anyone in this room familiar with the cryptogamic arts?" "David, you may enter on your creativity alone although the magic word was 'blow job.' You may enter immediately but please shut the fuck up. We need no scientific terminology here. You have entered the spiritualistic realm." The measurable effect on John after a few puffs on the bong plus innumerable sips of beer is rendered evident by the eight to ten seconds it requires him to pronounce the word "spiritualistic." Of course Alan, or anyone else in the room successfully determining eight to ten seconds is almost ludicrous.

Time has bounced up and down, gone from side to side, out through the windows and in and out of every body orifice in the room; before pitter-pattering in Alan's skull and flip-flopping its multidimensional fluid, static, ecliptic, parallelogrammatic essence over to the spot on the wall somewhere between Pamela Lee and The World Cup.

"Okay, everybody gather around. We have work to do. Who goes first? What spiritual force, entity, or soul must we make contact with?" John proclaims and queries. "I'd like to go first," comments a buxom and bespectacled older man who has on a badly askew hairpiece and is wearing a conservative argyle sweater-vest over a striped, button-down shirt. "Alright, Emanuel."

John sits upright and adjusts his hands over that mysterious little wooden object that is used as the pointer for the Ouija board. "Now, Emanuel, before I attempt to conjure the apparition of your choice, I would like to implore those materialized beings currently gathered to join in a unified focus of consciousness. Let us grapple with our demons, dragons, and neuroses to ensure that we are at a clear, transparent zone, most amenable to the desirable spirits. "Very well spoken, for an accomplished inebriant like yourself," quips David. "Shut up, bloke. I'm the leader here." "I thought all egos had to be set aside," Carla chimes in. "I wear my ego on my sleeve and any aim is true, my lovely."

Uproarious distractions aside, Alan is genuinely amused by John and feels if anyone can conjure spirits it will be the English comedian of the group, a title he feels John is earning well. "John, you have our utmost attention, please continue," Alan posits. "Grrrrghhhh," John clears his throat before continuing. "Emanuel, you have been chosen to select the object of our spiritual strivings. Please reveal the name we shall seek." "I would like to suggest that we pursue divine communion with the eminent English writer Aldous Huxley." "Wait," interrupts Jennifer. I'm afraid that has already been done pseudo-successfully. It's well-documented in that special book by Aldous's wife Laura. What was it called? Help me Carla." "I think *This Timeless Moment,* a very beautiful book by the way," Carla contributes. "Never mind, we shall proceed as Emanuel sees fit. Aldous Huxley it shall be!" John interdicts. "First, I would like to know the nature of the spiritual connection as outlined in the 'timeless moment' book," he adds. Jennifer speaks up: "I think they were able to get some sort of instructions toward a page number in a book on the shelf

which ends up having significant text of some sort within it. The participants seemed convinced at least." "Alright," John continues, steadily
controlling his hands to optimize their ability to receive instructions from
the other realm.

"Let's go!" "Everyone close their eyes. Tonight we are trying to reach
you, you scholar, philosopher, scientist, poet, psychologist, and brilliant
raconteur who gave us such wonderful gems like: *Point Counterpoint,
The Perennial Philosophy, The Doors of Perception, Island;* but probably most of all—*Brave New World.* We entrust you and beseech you to
make yourself known in some familiar fashion to us."

A long pause ensues. Intermittent burps punctuate long, drawn out
deliberations over the true genius of Mr. Huxley. Alan marvels at the
bizarre interplay within the even stranger context of a Ouija seance—the
sincere sense of respect and admiration for Huxley and an arguably
frivolous, undeniably intoxicated effort at resuscitating his spirit. Alan is
fairly certain that Aldous would not have disapproved.

"I ask again, in the name of our dear friend Emanuel's request, that if
you so desire to allow us in this—the latter part of the twentieth century—to feel your presence, then so be it." A momentary pause elapses.
"Excuse me, John," Timmy interjects. "Perhaps it would be more effective to ask more pointed questions. I don't know this Huxley dude well
enough myself but maybe someone does." "Hey John," Alan implores.
"What about asking if the events of the past several years have played
out as he expected when he wrote *Brave New World*?"

"Alright, Mr. Huxley. As we sit here tonight with candles flickering
and our minds focused on your extraordinary legend, we ask: Have the
events played themselves out as you foretold in *Brave New World*?" As
everyone watches the board carefully, the pointer—with John's hand
touching it—appears to move in the direction of the letter "w." "You're
moving it with your hand, you bloke," shouts Timmy. "No, I'm not.
Quiet down," yells John. "Watch carefully." The pointer stops on the
letter "w" and then slides onto the letter "a", then quickly to "i" and "t",
apparently spelling the word "wait." At this point, Alan feels that he has
definitely seen the word "wait" spelled out, albeit through the haze of
awareness induced by pot. Differentiating between so-called objective
reality and subjective, drug-enhanced perception is quite a juggling act at
this stage in the game.

The pointer continues with John's hands moving with it. The following letters are: "a", "n", and "d", which spell "and". Emanuel looks on
anxiously. Jennifer and Carla appear somewhat skeptical but interested.

Alan and Timmy look on intently but are spending equal time in intimate oral contact with the bong. John continues with the reading while everyone watches, most trying to figure out if he is volitionally moving it or if it is moving itself. "I am feeling the power. It is happening," exclaims John. The pointer moves and lands on the letter "s" and then it locates and hits the letter "e" twice. "Wait and see! Wait and see! He's telling us to wait and see. Oh myyyy!"

In an amazing acrobatic feat of proportions as grand as a porpoise in heat somersaulting in orgiastic bliss, John thrusts his torso forward, ricochets back forcefully and lands with a loud thump on his back before spasming into a fit of seemingly uncontrollable but harmless flailing on the floor. Countenances around the room alternate between expressions of concern and amusement. "John, control yourself," exclaims Jennifer. "I'm being moved by the spirit," John blurts in a fashion not dissimilar to a down-home southern U.S. TV evangelist.

CHAPTER 17

Alan needs a break. A little weirded out by the seance and dizzy from the pot, Alan stands up and excuses himself. He first goes to the restroom and then heads downstairs to replenish his glass. Before leaving, he asks Carla if she wants anything. She asks for a vodka orange juice. As Alan crosses the threshold of the kitchen, he notices a young couple passionately embraced in a heated, throbbing kiss. The girl looks up as Alan is pouring the drinks. "How's the supernatural going upstairs?" she stops to ask. "Quite bizarre, thanks. I'm wondering when we're going to be able to levitate the entire home. Do you two have any opposition if this should happen?" "As long as we're together—on the couch or bed or something—then no. It'll be fun!" "Wow, I'll let you guys know when it's about to happen," Alan quips. "Please don't!" she answers as he proceeds to spill orange juice on his fingers and then watches some dribble down the side of the glass.

The dogs growl as Alan passes by the patio doors. He wonders if they are picking up with their high sensitive auditory channels any psychic activity upstairs. Alan smiles at some people in the living room as he returns to the stairwell. As he looks up at the eclectic collection of art lining the staircase walls and leading to the hallway upstairs, a surreal palpitation seems to overtake all objects, including the walls themselves. The walls are not necessarily breathing but an organic sense of movement and change is taking place in an otherwise ostensibly static structure. Alan carefully climbs the stairs, trying very meticulously to keep the drinks still.

When he reaches the top of the stairs, he stops at the master bedroom door and leans into it with his shoulder. Luckily, the door is partially opened. It swings open and Alan slips in. A few lights are on and people are milling about. Timmy sits in one corner of the room and passionately debates John over some theory that has something to do with existentialism. Carla and Jennifer are cruising the World Wide Web on the PC by the window. The two chess players are permanently engrossed. Their game has progressed nominally but their attention is decidedly rapt.

Emanuel stands facing the fluorescent Jimi Hendrix poster that he attempts to be deciphering or at least visually absorbing. Alan is sure Emanuel is on some psychedelic. Music flows from hidden speakers located perhaps somewhere in or around the bed; the tunes are an interesting amalgamation of what sounds to Alan like the Indian sitar and tala drums. Hypnotic and alluring, the music rises to majestic crescendos and swings to mysteriously beautiful polyphonic harmony.

Alan carries Carla's drink to her and sets it next to the computer. "What's going on, dude?" she coyly asks. "I'm doin' fine. How are you?" "Great!" "What are you guys exploring here on the net?" he asks. Jennifer speaks up: "We're exploring a site dealing with what else? the paranormal and occult. It seems there's this group of kids in the states who fancy themselves vampires. Some take it a bit too far and their neighbors believe that they have actually killed someone. Quite bizarre stuff."

"Yeah, I've heard about that but in all fairness that kind of bullshit goes on everywhere," replies Alan. "Thanks for the drink, Alan." "You're very welcome, Carla." Alan petitions John: "Hey John, are we heading back into the astral plane anytime soon?"

"Yes, thank you Alan. Ladies and gentlemen, I'm aware that many of you in conjunction with myself are currently engaging in the communion of spirits of an amusing, but inebriant nature. Let me, however, redirect you to the task at hand, which is, of course: What can the antiquated mysterious Ouija board tell us about the other side?"

At this time, someone dims the lights and participants begin to get excited. Timmy comes up to the board and plops himself down into an instant lotus position. Emanuel tears himself away from Jimi Hendrix. Carla and Jennifer shut the computer down and join the group. While the chess enthusiasts continue their game virtually undisturbed by the announcement, bong hits across the room flow freely along as the antipodes of consciousness within all the psychic voyagers remain mostly happily and occasionally paranoiacally lit. The one common theme—other than the pot—that seems to unite everyone, is the sincere belief in exploring the psychic realm through the medium of the Ouija board. If not for the sincere belief that contact will definitely occur, it is for the sheer pleasure of participating in an activity so uncommon in modern times and at least partly defiant of so-called normal religious and meditative practice.

Once again, John brings the meeting to order: "Okay, will somebody please light the sacred candles?" Jennifer readily complies. "Now, I consider our last attempt to have been an undisputed success." There are some snickers and most of the individuals in the room are simply trying to balance out John's uncanny flair for drama with the expectations they have for reaching other realms via the Ouija board. "I would like to give another individual the opportunity to determine our next mystical direction. Timmy, do you have any suggestions?" "Sure, what about Lady Godiva?"

"Alright, Lady Godiva it is. Timmy, is there some historical background you can offer us for this Lady Godiva? The only image I can conjure is a beautiful blonde naked woman with a laurel in her hair, riding around a misty field on horseback. This image alone is satisfying, mind you, but for the purposes of our task we will need more." Timmy looks perplexed but a crackly voice emerges from the dark corner of chess aficionados to reply: "John, legend has it that she was the wife of the Lord of Coventry. Somebody please pass the bong. Thanks. She was a highly pious woman who induced her husband to found a Benedictine monastery. According to the story... Hold just a minute please."

Someone passes the bong over to the "chesster" and he immediately sucks the mouthpiece, inhales deeply, and a charming interlude to the story—a gurgling sound of water from the bong as it's being sucked—ensues.

The speaker continues: "According to legend, the husband agrees to lift a burdensome tax if his wife will lift her shirt, so to speak." Laughter and smirks fill the room. "Back to you, John." "Okay, thanks Kevin." John repositions his hands in accordance with the mandates of the Ouija board. Everyone is silenced.

"Glorious beneficent spirit realm, we have united once again to respectfully implore you to look with favor upon us modest, drunk souls and vouchsafe to us yet another historical persona. Please take us back to the time period of... Kevin, what was the exact time period?" "I think around 1050 or 1060." "Thank you. The time period we want is the very early millennium and the personality we seek is the icon of women's liberation, Lady Godiva."

All of the participants remain silent. John carries on: "Lady Godiva, if you are listening, could you please make yourself known in some demonstrable fashion?" At this moment, the door blasts open with the force of a hurricane to the infinite shriek of everyone in the room. "Laaaaady Godiiiiiva," slurs a young, sultry brunette who bursts through the doorway with a bottle of champagne in her hand and two companions by her side—one male and the other female. "I'll show you Laaady

Godiiva." Looks of horror and great expectation fill the room as her companions assist her in pulling her sweater down to expose her breasts to the entire room. For about thirty seconds, she parades through the room in an almost light, airy, angelic—but undeniably drunk—fashion to the complete bemusement of Carla and Jennifer and to the enthusiastic appreciation of the men. Her two cohorts pick up the bottle of champagne, apprehend their nearly naked friend and fly from the room. An explosion of laughter erupts to break the aghast emotional cloud that hovered only briefly. "Can you believe the wonders of the Ouija board? My case is unequivocally proven!" exclaims John.

Alan leans toward Carla and whispers in her ear: "Interesting party, huh?" "Uhhh, I don't know what to say. Sometimes truth is stranger than fiction." "Dammit, I never have my camera when I need it," exclaims Timmy. Emanuel sits with a slightly more expressive glaze, albeit a still aloof, sedate look. "Hey Alan, how are you doing, man? Are you feeling okay, mate? How many fingers am I holding up?" Alan knows that it is Timmy speaking to him. Answering the relatively simple question proves more difficult than Alan could ever have imagined.

The alcohol seems to fulfill its medical promise of overwhelming his digestive, absorptive capacities, throwing him immediately into a paroxysm, accompanied by profoundly dizzying psychotropic effects plus slight nausea. Without answering Timmy's question, Alan steadies himself and rises slowly. "The bathroom's through the hall, mate," Timmy calls out as Alan sprints in the appropriate direction. Upon reaching the toilet, Alan promptly drops his head within the rim, throws his arms around the bowl, and succumbs violently to the involuntary regurgitative spasms that effectively sap his body of every solid and liquid available. His vision is blurred and picks up bizarrely scattered images of light refracting through items such as the shower curtain.

With each illusory moment of respite between bouts of vomit, come concomitant mouth-waterings, heavings, and overall writhings, which drive the point home that he is plain and simple—a physiological system in revolt. "How pretentious," he wonders as his head throbs and that peculiar acid, digestive sour taste lingers in his mouth: "that I actually thought the 'I' was somehow above the animalistic proclivities toward obnoxious conditions such as disease or illness. Here I am at the disposal of the highly overrated drug of alcohol merrily wreaking havoc all over my body." He hears the door open. In his now blurred periphery, he barely constructs an image of a delightfully curvaceous, radiant figure. It is Carla.

"Alan, honey, are you okay? Is there anything I can do for you?" "No thank you. Really, please just leave. I don't want anyone to see me like this. I'll talk to you when I'm feeling better." He motions for her to leave and she complies, stating as she leaves: "Let me know if I can help."

Once again, he stumbles into the compulsory karmic vomitone tune which grates on him like a broken record. His drunkenness exacerbates his sense of alienation and awkwardness at being at a party with mainly strangers. The vicious fein, alcohol, has disoriented him and spiraled his mental framework into strange dimensions; his sense of self flies out through the window of the home and into the solar system to float around in limbo until his physical system decides it is time to once again accept a personality back into it. Alcohol is the devil. For this, at the moment, Alan is sure. Whatever Faustian agreement or construct Alan has signed has no foreseeable royalties and is sure to exact an egregious, excruciating toll. Alan must be flushing the toilet thousands of times, or so it seems. As he wipes his face with toilet paper, he stands to gaze at his reflection in the mirror. The glass, with his reflection in it, appears to undulate.

Alan starts to feel a little better. He washes his face with warm water and rinses his mouth several times. After drying himself off with a towel, he slides into the hallway. It appears that at least a few of the other party-goers are in states as debilitated as his, if not worse, leaving them wandering around the hallway; some are being lifted up by their lovers while others are left alone up against the walls and doing battle with their inner spirits. Jennifer comes up and pats Alan on· the butt. He walks past her and steps over to the master bedroom. He peers in and finds Timmy surfing the net for pornography.

"Hey mate. How are you doing?" "I'm feeling much better. Thanks, Timmy. Where are all the others?" "They're downstairs cavorting at the rest of the party. Maybe some food would make you feel better." "Dunno. I'm just gonna drink water for a while. Thanks."

Alan shuts the door. He turns and heads back for the stairwell, looks at his watch, and discovers it is about 2:00 a.m. Not really wanting to leave at this point and feeling somewhat better after his bathroom stint, Alan descends the stairs slowly and moves in the direction of the most noise, which happens to be coming from outside. He pulls back the sliding glass door and steps out onto the patio.

He is immediately greeted by John, Carla, Jennifer, David, and Emanuel. In the company of a few others, the group had been hanging out by the pool sipping drinks, munching on delectables, and smoking cigarettes. "Come here my young American who flew so high and crashed so low. Come sit down next to us and roast some more neurons on our nice little intellectual fire. The kindling has been a combination of philosophy, metaphysics, and psychology," John implores in a friendly, almost fatherly tone.

John continues: "Alan, my friend, the purification process seems to have been completed. You've successfully rid yourself of all of those noxious chemicals and liquids and stresses that I'm sure you brought with you from the states. You are now fully adapted and initiated into the European way." "Oh John, please," Carla amicably admonishes. "Alan, dear, how are you feeling?" she queries. "Much better. Thanks. I've been drinking a lot of water to clear out my system. How's everyone doing out here?" "Pretty well. Pull up a seat." Alan grabs a lawn chair and scoots up next to Carla and David. "Hey Carla, how did the psychic journey play itself out upstairs?" "Uh, basically after the stark naked debut of our dear friend Kim perfectly on the Lady Godiva cue, the guys were, how can we say, a bit too distracted to go on. I think their minds went on to more carnal things than the astral plane." "God, I'm sorry I missed that whole scene," quips David. He continues: "But how do we know, Carla, that the astral plane is just not a whole other dimension of carnal delights?" "Ha, ha, you wish," Carla replies, rather sardonically.

The moon shines at a quarter glow, casting odd reflections of the sun's light all over the backyard and the city down below. Alan watches the surface of the pool. Periodic ripples windswept on the surface refract this light into interesting mosaic patterns on the concrete floor of the pool. "Hey, watch this," John shouts.

He picks up an empty beer bottle and throws it in the direction of a large oak—toward the back of the yard. After a lightly sonorous crash into some bushes, a return shout can be heard: "Hey, cut it out, you bloke!" A slightly hairy naked back and buttocks of a man can be seen and then the long, flowing blonde locks of a woman underneath him. Just as quickly as they can be seen, they disappear back into the bushes. John bursts into an elongated, guttural uproar of laughter that is at once disturbing and pleasing to hear. Emanuel sits off to the side, next to the shallow end steps in the pool, quietly contemplating the previous series of events while attempting at the same time to enjoy the present conversation around him.

For the most part, people leave Emanuel alone to do what he wants. Only occasionally does he enter into conversation and that seems fine with those around him. In fact, some find him a bit peculiar, and therefore deliberately steer clear of him. Jennifer goes inside to make a pot of coffee. Carla shuffles up with her chair up close to Alan. "Carla, I apologize for my actions earlier. I'm really embarrassed by getting drunk." "Hey, don't worry about it. You're among friends." John gets up and strolls around the pool as if he is deep in thought. David edges up to a sultry brunette in the corner of the patio and engages her in conversation about fashion.

All of a sudden, Timmy appears on the scene. "All done with the Internet?" Alan asks him. "Yeah man, enough smut for my gut and licentiousness for my consciousness. I'm sorry man. I don't know what the fuck I'm sayin'. I'm pretty toasted, dude." "No problem, Tim." "Have a seat, please," Alan begs. "All right, mate."

The two men watch as John traverses ever so carefully the edge of the deck of the pool as if it is a tightrope. At the point of the diving board, John's arms begin to flail wildly as he loses his footing and begins teetering on one foot before he completely loses his balance and falls into the water. A tumultuous splash sends sprinkles of water showering all over the surface. Alan and Timmy break into boisterous laughs as does everyone else around the pool. Somebody throws a towel to John as he struggles to climb out of the brisk water. He pants heavily as he dries his hair and rushes inside to change.

"Hey Alan, have you ever seen one of these?" Jennifer holds out her hand and reveals a strange arrowhead-looking piece of stone not larger than six inches long. Alan takes the clumsy looking, irregularly shaped stone and asks her what it is. "It's a Clactonian flake tool; basically a prehistoric artifact some of the guys have been studying at the university. It's interesting to think of the progress we've made." She takes a deep drag on her cigarette and then continues: "Think about it, everyone," she raises her voice dramatically, exuberantly. "Man was once striking elephants with primitive tools, artifacts such as these; primitive pieces of flint or flake tools and now we've got the microchip technology to teleport our words all over the fucking world. It's brilliant really!"

Timmy and Alan gaze at the exquisite tool and marvel at the animated point Jennifer is articulately and quite beautifully making. Not only had nature evolved amazing advances in technological expertise and human ingenuity. It had also evolved a wonderfully attractive, intelligent woman such as Jennifer to slightly slurringly, but oh so eloquently, present such information to them in intellectual and aesthetic grandeur.

Her red hair shines under the light of the moon in a glimmering, magical way that seems to portend even greater advances nature would make than the ones these curious humans in their slightly intoxicated, but resolutely focused attention are currently considering. Nature is truly majestic, Alan muses, and on this night and on this patio, as everyone passes around the archaeological find from hundreds of thousands of years ago, all minds are struck with reverence and awe by the very notion that they are able to be part of it. Inextricably bound up with the very process itself, each participant knows in his or her individual way that somehow and in some way, each will contribute to the way the evolutionary process plays itself out. Alan's heart is content.

He rises and begins to do the rounds of saying goodbye, collecting a few phone numbers and addresses, and then heads toward the door. Carla begins to walk with him through the kitchen, living room, and out into the front doorway. "Alan, thanks for coming. I'm so glad you could make it. My friends really enjoyed meeting you." "Thank you. I've had a wonderful time myself. The party has been great." "Alan, where do you think you're going after your stay here?" "Probably up toward Liverpool, although a diversion to Wales would be most enjoyable." "Make sure that on your way out of town, you stop off at an oak tree and meditate a while. You know the Druids regarded oaks as sacred." "Oh really." "Yeah, there were many cults centered around the supposed magical essence of the oak. Christianity, of course, subsumed this concept, as evidenced by the frequent sighting of crosses and images dedicated to certain saints placed strategically by the tree." "That's pretty intriguing," Alan responds. "I'll make sure and stop to pay my respects. You're a very interesting group and I will not forget you." "Nor will we forget you, our American friend." David comes up and shakes hands with Alan.

Alan turns and heads for his car. The early morning has turned foggy and brisk. A fresh layer of dew blankets the grass in front of the house. Alan feels comfort in the solitude of returning to his peripatetic life, the journey that will soon be taking him to another place and another experience. He cranks the engine and accelerates slowly down the spiraling road.

Upon arriving at his room, he contemplates writing a letter to Ronia, but decides that he does not have the energy to do so. Instead, he opens up the original book on mysticism and picks up where he had left off, with the intention of only reading a paragraph or two before falling asleep. His sleepy eyes fall upon the following words: "Alan Watts, an erudite, jovial Englishman, published a book solely devoted to LSD—induced thoughts, titled, *The Joyous Cosmology,* in which he pontificates the cosmological bliss of experiencing a direct union with all living beings. Bearing in mind that Watts was not a trained scientist, he nevertheless has something interesting to say in *Psychotherapy East and West*: 'We could say that the cortex works as an elaborate feedback system for the thalamus by means of which the organism can to some extent be aware of itself. Because of the cortex, the nervous system can know that it knows; it can record and recognize its own states. But this is just one 'echo,' not an infinite series. Furthermore, the cortex is just another neural pattern, and its states are neural patterns; it is not something other than neural pattern as the ego agent is supposed to be, in the organism but not of it.' For Alan Watts, divine enlightenment came through liberating oneself from the constricting and debilitating effects of a societally produced ego concept." The pages start to crumble as the book falls gently upon his chest and he falls soundly into sleep.

Alan awakens around checkout time. He calls down to the front desk to ensure he has enough time to check out. He packs, takes his belongings downstairs, and sits down to compose a letter to send to Ronia.

> Dear Ronia,
>
> Had a pretty crazy, enjoyable night last night. I met and hung out with some interesting people in the Oxford area. Among other less notable things like getting filthy drunk, we had a Ouija seance in which we conjured the ghosts of Aldous Huxley and Lady Godiva. Just your ordinary night, I suppose. Am thinking about you constantly and hope that you are well. Let's talk soon.
>
> Love,
> Alan

He walks down the street, mails the letter, and then returns to his car. The day is sunny and probably about sixty degrees—perfect weather to travel. Alan flips open the road map and observes a northwestern path up to Liverpool. Times that he had thought of Liverpool were times that he thought of The Beatles. With Liverpool having this interesting connection and being one of the largest cities in England, he figures he should give it a go.

He drives all day through hills that are scenically dotted with verdant oaks that bespeak the mysteries of which Carla had referred. On her advice, he stops at a rest stop near Kidderminster and meditates by a statuesque, enveloping tree. Alan had seldom, if ever, given much thought to the significance of the oak. On this afternoon, however, he sits transfixed at the thick, curvaceous trunk with its towering, Gothic limbs and branches outstretched in majestic, almost foreboding repose. Various shades of dark red, brown, and black are interwoven in this sturdy living being. Alan is not sure of the average age of an oak, but each limb, with its multitudinous branches arched and perched in myriad directions, represents to him aspects or stages in human life. He fantasizes that the development of the oak mirrors the development of a human being. He ponders the information that Carla had passed along about the veneration of tree life. He also thinks back to the fairy stories told by the professor of Warwick. The ancient mind of Great Britain had interestingly coalesced with a lush environment—the production of distinct images, concepts, and identifications seemingly incommensurate with so-called modern thinking. The sanctity of the oak and the objective reality of fairies were not called into question. To do so would be blasphemy. The human mind accepted these concepts as you and I now accept that the sun rises in the east and sets in the west.

Alan had always found great intrigue in the duality of ancient and modern thinking. Was the brain simply less developed and therefore more receptive to delusions or daft explanations for the world around it, or did the so-called primitive mindset have a more intuitive, enlightened channel through which veracious, albeit mysterious phenomena could be directly perceived? Has the modern mind simply developed blocks or barriers that prevent it from experiencing certain objective phenomena? Alan leans against the magnificent trunk, which seems to wrap itself around him like some great cocoon. As he gazes at the ground around the tree, interspersed between several leaves is an unusual, protracted root, dripping sap which has trickled down its side and partially dried. Alan marvels at the strange, almost phallic nature of this root and the obvious similarities of reproduction among all living creatures. Gentle rays of sunlight seep in from beyond the branches, providing periodic warmth to Alan's face. He closes his eyes and faces the sky in an attempt to absorb the sun's magical glow.

Knowing that time is slipping past him, he stands up and returns to his car. He merges with the light traffic on the highway and builds up his speed to about seventy. Alan passes the industrialized outskirts of Birmingham and sees many signs pointing to various locales west, toward Wales. Although Liverpool is the destination, temptation gets the best of him and he sidetracks to Wales. Not really sure where to stop, Alan simply arbitrarily selects an exit near Shrewsbury and follows a small two-lane country road into the north section of Wales.

The transition between England and Wales is relatively undramatic and similar to transitions between any two states in the U.S. If not for the signs, he might not have known that he has actually left the country of England. Alan follows the twisting road into a bucolic, almost paradisiacal town called Llangollen.

Alan parks the car and strolls around the town, secretly wishing that someone would come along and mandate that he stay, forever. The town is pleasantly lost in time. Part Victorian and part Elizabethan, Llangollen blends a perfect arrangement of quaint stone-built shops and homes that hug the contours of a river that flows serenely through the town.

Quietude in the hills of Wales seems perfectly encapsulated by a carefully placed railroad station, churches and pubs that sit nestled amidst the hills, with trees permeating the landscape like protective guardians of the town's charming inhabitants. Elderly couples walk hand-in-hand beside the river as a young student walks his black shepherd along the main bridge in town.

Overhead, an eagle soars high as white fluffy clouds taunt the sun and frame the superimposed spires of medieval structures that take one back to another world. Alan drinks plenty of water and has a couple of aspirin to combat the slight hangover he feels. His body, while in its exhausted state, relishes the opportunity of meandering amongst the antique shops and cobblestone paths which transport him delightfully out of the twentieth century.

He steps into a pub and sits at a barstool. "What can I get you sir?" asks a young ebullient female bartender who seems excited about getting a customer. Alan takes a look at a menu and decides. "I'd like an iced tea and a hamburger, thank you." He looks around and notices only about ten other people seated at various tables and stools in the bar. He hands the bartender several pounds and begins to sip his drink. As he looks around, he notices a couple of middle-aged businessmen discussing finance at the bar. In the corner of the room sits a young, attractive couple, two kids, who giggle and stroke each other's hair in an intimate, loving manner.

Steady streams of sunlight filter through the blinds on the window and land against the back of the bar, subsequently illuminating and putting a gleam in the eyes of the vivacious bartender. She smiles at Alan, wipes off the counter, and asks: "Are you from the states?" "Yes, I am. My name is Alan. What's yours?" "Julie. Julie MacDonald." Alan shakes her hand and clears his voice before speaking up: "MacDonald. That's Scottish, isn't it?" "It sure is," she replies. "My name originates in an area of

Scotland called Paisley. Have you heard of it?" "Well, I'm familiar with the paisley print. I suppose it's all the same," he replies. "Yes it is. So how do you like the city we're in right now?" "I love it, actually; coming from the states where everything is so busy and hectic, it seems quite peaceful and very beautiful here." She nods in agreement but retorts: "I want the excitement of the big city. I'm bored here. Do you know where I want to go?"

"No, where?" Alan wonders. "New York City. I think it's fucking brilliant!" "Ha, ha, ha," Alan guffaws, as he imagines the stark contrast between Llangollen and New York City. "Julie, have you never been to New York?" "Nope. I really want to go." "Well, it's pretty cool. It's highly stimulating, energetic, and fashionable. Practically anything you want to do there you can do. When you go, make sure you see the Empire State Building, of course; the Metropolitan Museum of Art, and a Broadway play. Tell me, Julie. On my way in today, I passed a nice looking B&B up the road. It was a green and red sign in the lawn. Do you recommend staying there?" "Yes, I do. That's owned by Terry and Scott McNight. They are extremely pleasant and will not charge you an arm and leg." "Thanks, Julie." Alan eats his burger and savors his drink, relaxing in the laid-back Wales ambience. When he finishes, he pushes back his stool and exits the bar as he bids "Adieu" to Julie by wishing her good luck on getting to New York. He wonders if she will ever make it there.

With the intent of walking along the river for a while and then making his way to the B&B, he steps out into the cobblestone path and heads in the direction of a few miscellaneous stores on the other side of the street. He says hello to an elderly couple that he passes at a very slow pace. The man is wearing a blue and white tweed jacket with baggy brown trousers. On his head is placed a dusty top hat and he supports himself with a sturdy cane. The man's wife has her hair pulled back in a bun and she attempts to steady her husband's astatic gait by sliding her arm underneath his left shoulder and firmly gripping his hand. As he passes, Alan watches carefully that the distinguished man leans into the woman for support, as she clings tightly to him and helps him along. The woman's countenance is expressively humble and she gracefully wears a modest, almost ragged flower, pastel dress. To Alan, the woman bespeaks innumerable years of loving, unfailing support and confidence in the man she has undoubtedly chosen to spend the rest of her life with. Alan gazes closer although they are slowly moving farther away from him. He notices that the man is weary and tired from the years and this is made manifest by the way he seems to be incapable of raising or lifting his head, so that his chin is not touching his chest. The couple moves in a shuffling, slacken, but resolute and almost balletic manner that demonstrates not only a commitment and endurance to each other, but to life itself. Though only momentarily, Alan is moved deeply.

He peers into storefront windows that showcase various trinkets: candles, paintings, carousels, lamps, jewelry and clothes. Mostly, the items he observes represent a different era, a time when craftsmanship and style were more easily captured and represented by the human mind. Victorian and Renaissance sculptures, paintings, and antiques provide substance to the interior of many of the shops. Alan muses that during the Victorian and Renaissance eras, in addition to a proliferation of the intellectual achievements of man, there were certainly equal strides being made in the arts. There seemed to him to have been pivotal, critical time periods in human history in which men had awakened from a cerebral sleep or somnambulism and focused their energies on propelling and evolving their achievements to an all-time high. These spurts were intermittent and seemed to mirror the sporadic but predictable developments in an individual's evolution from birth to adulthood. Alan had read that ontogeny repeats phylogeny; the development of the individual repeats the development of the species.

Elaborating on that theme, Alan ponders the artistic endeavors and accomplishments that man had made, which were, in theory, comparable to the developments that occur in, say, puberty. After a lengthy period of innocence and prepubescence, the developing child is awakened, his nervous system is excited. This stimulation generates profound change in the direction of increased vigor, strength, vitality, and the emergence of reproductive capacities that assure the success of the entire species. As in biology, Alan theorizes elongated periods of stagnation and apathy were fortuitously interrupted by explosions of genius and creativity. These served as hallmarks of what man was capable of achieving. Alan gazes into a clock shop that showcases varieties—large, medium, and small— of mainly grandfathers and cuckoos with intricate designs and displays.

Beautifully constructed and deftly placed Roman numerals encircle golden inlaid vortices from which delicate, hypnotically rotating hands extend and flow like magic wands. The proliferation of clocks—the sheer inundation of timepieces—seems comical. Time, being, and abstract representation as opposed to concrete reality, are rendered almost surreal by the agglomeration of so many objects thrown together to measure it, albeit in a beautified artisanship.

Dusk descends slowly but surely on Alan, the clockshop, and the city, casting an alluring reflection of the horizon on the glass of the storefront window. Through the reflection, Alan reads a line on one majestic, towering clock in the corner of the shop. It reads: "Time Does Not Have A Stop."

Alan turns and heads in the direction of his car. The balmy air has turned chilly as Alan shoves his hands in his pockets and jogs part of the way. When he reaches it, he gets in, glances at his map, and then drives in the direction of the B&B. When he arrives at the house, he climbs a rather steep gravel driveway leading to a spacious lawn with a junker parked at the side of what looks like a barn; on the other side of the lawn is a peculiar looking clothesline covered with clothes. Alan throws the stick into neutral and glides up next to the junker, then stops and gets out. He notices a sturdy-looking gentleman in a dusty plaid shirt gathering firewood over by an apple tree. An attractive woman in a baggy white dress is removing clothes from the line and then folding and placing them into a basket.

Alan approaches her and introduces himself to her: "Hello, your place was recommended to me and I sure hope you have a vacancy tonight." "Hello there, young man. My name is Teresa, Teresa McNight." "It's nice to meet you, Mrs. McNight." "As a matter of fact, we do have a vacancy." "And the price may I ask?" "Fifteen American dollars." "Great." Alan reaches into his jacket, does a few quick calculations in his head, and hands her the money in English pounds. She hands him the key and explains what time tea will be served in the evening and breakfast in the morning.

Alan carries his bags into the living room. A large comfortable room with deep burgundies and purples captures two stunning works. On one wall sits a rich, elegant tapestry that quaintly depicts colonial England. On the other wall hangs a large oval mirror surrounded majestically with a golden Italian frame. A plush Oriental carpet blankets a dark brown hardwood floor. A carpeted, spiraling staircase leads upstairs where Alan will be sleeping.

On his way up the stairs, Alan looks down and notices a luxuriously decorated dining room with crystal plates and glasses neatly arranged on an impressive mahogany table. He locates his room and, upon entering, drops his bags on the floor. Noticing that his door is unlocked, he attempts to lock the door with his key, and realizes that he cannot. He figures that either Mrs. McNight had given him the wrong key or the key is intended for the front door of the house. His room is comfortable and casual, blending an art nouveau look with European country. A blonde deco dresser with a partially cracked mirror stands next to a closet door which opens to reveal bronze antique towel and bathrobe racks. The bed is queen-sized and made of oak. Two plush comforters, with vertical and horizontal red and white stripes, sit neatly folded at the foot of the bed. The upstairs, like the down, is mainly hardwood with rugs placed in the bedrooms and bathroom. Alan rests on his bed for about an hour before going downstairs for tea time. Luckily, it is being conducted in the dining room.

When he enters the room, he notices a shimmering crystal chandelier; its warm illumination is drawing out a rich burgundy from the walls of the room. Against all four walls,sit beautiful large colonial style chairs with soft white cushions and flower-patterned designs of red and blue. In the chair sitting next to the doorway which leads to the kitchen, sits an elderly woman with teacup in hand. She chats gingerly with another woman standing next to her, who appears to be her sister, or cousin—due to a striking resemblance. They both have luminescent, hazelnut eyes and brilliant smiles. Their eyebrows and cheekbones are in synchronicity as they speak.

On the other side of the room, there sits a man who looks like he is in his mid-thirties. With his legs crossed and his hands carefully holding his tea cup, he has long dark wavy hair that partially conceals his eyes that can barely be seen through dark-framed glasses. His shirt is a fading tie-dye pattern and he wears blue jeans and tennis shoes. His eyes are intensely fixed on the bookshelf, which houses an eclectic mixture of antiquated titles that range from politics to natural history and possess mostly dusty covers. A porcelain teapot and cups are nicely arranged on a cart near the kitchen doorway.

Alan says hello to the ladies as he pours himself a cup of raspberry herbal tea. "How are you this evening, ladies?" "Fine, thank you. And how are you?" replies the seated woman, who smiles in a comforting, soothing manner. "Very fine, thank you," Alan responds, smiling back a heartfelt expression. Mrs. McNight passes briskly with a tray of cookies in her arms. "Hello, Alan. How is your room?" "Very nice, thank you. Quite comfy," Alan comments demurely. "Your home is very beautiful." "Why, thank you," she replies. "I was wondering, Mrs. McNight, is the key you gave me the proper one?" "Yes, you'll find it works in the front door." "Oh, there's not a key for my room?" "No, Mr. Agrippa. We do not lock the doors in this house. I'm sure that you will find it very safe. I've been doing this for twenty years and there's never been a problem."

She smiles in an omniscient, almost smug, but mostly sincere and warm fashion, that to Alan is reassuring. "You'll have to forgive me," he responds after realizing that he might have sounded unwarrantedly concerned, if not paranoid. "I'm from the states, where safety and security are sometimes precarious states." In response to his statement, she simply smiles with a look of condolence. Alan walks over to the dark-haired gentleman and introduces himself. "Hi, my name is Alan, Alan Agrippa."

"Hello." The man seems slightly startled but attentive.

"My name is Richard O'Donnell." The two men shake hands. "It's nice to meet you, Richard. What brings you to Wales?" "I'm actually on vacation. I work in Dublin and thought a little excursion would do me some good. What about you?" Alan sits down on a couch next to Richard. "I'm on vacation myself. I had been in London for a while and decided to make my way up into Scotland. Wales seemed a nice stop."

"It certainly is," Richard confirmed. He goes on: "Wales really seems like uncharted territory when you compare it to the modern, industrial complex."

"It really is pristine," Alan eagerly agrees. "The landscape seems perfectly entwined with the man-made structures. A perfect harmony seems to have been reached. So Richard, what do you do in Ireland?" "Quantum mechanics. I'm a physicist with a research group in Dublin." "That's pretty interesting," Alan remarks, with obvious zeal. "I basically know very little about quantum mechanics. I've perused works by Bohr, Schrödinger, and Einstein, but I'm sure I could learn a thing or two from you."

Richard laughs heartily as he takes a sip of tea. "It's basically the study and applications of atoms and their nuclei and of molecules and the various particles involved: the general properties of bulk matter. My colleagues and I are conducting studies based on the Bohr model that indeterminacy is part of the order of nature and that uncertainty—in terms of definition and application—is inherent with respect to quantity. Among other things, we're trying to figure out exactly how those little buggers, atoms that is, operate and whether or not light should be considered a wave or a particle. These are sort of macrocosmic overviews of some of the areas of quantum mechanics."

"I'm glad you mentioned macrocosmic," replies Alan. "In terms of macrocosmic theories of quantum mechanics, are you familiar with books such as *Tao of Physics* by Fritjof Capra, books that speak of the fascinating parallels between modern physics and Eastern mysticism?"

"Yeah, actually I am. I tend to find those concepts interesting; you know, the intuitive notion that space and time are inseparably linked is something shared by mystics and physics alike." "The idea that everything is interconnected?" Alan attempts to clarify. "Yeah," Richard goes on. "We definitely have a situation where, in modern physics, the universe is conceptualized as an amazing congruence and interaction which involves the subject and his or her environment: a reciprocal arrangement, if you will. I certainly see phenomenal correlations between this essential concept and integral elements of, say, Zen Buddhism." "And Chinese Taoism," Alan adds cheerfully. "Yes, Taoism," responds Richard. "Just think of the yin and yang. We have yin, of course, the dark, mysterious, feminine element and then we have the yang, the explosive, male, creative half. Now, these two opposing, yet cyclical, processes are the supposed underpinning of the universe. For thousands and thousands of years, thoughtful men and women listened and watched closely the vicissitudinal nature of nature, if you will. Constant transformation is the natural process and I think this confirms modern physics notions."

"When one conceives of space and time," Alan begins to query, imploringly, in between sips of tea; "is not the most important question one that understands that space and time are merely constructs of the mind and not objective things in and of themselves?" "Of course," replies Richard, enthusiastically. "That was what Einstein was all about. The position of a moment in time or an object in space is determined by it being in relation to another moment or another object. Relativity. Taoism. Two sides of the same coin, if you will."

"Richard, the organization of the brain. Can you touch on how you see the structure and function of the brain in the midst of modern physics and eastern mysticism?" "Well, Alan, you mention something that falls into the realm of neurology; psychology, biology, chemistry, neurophysiology—many areas that approach matters from a slightly different perspective than my specialty, quantum mechanics." "Sure."

"Back in 1953, an American chemist named Stanley Miller, performed an experiment in which he mixed a batch of several gases and then subjected these gases to electrical sparks, an imitation of lightning over the earth. After a short time, the fluid showed evidence of protein, or at least amino acids, the building blocks of protein. He also succeeded in producing parts of nucleic acids which, of course, store and translate genetic information. Now, I'm going way back, but the point of this is to suggest that the biological origins of life on this planet—which have led to the specialization and highly advanced nature of the human brain—are a result of chemicals or gases found throughout space. This hints that life could have originated elsewhere and landed here via a meteorite of some sort. Now, everything is a result of complex interchanges—among molecules, for instance. The human brain is arguably the most incredible mass that has evolved on the surface of this planet. It is an organism that provides us an almost infinite capacity for pleasure, intellectual stimulation, and creative virtuosity, I must say. Much about the world we live in is truly awesome, spectacular adventure."

Alan smiles in great amusement. There is a reasonableness and a humaneness about Richard that actually surprises Alan. Richard's affable, casual nature pleasantly contradicts the stoic, detached and highly technical stereotype of a quantum physicist evoked in Alan's mind. Richard conveys a loose, flexible, open-minded demeanor, which seems to shiningly underscore the very tenets of relativity. Methodical and scientific, yet jovial and relaxed seem to Alan to be remarkable symphonies of molecules that make up his newfound friend, Richard O'Donnell.

Richard excuses himself momentarily to replenish his tea. When he returns, Alan speaks up: "Richard, are you familiar with the book *Neuropolitique* by Timothy Leary?" "Timothy Leary—as in 60's guru?" "Yeah. He wrote an interesting book called, *Neuropolitique,* in which he discusses various circuits of the nervous system, one being the cyber-electronic circuit. Within this concept he refers to the idea coined by Dr. John Lilly as 'metaprogramming,' which is basically awareness of programming one's programming, in terms of modifying one's cognitive processes in order to effect behavior change. Leary theorized that what Lilly was talking about was an Einsteinian, relativistic awareness or intelligence that recognized Euclidean, Newtonian, and Aristotelian systems as just three among billions of quantum programs of experience. I guess what Leary hypothesized was a breakthrough in psychology that occurred concurrently with the revolution of physics: the idea that the nervous system could metaprogram the nervous system, or essentially re-imprint itself."

"That's pretty fascinating," responds Richard with enthusiastic, rapt attention. Richard picks up: "You mentioned John Lilly. That theory of metaprogramming was developed in the milieu of the isolation tank, a similar environment portrayed in the movie 'Altered States' with William Hurt, right?" "You got it, Rich. John Lilly wrote *The Center of the Cyclone* and *Simulations of God,* among others. He did extensive research with the drug Ketamine to achieve higher states of awareness. Very fascinating man."

Mr. McNight has thrown a few logs in the fireplace and ignited a rip-roaring fire. The incendiary glow and warmth emitted are welcome reminders that despite man's loftier thoughts about expanded awareness and relativity, he is still in touch with nature's primordial incandescence. Alan figures he will give Richard a respite after picking his brain. He wanders over to the fire and warms his bones for a while. The soothing retinal images of luminescent, dancing, smoothly prancing flames give rise to neural embers and flickering hypnotic revelations of the mysterious discovery of fire. The crackling of freshly burning wood spirals its way through aural canals echoing the ancient yet eternal eminence of fire. A soft, orangish glow blankets the bookcase, revealing immaculate leather binding that has withstood almost as many ages.

"Goodnight, Richard. It was nice to talk to you." "See ya, Alan." Alan waves to the two women and makes his way back up to his room. He pulls out his wallet and removes the calling card. He picks up the receiver and dials Ronia's number. The phone rings four or five times before she answers.

"Hello." "Ronia, this is Alan. What's going on?" "Alan, sweetie, where are you? I miss you so much. What's going on?" "I'm in a home in Wales. It's really beautiful here. Earlier today I walked around a pastoral little town. You wouldn't believe it. It's wonderful here." "Are you doing okay, Alan?" "Yeah, I'm doing great. Just a little bit ago, I met a really interesting guy who's a quantum physicist. We had an intriguing conversation. What's going on with you?"

"I've got some great news, Alan. I found some incredible rates on flights to Scotland. I just submitted my paper which will be evaluated for the next few weeks. I can take some time off and would love to catch up to you. Can we plan on meeting?" "Yes, definitely," Alan responds. "I was planning to drive up to Scotland within the next few days. We could meet in Edinburgh. When can you break away?" "I can get a ticket to fly out in a few days. Will that work?" "Yes. What time do flights leave? I'll pick you up at the airport. We'll find a place in Edinburgh. It will be awesome!" he effuses. "Alan, here's the info." He hears her fumbling with paperwork. "There's a flight leaving in the morning. I can get there at 11:00 a.m. How will I know where you are?"

"Tell me your flight number and I'll pick you up at the airport." "Okay," she replies. "Let's see. The flight number is 1128. I'll call and leave a message with Jim and Mary if there's a problem. If you don't hear from me, it means I'm on the flight." "Great. Ronia, I can't wait to see you." "You too, Alan. Goodbye!" "Goodbye." Alan sets the receiver down and cheers silently to himself. Ronia seems genuinely excited to be seeing him soon and this makes him feel blessed.

Roaming away from the bed, he walks over to the backpack and removes a cigar and matches. He walks over to the window, lifts the pane, and sits in the sill with the freshly lit end of the cigar pointing outward. Other than an occasional fluid movement of his arm in taking felicitous drags of smoke into his mouth, he is motionless. As he methodically blows steady streams of grayish white smoke into the night air, he gazes up and reverently beholds the marvelous constellation, "Hydra." With varying luminescence, the twinkling panoply fills the great solar system like thousands of Christmas lights covering a mammoth pine. Like a navigational compass for a ship's passage, Alan points with the embers of the cigar and outlines the interesting dimensions of one of the few constellations that he can actually identify. First, he outlines the six stars directly under Cancer which seem to form a serpent's head. Alan points out Alphard, the brightest star in the vicinity, which has the definition, "the solitary one." He ponders the mysterious Greek Hydra, the serpent with many heads: the serpent that was laboriously killed by Hercules. Alan remembers from what he had studied that Hydra possesses something like two hundred and twenty nine stars and covers an area of something like 1300 square degrees.

As sporadically twinkling starry lights infinitely light up the moody, all-enveloping nightly backdrop of elegantly deep shades of midnight blue and black, Alan's memory bank falls back upon a magical time in the history of man. At least 5,000 years ago, the ancient Sumerians who lived in the Near East began naming many of the constellations which man can still recognize today. Various gods and goddesses represented in the minds of these people were portentously projected onto the night's sky. Mythological persons, objects, and sundry representations of natural phenomena were delineated and illustrated beautifully by the magical constellations. Throughout Phoenicia, Greece, and the valleys of the Tigris and Euphrates, the cognitive torch was heroically lit and carried on by the proud perpetuation of the stellar concepts that had originated in relatively modest Sumeria. They were modified appropriately along the way by notables, like: the Greek poet, Aratus, who wrote *Phaenomena*; the Greek astronomer and mathematician, Ptolemy, who wrote *Almagest*; and of course Magellan, who valiantly circumnavigated the earth in the sixteenth century, realizing along the way that a substantial part of the southern sky was not divided into constellations. This, of course, led to the formation of the "modern" constellations aside from those of mythological significance.

Alan takes one last puff on the cigar, then extinguishes it and throws it down in the grass. He shuts the window and returns to the bed, upon which lies the book on mysticism—the one from the voodoo shop. Randomly flipping through the pages, he happens upon a page that reads at the top: Paul Sédir.

Alan begins to read: "Paul Sédir took up divination by mirrors in which visions are produced as a seeming result of seeing in consciousness what is normally subconscious through the gazing into various discs, vases, or crystals. Psychologists study the strange effects to which terms such as automatism and hallucination were interestingly applied."

Alan feels that he had seen the workings of his subconscious this night, in all of their grandeur and conceptualization of love for another mortal—Ronia. He directly experiences those intimate feelings and emotions of warmth, acceptance, and raging lust for the wonderful creature he will soon be reunited with. The "mirror" into which he had gazed, that catapults him into luscious accordance with his subconscious, is not a crystal ball, a vase, or the beautifully ornate antique mirror hanging on the wall in his room. The mirror into which Alan has gazed, the quintessential reflection of his very self, is the paradisiacal canopy of the night sky, with its billions and billions of stars that somehow seem less than distant, more palpable to Alan now than ever before.

As Alan turns out the light in his room and lies down to sleep, he feels at peace with his surroundings, although he is by himself, in a country far from home. From his bed where he lies with his head on the pillow, he can still see out the window and into a night that is strangely his. Before his consciousness is once again suspended and ebbs into sleep, a realization occurs that he believes he will hold forever. His nervous system is an extension of a planet that floats through a solar system in one galaxy among a multitude. Our local group of galaxies—containing the Milky Way, the Andromeda nebula, and many smaller systems—is actually in the outskirts of the Virgo cluster of galaxies. Nearby galaxies are moving away from us at speeds increasing proportionately with distance. The universe is essentially constantly expanding. The last thought Alan has before drifting off into the horizon of sleep, seems to sum it up best: There is infinity within and infinity without.

The morning sun greets Alan gingerly, casting its warm, soothing rays on the right side of his face. Cool breezes had comforted him through the night and now, getting out of bed seems a difficult prospect. He reluctantly pushes back the sheets and stretches his tired muscles. Rising slowly, he carries himself to the shower and rinses off. The shower is down the hall and Alan is glad that no one is trying to use it at that time. He gets dressed, throwing on blue jeans and a button-down shirt, with his usual black shoes. Listening carefully to the sounds in the house, Alan determines that some of the people are still sleeping and some are downstairs eating breakfast.

He loads up his things and traipses downstairs to find company in his newfound friend, Richard. "Good morning, Richard, how's everything?" "Fine, mate, and you?" "Wonderful. I'm meeting up with my special lady friend within a few days. I'm pretty excited!" "Is she American?" Richard queries in a friendly tone. "No," Alan responds. "She's a lovely French girl who has somehow found it in her heart to bestow upon me her immaculate charms." "Aha," replies Richard. "The French girls are charming, indeed. Depeche Mode—French fast fashion. The French are very stylish and many of them are pretty sophisticated."

"Richard, you mentioned Depeche Mode. That's a magazine, right?" "Right."

"Well, it happens to be the name of one of my favorite bands. I sure hope Dave Gahan keeps it all together and continues to mesmerize us with cool music." "I'm a Depeche fan myself, Alan. Those guys were the forerunners and continue to be innovators of the electronic stuff that is so cool." "You're right," Alan concurs.

"They coalesce a surging industrial back beat with a synth pop flavor. Quite an effective combination if you consider their intriguing lyrics, as well." Richard passes Alan the coffee. "So Alan, what did you think of the O.J. Simpson case?" Alan ponders the question only for a few moments before replying: "I thought it was a tragedy that he was originally acquitted in the criminal trial. At least some vindication arose in the civil trial where they found him guilty. The man was unequivocally guilty and the case unfortunately polarized whites and blacks throughout the United States, something we didn't need to happen. What did you think, Richard?" "I—as well as most everyone else in Ireland—feels that the bloke did it. What it has to do with race I really don't know. Shouldn't one be held responsible for one's actions, independent of race?" "My sentiments exactly," Alan replies. "Will you pass the rolls, Richard? "Sure."

Alan proceeds to finish his breakfast of fried eggs, sausage, and toast. After emptying his coffee cup, Alan says one last goodbye to Richard

and then departs from the table in search of the McNights. He discovers
Mrs. McNight in front of the house. He thanks her cordially for the
night's stay and hands her the key. She asks him what direction he is
going to go and he answers simply: "toward Edinburgh." She offers him
a quick tip on scenic directions to the highway. He takes his bags to the
car and begins the next leg of his trip.

Alan speeds along a heavily tree-lined route, which begins to gradually metamorphose into a more industrial setting on the outside of Liverpool, England. Magical English words that Alan had grown up with—
like Manchester, Chesterfield, Blackpool, Sheffield, and Mansfield—are
appearing on the street signs. The ever-winding highway takes Alan
through an ever-changing landscape in which he begins to think of
Liverpool and its evolution of The Beatles; a group of otherwise working
class young dudes tapped into a musical wavelength which ended up
resonating throughout the world. A revolution of the entire music scene
and an influence on innumerable artists ensued.

The predominantly naturalistic settings of Wales and rural England,
with their towering oaks and lush willows, give rise to smokestacks and
brown rustic warehouses and factories. Mass-produced tenements and
hopelessly knotted freeways begin to remind Alan that he is in fact in the
20th century. As he enters downtown Liverpool, its modern industrial
feel is underscored by an antiquarian presence to the buildings and
streets. In conjunction with an overcast sky, an image is created that
seems incompatible with The Beatles. It does not seem possible that four
chaps with cute, eternally fashionable haircuts and sentimentally laden
lyrics and melodies would emerge from a city with such a cold, harsh,
biting, almost hard-edged essence. To Alan, Liverpool seems the
quintessential blue collar, middle-class, hard-working city that must have
been unsettled, if not shocked, when its eternally most famous sons went
from bubblegum pop into transcendental, Indian mystic musings. In
Alan's mind, the juxtaposition of stoic, cold industry with colorful
Ramakrishna musings and images of The Beatles is a humorously stark
contrast. Alan decides that the decidedly drab, almost haunting street he
has discovered could use a splash of Sgt. Pepper color and design. He
spots one of the only colorful icons in the neighborhood—a multicolored
flag, that depicts sundry renditions of British insignia and soccer balls—
in front of a traditional English pub.

He pulls the car over and feeds a meter before stepping inside to a
dark, slightly musty bar with a wide array of sports events commemo-
rated through posters and flags on the walls. Alan steps up to the bar and

orders a cider. The only light comes from natural rays that trickle through the windows and the front door. Sitting to Alan's left is a grizzly-faced biker with long, straight black hair that is slicked back with what is hopefully gel. In the man's right hand is a precariously held Marlboro cigarette with an extended strand of ash that hovers delicately over an amusing white ashtray in the shape of a voluptuous, buxomly endowed woman with big, bright red lips. The man's face, although possessing darkened, cavernously concave sockets that enclose beady, blood shot orbs, is chiseled in a Romanesque countenance that is distinguished and almost thoughtful. A dusty, fashionably tattered bomber jacket made of dark tan leather covers his torso boldly. On the back of the jacket is a large red and white American bald eagle.

To Alan's right—over by a wall with a dart board—are five twenty-something collegiate types, tossing darts and stumbling about drunkenly. Strangely enough, they look American, with baseball hats and plaid flannel shirts and blue jeans. Alan grabs his beer and walks closer to them. He sits down at a table within earshot of their voices, which seem to be babbling on about topics like sports and women; typical of any American bar except for the undeniably distinctive English accent. "Hey Eric, I got the tickets to the Manchester game which I promised. Sally and Carol are going with. Is that cool?" "Is that cool? Sure. As long as I'm going with Sally. You know Carol drives me fuckin' crazy sometimes."

A tall, thin freckled-faced kid who is widdling his dart incessantly into the bull's-eye, speaks up: "You fuckin' blokes. I can't believe you're deliberating over who shall take whom to the fucking football game when the broads in question are two lusc, luscciouuuuuussssss plums like Carol and Sally." He amusingly slurs in a way that suggests a brain functioning more like an engine whose pistons are overfiring.

"How bout you give the goddamn tickets to me? You guys fucking stay at home. I'll take the two fawns myself." One of the guys erupts vociferously. "Oh, you'll take the two girls. Right, mate. And who'll give you the fuckin' penile implant it'll take for you to handle a real woman once in your life, let alone two?" "You bawstard." The two immediately engage in a playfully raucous wrestling match as the others sit back and laugh.

One of the guys, who is wearing a Black Sabbath t-shirt, approaches Alan.

"Hello, mate. What's your name?" "Alan, Alan Agrippa." They shake hands.

"Alan, it's nice to meet you. My name's Jason and the guys over there—that's Beavis and Butthead—times two." Alan chuckles and then asks sarcastically,

"What are you guys doin partying at this early hour? Don't you have anything respectable to do?" His sardonic flair immediately endears him to Jason. Jason replies, "Well, mate, when five guys stay up all night trippin', what's left for them to do the next day but drink beer and throw darts?" "Good point," Alan responds. "So you're an American, aren't you?" "Yep, the grand ole' U.S. of A." Alan proudly responds. "So what brings you to Liverpool?" Jason gregariously queries. "I'm on my way to meet up with a lady friend in Edinburgh. I'm in the midst of a wonderful tour of Great Britain. Your homeland is quite impressive to me." "Why, thank you," Jason responds in a feigned redneck sort of Yankee accent.

"So, Jason, I take it you guys are students or something." "Or something," Jason sneers as he gazes out over his humorously inebriated entourage. "Yeah, we're students. I'm a history major. In the group, we've got an economics, psychology, political science, and business major." "So, while trippin' last night, did you guys have any revelatory, visionary insights into the nature of man or the universe, or anything?" "Heh, heh," Jason chuckles, looks around as if to make sure there are no unwanted eavesdroppers, and then continues: "Oh man, you wouldn't believe it. I saw tracer trails of lights that were like extraterrestrial fire-crackers. You would not even believe it. At times, I was on the outside looking in. In terms of revelations or visions, would communication with aliens count?" "Aliens?" Alan sounds and actually feels intrigued. "Yeah, dude. We drove out to this hill on the other side of Oldham and a fuckin' UFO landed in this field. A bright—no, overwhelmingly iridescent—strobe hypnotized all of us. It was outta sight." Alan scoffs, but is certainly entertained by what he hears. "So tell me, Jason. What happened? Did little green men with oval heads and squinty black eyes take you in and perform mad science on your testicles?" "No, man. Nothing like that happened. But there was this magnificently glowing sphere that hovered before our eyes and then swooped down magically and completely inexplicably." "That's pretty wild, Jason."

Alan swishes down his beer and begins to look bored. It isn't that Alan feels incompletely entranced by the idea of extraterrestrial contact. It's just that Jason's highly entertaining story reveals a not so reliable source. "Alan, it's nice to meet you, man." "You, too, Jason. Take care." Jason goes back to the dart game and Alan gets up to leave the bar. When he gets to his car, the sun is slowly penetrating the cloudy veneer and crisp, stalwart winds blow sturdily through. He climbs into the driver's seat and starts the engine.

CHAPTER 18

As he drives away from the bar, he notices the group of guys slipping out the door and spilling out on the sidewalk. Alan knows what the day after tripping is like and with this thought in mind, looks on with not exactly envy, but mainly a sense of appreciation and nostalgia for what these young men are exploring and experiencing. They represent Alan at a different age but if there were any facets of a common thread, or a theme of life that he definitely shares with them, it is this: the spirit of adventure; camaraderie, and delightfully happenstance approach to living.

The engine roars as Alan speeds past Manchester and up through the scenic Scottish hills, and on toward Carlisle. He passes by rolling, verdant plains that lie intermittently dotted with lazy, grazing sheep. The highway is alternately straight and winding with each passing mile and Alan's comfort in his solitude grows increasingly. His discovery is that driving along a European highway is as much about watching the scenery and every imaginable high-performance auto as possible, as it is about getting from point A to point B. It seems that every few minutes he is passed by a BMW, Audi, or Mercedes with drivers completely comfortable taking hairpin turns at eighty-plus miles per hour. In the U.S., Alan is extremely confident in his powerful, competent driving. In Europe, he is greatly humbled by the driving expertise around him.

About three-fourths of the way to Edinburgh, Alan pulls over in a small chalet style Danish village. He parks in front of an Alpine restaurant and walks in for lunch. After sitting down at a table by the front window, he reaches into his backpack and pulls out a pen and his pad of paper. He begins to write:

"Am on my way to visit and hopefully spend ample time with a woman who is a strange mixture of brains, beauty, and adventure— someone who encapsulates an almost extragalactic, mystic, ethereal nature that is simultaneously haunting and comforting. Like the ineffable grand epic of godly proportions, *The Odyssey,* the search or journey that I have undertaken seems a powerful coalescence of the willy-nilly nature of both gods and men. As geographical space contracts and expands around me, so is my soul being manipulated into forms and structures of a tumultuous nature. The ostensible emptiness of the landscape is soon fleshed out by the development of the city. Preliminary pains of loneliness and isolation within become very quickly transmuted into voluminous diaries of personal histories and experiences which will be with me always. The tides are eternally connected to the shadows and luminescences of the moon. The idiosyncratic demands and limitations of our environment certainly shape us and render us amusing characters or puppets in the magnificent theater of life. Odysseus, Athena, Zeus, Menclaos, Telemakhos. All magical names in the widespread sojourn across land and sea. All of the loves; the lusts and heartaches; the music and the drama; the lives and deaths and the communion of men and women with the spirit world; that part of man left unexplained; uncharted territories—dimensions, maps, and stratagems of consciousness—beguiling and hypnotizing. The grand epic of life itself for a multitude of mortals who had crossed both geographical time and space while equally exploring their own physiological and psychological systems..."

"Sir, can I take your order?" The waitress' words take a minute to register.

"Sure. I'll take an iced tea and the grilled chicken salad. Thanks." Alan glances at the window and catches sight of a small child grasping the string to a balloon. A woman, who appears to be his mother, approaches him quickly and he suddenly releases the balloon. To the woman's obvious chagrin and some amusement, the colorful orb ascends slowly as a sudden forceful wind temporarily stunts its climb. She smolders, as if to say, "Now see what you've done, Johnny." Alan notices the look of excitement in the boy's eyes, which remain fixed on the floating spectacle.

"A crack in the sky and a hand reaching down to me. All the strangers came today." Alan ponders the lyrics to David Bowie's, "All You Pretty Things," while also considering Icarus' majestic flight to the heavens to procure the power of fire for man. Bowie had in a sense done that, Alan muses; that is, brought the power of electrifying music and vouchsafed it to man. "Making love to his ego, Ziggy sucked up into his mind." Just as grandiose as Alan's trip seems to him, he is equally aware of the hedonistic, self-indulgent aesthetic it holds. "He's told us not to blow it, cause he knows it's all worthwhile." Alan revels and deliberately perpetuates the Bowie lyric vignette in his mind.

The meal arrives and he devours it in minutes. When Alan is finished, he pays the tab, gathers his things, and heads for the street. He stalls for a while in the undeniably pleasant but borderline gaudy scene of the town. Windmills and butter churns punctuate quaint, flower-landscaped streets as lovers and siblings gracefully, casually meander. "New York's a go-go and everything tastes nice." Alan steps into a Cinnamon roll shoppe and indulges in an absolute delight of a dessert. Hot, spicy, sugary, dripping cinnamon and butter bathe a perfectly delectable roll that caresses Alan's throat as it slides down. He reaches into his backpack and pulls out a cigar. He unwraps it, lights the end, and takes a careful, thorough drag. The rich, aromatic tobacco nicely complements dessert. Alan looks around in pure, mostly undiluted epicurean rapture at the town but his attention is directed elsewhere—at the sky.

The vast expanse cradles in its gargantuan canopy a light grayish mist of cloud. It spirals in long streams that carefully encircle the sun, and scatter multi-layered rays into myriad streaks of orangish, yellowish, and white colors. A luxury airliner flies in the distance, penetrating the cerulean backdrop before slowly disappearing from sight. Alan takes leisurely puffs as he walks around the edge of the shops and down a picturesque street that winds for a couple of blocks. He maintains and relishes a sense of charm at the amusing portrayal of Denmark in the midst of rural Scotland. Off to the left lies a man-made pond that has in its center a little bronze mermaid that depicts one of Hans Christian Anderson's characters. It is perched on a rock as a flock of swan swims elegantly around it. Kids sit on the other side of the pond and frolic in the grass while occasionally stopping to feed pieces of bread to ducks. Colorful shops that line the streets brilliantly showcase boxes of cheese and chocolates wrapped in ribbons depicting the Danish flag.

Alan begins to make his way back to the car. He extinguishes the moist, tattered cigar and gets back into his car. After briefly scanning his map, he embarks on his scenic journey upward through the foothills of Scotland to reach regal Edinburgh. Soon he is passing surprisingly verdant, lush hillsides which dismay in their stark contrast to the barren, rugged terrain that covers much of the country. Flocks of sheep happily graze off patches of grass that cover huge rocks. Herds of goats traipse on alternately changing landscape that reflects arid valleys, plains, and ravines before shifting to fertile fields with bounteous willows and oaks.

He ponders snippets of Scottish history. In very early A.D., Roman armies occupied sections of southern Scotland and defended it from the attacks of the Caledonians, or Picts. The Antonine Wall was built to separate the warring factions. Alan is cognizant that when the Romans first lost control of southern Scotland, they erected Hadrian's Wall. Apparently the wall had failed to control the Picts, who continued to successfully penetrate the south. Disparate shadows from intermittent passing clouds dance on the highway. Alan gazes into the distance and notices a contrast of light projected onto rocky cliffs. The cliffs jut like sawed gun barrels superimposed on the great sun. He contemplates the influx of organized Christianity when, around the time of 563 A.D., St. Columba—who proselytized from his monastery on the small island of Iona—converted the king of the Picts at Inverness. This would later give rise to the conflict of Irish Christianity with Roman Christianity. Rome won out and this of course had been a pivotal step in the European infiltration of Scotland.

Alan feels the lion's roar of the engine as he barrels down the highway. The highway covers land which had once been the battleground for invading Norsemen. They had traveled by sea from the north to inflict their overlordship; starting with places like Shetland and Orkney and moving brazenly into the Hebrides and all along the northern and western mainland. During the 11th and 12th centuries, the Scottish kingdom gradually loosened and then extricated itself from the grip of the tightly held reigns of the Norse. It seems to Alan that the influx of England into Scotland began around the time that Malcolm III married the beautiful Anglo Saxon princess Margaret. Having spent several years in England, Malcolm III brought English ways with him into Scotland, instituting the first hints of Norman feudalism. Scotland, between the years of 1153 and 1286, had experienced what some have called its golden age. It experienced a peaceful and progressive period until Margaret, Maid of Norway, died. It had been decreed that she should marry the son of Edward I, king of England. Edward became John de Baliol's suzerain, which resulted in Baliol aligning with France to attempt a revolt.

In 1297, William Wallace, who has since been popularized through countless tales, including the one told by actor Mel Gibson in the movie "Braveheart," challenged the English at Sterling Bridge. The Scots were victorious. Edward eventually sought revenge on Wallace, but Robert I, the Bruce, was soon bashing the English again in 1306. Robert the Bruce fought valiantly against Edward the II's ineffectual troops. In 1320, a letter from the Scots to the pope proclaimed: "So long as a hundred of us remain alive, we will never be subject to the English king."

Alan winds past highway signs indicating upcoming modern cities and suburbs that now pervade this magical land. Kendal becomes Penrith and Carlisle segues beautifully into Gretna, where Alan decides to stop for a break. The western coast of Scotland is not simply beckoning Alan. It is irresistible in its windy, salty, energizing air and its billowing, ominous fog, which rolls tenderly over crashing waves and powerful rocks. Alan drives to a section of land that protrudes pleasantly over an isolated cove of the Irish Sea.

Seagulls hover angelically and appear to Alan to be organisms that are not separate but actually inherent components to the breathtaking, nautical surroundings. He watches with great amazement as their wings flutter and feathery bodies hover in unison with the motion of winds that sweep forcefully over the waves. Alternate surgings and retractings of the birds develop a rhythmic, poetic balance interrupted only momentarily by a sudden dive into the water for fish, or drops upon sandy rocks for respite. Alan reaches into his bag and removes some drinking water. With the car parked strategically overlooking the ocean, Alan feels as if he holds the essence of Scotland in his hands. He steps out of the car and reclines on its hood. Alan clasps his hands behind his head and begins to relax by the edge. This great promontory towers majestically above the breaking waves that hauntingly recall the spirit and history of the land.

Alan ponders The Hundred Years' War between England and France in which Scotland sided with France. He muses over the seminal figures in Scottish history: Mary, Queen of Scots, who, having returned to Scotland after the death of her husband Francis, greets the newly established Reformed Church with something less than open arms. Later, Mary married the Earl of Bothwell, who was believed to be the murderer of her former husband, Lord Darnley. As a result of this controversy, a sedition supplanted her with her baby son, James VI. Mary fled to England and was executed under Elizabeth's reign. Alan faintly recalls the dichotomous leadership of James VI and Charles I, the former ruling his people with relative diplomacy and tact; the latter imposing arguable impudence and interference across the land.

As Alan's visual focus scans the distant white caps and rippling tides of the water, his mind scans over the Scottish Civil War and its subsequent Restoration and Glorious Revolution. He is only vaguely aware of the current state of affairs in terms of the union between Scotland and England in their courts of law. He knows that there has always been alternate friction and harmony between the two nations but is certainly curious about the present situation.

At first consideration, it seems to him to be unfair that Scotland has relinquished its autonomy to England. He knows that in 1707, a treaty of union was formed between England and Scotland and it essentially surrendered the Scots' political independence. Scotland would be represented in London by forty-five members of the House of Commons and sixteen peers in the House of Lords; that after the death of Queen Anne the two countries became ruled by the House of Hanover.

Alan turns and slides off the car, coming to a firm stand on the ground. He starts to stroll leisurely along the edge of the precipice, noticing with great interest how the alternately jagged and smooth rock formations that line the edge are a strange mixture of eroded, exfoliated, but ever-rejuvenating organismic deposits. The area bespeaks millennia of glacial shifts, seismic eruptions, and oceanic upheavals that have shaped the now breathtaking, awe-inspiring terrain. Tectonic violence and chaos had, once-upon-a-time, formed this landscape and waterscape perhaps with the prescient awareness that it would soon enough be teeming with life of a different sort—that of humans and other animals who would carry on in equally dichotomous strains of violence and peacefulness. The gentle sounds of waves crashing against the boulders way down below soothe Alan's brain like a warm, caressing drug that nestles its way along the corridors and contours of his nervous system.

He watches as a septuagenarian couple meanders arm-in-arm, absorbing the same views and perhaps the same perceptions. They walk up to within ten feet of Alan. The gentleman—who wears thick, black spectacles and has a grayish beard and long, sheepswool overcoat—calls out to him: "Hey sonny, how are you?" "Fine, thanks," Alan responds." How are you all doing?" "Great!"

"Excuse me, sir," Alan implores as the couple walks by. "I couldn't help but wonder, sir—being the somewhat ignorant tourist that I am— what exactly happened in Scottish history after the time of the treaty between Scotland and England in 1707—in terms of the relationship between Scotland and England?"

The elderly gentleman turns and smiles at his wife, as if greatly amused that he has been called upon to expound on this subject. In answering Alan, the man removes his hands from his pockets and makes a dramatic full sweep with one arm as he segues into his answer:

"For many, many years, the British Parliament ignored the Scots." The man is now truly beside himself. "You see, young man; the Jacobite risings of 1715 and 1745 that were designed to restore the descendants of James VII and II were mainly the work of the Highlanders. They joined the Jacobite side. Now, the Earl of Mar failed miserably."

The man's voice takes on a raspier, more cigar-nurtured essence: "In 1745, the 'Young Pretender,' Charles Edward, landed in Scotland, took Edinburgh, and invaded England. When the Highlanders failed, the Lowlanders were not terribly disappointed."

Alan questions the man: "Sir, didn't the eminent Scottish writer Sir Walter Scott deal with the Jacobite rebellion in his novel, *Waverly*?" "Yes, he did, young man. That was Scott's first novel and it brilliantly captured the true horror of civil war. I must say, as an American you are remarkably inquisitive. Shall I continue?" "Oh, please," Alan responds. "As I was saying. The original discontent with the Union gradually metamorphosed... (Alan marvels at the eloquence with which the man uses the word, metamorphose) into acceptance because, of course, profound economic development was fostered. So you see my friend, the relationship between England and Scotland has always been one of love and hate."

Alan smiles and shakes hands with the gentleman and his wife. "Thank you for taking time out to speak with me." "Certainly, sonny. You have a grand trip." "I will," Alan responds. He watches as the loving couple continues on their way. The man had spoken with a sense of pride in his homeland and a knowledgeable, concerned perspective that only comes from an individual who has spent seventy plus years contemplating, questioning, and observing. Alan takes one last look around him and a deep breath of ocean air.

He climbs back into the car and starts the engine. He heads northeast toward Edinburgh not with a complete sense of urgency, but with definite plans of arriving on time to meet Ronia. Allowing for extra time in case something unexpected should arise along the way, he relishes the sight of grayish blue misty clouds that float through the sky like slowly oozing molten lava. Alan adjusts the radio to an alternately progressive/popular station—for he is not sure if there is a difference these days—and sits back to enjoy the ride. Within minutes, he slips into that semi-conscious mode one typically experiences when they are traveling a path they have traveled before. The fact that Alan has never driven this path does not seem to matter.

Occasionally, he looks in front of him while in his peripheral vision he picks up sporadic points of interest. His mind's eye remains comfortably fixed on the image of Ronia: the immense outer beauty she possesses and all her energy and charm she so elegantly exudes. The borders around this image are not merely fuzzy but actually limitless in terms of a sort of gestalt of her being and an insignificance to anything else.

Although the mind is truly vast and capable of innumerable simultaneous thoughts or ideas, Alan's at the moment is completely and inescapably consumed with Ronia. It is not an image or a memory or even a concept of her, but her actual essence that seems to infect every port in the vessel of his mind; every nook in the recesses of his awareness; every cranny in the walls of his consciousness; every fissure in the dam of his unconscious; and every compartment and crevice in the voluptuous, curvy, spiraling universe of his cognition. Who is actually driving the car at this point is an utter mystery. He is already with Ronia and some other, sycophantic mush of an entity is somnambulistically struggling to catch up.

The car does finally arrive in the city which blends medieval castles with modern technology as beautifully as Beethoven composed fugues: Edinburgh, Scotland. Alan's first stop is the bank where he immediately makes a sizable withdrawal. He then parks the car and begins to wander around on a search for the most romantic place to stay in town. He performs this survey by stopping into a variety of coffee shops and retail outlets and taking a poll.

One suggestion is the Orkney, a Byzantine style, moderately to highly priced hotel that overlooks a majestic 17th century clock tower. Another option is the Elice, a cottage on the outskirts of town with pleasant views of rolling hills surrounding the inspiring Edinburgh skyline in the distance. The one Alan chooses, however, is a Viennese-owned and operated chateau called, "The Waltz." It is a dark, charcoal Gothic structure with two towering spires and a large wooden door. The door leads to an interior courtyard that has a heated pool surrounded by Venetian-designed flower pots filled with radiant long-stemmed roses in vibrant red. What sells the idea to Alan is the fact that hanging within the courtyard is a string of glowing orbs—mobiles in various colors, shapes, and sizes depicting the planets in our solar system. From the large, orangish glow of the sun to the multi-layered rings of Saturn, everything is captured magically. The mobile planets are connected by an almost invisible cord that swings through the courtyard along tree branches and wooden posts as the wind ensures proper orbital function. In one corner of the pool is a flame thrower that is timed to emit wonderful, dramatic flashes of fire. Background blues music that sometimes changes to jazzy numbers by Frank Sinatra and Tony Bennett completes the surreal, but romantic picture.

Alan walks back through the lobby and up to the front desk. After asking for a room with a view of the skyline, he is promptly led to a plush, airy suite equipped with luxurious decor. A misty green large leather couch is centered neatly in the middle of the spacious room and spread out on the floor in front of it is a broad, silky white oriental rug with a colorful mosaic pattern. The rug's edge extends to a minimalist nineteen-fiftyish oak coffee table upon which sits a retro tin lamp and a black and white photo book on architecture. French tapestry with a fine willowy texture covers large windows in a way that tempts the eyes to gaze out over the magical city, steeped richly in history.

Alan falls into retinal ecstasy as he catches a glimpse of the sun melting beyond the cityscape. Through the intricate designs of an office building's apex, one can visually roam verdant hills that frame the Edinburgh cityscape. In the distance stand ruins of ancient castles that bespeak a medieval underpinning or fabric that is distinctly Scotland. Knights in shining armor had once galloped through land that is now a bustling metropolis. Businessmen and women scurry along paved roads that cover ancient battlefields where valiant clans had violently clashed. The perennial mythologies of elves and spirits are now transmuted into modern day superstitions of placing crosses on the walls of houses and dangling in the rear view mirrors of cars. In the city there is a vibrancy and easily discernible heartbeat that permeate the insides of the buildings. Alan picks up on a kindness and a passion toward living that the Scots exemplify like no others. He feels safe in this city of Edinburgh and thankful for the Scottish genetic contribution to his make-up.

He lies back upon the bed and slips into a daydream. Philosophy had always been a companion to Alan, but he isn't sure where it had ever gotten him. Being in the exotic location of Europe has generally stimulated in him an interest or proclivity toward asking himself questions about everything: from how we got here to where we are going and what higher purpose or design exists, if any. Arriving in Edinburgh and being at the threshold of his reunion with Ronia, Alan's thoughts are stimulated and driven for whatever reason by the burning curiosity for knowing and understanding the various purposes for living: the ones that people hold true.

He forms a ledger in his mind upon which he lists some of the reasons or drives that seem to keep people living. The list starts with things like: love, money, power, lust and continues with: creative fulfillment, artistic and aesthetic appreciation, pure unbridled fun, and religious satisfaction. He wonders if all desire was quelled or suspended in humans, would they merely die? He begins to consider the strange desire that must go into building and the construction of buildings that will long outlive their designers and developers. Is this just another example, like parenting sometimes is, of humans attempting to achieve immortality through what they can create? Alan quickly makes a mental leap to the desire that for many is all-important, namely, the religious pursuits; including the idea of reaching some sort of ethereal, heavenly place for all eternity based on their performance or behavior here on Earth.

Alan juxtaposes this concept with the quantum physics notion of divine play or chaos, in which what we are experiencing at any given moment is simply a nuance, variation, or theme in a grand production that involves an infinite number of atoms dancing, prancing, and intermingling in ever multidimensional ways. Can humans ever be truly happy accepting that this whole process is based on randomness, a roll of the dice, so to speak, in the great cosmic casino hall? Alan pictures an enormous casino— thousands of times larger than the MGM in Vegas— in which the great cosmic instigator occasionally deals a hand or cashes chips in the divine drama of life. As the planets rotate and revolve, so does the Roulette wheel as millions of players pick their choices or numbers in the game of life. Just as there are varying hierarchies within the Las Vegas game—such as, player, booker, dealer, guard, and casino owner, so throughout the universe could there be varying hierarchies of life forms vying for disparate rewards and reinforcers to keep them going.

"Desire... What a strange thing," Alan wonders. It can drive a man to love. It can drive a man to create. It has even driven men to kill. If Prajna in Buddhism necessitates the extinguishing of desire, does that ensuing enlightenment necessitate death? If we ascetically deny ourselves pleasures, are we closer to understanding? Or does the relentless pursuit of every carnal, spiritual, and artistic high known to man achieve the same result? Alan ponders the deviant fundamentalist Christian who resolutely denies himself the fruits of the world in order that he may see paradise upon death. Alan contrasts this man with the unrepentant hedonist who shuns any spiritual transcendence in opting for a temporal, self-indulgent path. Who is really better off? Alan ponders the bleak existential dilemma of our inherent isolation in an unforgiving, uncomforting world, a state that is sometimes mitigated by the attachments familiar to the dichotomous set of men he considers. Through spiritual strivings, man feels satiated and transcendent. Through giving in to one's physical and materialistic strivings, man is concomitantly satisfied. Alan thinks back to his childhood, in which he was sent to learn the Christian path. He quiescently accepted the basic tenets and absorbed them into his psyche. Were they simply words imparted by well-intentioned elders who simply tried to pass on what they considered reality for what was really misinformation and misinterpretation? Or was it divine law truly vouchsafed to man? In his early adulthood, Alan had read *Anna Karenina,* by Tolstoy, and with fondness recalls the lines exchanged by Lewin and the priest:

"'Do you believe in all the teachings of the Holy Apostolic Church?' the priest went on, turning his eyes away from Lewin's face and folding his hands beneath his stole. 'I have doubted everything, and I still do,' Lewin replied in a voice he himself found unpleasant, and fell silent."

Alan ponders the notion that the idea of God—as promulgated by the Judeo-Christian-Islamic laws—can be considered merely that, an idea or concept. One's safety net is, in a sense, pulled out from under him; giving rise to the notion of an acrobat hurtling through a decidedly differently structured—if at all structured—circus of a universe. This is considered by many to be a very liberating, comforting notion in itself while to others it is horrifying. Is there meaning or is there no meaning? Does meaning come from asking if there is any meaning? Alan begins to build layers of questions that he feels are partly a result of stream of consciousness and partly logic and rationality. The anticipation and excitation of seeing Ronia soon are launching Alan into a philosophical reverie that bounces from subject to subject like a pinball. He smokes a joint and within a couple of hours falls asleep. Soon he will be reunited with Ronia—not in his dreams—but in Aristotelian, objective, linear reality.

The next day, he arrives at the airport freshly bathed, shaven, and with the slight scent of fresh Italian cologne. The airport is delightfully European—delightfully international—as realized by the numerous postings of destination and arrival cities from all over the world, particularly Europe. Alan scans diverse skin colors and facial structures of the ticket agents and sundry ground personnel while relishing the overall multicultural exoticism to the place. He locates, on one of the information boards, Ronia's flight from London, noticing that it is due to arrive on time. Being thirty minutes early, he waits patiently at her gate and watches with wondrous amusement the truly multidimensional forms of humans exemplified on representative display in an airport.

Choosing a seat that has optimum viewing capabilities, he quickly begins to peruse the myriad masses: hordes of people shuffling through the terminals like cattle. He notices fat people—very fat people—and skinny people: gaunt, emaciated, downright famished people. He observes bearded people, people with hats, people with long hair and people with no hair. He sees stunning, fashionable, and beautiful people who don the trendiest European fashions and he witnesses horrific displays of hopelessly outdated, misfitting ensembles that pathetically cover aesthetically devoid, unrepentantly corpulent, helplessly unkempt frames. He pores over people in jeans, slacks, dresses, overalls, business suits, shorts, t-shirts, skirts, sweaters and leather jackets—all representing various shades of blues, greens, reds, yellows, and grays.

Black is a common color theme among many of the clothes and Alan is sure that any Parisian fashion consultant would have a field day dispensing proclamations of alternate stamps of approval and vehement disgust for what can be seen. Alan takes particular interest in low-cut shirts and dresses on women, looks that sophisticatedly expose emerging, shapely cleavage. As he takes additional interest in shapely, curvy hips and waists, he feels that he is not so much participating in a sexist, voyeuristic exploitation of women but actually engaging in the most promising aesthetic ritual that has ever evolved from the higher cerebral cortex—an appreciation and adulation for the female form. It moves the hormones and other chemicals in his body in an ostensible fashion as he cradles within his field of vision the sight of a nice, muscular soft nape and buttocks of a frame that moves angelically. To watch a woman walk in an elegant, smooth motion like this, is always something that Alan treasures. It is often a moment of calm, a moment of transcendence from everyday concerns. To see a beautiful, shapely woman carry herself in confident, sensual repose is to Alan not base, blue-collar amusement. It is the highest form of visual art.

As he retinally parades through the crowd, he begins to imaginatively replace the overall modern forms of dress on the crowd with styles and fashions from other centuries. He imagines Egyptian loincloths, Semite mosaic dresses, and Minoan tiered skirts. Greek chitons replace Laura Ashley sundresses. Byzantine draped tunics cover flesh normally concealed by baggy Levis and flannel shirts. Intricate tunics with multiple folds encompass frames that normally don t-shirts and shorts. Colorful hooped skirts, broad-brimmed hats, frilled cuffs, and laced bodies can now be seen all around. The women carry delicate, Oriental fans and the men carry rifles and walking sticks. Alan is suddenly awakened by the announcement of the arrival of Ronia's flight. His heart begins to beat wildly and a quick shiver races over his spine. He watches closely as the ticket agents open the jet bridge doors and the passengers begin to trickle out. One by one, exiting passengers are being greeted by friends, business associates, and relatives. All are completely unfamiliar faces to Alan as he waits patiently for his nymph, siren, and muse. Anticipation breeds nervousness, excitement, and mounds of adrenaline that well inside him as he holds his breath and awaits the heavenly sight of his angel.

Despite himself, fragmentary tears of joy simmer around the edge of his eyelids and moisten the corneal structure of his ocular sensory awareness. Eternities slowly elapse before he peers through an extension of the line that curiously contains a cowboy, an Indian guru, and a stoical, highly repressed looking businessman.

Behind them all, in satiny blond curls, glowing, smiling countenance and shiny black leather jacket, emerges Ronia, in such a composition of radiance that makes Alan believe she is combustible. A blood-red warmth pervades his body and face as he anticipates her touch. When she is free to rush to him she takes advantage with glee and exuberance, literally running up to him and throwing her arms around his neck. He holds her closely as he glows with pride at the peripheral sight of men gawking, seemingly unable to take their eyes of Ronia. "How are you doing my love?" she implores, before sliding her hand over his left cheek and kissing him on his right. With his arms tightly around her, he answers her with an intimate, caressing kiss that gently places the side of her mouth and part of her cheek within the sphere of his lips. He savors each moment of touch and smell—the aromatic, velvety perfection of porous fiber in her skin. Feeling at this moment that he could devour her, he is upon further speculation disappointed that this is a virtual impossibility. "I have missed you dearly," he utters in a half-hearted fashion; for he believes through touch he is conveying everything. She smiles ebulliently and informs him that she has a checked bag. He grabs the bag she is carrying and they begin to walk to the baggage claim area. "I've arranged a hotel in town and I think you're really going to love the city," Alan somewhat nervously informs her. "Alan, that sounds wonderful. I am so glad to see you. It seems like it has been eons since I have. Cosmic forces have kept us away but they have divined that we should be together again. I am sure." He pulls her closer with his arm wrapped around her waist as they make their way through the exit doors that lead to baggage claim.

When they collect her bag, they depart the airport and drive into downtown Edinburgh. The outline of the cityscape evokes a spark in Ronia as Alan clings to the highway as if he has driven here his entire life. The city is teeming with life as Alan has the uncanny realization that it is divinely ordained that they should be together—in this time and place. Enraptured by the closeness of their bodies and the resurgence of neural connections that had been dormant, Alan is biased against articulating anything with spoken word, but he feels there is not much else to do in order to absorb more of her essence.

"So how was the flight?" he asks. "It was fine. It was smooth—not much turbulence, thankfully." "That's good. How are Auntie and Uncle?" "They're fine. They're not completely apprised of everything that's going on, but nor am I, so I guess it doesn't matter." "I love your spontaneity," Alan replies. "Considering I've been surfing the rays of cosmic consciousness, merriment, and chaos, I don't suppose it hurts if you'd like to come along. Hopefully, your research affairs are in order." "They are. I've wrapped things up for the time being and am thrilled to have some time off to relax—other than the moments in which I'll be savagely groping you and hopefully taking you to the heights of pleasure, that is."

Hormonal balances are shifting within Alan like a flame burning a cinder around every new word that she speaks. The clouds have parted and deposited through invisible rains this droplet of spunk, energy, lust, intellect, and voluptuousness. She is heaven made manifest through feminine exceptionality: everything desirable and good in the world with French blood pumping in the veins. Alan hangs on her every word and takes momentary respite from listening to audible ambrosia only to shift his vortex of pleasure to the gazing into crystalline, pleasantly icy cerulean eyes. God exists, and Ronia is incontrovertible, axiomatic proof.

The car barrels past bucolic cottages nestled in the valleys and plains that surround Edinburgh. He takes a long, scenic route through winding country roads traced with rows of oaks and fields that flourish with buoyant sunflowers and grazing cattle. He points out to her noteworthy sights as if he is thoroughly versed in this land and has lived here for centuries.

As they soar along the main highway into town, she turns toward Alan and asks: "What have you been doing with yourself?" "Well, I've been traveling through this country with my head basically in the clouds, my mind fixed on the road, and my heart terminally on you." She smiles with a radiance that simultaneously chills and warms the soul. "I didn't mean for you to talk about me silly," she responds lovingly. "But it's certainly okay that you deviated from my expectations, of course," she adds as she delicately strokes his right cheek and fingers his bangs before pulling them back gently from his eyes.

Sensing not only her embarrassment but also her frustration, he goes on: "I've been exploring the Great British rural mindset and landscape. I've made mental and written notes along the way and probably had one or two knock down, drag out revelations along the way. I've seen brilliant contrasts between what would be colloquially referred to as archaic, ancient elements to the place and the differing novel, innovative, modern developments that have propelled Europe blisteringly toward the 21st century. I've entertained divine ponderings over the state of human consciousness in relation to the state of the cosmos and I've spoken to people about some of the most mundane, matter-of-fact topics you could imagine."

Suddenly, Alan swerves to miss a white object—that looks like a cat—blowing across the road. It turns out to be a bag. He feels his pulse quicken and his heart race. Gradually building and regaining speed, he continues: "I've been referring back to my book on mysticism from time to time and gleaning insights which I subsequently integrate into my view of the places and people I encounter. It's as if my frame of reference and locus of consciousness is constantly colored and flavored by the mystical ponderings. Each place that I go seems to affect me in a different way; chemically, intellectually, and spiritually." Ronia smiles and leans to kiss him.

They soon arrive at the hotel. He grabs her bags and leads her through the Baroque corridor and spiraling staircase up to their room. If anything, the hotel magically encapsulates the dichotomous nature of the city, geometrically and poetically coalescing both old and new in a sort of yin and yang harmony. He unlocks the door, pushes it back, and allows Ronia to step through the threshold. She enters the room with some hesitance, allowing her senses to grow gradually in touch with the odd, but aesthetic array of furnishings and art that fills the space.

"Alan, this place is so, how do you say it, bizarre. I love it." He closes the door and sets the bags down. She runs to the windows and looks out over the city that is bustling with the erratic, busy hum of the day. "Alan, I want some Cappuccino." Okay, let's go get some Cappuccino." "I need to do something first, however," she speaks in a surreptitious manner that taunts him.

She assertively slithers up to him, pushes him back on the bed, and descends her lips to his like a cat to milk, first observing the intended delicacy, then closing her eyes and leaning to commence the lap of gustatory pleasure. As she straddles his waist with her petite legs and firm buttocks, Alan becomes erect and his hardness presses comfortably into the vortex of her thighs. His hands slide caressingly along her back and buttocks as the silky lips of her mouth undulate with the moisture in his and she gradually relinquishes the strain to stay hovered above him.

She lets go and falls lightly into his body. Intermittently, she pulls her head back in order to gaze into his eyes, that serve as media for him to visually plunge into the dainty, yet luscious figure that she cuts. He had forgotten in her absence the softness and translucence of her skin and the breathtaking contours of her body. He deeply inhales the fragrance of her hair like a starved opium addict reunited with the burning, spicy scent of his sacrament. She bends her back like a half moon curve of the rubber tube in an opium pipe that bends willingly to the one who gratefully envelopes the mouthpiece and sucks in the transforming essence of hedonistic rapture.

With the fingers on his left hand dexterously unfastening her belt and unbuttoning her jeans, his right hand slides along the curve of her lower back before slipping into the satiny lace of her panties. He can feel her breathing more heavily and becoming more vigorous in her kissing. As he slides her jeans off and then her panties, she tilts her head back to expose her creamy neck to his kiss, while she pulls his pants down and mounts him with slow incremental movements—movements that systematically titillate his nerve endings with alternate contractions and moist, cool, and warm gyrations of flesh. She envelopes him into the folds of her body and they lead each other into seismic, symphonic moans and palpitations of orgasm.

He holds her momentarily, while still inside her, as she strokes his arms and chest and cuddles his head on her shoulder. She revels in the strength and serenity of his body. "Will you tell me something?" he whispers. "What do you want to hear?" she asks as she smiles in response to his pleasantly quirky question. "Speak the first thing to come to mind." "Ummm, alright," she responds. "Before you come alive, life is nothing; it's up to you to give it a meaning, and value is nothing else but the meaning you choose." "Sartre?" "Yeah, Sartre," she hums in a mellifluous, soothing intonation that would have made Jean Paul more than proud.

The words ring in Alan's ear. As he lightly taps the curves of her virginal white buttocks with his fingertips, he marvels at the confluence of brains and beauty that are divinely manifested in Ronia. Alan cherishes her touch but also craves nicotine. He sits up and reaches for a cigar. She wraps a sheet around herself and joins him. Her hair is ruffled beautifully. As she casts a silhouette that permeates the sunrays spilling on the floor, Alan can understand how carcinogens are glamorous. "So what do you want to do today?" he asks. "Be with you and soak up the vibes of the city, dude." She giggles in a mischievous, loving elfish fashion. While choosing not to ask her how long she will be with him, Alan simply focuses on enjoying and savoring the day. He opens a window in order to allow the smoke to trickle out.

As he puffs on his cigar, he tells her how beautiful she is and then removes from the table a tourist guide that outlines activities in the Edinburgh area. He shows her advertisements depicting four star restaurants, swank museums, opera and ballet houses, and symphony options. Alan pontificates on the high-culture, upper echelon nature of the city that seems to have many of the amenities of a bastion of culture like Paris, France.

"Alan, I feel like doing something basic today such as taking a stroll through the park, watching the skyline, or just being together in the city, soaking everything up." "Those are my sentiments, exactly," Alan concurs. "Simplicity it is!" Ronia opens her bag and removes a dress. She drops the sheet and heads toward the bathroom. Her cigarette is still lit and it dangles from between two of her fingers on her right hand, which swings rhythmically as she sashays nakedly with her back facing Alan.

He studies the way the light from outside shines in and illuminates the elegant contour of her spine and the sensual ripple of muscles that lines her back from the nape of her neck to the shoulder blades—through the delicate framework of her mid-back—and down to the soft curve at the apex of her buttocks. Her legs are lean and shapely and she walks in a sort of confident stride that bespeaks the myths of Athenian goddesses.

Leaving the door to the bathroom open, she begins to run some water for a shower. Alan steps a little to his left in order to watch as she opens the shower door and melodically immerses herself in the steaming water. Although fully sated in his post coital state, there is something quite magical about being in this room with a richly burning Cuban cigar and a beautiful French girl—something that seems to go beyond physiological rapture.

He puts the cigar out in the ashtray and begins to dress. He orders Cappuccino through room service and then retrieves his original book on mysticism. While turning to the bookmarked page, he audibly tunes into the hypnotic sound of the water falling in the bathroom.

He begins to read: "He felt that society... Wait a minute," Alan wonders. "Who is 'he'?" So he scans a few sentences up and remembers he had left off at Alan Watts. Alan continues to read: "He felt that society placed a vicious double bind on the individual by making it appear to the individual that society's commands were the individual's innermost thoughts or self. When God says, 'Ye shall love your neighbor as yourself,' this is a futile proposition. To love is to be spontaneous and one cannot be forced into being spontaneous. A similar situation occurs in cases of schizophrenia. A child is beaten as she is being told that she is loved. This horribly ambivalent message creates a no-win situation for her. In order to be one with one's self and one's surroundings, there must be freedom and consistency between thoughts and occurrences. For many, this liberation is achieved by transforming consciousness toward a mystically enlightened state." Alan closes the book just as the shower is being turned off.

"Alan, darling, this apartment is awesome!" "It is pretty cool, isn't it? Wait until you see the courtyard downstairs," he replies. His senses are alert from the nicotine and his body is pleasantly sore from the sex. A refreshing wind periodically blows through, infusing the room with fresh supplies of oxygen. Alan listens as Ronia goes about getting prepared. The welcome sounds of hairspray, makeup application, perfume bottles, hairdryer and brushes remind Alan of the serenity and joy that only living with a woman can bring.

"Alan, darling, I'll only be a minute," she mentions, as she steps into the living room to retrieve some clothes. They both hear three knocks on the door. "What's that?" "It's just the guy with the Cappuccino. I'll get it."

He makes sure that Ronia steps back into the bathroom before he answers the door. He tips the attendant two American dollars and then sets the drinks down on the table. "Alan, you sweetheart," drifts the soft voice from the bathroom. "Do you want cream and sugar?" he asks. "Yeah, a little of both, please. Thank you." Within minutes, she emerges in a burgundy and white cotton dress that hugs the curves of her body. She leans to kiss him before picking up her Cappuccino and sipping lightly. Alan takes a sip from his and then rushes to get ready in the bathroom. When he is done, he throws on some jeans and a button-down shirt before noticing that Ronia is leafing through the book he had purchased from the voodoo shop.

"Finding anything interesting?" he asks. "As a matter of fact, I've just been scanning over the intriguing notion, which was actually discussed at a symposium here in Edinburgh back in the 1800s: 'that the self is the so-called supra-individual ground of man's consciousness, the field or continuum in which man experiences the world.' It goes on to speak of the perplexing concern of what happens when we die, in terms of whether death is total annihilation of that center of being or if it's simply a quelling or transforming of that particular essence into a larger whole that continues to think, feel, and generally perceive. The coffee's good by the way; just the right amount of richness with a touch of Mocha." "Did you say Moksha?" Alan inquires, sarcastically. "I wonder how my friend Peter and his Moksha Revellers are doing, by the way." "Oh, you just reminded me."

She sets the book down and dashes to one of her bags, through which she quickly scours and comes up with a colorful advertisement that reads: "Party For The People: An Intergenerational, International Love Fest concert featuring Smokes on Dopes, Starphase, the Trashcan Picassos, Galactica, and the Moksha Revellers." "It's coming up in a couple of weeks. It's taking place at a racetrack outside of Dublin and I knew that you'd want to know about it." "That is so cool!" Alan exclaims.

"We've got to go!" he blurts, without thinking about the implication that she will still be with him. He sets the leaflet down and picks up his backpack. As they lock the door and head for the lobby, they resume their talk about the self: "So, Ronia, the debate mentioned involved the individual self with the greater self—the atma with Brahma. I suppose that one can differentiate between the self in man and the infinite self but perhaps the two are actually one in the same." "I think that this lecture dealt with both the divergence and convergence of the self and selves. It seems the participants were open-minded to all possibilities. It sort of makes one—or all—wonder if we simply emerge from the void, take on individual characteristics, smile, laugh, and cry for a while and then simply return from where we came. Or, perhaps, we rise again in various manifestations as new forms of life or energy: matter transubstantiated."

Alan leads her to the spectacle of the courtyard and describes to her its nocturnal magic. "Wow, this is pretty cool. How did you ever find this hotel?" "I did a little research and systematically narrowed down my choices until this one stuck out as the logical, or delightfully illogical choice. It reminds me of a David Lynch film. It doesn't make sense—that's why I love it."

He continues, as they walk around the pool: "You mentioned the Void. I love that expression, the Void. It's interesting that as conscious, sentient beings that are true fulfillments or evolutionary exemplars of matter, we can nevertheless conceive of nothingness: the absence of matter as we know it—the Void. I always picture a black hole when I conceive the Void but I suppose any picture at all is inadequate." She giggles and then responds: "The idea that we came from nothing is quite contrary to the Biblical concept of the Creator. But I suppose it isn't too difficult, come to think of it. That version involves an origin in dust and ribs, quite humble beginnings, anyway." "But at least something. At least matter," Alan proudly proclaims. "The notion that we could have come from some higher intelligence—whether God-like or alien-like—is truly a perplexing notion to grasp. It covers the whole spectrum and any possibility seems miraculous and quite bizarre," he adds.

CHAPTER 19

They walk through the corridor leading out into the street. The sun shines warmly through misty, displaced cloud cover and otherwise cerulean, deep sky. They begin to walk along the sidewalk in the general direction of the lush hillside that carries the castle at its apex. In the foreground, of course, stands the impressive National Gallery of Scotland, that on this day contains hundreds of passers-by moving in all directions. "God, this city is beautiful," Ronia rejoices. "Look at the houses on the thoroughfare over there. They are the reason Edinburgh is called 'Auld Reekie,' meaning 'Old Smoky'," she adds.

Alan enjoys the facile way in which Ronia can segue between such diverse topics as the philosophy of the soul to the history of Edinburgh. He pulls her from the smoky aesthetic of the homes back to the haunting, atomistic aesthetic of the Void. "So, as corporeal entities floating through a universe, the design and meaning of which is a hopelessly unsolvable mystery, can we not at least expect to know where we go when we shed our mortal coils and shuffle off our bags of limbs?" "I suppose we shall never 'know' if the 'knower' that moves on becomes swallowed by an infinite knower or simply returns to that of which it was always an integral part or manifestation." She adds: "Will the 'I' that now questions ever truly answer the question if the answer to the question is in the very dissolution of the 'I'? I don't know." They let out an uproarious laugh.

The perfect happiness and meaninglessness of the moment with her is in a sense better than knowledge. Alan stops questioning and pondering long enough to as fully as feels possible relish the tangible essence and pleasure of simply "being" with her. The whys and the hows of the situation—him being with her—are eclipsed by the direct perception of its very happening. Whether this perception is simply a process of a small self or a much more vast entity seems incidental. Whether the seeming of it as being incidental is a process of a small self or the grand self, it really, objectively doesn't matter. Anyone would agree.

The two lovers stroll off the sidewalk and down along the grassy valley between the Gallery and the Castle. They throw their coffee cups in the trash and find a somewhat secluded spot near a tree where they recline for a few moments. Although full of energy, there is something calling them to become idle for a while and soak up their surroundings. "So, your research projects are in order and you decided to come join me in the Scottish hills. I'm absolutely delighted." "This much is true, and I might add that I'm very glad to be here. You know, Alan..." She rests her head on his shoulder. "I wasn't quite sure when I originally made plans to come see you exactly how much time I'd be able to spend or how much you'd like me to spend. At the last minute before I left, I realized that it's pretty flexible, um, how much time my sabbatical or time between semesters can be. Basically, this coming semester will involve a lot of autonomy for me. I'll be able to construct pretty much an independent project that will allow me to work at somewhat of a distance if I want."

Alan takes a moment to allow the words to sink in. He has hoped that Ronia would be able to come see him and the idea—as implied through her words; that she can share with him his adventure for a lengthy time— makes him immensely excited. He thinks carefully before he speaks to her. "I am going to be continuing my sojourn over to the mainland and without imposing any pressure on you, I would be elated if you would join me." It suddenly occurs to Alan that he not only has a love affair with this woman, but he is also slowly falling in love with the part of his imagination that conceives a mystical journey in which the two lovers travel far and wide geographically and within themselves.

Through the use of meditation, exercise, nutrition, psychedelics, academic study, poetry, alchemy, and European travel, they will ascend and evolve to a level that will be meta or supra human. They will commune happily and raucously with that divine essence—that eternal self; that creator of everything and nothing; that ineffable, cosmic trigger of solar system synchronicity and chaos. Two souls will coexist intertwined with senses united, not divided, while delving majestically into that moon swept dark blue oceanic underworld of the great sylvan abyss. They will travel briskly over mountains and seas with destinations, perhaps never known, but always with the driving, relentless passion to hopelessly inundate and transubstantiate themselves with the eternal now. Celestial mathematics and the harmony of the natural senses will serve as guideposts into uncharted vistas of intergalactic delight. Brilliant sunsets and honeydew rains will make them forget all life's tragedies and monstrosities. They will openly laugh in the face of violent aberrations of nature, open their arms across the Milky Way and gladly embrace the cosmic genetic plan. Any consideration for ultimate outcome will be rendered perfectly obsolete. They will forget themselves by indulging themselves.

Before she can answer him, he quickly but gently stands up, cradles her head and firmly lifts her as he rises. "Come on, let's go," he says. He grabs her hand and they are off to see the city.

First grabbing a trolley, they make their way to Old Town's Royal Mile, with its cobbled roads and intriguing arts and crafts shops. They walk around and imagine themselves in the 1500's and then the 1600's. The sun shines brightly upon the city streets, while casting iridescent glares off bikes and motorcycles parked on the curbs. Next to a cobbler's shop, young mothers leisurely stroll, pushing baby carts and talking casually about politics and the weather. Across the street sits a bustling ice cream parlor that has its doors open and several tables in front on the sidewalk. Large parasols shelter those seated from the comfortably bright but ice cream-melting effects of the sun. "Do you want some ice cream?" "Sure," Alan replies.

"A scoop of chocolate will be cool." They walk in and come out with two chocolate ice creams. Without much conscious decision making, they head in the direction of an ominous, smoky Gothic church that sits nestled between two modern office buildings about a half mile down the road. Alan is once again in the presence of a woman and pleasurably succumbs to the warmth and contentment that he had missed while they were apart. As he licks on the icy, dripping chocolate, he transfixes his gaze onto the porcelain skin that paints her beautifully sculptured high-cheekboned face. When she moves, it is as if she becomes a physical embodiment of the so-called physics chatter happening all around them. With fluid grace and composure she holds her head in elegant repose as the silky locks of gold angelically frame the mouth and lips that succu-lently consume her treat. He tactfully takes notice of the differing man-ners in which they walk: him with a strong, resolute stride and her with a balletic, delicate prance. Again, her rigorous and adept intellect strikes resonant counterpoint with her physical softness and beauty. Physically, she is vital and ebullient, but only in the sense that a rose evokes power or a mandolin "rocks." Both objects—the rose and the mandolin—pos-sess the latent capacity to create alternate effects, but only beneath the veneer and conception of another intention. Subtle and misleading, the relative suppleness and grace of a woman often masks a virile robustness in physicality—an inherent capacity toward strength which is often overlooked.

Feeling the antiquated cobblestone beneath their feet serves as a welcome reminder that there had been life outside of the 20th century—a life perhaps more substantive. Privilege is a word that comes to mind as they walk on a surface very different than staid, corrugated, 20th century industrial concrete. The so-called benefits that we all supposedly enjoy in the present more industrialized world seem somehow unimportant when considered while taking steps on a path more edifying and aesthetically stimulating—that of the 15th century.

"Alan, look to the east." Ronia points to the eastern sky and smiles a smile that could sail ships. In the distance, hovering majestically over the city, are two hot air balloons—one orange and the other blue—floating in unison through the clouds like great protectors. Alan ponders these orbs that float in a manner that seems to foreshadow the future of aviation technology, while reflecting elements of aviation history.

Balloons hover in a manner not dissimilar to an eagle or a hawk, combining the best elements of flight that occur spontaneously in nature. Coalescing the fluid, progressive strokes of a mallard with the soaring elegance of the albatross, a balloon seems more a variation or nuance of nature made manifest through flight, than an artifact imposed by man onto the fathomless vastness of sky.

Boldly renouncing the arrogant attempt to control nature or build against it—a balloon, more than any other flying machine—is constructed to merge with the winds and allow them to dictate the manner in which it traverses its course. The one who flies a hot air balloon must be sensitive to the climate around him as much as the internal functions of his flying machine. Alan recalls that hydrogen, the lightest of all gases, lifts ninety-three percent of the weight of the air displaced. He knows that hydrogen is highly flammable and can create explosions with certain mixtures of air. He recalls that helium is chemically inert and non-flammable. When ninety eight percent pure, it lifts eighty four percent of the weight of the displaced air. "Balloons are amazing, aren't they?" Alan asks Ronia. "Yes, they are. They are spectacular," Ronia exclaims. "It's pretty incredible how they move." Alan feels she has been reading his mind.

"Have you read anything about the dynamics of their flight?" Alan asks.

"Yeah, I know that gas contained in an elastic balloon expands when heated or brought to a higher altitude where the air exerts less pressure.

When it becomes full and taut, the added expansion builds an overpressure that expels some of the gas through a hole in the bottom. Sometimes that's when they have to throw the ballast on sandbags out to reestablish equilibrium. I know the gas should be the same temperature as the outside air." "Wow, the Ph.D. is yours!" Alan responds. He adds: "Did you know that in 1650, a Jesuit monk named, Francesco de Lana, proposed that a hollow sphere from which all air had been pumped would rise into the air, similar to how a bubble rises through water. The problem was finding a weightless container that had adequate strength; of course, reversing the idea led to the balloon." "Wasn't it a Frenchman who first traveled in a balloon?" she asks.

"Sure was," Alan replies. "I think his name was Jean Francois de Rozier back in the late seventeen hundreds." "Alan, what would you do if you were flying in a balloon?" "After quickly overcoming my fear of heights, I guess I would fly as far as I could and gaze out over the land below me and observe with great interest the varying topography and the miniature people going about their business. I'd also sit back and fritter away my days with a fully stocked supply of wine, cheese, and something to smoke, preferably something mind expanding. What about you?" She places her forefinger on her chin in studious repose and rolls her eyes until both her pupils fixate on the balloons. She giggles and smiles effusively while her cheeks redden slightly, before answering:

"I'd probably hop into the basket and sail into the far reaches of the sky, hoping to stop off at the peaks of some of the world's most impressive mountains like the Alps and the Himalayas. I would stop for a cup of tea, leave a little flag with my name on it, and then sail on into the sky." Alan feels a chill up his spine as the wind picks up.

He and Ronia approach the church with some caution and immense intrigue. The doors are large, ironclad wooden planks surrounded by bronze panels, which depict various images of Jesus carrying the cross and being crucified. Pointed arches lined with myriad, elaborately designed geometric patterns are the apertures that funnel in cascades of light from both sides of the door. Towering spires that mirror giant redwoods in a forest erupt from the roof. On one outside wall, depicted in stone relief, is a ship with flowing sails. On another wall are a series of sculptures with images depicted in exquisite detail: images of shivering men with shaven heads and flowing tunics. On all sides of the structure, there are multitudinous forms of windows in stained red, pink, yellow, and green glass. The overall color of the church is a dark charcoal and black that speaks of centuries of weather, burnings, wars, and pollution.

A lofty, monolithic central spire emerges from the front—an ominous but victorious signal that this structure had been built with the infinite in mind.

After ascending the flight of twenty steps that leads to the entrance, Alan and Ronia are amazed to find a schedule posted on the door informing passers-by and regulars of services being held weekly at the church. As Alan pulls back the sturdy, creaking door, he and Ronia notice that the inside is relatively devoid of people. Several rows of pews lead to an altar barely visible through the illumination of multidimensional rays of color that refract mystically from the windows before landing in giant streams across the aisle.

Alan notices an hourglass configuration of stone that stands in the backdrop of the altar and encloses in its upper opened position a large cross that is inlaid with various colored gems between strips of bronze. The structure glimmers as the door swings periodically open.

A silence and dustiness shuffle the emotional cards into a dimension of quietude and introspection. Alan can hear his heartbeat in rhythm with Ronia's delicate steps as they meander through only the foyer of the church, afraid to venture further. On a long rectangular mahogany table to the left sits a dazzling collection of photographs and sketches of Gothic churches that represent styles from England, Belgium, Germany, Spain, and France. Several pieces of smoky parchment paper contain text; upon closer inspection, Alan can make out vivid descriptions of the decorative elements in some of the churches.

He reads: "Enrichment and elaboration of style. Mirrored structure. Sentinel-like pinnacles capped buttresses and receding moldings of doorways were supported by clonnettes interwoven with amazing figures of saints and angels. Arched tympanums covered the doorways and windows evolved into bar traceries and stone bars." The esoteric language is interestingly strange to Alan. He reads about "H" shaped lead cames and "X" ribbed vaultings. He peruses the narratives casually, until he gets to a section on the design of gargoyles. He slows down his reading and focuses on digesting the information as he learns that gargoyles have been fashioned into various arrays of animal and plant forms. "Hey Ronia, look at this."

He motions for her to come over. She tears herself away from studying a painting of a 13th century monk to see what Alan is talking about. "Yeah, what's going on?" she asks. "It's talking here about the formation of gargoyles which seems strange to me, given we're in the midst of Christian surroundings. I don't know. Something about their spooky, dark, ominous overtones seems a little more diabolical than what I would think acceptable to conservative Christian orthodox sensibilities." "I know it seems paradoxical at first," Ronia responds.

She continues: "Didn't you one time mention to me back in England something about the belief existent among some Medievals that God—or the divine—is often exemplified most aptly in that which is grotesque, monstrous, or almagamatedly perverse?" "There are certain piots who did portray through visual art such curious phenomena as: part human, part animal mutations; mythological oddities like gryphons with tails of bows and arrows, odd-looking dwarfs, combinations of dragonflies and lizards, and chimeras and sea sirens. The seminal writer, Umberto Eco, has poetically captured the essence of this idea in his novel, *The Name of the Rose*. I've got to tell you, though. There's something about these little devilish creatures that seems incongruous with the angelic icons of Christianity." "I suppose it underscores the theme of opposites, the theme of extremes and incongruities—that points to some higher truth." "I think you're right, sweetie." Alan leans and kisses her on her forehead. The sweet smell of her perfume, intermixed with her natural aromas, provides welcome olfactory pleasure in the midst of such a musty place.

He takes her by the hand and leads her to the opposing wall, which is lined with several paintings. Elegant, realistic portrayals of saints and venerated monks depict solemn, dedicated expressions surrounded by soft, glowing colors that enhance an ethereal, or otherworldly nature to the portraits. Alan is impressed that a place with such measurable wealth, in the form of priceless art and relics, can remain unlocked, unattended, and unviolated.

Suddenly, one can hear the voices of Swiss tourists who have entered behind them. Alan asks Ronia if she is ready to leave and she motions for them to go. They push the monumental door back and descend into the brightly sunlit streets. On their way back to the hotel to get the car, Alan asks a policeman for a recommendation for a good Italian restaurant. The lovers retrieve their car and drive up to a place called Sal's. They enter the restaurant and scan the menu before placing an order to go: two plates of rotelle pasta with marinara sauce, half a loaf of garlic bread, and a bottle of French Cabernet.

Jumping back into the car, they proceed to barrel up Princes Street while making sharp twists and turns, before arriving at a lush, heavily shaded park that overlooks a stream just outside of town. Alan pays attention to the precious silence that is broken only by Ronia's intermittent, delicate breath. The pulse of the city is still within their perception but the park possesses a tranquillity more reminiscent of the countryside Alan had driven through in western rural Scotland.

They stop at a knoll that sits immersed in an almost tropical-looking setting commingling rocky, grassy trails of trickling springs and vibrant foliage-lined pond. A bevy of vibrant waterlilies floats on the surface. Alan and Ronia choose a secluded spot near a shaded brook and spread out the meal. Luckily, Ronia carries in her purse a portable corkscrew. She hands it to Alan with delight and watches animatedly as he pops the cork. Not having any wine glasses, they take turns drinking directly from the bottle. Biting into rich, spicy sauce and plump, juicy pasta, they savor the garlicky content that is copious to the point of quickly opening up pores and nasal passages. Zesty, tangy marinara sauce tantalizes the taste buds, which are soon bathed in a blissful torrent of Cabernet. Not having glasses doesn't really seem to matter. Gulping red wine from a bottle adds a welcome element of savagery and impulsivity to the otherwise serene picnic.

"Alan, will you please hand me that book on the mystical—not the voodoo reference guide—but the other one." "Sure." Alan reaches into the bag and removes a cigar and the book on mysticism. He hands the book to Ronia and lights the cigar for himself. She begins to read quietly to herself from the point where he had left off. Birds chirp high in the treetops and leaves rustle in seeming rhythm with the wind. Alan softly puffs on the cigar as he alternately watches Ronia and stares at the periodically rippling but mostly placid surface of the pond; and the interesting way the water trickles over lily pads, and leaves microscopic droplets resting on their tops like tiny universes of trillions of microbial forms. "Alan, can I read to you from the book?"

"Yes, I would love that. Only one thing: While you do that, I would like to concomitantly scribble down ideas in my notepad based on what your reading inspires—top of the head sort of stuff. Is that okay with you?" "Yeah, what an interesting game. Okay, here I go!" She takes a gulp from the bottle and wipes her mouth on a napkin, creating what to Alan looks like a stunning work of lusty, steamy surrealist art—a beautiful composition of smeared red lipstick with Cabernet. She reads: "While the sundry paths toward enlightenment are many, such as meditation, philosophical musings, and psychedelic substances, etc., the actual end result—whether it be newfound insight or profound anxiety—is often a precarious outcome."

Alan reaches into his bag and grabs the pad of paper and a pen. He quickly begins to write while sipping his wine and feeling the salubrious warmth of the sun's rays on his face: *"Rhythmic, undulating, pulsating, vacillating and transmigrating aurally stimulating nuances have smoothly and effervescently penetrated my blood brain membrane transporting whimsically, musically into a perpetually alternating and transcending universe; seemingly hovering, phantasmagorically elevating—vastly distancing—no mundane reality."* He stops and prompts Ronia, "Okay, continue reading please." Ronia speaks up: "Voluminous accounts of the mystical experience parallel dramatically case histories of schizophrenic hallucinations. When observing many individuals who have had intensive mystical experiences, we see persons who exude a marvelous ambience of calm, peacefulness, and adaptability; whereas a myriad of others who have crossed a similar threshold of consciousness appear lost in a haze of mindless, irrational chaos." Alan keeps writing: *"yet perfectly encapsulating geographical infinity—the coordinates of a circle with a center nowhere but a circumference everywhere—which brings me to the knowing of the not-knowing."* Ronia's voice begins to layer what he writes: "How is it that some individuals possess the ability to delve the inner reaches of their minds, returning with keen, rational, refreshed perception whereas others become irreversibly lost in a forest of obscurity?"

"Swallowing, dropping, falling, cumming slowly deeply cutting frailty encompassing none but enveloping all on an eternal whisper echoing down an infinite tunnel brushing cusping sanctuary sought in a Vietnamese brothel scouring dripping fasting gripping slipping through death's clutching on a spiraling organic rocket..." "When Thoreau and Emerson voluntarily renounced the world, withdrawing into the woods far removed from any social contact and deep into the introspective realm of the mystical, they not only avoided suffering any..."

"Forgiving nothing, forgetting everything from beginning to end in a heart-filled shell bent on bending, breaking, saving, destroying..." "impairment in their communicative..." *"calling, feeling, hearing the enemies and friends coming and going..."* "abilities but actually displayed a greater repertoire of language..." *"studying and confounding, weeping tremendously throughout an echo park..."* "Upon returning, many schizophrenics are apparently incapable..." *"Fast, fun, and furious; a frolicking ball rolling and fucking..."* "of executing the simplest of coherent sentences, whereas accomplished mystics shine with oratorical prowess..." *"reflecting and pacing, spawning and throwing an eternal knowing..."* "Teilhard de Chardin, an early Jesuit mystic, was quite adept at delineating..." *"and no-ing, passing, wiping, scouting, and*

impregnating—a spherical follicle floating to its meaning..." "the fine balance between conducting oneself in a "normal," practical manner while simultaneously pursuing..." *"overlapping and supplanting..."* "the divine..." *"Fidgeting and squeaking..."* "In The Divine Milieu he speaks..." *"scratching through mentating..."* "of finding God..." *"A passing and an ending..."* "in everyday pursuits..." *"into the knowing..."* "and finding..." *"of the not-knowing."*

"Whew!" Alan sets his pen down and Ronia stops reading. She has seen him frantically writing and is burningly curious to know what he has written. Equally, she is excited by what she has read. The delving into the unknown and the attempt at grasping the intangible is just what her brain needs in its wine-enhanced, receptive state. The sun shines brightly as they finish their meal and focus on the wine. "May I see what you wrote?" she asks. "Sure, let me clean it up a bit." Alan peruses the words to check for spelling accuracy on words like, "phantasmagorically," "encompassing," and "transmigrating." He then hands it over to Ronia. She pores over the words as if she has just discovered an ancient hieroglyphic text and is the only one privileged enough to study it. Her lips remain closed and only her eyes fluttering in saccadic waves reveal the intense neural activity being expended.

"Alan, this is a trip. Rhythmic, undulating, pulsating. Phantasmagorically elevating. Swallowing, dripping. Frolicking and fucking. Grinding. Cogitating. My God, this not only bespeaks practically the language of the universe, this reeks or, rather, pleasantly exudes, a most charmingly lustful and cosmic ambience. I don't know if it's the wine or the poem, but I've suddenly got the chills." Alan revels in pride. "Thanks, Ronia. I just sort of slipped into this state of—I don't want to say unconsciousness—but altered awareness of some sort, in which I felt that I was simply transcribing or emoting an experience and understanding that goes beyond me or my personality. It was quite cathartic to write, actually. Do you ever feel that way—that we're simply individual funnels or receptacles screening through material that is floating all about us, that Huxley's 'Mind-At-Large' concept holds true? Do you ever think that Platonic ideals or prototypes of thought actually exist as entities independent of the individual human brain?" Ronia stares at Alan in a deliberate, focused manner which suggests that she is attempting to comprehend the multifaceted elements of the question and marveling that Alan would compose a question in such a way. "Really, that is an interesting idea, that there are universal forms or ideas that exist as entities in a realm that the human brain is only able to tap into for periods of time, without actually tangibly grasping—universal forms that are seemingly and incongruously fleeting or only capable of being manipulated and perceived at critical times."

Alan can see in the distance a couple throwing a Frisbee. Beyond them is a soccer game taking place among two teams, one with brilliant orange jerseys and the other in navy blue. To the left of the brook stands a sculpture: a sort of water fountain depicting a monk, with hands clasped, head bowed, and a dove on his shoulder. Alan ponders the playfulness and serenity of the scene. Its bucolic and pastoral mood seems perfect for what he is about to recommend.

"Do you feel like tripping?" "I think you read my mind. Yeah, that sounds like fun." He reaches into his bag and removes the foil that contains the acid—the supply he had meticulously avoided until he was reunited with her. After glancing around to make sure no one is watching, he carefully unfolds and removes one tab that he promptly tears in half. "Yeah, that's all I want to do," she remarks while watching him with detail. He hands her the bottle and the half tab and she swishes it down. He places his piece on his tongue and lets it naturally dissolve for a few seconds before chasing it with Cabernet.

He lies back and supports his head with clasped hands. Ronia nestles her head close to him and closes her eyes. He had always noticed an idiosyncrasy to the words spoken between ingesting a psychedelic and the actual effects occurring. The words exchanged between participants always carried a shadow of anticipation and an excitable, celebratory, almost sacramental tone about them. It was as if the purpose of speaking during these intermittent moments was simply to fill time and make one last, ordinary human communication before stepping into the other world. Communication would still be possible once the drug took effect, but it would be of a wholly surreal, enriched, mystic-philosophic nature. At NASA, ground control always makes a ritualistic, obligatory gesture to the crew before a shuttle is launched. This is no different.

Alan strokes Ronia's hair softly and gently, running his fingers through the silky strands like they are of precious gold. Her cheeks are curvy, well-defined structures reminiscent of Parisian marble that had been skillfully chiseled and sanded over centuries with perfection of contour and smoothness in mind. Her neckline—which merges in beautiful, tendrilous waves of flesh into her cleavage—become slightly moistened with minuscule but aromatic droplets of sweat that heave in unison with the graceful arching of her chest.

The sounds of robins and bluejays chirping in the treetops become increasingly more audible: sonorous fragments that fall like sentient jewels in a basket of bliss. Visually, the tips of the branches on the limbs of the now shimmeringly emerald trees glisten and almost sparkle with magical reflections from the sun. While distinct, sharp perceptions become more in-tuned, a monolithic wall of silence and stillness pervades the rest of the frame of reference. Alan looks into the macrocosmic wonder of the lush conglomerations of leaves in multitudes of geometric, kaleidoscopic arrays: patterns of veins spreading through various shades of green like trails of spider web. Webs are spun skeletally to support the mass of leaves, which subsequently supports micro-organismic activity certainly not visible to the naked, sober eye. Alan imagines that each acorn and discarded cupule represents a soul emerging from the abysmal, sap-spawned, deep-rooted antiquity of tree life. Sylvan birth had gestated and unfurled these glorious orbs. Nuts of energy had blossomed into ovoid kernels that would shine in magnificent, teeming energy and shuffle and cast off their shells to become happily eaten by squirrels that had correspondingly evolved in the grand interplay of the life chain.

Alan leans his head toward Ronia and kisses her gently on the cheek. Immediately, he sinks in the rapturous void of consciousness brought on by the softness and blood-warmed skin of her face. Her entire body generates warmth and vitality that suddenly envelop all of his senses. Spontaneously, the universe incarnate lies there next to him in majestic distaff repose, a model or prototype of the vast celestial artwork that would soon illuminate the night sky. The cool wind is both haunting and soothing. As Alan's pulse quickens, his mind races in tandem, hoping to catch up to the baton and frantic pace set by his physiology. Cartesian revelations of duality abound. His mind begins to cogitate over the nature of mind and the mind of nature. He considers the poignant quote from Joseph Campbell:

"But if there is no divinity in nature, the nature that God created, how should there be in the idea of God, which the nature of man created?" Alan feels his heart beat profoundly, pumping the tides of cells and fluids that enliven his otherwise lifeless corporeal bag of limbs. "Where is the heart of the tree?" he wonders. "Is it in the branches? Is it in the trunk? Perhaps it is in the roots, mysteriously pumping in the underbelly of the earth." Divinity is all around. Deep, sensual, melodic crystal blue becomes cerulean ambrosia. Vibrant, titillating, exciting reds become passionate crimson. Browns, greens, yellows, and oranges coalesce into a symphony of color that elevates richness and texture to a visual high. A

gargantuan chasm or aperture could tear open in the sky and unleash a
litany of angels, celestial bells, and heavenly harps. At this point, Alan
would have been prepared. He only wonders: "Would the colors and
grandiloquent display compare to what is before me now?"

"How are you feeling sweetie?" he whispers into her ear. Ronia's
eyelids flutter momentarily like butterfly wings before revealing two
exotic, multi-hued marbles that are glossily mesmerizing; a knowingness
and a sated glimmer exude from their core. Her mouth cracks open
slightly before erupting into a brilliant, all-encompassing countenance. "I
feel wonderful!" she responds. "I feel as if I've channeled or harnessed
an intergalactic, opium-like serum that is simultaneously mind expanding
and soul enriching. Heavens opened up a bottomless, sinewy river or
ocean of paradise and I'm taking a perpetual swim." "Ronia, look over
there." Alan points to an ivory cat frolicking in a hedge by the water. It
seems to be playfully yet seriously chasing either an insect or a rodent.
The feline eyes pause to gaze in the direction of Alan and Ronia. Alan
has always enjoyed cats. Their relentless independence and lovable,
curious nature have proven sources of endless hours of amusement
gained simply by sitting back and watching their behavior.

For what seems like hours but were probably only seconds—or perhaps it is the other way around—the two humans gaze in absolute wonder at their evolutionary counterpart in the family of animal known to
Ronia as Felidae: lions, tigers, leopards, lynxes, jaguars, and their cute
little siblings—the domesticated short hair cats. Crystalline blue eyes
emerge from the bushes and then are diverted to the object of pursuit—
now clearly visible—a brown mouse, that scurries and tries to burrow an
escape route and then attempts to outrun the scratches and potential bites
of his hunter. The hunter and the hunted seem to Alan to be normal roles
in the game of nature and the game of life. However, in the sensitized
state, this seemingly normal, necessary process of cat and mouse has an
outcome that he feels he is now unable to unflinchingly watch. Alan
stands up and lifts Ronia to her feet. "Let's walk around a bit," he
exclaims. "Okay." They gather up their stuff and begin to walk along a
hiking trail that meanders through tiny streams and thick woods. A tinge
of vertigo and a long series of distorted images color their walk.

"The wine was pretty tasty," she remarks. "Yes it was. Red wine is
truly comforting to the soul," Alan muses. "The woods are so placid.
Look at the orange and green, how the two colors intertwine and bleed
into one another in a sort of fugue," he adds. "Alan, nature seems to
flower into assortments and patterns of colorful, vibrant arrays. There

seems to be a desire or plan to unfold a collection of designs in texture and color; an effluence of diversity and of kaleidoscopic combinations seems to be nature's way of perpetually outshining itself. It's all quite marvelous if you think about it."

Alan smiles and puts his arm around her. What seems to be a glow or perhaps ambience, or it could just be pheromonal release, emanates around her. He thinks that he can actually see an energy field or mist seeping from her pores.

"Ronia, I understand what you're talking about when you refer to the diversity or multi-faceted interplay in the dimensions of nature. In states like this, I feel I can more vividly realize otherwise abstruse concepts like classificatory breakdown of species—genera, families, and higher categories like phyla and kingdom. The microcosmic world of teeming organisms becomes an observable, analyzable subject and my eyes—the lens or the petri dish through which the subject is studied. The richness and the vitality of the natural world opens up before my eyes, which have become, truly, windows of the soul. The soul of nature is revealed through swirling patterns of life and efflorescent multitudes of species. We are hurtling through this Milky Way, a spiraling galaxy with a hundred billion stars and each human possessing a corresponding number of neurons in their brains. There are probably one hundred million species of organisms on our planet all vying for their place in the grand stage of life. Ronia, within studying anthropology, are you familiar with and can you explain some of the classifications of life?" She gently kicks a rock on the path, clears her voice, and begins to speak:

"Well, there are about a million and a half species documented along the lines of insects, higher plants, protozoa, algae, fungi, monera, viruses, and other animals. There are about two hundred and fifty thousand higher plants: dicots, monocots, gymnosperms, ferns, bryophytes, and others. In terms of animals, they total approximately one million, ranging from: lepidoptera to echinodermata and then to nematoda and onto porifern, chordates, arachnida, and diptera. The whole spectrum really. Wow, I really feel awesome!" "I feel awesome, too," he concurs.

"Ronia, think about evolution. We—and when I say 'we' I mean life itself, came on the scene about 3.9, 3.8 billion years ago. Correct me if I'm wrong. Unicellular organisms were first to appear. Higher organisms began about 1.8 billion years ago. Then we have the Cambrian explosion 540 to 500 million years ago. The human mind evolved probably a million to 100, 000 years ago. It's amazing how we've progressed to the stage we are at now: self-reflective, conscious, intelligent creatures roaming, exploring, and delving our environments." "Yeah, you mentioned progress. Some biologists and philosophers take issue with the implications of a term like, 'progress.' They feel a term such as progress implies direction or goal orientation, contending that DNA has no goal. Goals come later when organisms adapt to their specific environmental needs."

Alan cannot remember a time when he was so pleased to stand corrected. Ronia's erudition in the midst of a substantial psychedelic trip is a glowing confirmation that the human brain is DNA's crowning achievement; whether or not it ever had a goal in mind.

They walk steadily through fallen leaves and rocks scattered on the trail. Occasionally, a biker or a jogger sails past them, but for the most part, the woods feel completely theirs. A protective canopy of towering branches shades portions of the path, providing momentary respite from the sun. Neither Alan nor Ronia is really dressed for serious hiking, so they approach the trail slowly. The drug is inundating the walk with not only philosophic, evolutionary discourse, but also perceptual enhancements and other alterations.

A hypnotic trance-like malaise permeates their perceptual fields, casting an undeniable "other-ness" on the place. The woods seem to breathe their essence and pulsate with a vibrancy and aliveness that simultaneously draws them in and repels them. There is always at least a fraction of psychological or physical discomfort for Alan when he trips, but he views this as a right of passage for entering the glories of the other side. Gestures of smiling at one another and hand holding inhabit most of the communication between the two lovers. Words almost seem futile in conveying the profound joy experienced, so should often be avoided. They soon arrive at a clearing in the path. A ledge that strategically overlooks a valley provides ample views of innumerable rows of pines and acres of yellow stalks of grass that sway eternally in the wind.

Alan grasps Ronia's hand and leads her down into the valley where they develop long, strenuous, exhilarating strides while flailing their arms in fun before collapsing and falling into each other's arms. They both let out uproarious laughter and roll rambunctiously in the grass, before stroking each other's faces and kissing like mad banshees. Alan relishes the sweet, moist kiss complemented by a fresh scent of sunflower. Ronia fondles his muscular back and abandons her face in his chest. The sun's rays refract through infinite blades of grass, leaving streaks of light and shadow spewing discordantly on the ground. In the distance are trees that seem to watch over protectively and presciently. Silence of nature is soothing and sedating. Love is good and Alan is cherishing it. Hours elapse with the two pausing periodically for smokes and sips of water. Their nervous systems are relinquishing control and simply allowing them to be imprinted and caressed by the elements.

Dusk eventually arrives and Alan turns his head toward Ronia to speak: "I was thinking of eternity a minute ago and the thought sort of scared me. You know, eternity in terms of all that ever was or ever shall be: the mountains, rivers, oceans, deserts, and plains. Will the planet still be here after millennia have passed, or will some spaceship—perhaps a neighbor with a comet—swoop down and take those humans it wants for future colonization and leave the rest, or perhaps worst?"

"That's a comforting thought," she replies sarcastically. "Well, it's a very sobering thought, I know. But I'm serious. Will the sun eventually grow too hot, or too close and extinguish life as we know it, or will the earth perpetually float within this solar system—a constant reminder of the civilization, if you can call it that, that once was?" "I don't know," Ronia replies solemnly and contemplatively, as she gazes at a pinkish and lavender hue on a hillside that is beautifully superimposed on the horizon. "I'd like to think that if the earth simply totally evaporated or burned out, that it had already grown to be uninhabitable and that all the humans had died of natural, painless causes—in advance."

"What if?" Alan begins in an almost hushed whisper... "The purpose or—forgive me—purposelessness of DNA, resulted in humans success- fully migrating into outer space and colonizing more inhabitable realms; and they looked back on the events on planet earth as if upon some dis- tant dream?" "I will worry about the battles and wars waged in the pro- cess of so-called colonization of other realms, be they planets, stars, asteroids, or satellites. Can you imagine? Think of what Europeans did to the American Indian. It's simply horrible to conceive. What if man encounters alien life that happens to live in a paradisiacal realm for which man is instantly envious? All hell would break loose." "Ronia, I wonder what effect cloning will have when the time comes. Perhaps we will send copies of ourselves out into space to experiment and test out the new environments before we actually go there."

The sky turns a misty grayish blue and it is one of those magical times when both the sun and the moon are clearly visible and both vie for man's attention. For above the eighth of the sun's horizon is a three-quar- ter moon beckoning the incipient night and cuing the sun that the celes- tial shift is changing. Among priceless works of art in a swank museum, an arriving security guard lingers with the guard at post. They discuss any relevant events before making yet another revolution. The sun and moon do likewise: watching over every one of us, each of us a master-piece in the great cosmic gallery. We alternately curse and praise the celestial orbs but always know that they are there at least partly for our protection. So it is with museum guards.

"We could start heading back," Alan suggests, as he is a little con-cerned that there will not be enough light for the trail. "Okay, will you give me your hand?" Ronia reaches out her hand to him and he lifts her up. They take one last look at the valley and then begin the trek back.

Alan opens the door and when she steps in, he throws the bag into the back seat. They are still undeniably tripping. Alan approaches the steer-ing wheel with only some reticence and mainly eager anticipation. He believes that he is fairly well cognizant enough to maneuver the vehicle competently and simultaneously he is looking forward to the opportunity of driving through scenic and now—magically glistening, though dark hills. Darkness has descended but through the headlights one can see the voluptuous curves of the hills and spiraling, tree-lined roads quite clearly.

The engine hums as Alan adjusts the radio until he lands on a station playing Elton John. The sound is soothing as the lyrics—"high as a kite," from the song "Rocketman"—float serendipitously through the speakers and then are quickly followed by the sweet melody of "Your Song," that caresses their fertile aural canals. Alan turns to Ronia and asks her how she is feeling. "Fine, I've just been thinking how nice it will be to get back to the hotel, smoke a cigarette, and take a long, luxurious candle-lit bath."

Alan cannot decide which is more pleasant: the thought of performing the actions she describes, or hearing her mellifluous voice articulating them. Her silhouette is translucent as he responds to her: "That sounds wonderful," he replies, while readily realizing the dual nature of his response. He adds, "You know, your lips could tell lies and cast hideous, monstrous dispersions my way and I believe they would hopelessly fall on welcome, gracious ears. For your voice is more beautiful than the siren's cries of Atlantis and the holy host of choruses performed by seraphim and cherubim at the very gates of heaven. The intonation and tone bleed of a serenity that can only be found with the fountain of youth."

It is very dark in the car but as they pass an illuminated highway road marker, he can see her blushing, vibrant crimson cheeks—a pulsating human contrast to the machination of the car. "Alan, that is so sweet." She slides her left arm around his neck and rubs her cheek next to his. He cracks the window to let some air in. To say or do something which ostensibly makes her happy brings him a warmth and contentment that are unparalleled. As the car races along the road, he focuses on the passing white stripes and makes sure to take every precaution to keep the car centered in its lane. "I want you to see the hotel courtyard at night. If we just want to relax in the room when we get back, then maybe tomorrow night we'll go for a couple of drinks." "That sounds good. Whatever you want to do."

"Ronia, do you ever get sort of caught up in the mire of religious-laden ideation when you trip, in terms of conflict or neurosis over early religious programming?" "You mean in terms of how I was raised religiously?" "Yeah, like what your church, school, and family inculcated you with?" "Ummm. Not too often. My brain is very well suited or geared toward psychedelics. Very seldom do I have a so-called 'bad trip.' Why do you ask?" "Well, at times I slip into a slightly zany state where my perception, both visual and intellectual, is colored with religious perspective—religious in the sense of annoying precepts or tenets from a literalist view and from early Protestant messages scripted on my brain. I'll find myself decoding words that people have said or unusual things that are going on in a decidedly religious vein. It's as if a battle of souls is going on and I've either given myself to the dark side or at least am skating thin ice in the roller rink arena of 'good' versus 'evil.' It's hard to explain."

"Well, Alan, it's obvious that all of us—to a great extent—are products of our environment. Things said and taught to us as small children will arguably be floating around inside our heads throughout our lives. I think that is the basis of psychoanalysis: to purge ourselves of those demons. Perhaps in psychedelic states, structures—or avenues—in the brain, that have been repressed or temporarily quelled, arise and rear their ugly heads. A belief can be a terrifying thing. Individuals grow and develop independently, but often fall back on a basis of thinking or world view shared by their families, their societies, and their cultures." "Yeah, you're right. That's very interesting. It seems to be a slow, gradual process to work through one's impressions and truly formulate, or implement independent, thoughtful, more salubrious ideas. I believe it's possible. It's just tedious." "Arguably, Alan, it's the goal of humanity to learn from the past and take logical, rational steps to evolve to a higher plane—to ascend the evolutionary ladder of thought that is more scientific, more accelerated, and more humanistic."

"Alan stop!" She shrieks. Alan slams on the brakes and skids about twenty feet in the road while gripping the wheel to prevent the car from spinning. It turns slightly and lands about ten feet from a buck in the road. Towering antlers climb from the head of a stationary white-tailed deer, blinded in its tracks and staring into the headlights. Ronia covers her mouth to conceal a haunting moan as Alan gazes in front of the car. He can see the piercing hazelnut and black eyes of this princely looking creature that he almost killed. Its tall, muscular frame is contracting and expanding as it licks its lips and maintains perfect, direct eye contact with the car.

"Alan, look. It's the most beautiful creature I have ever seen." About ten seconds elapse for Alan to make out twenty twisting spikes of antlers that form a majestic natural crown. The deer springs from the road and gallops through a thick brush to the left of the highway. "Watch out, Alan. Sometimes they travel in groups. There may be others following." Alan's heart races and pounds. A tangible maelstrom is going on in his chest. "Oh my God! I can't believe what just happened," Alan exclaims. "That was absolutely awesome."

Alan slowly builds speed as he struggles to regain composure. "That was absolutely amazing. What are the chances that the deer would cross at exactly this time?" Alan's drug-nurtured brain is carefully concluding that the incident has profound mystical significance. The regal-looking athletic creature had focused on them with very large, penetrating eyes, that looked part fleshy and part glassy. It seems to Alan that an almost cosmic connection had definitely taken place. He is mesmerized and astonished. He emits a nervous giggle and continues to marvel at the episode. "This exotic, wild, marvelous creature has been spawned from the forest to appear and greet us with its mystical gaze. The world is wonderful," he exclaims. Ronia smiles ebulliently. "Alan, it is pretty wonderful."

Off in the northwest distance—through a veil of grayish blue, almost fairytale clouds—shines a full, corpulently glowing moon that casts a vista of light all around. Alan resumes his course toward the hotel. When they arrive, he leads Ronia to the room. Although only having left the room that morning, everything seems strangely different and distant. The sheets on the bed have been neatly made but all the items on the table and the clothes strewn around the room are still in disarray. All of a sudden, the reality sets in that Alan is thousands and thousands of miles away from home with a woman that he has not known very long. This thought makes Alan feel temporarily not himself. He sets his bag down on the bed and as Ronia lies back on the bed, he pulls up a chair and sits down. Physically, his situation is one of ambiguity. He knows it isn't rational but he meditates on the fact that his mind is alert but he is physically tired. "How can that be?" he wonders.

"Are the mind and body really that separate? Should not the one always be in accord with the other? Shouldn't we dispel the sense of duality altogether? Perhaps, if there was no sense of duality, I could not have possibly imagined that my mind was alert and my body tired. Perhaps I would feel either alert or tired and that would be the basic state of my being. Maybe the 'I' that seems to be perceiving anything at all is simply a manifestation of a physical body that is tired, or a mind that is alert."

"Ronia, back to what we were talking about. It's interesting to ponder the extreme damage wrought by a fundamentalist background. Think of the American cultists like Koresh and Applewhite that led many to an early grave. They both had very Christian backgrounds. Now, of course, that doesn't happen to everyone from a strict religious background. It just so happens to be a typical feature in the backgrounds of people who end up doing crazy things. Religion more often than not should uphold its ideal of peace. Instead of waging wars in the name of God—and instead of breeding paranoid, conformist automata—religion should be more in line with the tenets of something like, humanism. Mutual respect is important. Tolerance is important. Love is important. Care for the earth is important. Appreciating and accepting diversity are important." For fear of sounding too preachy—if he hasn't done so already—he slows himself down. Ronia has been listening intently. "Some of your iconoclastic rockers like Marilyn Manson are proud to debunk orthodoxy, particularly with regard to conservative Protestant views. Are they not?" she queries, rhetorically. Alan guffaws. "I'd say so. Many of them very articulately express their strong indignation at having been raised in restrictive environments. Anyway, on a positive note, many of the positive ideals of something like Christianity can be realized while pursuing the psychedelic state. It's not just the bad. With proper focus and preparation one can realize and exemplify the tenets of peace, love, openness, and the other hallmarks of Christian theory. That's the upbeat, optimistic view. Give me a kiss, girl." He jumps on the bed and presses his lips against her mouth. Her moist, soft lips are ambrosia at this moment. He quickly sits up and goes to the window, immediately pulling back the shades to reveal the city lights. Then, he steps to the bathroom and begins to run a hot bath for Ronia.

"Do you want that cigarette now or later?" "I'll take it now, thank you." Alan reaches into the bag, removes a cigarette and the lighter,

lights it and then hands it to her as she rises to greet him. "Thanks."
"Sure." As the bath water begins to rise, he begins to slowly undress her.
She closes her eyes and continues to drag on the cigarette as the cotton
slips off her slender, muscular body. She is radiant and regal as she
stands with her waist and hips slightly tilted—one hand resting on her
waist, with the elbow of the same arm slightly bent. She is irresistibly
succulent in a manner Alan likens to a raspberry and chocolate pastry
dripping with warm icing.

He saunters into the bathroom and shuts the water off. He then returns
to the main room and gravitates to her flesh unavoidably. Sliding one
hand along her inner thigh, he begins to tenderly stroke the curves of her
physique. With his other hand, he reaches up to massage her neck as he
kneels to kiss her buttocks. As he reaches the silky fold between her legs,
two fingers gently merge with moist, warm beckoning mounds. Lifting
her firmly from the floor, with arms tightly around her, he spirits her to
the bed upon which he immediately begins to make love to her as he
drops savoring, delicate kisses upon her mouth and neck.

The burning cigarette, which has been dangling between two of her
fingers, falls to the carpet, a solitary casualty in the throes of passion.
Alan leans over and extinguishes the nicotine ember by pressing it into
the carpet. Simultaneously, he kindles the torrid body, which is now
straddling his torso. Ripe, erect nipples protrude through his fingers; that
coddle her breasts like tender, freshly budding fruits. As he plunges her
depths to the increasing sighs and moans of pleasure that sway with his
movements, her body seems to flower into coital rapture; his semen is the
pollen that fertilizes and unfurls her dormant state of homeostasis into a
brilliant, turgescent maelstrom of pulsating pistils and stamens. Their
bodies converge into a symphony of chemistry—a sojourn in sentient
melody.

He closes his eyes to reveal the splendor of cerulean Rocky Mountain
columbines, the Cabernet Mariposa lily, the tortuous, tempting curves of
the Gladiolus, Snapdragon, and Hollyhock: all integral facets, testifying
not just to the floral vista they had savored earlier in the day, but to the
act of coitus—a fitting parallel—between mammal and plant. The inherent stimulation in the natural process beckons floral and human species
alike, inviting them to the eternal, Kama Sutra dance of life. Alan and
Ronia quiver and gyrate into a cyclone of ecstasy and transcendence;
their bodies left pleasantly limp and exhausted on the bed.

"The bath water is probably still hot. Do you want to get in?" "Yes,"
Ronia replies, while rolling her eyes and smiling in a gesture that com-

municates she is sated. She is content and the bath will simply complete the evening.

CHAPTER 20

As she slithers into the bath, Alan clasps his hands behind his head in a position that comfortably cradles his very human skull—magically, paradoxically alit with a consciousness of hedonism and spiritual stimulation—that somehow belies the base, corporeal animal shell that lies motionless in his hands. Minutes—which feel strangely like eons—elapse before Alan drifts off into sleep. Not hearing her finish her bath, he simply awakens to feel her warm, naked, slightly moist body slide in next to him. Soft, magnetic flesh envelops him peacefully. He turns to kiss her and falls back to sleep.

His mind wanders into an odd territory: an amalgamation of topographical splendor that combines snowy, misty vistas of mountain ranges and peaks blanketed in pines with a cloud-covered valley of shimmering, glistening lakes and smooth, rolling hills. Varying shades of amber and sienna limestone rock protrusions emerge from an alternately arid and fertile ground—arguably uninhabitable in its frigid and simultaneously scorching climate. No forms of multi-cellular life are visible as Alan's focus scans the terrain in a rapid, sweeping movement indicative of being in a plane or other modern aircraft.

As he passes over a jagged, grassy promontory, he finds himself nervously but blissfully aloft streams, tropical rapids, and oceans of currents that combine features of rivers, lakes, ponds, waterfalls, and oceans all converging in a whirling, centrifugal force: a vortex of raging waters colliding at full force and scattering into billions of atomistic, chemically retracting particles that float into a kaleidoscopic array of slowly evolving tadpoles and other spermatozoic organisms. All of them scurry into multidimensional realms of biospheric milieus composed of divergent flora and rock. Like holding up a viewfinder and selectively clicking on different scenes, Alan vacillates from one unique dimension to the next.

At one moment—while hovering hypnotically above a thick verdant rainforest intersected by a convoluted stream with multitudinous boulders and in another, a spacious rustic valley dotted with prickling, extraterrestrial-looking cacti and Joshua trees—Alan feasts upon the divergent geographies like delectable entrees; his eyes are the knife and fork voraciously feeding his starving brain.

Suddenly moving into misty alabaster cloud cover, Alan becomes enveloped by a cumulous blanket that feels refreshingly cool and moist. White, heptagonally mechanical Escherian birds begin to take shape and form from the clouds and attain flight in an organized pattern and direction. They swiftly and deftly flap their wings in a repetitive, rapid motion until soaring high above rumbling volcanoes that spew mounds of liquid steaming, seething lava that drips like taunting chocolate syrup down the sides of ice cream.

Majestic, towering spires—obelisks of molten rock—jut up in a city-like skyline that becomes torrentially poured on by hail, snow, rain, feathers, shoes, crayons, raisins, peanuts, trashcans, and lions. Cylindrical, multi-hued trinkets of toy soldiers, thimbles, spools, record players, motorcycles, and hats conglomerate in a giant basket held up by cranes in a now desolate post-nuclear war-like city of shambles. Dilapidated, burned and ravaged tenement buildings sit hopelessly vacant on crumbling foundation-torn streets and sidewalks that emit haunting, spiraling funnels of smoke into chambers and vessels of ashy, charcoal firmament. The busy microorganismic fish now swim merrily through a vacuum: an aperture torn open through the sky. The winds pick up and blow tablets or capsules of aeronautical delight into brisk synchronous waves of flight across barren fields and rugged, rocky mountainsides. The fish, or spermatozoa-like creatures that are spawned from a stream, become magnified into visible translucent structures of delicate neural and corpuscle strands interconnected in intricate webs of alternately fine and tenuous, membranous texture and varying color. Their anatomy seems like the sky and the earth—varied geometrical compositions conduct otherwise chaotic patterns into congruous, interweaving symphonic form. Rich, bloody reds and haunting, melancholic grays and black are offset by ivory and pearl. Everything in the dream-field of vision has cellular awareness and presupposes a divine origin.

Alan awakens momentarily to the gentle touch of Ronia's hand on his lower back. He leans into her body so as to sense it only for a moment, the soothing warmth of her skin and pleasant curves of her frame. The serenity of night and the placid, fathomless abyss of sleep wash over any distinct impressions and carry the two lovers into the dawn of the next day.

Ronia is leisurely making coffee and tidying up when Alan arises. "Good morning, sweetie," she calls out. "Good morning, beautiful," he replies—his voice only a gruff, muffled approximation of what it is normally. "How did you sleep?" "Fine, how about you?" she responds. "Actually, I had really strange, paradoxical images floating around in my mind; everything from thimbles to fish, to horses all carried on as if they belonged together. It was a veritable field day for an analyst." "Sounds interesting. I simply had to settle for a perfectly passionate delicacy of fawning over your body while you were making love to me," she quips. "Oh, God."

Alan lifts his cumbersome frame from the bed and staggers in his caffeine-deprived state over to kiss her. She turns and locks lips with him while he pulls back the bangs from her face. As the coffee machine hums, he reaches into the cabinet, removes a mug, and inserts a touch of sugar before methodically pouring himself a cup. The wind outside is lightly rustling trees and the window panes. Ronia has opened one of the windows to let some fresh air in.

Alan pulls up a chair to the table and watches as she gets dressed. In the silence that exists between them at this moment, Alan treasures the simplicity and tranquillity of basically being with someone; in body, mind, and spirit his self has merged with hers. They have carefully constructed bridges that interconnect the gaps that normally separate us as individuals. Through a series of conversations, voluptuous exchanges of touch of flesh—and merging of sweat, semen, and pheromones—infatuatingly, they have absorbed one another. In the trans-millennial field of time, they have achieved for at least a matter of hours a spiritual rapprochement—an ethereal, transcendent, but very real communion—that may not last forever, but seems in its own special way something that will go beyond forever.

Alan takes a sip from his coffee and gently sets the cup down. "Hey, if you want, we can drive into Glasgow tomorrow and explore the surrounding areas like, Paisley. What do you think?" he asks. "That sounds like fun, actually," she replies while brushing her hair. "Alan, then maybe we can drive up into the highlands later in the week or something." "Sure, we can. Anything you want," Alan concurs.

They get dressed and load up the backpack. After going downstairs, they grab some breakfast and head off to Edinburgh castle. The day is spent pleasantly touring Edinburgh castle and walking the streets vigorously, soaking up the ambience that is distinctly Edinburgh. At night, they go for dinner at a Thai restaurant and then after-dinner drinks in the courtyard of the hotel. "Alan, this place is so fun. It's laid-back and hip," she remarks, in between sips of a Margarita. "You're right. I like it here and think that this is the sort of place where I could live." He gazes at the mobiles that swing hypnotically in the night air. Dreams have pervaded his life for the past several weeks, as have realities that he did not know were possible. Across the table, in the soft moonlit glow that frames his lover, is an image of beauty that equally exceeds his imagination. The stars shine brightly as he leads her back up to the room that he truly never wants to leave.

Princes Street is illuminated with an early morning radiance that emerges uniquely from the sun's stream of rays that spill majestically through Gothic spires and antique clocks of the cityscape. Buses and pedestrians bustling amidst the streets are the pulse and the heartbeat of the modern city; which to Alan belies, momentarily, the rich Scottish history and the mythical, fairytale nature of the land. After having some coffee and checking out of the hotel, they load up the car and head out to the highway toward Glasgow at about 11:00 a.m.

The cloud cover above them is a moody melange of haunting grays and whites as they race past fields of grazing cattle and the lush, rolling hills of central Scotland. "Alan, yesterday—or, actually—the last couple of days were truly magical. Everything had its proper place and importance; as if it had been celestially arranged. Basically, I had a splendid time and just wanted to let you know." "Well, I'm not sure what I can do for an encore today. But anyway, I'm glad you had a wonderful time. It was special for me, too." Alan carefully maneuvers the car, as it careens around tree-lined turns near the town of Bathgate. Ominous shadows from the clouds leave varying patterns on the landscape which seem to mirror the patterns of color on the hides of the cattle. Alan takes in the scenery and thinks of the amoeba-shaped patterns as precursors or prototypes for that psychedelic pattern that had revolutionized fashion and become imbedded in the minds of just about everyone: the pattern that originated somewhere southwest of Glasgow in its eponymous namesake, Paisley, Scotland.

"Alan, will you please pull the car over at the next stop? I'd like to take a break if we could." "Sure, I think there's a place just ahead." Alan exits at a stop near the town of Coatbridge, just east of Glasgow. He pulls the car up to a gas station. They get out of the car and he begins to pump the gas. Ronia goes into the convenience store and buys some bottled waters and candy. Adjacent to Alan's car—on the other side of the pumps, to the right—sits an orange, dusty, slightly dented VW van. Its occupants—who come barreling out the side with the door swinging wide open—are members of a soccer team, or football team, depending on how you name it. Four or five guys in their twenties—some cleanly shaven, others with long hair and shadowed faces—climb out of the van and begin to walk around and stretch. One of them is on crutches and has his left knee wrapped up in gauze and a tan cloth wrap. He leans against the side of the van as the others mill about.

Alan calls out to him, "Hey mate, what happened to your leg?" The young man looks up, spits out a clump of chewing tobacco and answers somberly, "ACL surgery. I fuckin' twisted my knee like a rubber band and it left me hobblin' about. So I had one of those medical butchers slice me open and put it back together with pins and all. Now it hurts like a motherfucker. It should be better in a couple of weeks, though." The lad speaks with a rustic, hurried English accent that to Alan seems northern English. Alan feels he is getting good at detecting the origins of accents. "Sorry to hear about that, mate. Soccer—I mean football—seems quite aggressive. It's fun as hell to watch but it seems the body takes a punishing." "Yeah," the young man answers.

"You fucking throw your whole self into it and before you know it, you're so involved passionately and all that you forget yourself and become sort of prone to gettin' all battered around like a shirt in a fuckin' drier or something." Alan laughs.

"Sort of like life, I guess." "Yeah, man, it's a lot like life. Football's a lot like life; I guess you could say." "Will you play again?" "Yeah, definitely!" "Then the best of luck to you." "Thanks." Ronia returns to the car with a bag of goodies. Alan has finished pumping the gas and goes inside in to pay. When he returns to the car, he says goodbye to his new acquaintance and tells him to take care. "Did you make a friend, Alan?" Ronia asks as he slides into his seat. "Yeah. That kid tore his ACL. I guess that's some sort of ligament in the leg. He said he's in a lot of pain."

Alan starts the engine and they resume their course into Glasgow. The near virginal countryside gradually segues into industrialized city markers, like: warehouses, factories, car dealerships, office buildings, power plants, multiple housing complexes, powerlines, amphitheaters, twisting freeways, monolithic shopping centers, and of course, the ubiquitous beer pubs. Alan and Ronia drive into downtown along a busy street that is dotted with colorful flags on towering poles. The flags depict symbols, pictographs, and ideograms that encompass a wide, visually impressive array of cuneiform and hieroglyphic images apparently on display at a local museum.

A caption above the symbols reads: "From Cuneiform To Cyberform: A Retro and Projecto-Active Overview of Human Modes of Communication." "That sounds interesting," Alan remarks, after he reads the words aloud. "It sure does," Ronia replies, her head leaning and her eyes glaring to see the flags. "Please take me, Alan. Please." "Ohhhh, alright," he replies sarcastically, as if he really is just acquiescing for her.

As the car soars past the signs, Alan notices with great amusement how there seems to be a gradual evolution or synchronicity along the signs that begin with cuneiform script and go to modern computer codes. Obviously, the intent of the exhibit is to trace the history of communication, a not-so-modest challenge. He notices how the basic elements that form cuneiform closely mirror the bits and codes he has seen in computer scripts. From disparate languages—although separated by thousands of years—emerges an uncanny pattern or symbiosis. A common thread runs through cuneiform, hieroglyphic, hierotic, demotic, modern word signs in alphabetic writing, and computer codes that is readily apparent by visually scanning the flags.

Soon, they find themselves at a busy intersection that encompasses in its quadrants a restaurant, a convenience store, a gas station, and a police station. Alan drives slowly alongside an amusing pedestrian. A rather large, waddling woman dressed in a baggy, colorful floral-patterned dress is leisurely walking her dog: a scruffy, furry little white poodle with a bright pink ribbon dangling from its neck in tendrils that bounce in unison with the funny way in which the woman walks.

Alan rolls down his window to ask her a question: "Excuse me, ma'am. Could you please let us know of any hotels in the area?" "Sure," the woman replies. She points in what seems to be the northwest direction. "Just take Westchester Avenue up about five blocks and you will see a few places. Their prices range from about 25 to 30 pounds." "Thank you ma'am. Nice dog by the way." "Thanks sonny."

Alan rolls up the window and begins to steer the car in the proper direction. "Funny, strange-looking but nice woman that was," he remarks to Ronia, who is now gazing out her window animatedly, seeming to be anxiously awaiting the opportunity to explore the city. "Yeah. She was very friendly and helpful. I only wish that she would take some fashion advice to the likes of Gaultier and Mizrahi. Her pleasantly frumpish, dowdy image cuts a surprisingly happy-go-lucky, casual beauty about it that says, 'I really don't give a fuck!'" Alan chuckles mischievously.

As he follows the woman's directions, he notices a brownstone, multi-storied hotel set back scenically off the road by about fifty yards.

Surrounded by verdant, rustling oaks, it holds in its foreground an arc-shaped, stone-lined driveway that directs one's focus to something else. Two Oriental lion sculptures hover ominously in the back and four giant vases contain radiant, blooming long-stemmed roses that peer at passers-by like tempting, almost taunting gnomes.

Alan commandingly pulls into the drive, parks the car, and leads Ronia to the front desk, at which time they check in and then quickly depart—with their bags in hand—to a room which overlooks an elaborate stone fountain on the outside. A winged, fairy-like mythical creature with neck extended reaches for the sky and emerges majestically from a funnel of streaming juts of water that propel upward in towering, scattering monoliths. The monoliths rise in unison with certain beats in the accompanying programmed music—classical—and then come splashing down in a pool of water. The water is left cerulean from deep tiles that, on closer inspection, reveal intricate shapes and designs of mermaids and other sea nymphs.

In the distance far behind the fountain, stands the rustic, industrial skyline of Glasgow. Alan sets the bags and the backpack down and asks Ronia where she wants to go first. She coyly requests that Alan take her to the museum.

After resting for about thirty minutes in the room, they descend to the lobby to ask for directions to the museum. Alan has difficulty understanding the clerk's pronunciation of the name of the museum but it sounds like, "The Seasons," and he is fairly certain that he can locate it based on the map. Alan tips the clerk a dollar and then they are on their way.

Within twenty minutes, they arrive at a white concrete, rectilinear I.M. Peish looking structure; a stone marble inlaid entrance and sundry geometrically sophisticated pieces of modern sculptures lie strewn across a lawn in apparent random fashion. Prominent white statues of gods and goddesses line a long narrow corridor that seems to lead to the main entrance to the museum. Colorful murals, depicting the same symbols he had seen in the flags earlier, hang elegantly on the walls. Alan and Ronia walk hand-in-hand down the corridor that is breezy and perfectly captures a long stream of sunlight that illuminates the faces on some of the statues. As they enter the lobby, they stop in front of the information and ticket desk to inquire about places to smoke. They are told by an attendant that they must walk outside to a patio. They can get to it through an exit about twenty yards away. They step outside, where he lights up a cigar and her cigarette. "Alan, look over there." She gestures toward what looks like a Rodin sculpture of a muscular giant of a man who seems to be swinging a disc. The sculpture stands near a man-made pond that has—adjacent to it, off one of its corners—an ivy-laden cabana with two benches.

The two lovers make their way to one of the benches and sit down. While puffing on the cigar, Alan reaches into his bag and begins to read in his now favorite book on mysticism: "Like the early Gnostics, Teilhard de Chardin took a very symbolic and mystical interpretation of biblical scriptures. The significance of the ascension was not in its objective validity but rather in the symbolism of an individual identifying himself with the spiritual to the extent of renouncing his own physical existence; to become unified with the spiritual."

Alan pauses to clear his throat. He then continues: "With this perception, we can see a commonality between Christianity and Buddhism. One's highest aim is to strive toward identifying oneself with the spiritual by overcoming the mayaistic illusory world of the senses. Isn't it interesting that what is considered spiritual perfection in India—a completely aloof, withdrawn individual—is considered insane in the West? In an industrialized capitalistic society bent on economic dominance, there is not much tolerance for a sedentary man of meditation, unless of course he is a hieratic representative of a major money making organization like the church. Now that's justified religion." "Alan, that's interesting—the duality of the contemplative, the producer of spiritual wealth, and the capitalist, the producer of material wealth. It seems that man seems to want to strike a balance between substantive, internal satisfaction—based on a lofty ideal—and the pursuit and accumulation of material prosperity and satisfaction."

"The great enigma of living, I suppose," Alan responds. "We are born on to this planet with so many years. We cannot take anything with us when we leave. Surely, man does not want to leave as his only legacy that he was a really adept merchant who bought and sold material things. There must be a higher satisfaction or ideal to be attained. The brain needs something more than food, sex, homes, car, and fine clothes. There must be a connection to something greater: a merging with some higher awareness. I think it is necessary." Alan punctuates his sentence with a steady exhalation and a rich stream of cigar smoke.

He watches with intense amusement and pleasure an interesting glimmer off a metal panel connected to a futuristic obelisk structure in the eastern section of the lawn. The—at times—seemingly awkward, but overall palatable arrangement within this area serves the purpose of enveloping the viewer like a cocoon. Meditating in this garden prior to entering the main exhibit hall is in a sense the preliminary stage in a metamorphosis. Ronia walks with her lit cigarette over to a concrete waterfall exhibit that creates rippling waves as the water trickles, casting shimmering light waves into any perceiving retina. She turns to speak to him: "The interesting dilemma that I think we all face is how to capitalize on the easiest congruence between material and spiritual betterment to the least detriment of those around us. How can we accumulate a lengthy array of meaningful, pleasurable experiences in our time on this planet and maximize them to their fullest potential?" "It's very complicated, my dear," Alan responds as he extinguishes his cigar in the ground. "Are you ready to go in?" he asks. "Yes. Let's go," she responds.

They purchase two tickets and quickly enter a large exhibit hall that houses sundry displays of modes of human communication, with historical, experiential overviews of each. Alan wanders up to a large mural that describes cuneiform. He reads about the ancient writing of Persia, Babylonia, Assyria, and Chaldea. He learns that the Sumerians more than likely inverted cuneiform and that it was based on pictographs. Alan tries to imagine what it was like in this time frame, when man constructed rudimentary symbols to depict things he was trying to say. He analyzes the wedge-shaped marks and thinks of them as little musical instruments or codes that express more vividly a musical harmony than a spoken word. Ronia directs Alan's attention to a chart, which outlines various families of languages: Indo-European, Afro-Asiatic, various other African, Ural-Altaic, Paleoasiatic, and Caucasian.

Ronia describes to Alan her knowledge of Kechuan, which the Spanish priests in Mexico and Peru discovered. She explains that Kechuan is the language of the Incas as well as the Aztecs and the Mayan civilizations. "Alan, human language is something that is remarkable in a respect that correlates to what we were discussing a minute ago on the issue of discovering meaning in life or some higher purpose. Isn't it the SETI organization in America that is actively searching for extraterrestrial signals out there in the great beyond?" "Yeah: Search For Extraterrestrial Intelligence. I'm aware of that."

"Well, isn't it bizarre that in our search for meaning upon this planet, one of the hallmarks in connection to others—to the larger group—is language. The question is, 'Have we throughout a period of thousands of years reached a point where human communication is not enough?' We have developed thousands of ways of expressing ourselves, yet, does life have any more meaning for us? In the seventeenth century the mathematician and religious thinker, Blaise Pascal, said that if, in fact, man was a mere reed in relation to the power and size of the universe, that at least he was a 'thinking reed.'"

"Pascal was a Christian," Alan replies. "It was very important for him to conceptualize man as special and unique, symbolic of God, if you will. Aristotle, of course, conceived that the earth was not at the center of the universe and that man resided high up in the hierarchy of living things."

"I know, I know. The point I'm trying to make though, is: What does man need in order to attain a transcendent meaning to life? Is it communication with his fellow man or is it something greater, perhaps communication with other intelligence out in space—if not this galaxy, then somewhere else 'out there'?"

Alan grabs her hand and leads her to a bench situated in front of a large photograph—of a mainframe computer—which looks like it was taken in the sixties.

"Perhaps that is DNA's purpose," Alan responds, adding: "to evolve to a level in which vastly disparate locales in the universe develop modes of communication amongst themselves and create some intricate cosmic village. Some astronomers estimate that there are something like six hundred and forty planets like earth in our galaxy alone." "Alan, sometimes I wonder what the ancient Egyptians were communicating with when they etched intricate symbols on walls. I wonder if there were extraterrestrial communications going on with so-called 'primitives' who were simply more adept at receiving the signals." "Ronia, sometimes I wonder about the role that psychoactive plants and vegetables have had or could have in the scheme of things—in terms of tapping into a certain cellular awareness or communication with other life forms. Perhaps these substances have been left for us to discover and implement to such a use. Wouldn't that be strange?" "Definitely."

Alan and Ronia gaze up at the mammoth, cumbersome, imposing machine and Alan is sure that they are both thinking the same thing. Advances made in technological communication had been so rapid through the years, that just about anything was possible.

They stand up and stroll down a long hallway that holds on its walls various images of Egyptian hieroglyphs and Chinese script. The various arrangements of squiggles and symbols were man's attempt to symbolize those objects and things that were salient and of specific meaning to him. Animals, tools, weapons, hygienic and cooking devices were all represented in various form. The breadth of expressions is obviously diverse and seems to symbolize in its very essence the rich diversity of human life on this planet. As he fills his brain with the seemingly endless examples of pictographs and ideograms, Alan ponders the hypothetical: that Marshall McLuhan's global village—which is now being realized through the World Wide Web—would some day be replaced by something much more grand: a cosmic village connecting various points throughout the universe. What kind of life exists elsewhere? What modes of communication will connect these beings? What plan does DNA have in store for all of us?

CHAPTER 21

The next two hours are spent leisurely but inquisitively meandering through the wings of the museum while inundating themselves with the myriad displays of just about every extant and obsolete language ever known by man. They stop for some iced teas and rest for a little while on an open-air patio adjacent to a refreshment stand. Interesting, modernistic chrome colored tables and chairs overlook a rather murky pond. The sky presents a marvelous canopy of white and gray clouds that hover in gloriously monstrous and beautiful arrangements: geometrically harrowing but graceful feats of circles, squares, rectangles, and triangles with delightfully no perfect angles but those which the overly linear mind imposed upon them. Staring at the chaotic curves of atmosphere proves refreshing artistic relief from the orderly, structured figures depicted on the inside walls.

Alan philosophizes about the dichotomous hemispheric evolutions that had mysteriously dropped from space and been organically fertilized to exemplify the opposing forces—the yin and the yang of life. Left-linear. Right-revelatory. The working brain that perceives clouds in their unencumbered, majestically sensual configurations is itself a bizarre, contorted, convoluted array of form. After all, the brain's physicality is nothing more than a mass of oozing, dripping neural jelly that lies encased in a rather ordinary cranial shell. "But oh, we can do so much with it and how it delectably craves and savors stimulation," Alan muses. "Alan, look!"

Ronia motions toward what appears to be a cat roaming through some bushes by the pond. In its mouth there appears to be a felled robin. The cat determinedly gnaws the flailing bird's neck until it lies perfectly motionless in the cat's jaws. The felicitous but focused feline scampers up to the edge of the patio and drips the bird's carcass on the ground, within sight of anyone on the patio who might have been interested. One woman gasps. Another turns quickly away. "Nature can be vicious," Alan exclaims. The cat sits prostrate, proudly by its prey and gently turns his head from side to side in what appears to be a sort of victory prance. Alan giggles as Ronia looks the other way, aghast.

"Do you want to go back inside?" he asks. "Sure." They throw the cups away and begin to make their way over to a display, which explains a little bit about Egyptian writing. It outlines how Egyptians coupled pictographs and phonetic signs called determinatives, that served to indicate the meanings of the phonetic words that had different meanings but identical consonants.

Alan gazes at a mural that portrays a glossary of computer terms, with respective pictures to denote their references. Analog computer. Bit. Encode. Flow chart. High-level language. Machine language. Problem language and Procedural language. Off to the left, hangs a huge black and white photograph of Univac I, the first mass-produced electronic computer. He reads that the Univac I implemented several thousand vacuum tubes and was less powerful than a personal computer. "Alan. Do you want to go outside again?" "Yeah, that sounds good." They step outside onto a different patio area. Various bronze sculptures peer out of lush, tropical ivy and beautifully landscaped hedges.

Alan and Ronia sit beneath a towering, drooping willow. "Can I have a cigarette?" Ronia asks. "Sure." Alan reaches into his bag and removes a cigarette and the lighter. He then grabs the original book on mysticism for himself.

As Ronia lights her cigarette and begins to blow an elegant stream of smoke into the arching limbs of the tree, Alan begins to read where he has left off: "In the Orient, there has always been a ubiquitously overt striving for the mystical realm. Buddhism and Hinduism are two major world religions that wholeheartedly embrace the precepts of divine contemplation and spiritual transcendence. Nirvana is that state of utter bliss in which one has successfully merged with the universal essence and therefore escaped the vicious cycle of birth-death-rebirth. One has denied the illusory sensory world and withdrawn into a perfect style of contentment and absolute knowledge of the divine. The atman or (soul) has been united with Brahma or (God.) An expression of this is samadhi or state of perfect enlightenment. Whereas one who has attained absolute Nirvana is considered to have reached the culmination of spiritual development and will not return, a Bodhisattva is one who has tasted the waters of eternal bliss but voluntarily returns to the mundane world in order to instruct and guide others to reach Nirvana."

With the sun gleaming through intermittent spaces in the lofty, flowing branches and with Ronia's curvaceous, elegant silhouette superimposed on this rather interesting garden, Alan tunes into the crystalline, piercing chirps of the birds. Cackles of myriad species have emerged within minutes as his mind recedes into thoughts of the seeming permanence of consciousness and the seeming permanence of life.

Alan muses how the various manifestations of life that are around him now are simply momentary vibrations or materializations: spirit made flesh, the incorporeal made corporeal, the formless made form, the structureless made into structure, and the great purposelessness of matter transmogrified into eternal purposefulness. The purposefulness that Alan conceptualizes is the sense of life creating meaning for other life. The inflections of thought and the subtle incantations of communication among chromosomal forms of life would perhaps never reach some universally resounding crescendo but it means something nevertheless. Visionaries among the spectrum of human life had hypothesized that man would reach monumental proportions of accomplishment in the domains of religion, art, science, and technology through his uncanny ability to synthesize and assimilate dialects and utterances into a unified, advanced, but instinctual language. The vast, disparate strands of DNA had mysteriously evolved and left scattered all over earth's crust would one day reach some sort of rapprochement, a harmonious, sanctified vision and understanding that would definitely propel the human race forward toward whatever grand goal or scheme it had in store for itself.

Alan places the book back into his bag. In the distance is a grossly distorted, contorted head bust which depicts a man in obvious agony. Alan focuses on large, rippling swollen lips that twist and turn, revealing gnawing teeth and an exceptionally strained jaw. The eyes are horrifically dilated, blisteringly opened orbs that reveal a witness to absolute terror. The head is large and possesses muscularly atrophied, voluminous cheeks that swell as careless wafts of coarse mane fall agonizingly over a heavily wrinkled forehead.

To Alan, the sculpture seems strangely out of place in such a pastoral setting. On the other hand, it seems to underscore and highlight the juxtaposition of opposites. Man had always struggled to sustain his existence in a world where moments of strain and strife were sometimes punctuated with climaxes of ecstasy and serenity. The interplay of pairs of opposites seems to be the way of nature. So it is fitting—Alan decides—that this symbol of man's arduous task of living is situated in the midst of such a placid setting. "Ronia, how are you doing, sweetie?" "Wonderful. How are you?" "I'm doing fine. I was just thinking about things. Do you want to move on shortly?" "Yeah. I think we've seen just about everything." Ronia grabs the bag and wraps the straps around her arm. They walk back through the museum and out to the car. "Maybe we can go back to the hotel and rest for awhile before dinner," Ronia suggests. "Alright, sounds good." Alan starts the engine and regains his bearings on the map.

It is late afternoon when they arrive back at the hotel. The room is pleasantly clean. While Ronia begins to use the phone to call England for school matters, Alan goes downstairs to get some postcards. He picks out mainly skyline views with phrases like, "Welcome to Glasgow," or "Greetings from Glasgow." As he sits in the room and fills them out, he overhears Ronia discussing something about her research proposal. As Alan writes notes to his family and a couple of friends, he notices her conversation deals with seemingly esoteric statistics phrases like, "correlations," "covariance," "analysis of variance," and "distribution." Knowing he is listening is surely affecting the course of her conversation. As we all frequently do when discussing our vocations while we know others are listening, Ronia is casting an overly erudite, important light on the subject of her research. She begins to wrap up her conversation. "How are things going?" Alan asks. "Fine, we're just ensuring that our study is longitudinally cohesive, or statistically valid."

Alan approaches the postcards assiduously, assuring that everyone back home is apprised of the details on his travels: the details that would be salient to them. When he is finished, he sets the cards on the bathroom countertop near the front door. He then walks over to the window and looks out at the glimmering fountain. The sun is shining down and casts a glistening sparkle all over the surface of the cascading pool. A few rambunctious children chase each other in circles, some slipping momentarily and splashing gleefully into the water.

Alan smiles and turns toward Ronia, who is now lying peacefully upon the bed with her head resting sideways on the pillow. Alan slides over beside her and lays one hand on her hip while he bends his other arm and leans his head on his hand. He becomes almost hypnotized as he watches the gentle pulse on her neck. Soon, they are both asleep.

They awaken sometime in the early evening between seven and eight. Dusk has left a misty blue sky, which gradually fades to whitish gray. Alan walks to the window and pulls back the shades to reveal distant hovering clouds that swing majestically in various shades of pink and reddish orange that segues into midnight blue. "Do you want to go to dinner pretty soon?" Alan asks. "Ahhhh," Ronia yawns. "Yes, where do you want to go?" "I don't know. Do you want to go get a pizza somewhere?" "Um, sure." Ronia rises slowly and creeps up to promptly lay a juicy, succulent kiss on Alan's cheek. "Let me freshen up a bit," she remarks, before retreating to the bathroom. Ten minutes later, she emerges an ebullient, mesmerizing beauty; her blonde, silky hair is pulled back in delicate sinewy strands that converge playfully in a pony-tail that falls lightly on the nape of her neck. Her smooth, translucent skin is soothing when gazed upon or touched. Ronia is wearing a colorfully red casual dress that covers her frame almost diaphanously, temptingly revealing her muscular, toned calves and slender thighs. As she gathers a small black leather handbag, Alan notices with great pleasure how her pearl white arms and shoulders emerge dazzlingly and beautifully in svelte but voluptuous form. This convinces him—not that he really needs any convincing—that women are very different creatures from men. "I've got the keys. Are you ready?" he asks. "Yeah, let's go."

On the way out of the hotel, Alan asks the clerk for directions to a decent Italian restaurant. They end up at a place called, Carmine's, which turns out to have one of the best pizzas Alan has ever eaten. Thin crust and juicy, spicy tomato sauce support tastefully oozing layers of melted mozzarella, pepperoni, and mushrooms. Alan scans a wine list before ordering a bottle of French Cabernet. They toast to continued hedonism and intellectual stimulation.

After a couple of pieces of pizza, Alan clears his throat and speaks up: "Maybe we'll move into Ireland pretty soon. Isn't that concert coming up sometime in the near future?" "Yeah, the Moksha Revellers. I know they'll be glad to see you." "Maybe we'll load things up tomorrow and stop off at some key points along the way as we roar into Ireland. Would that be cool?" "Yes, I think that would be fun," Ronia replies with a gleam in her eye.

When they finish the meal, they take a leisurely stroll down the side-walk that runs from the restaurant to a precipice that looks down upon the lights of the city. Twinkling lights bristle with energy and shine with brilliance that simultaneously encompasses the undeniable essence of industry but also a surprising, uncanny feeling of nature. He holds her lovingly in his arms as she smiles with effervescence and a look of gen-tle, calm renouncing—renouncing in the sense of voluntarily giving up any need for the usual control or preliminary planning for where they are going. Ronia is gradually and comfortably embracing a spirit of spon-taneity and caprice that Alan had adopted early on in his travels. They lean against a large, antiquated oak and listen to the sweet sounds of night; the quietude and solitude of nature serve as a backdrop or amphitheater to the symphonic offerings of crickets chirping and light bugs conducting a moving, harmonious display that rivals the Philharmonics of London, Sydney, and Milan.

They return to the hotel at about eleven and stay up late surfing the channels on cable TV. This night, Alan dreams of falling—falling into a vast abysmal lake surrounded by towering pine-laden mountains that stand as monstrous, imposing giants which seem to be monitoring his fate. He struggles, as if bound with chains, and his body severely contorts and strains to break free. As he sinks lower and lower into the depths of water, he feels the very real sensation of being immersed in a tepid, honey-textured sea of not simply water but a sort of mixture of water, seaweed, and an indefinable substance—a sort of amniotic-like goo, that is simultaneously comforting and terrifying. Visually, he perceives strange amalgamations of seahorses and starfish that dangle almost artificially like mobiles suspended in air, although these objects are clearly in the depths of water. Instead of possessing normal anatomy, the structures of these creatures have unusual curves and forms that belie their classifications. Their eyes are larger and beadier than normal and their sponge-like encasings are a more brilliant orange—with spores that emerge in detailed, cavernous craters that open up into other worlds. Alan fears looking too closely at these apertures that spot the oddly structured sea life. He feels that if he watches too closely, he might be sucked terminally into their infinite, enigmatic spheres. As he floats closer to the surface, he becomes surrounded by schools of dolphins, stingrays, and sharks that are all covered in sky-blue shiny skin that reflects the outline of mountains. Gazing up to the surface—as he finds himself gasping for air—he sees through the rippling translucent waters: snow-peaked Alpines that continue to beckon him with a subliminal, barely tangible voice that he encodes as a message telling him that he must swim and push toward survival. He begins to lunge with broad, painstaking strokes that carry his body cumbersomely but successfully to the surface. Upon reaching the surface, Alan thrusts his head into open, icy air that refreshingly caresses his throat and brings him to a more "awake" consciousness. Dog-paddling in swift, repetitive motions allows him to look around at the vista of mountains, superimposed by a thin veil of charcoal misty clouds. On a plateau that juts from one of the hillsides stands a castle surrounded by pines. The entire castle is darkened, except for one of its windows, that is lit by candles and frames a woman's venomous silhouette. Alan squints in order to see more clearly as voluminous, chilly waves periodically wash past him. He realizes that it is Ronia in the window and that the distance between them is unconquerable. For although he seems to possess the power to swim, with each stroke in his efforts toward the castle the ocean of water expands and creates more distance between them. Meanwhile, she stands motionless, in a mannequin-like state that seems ethereal or hopelessly otherworldly. The air grows increasingly cool and the winds begin to pick up.

Suddenly, Alan awakens. He has broken out into a vigorous sweat but very relieved to find Ronia sleeping peacefully next to him. He momentarily rests his cheek against hers and in this closeness finds great comfort. Within minutes, he is back to sleep.

In the morning they dress and pack. Before checking out, they stop off at a restaurant to eat breakfast. Once he has eaten and had some coffee, he feels refreshed and thankful that the dream has passed and he is back in wakeful consciousness. They enter a convenience store adjacent to the restaurant and promptly purchase a map on Ireland and a couple of guidebooks. As they make their way toward the Scottish coast, they decide to stop off in Paisley, a quaint town that possesses a variety of antique and arts and crafts shops. They park the car and decide to walk around a bit. Storefront windows showcase ties, scarves, and raincoats designed with various shades of paisley and argyle designs. Alan notices a travel business and decides to get some information about transportation to Ireland. For some reason, he has temporarily neglected to consider that one must cross the North Channel to get to Northern Ireland from Scotland. They enter the store and after asking an agent, quickly discover that one can travel by boat or plane for a couple of hundred dollars. With a phone call, Alan makes arrangements to return the rental car. He purchases two tickets on a boat that is pictured as an elongated submarine-like craft that looks like something from a James Bond film. It will take a day to get there.

Upon leaving Paisley, Alan and Ronia drive for a couple of hours to the dock from which they will be departing. Luckily, they are able to return the car about a mile from port and they take a shuttle to the dock. They board the sea vessel and make their way to two comfortable seats surrounding a table by a large window that overlooks the gentle seas.

A waiter arrives shortly to take their drink orders: for Alan, a Bloody Mary, and for Ronia, a vodka tonic. They sit back and relax as the engines are started and the boat begins to scurry through the bay. Alan asks Ronia to read to him about Ireland.

She picks up the book and lifts her voice: "In 1845, the population of Ireland was around 8.5 million. In 1851, it had declined to approximately

6.5 million. This precipitous decline can be largely attributed to the widespread famine and fevers accompanying the failure of the potato harvest between 1845 and 1847." Ronia's voice is sweet and mellifluous as it hovers barely sonorously above the relentless hum of the engines and the crashing waves.

"Further, increased industrial expansion in Britain ensured that a steady flow of emigrates from Ireland would continue. Within Ireland, renowned religious conflicts can be traced back to the English efforts to impose the Protestant Reformation upon Roman Catholic Ireland."

Ronia takes a long sip from her drink and casts a quick glance out the window. Alan listens attentively and watches her absorbingly. As she speaks, a slight quiver in her lower lip adds an anxious, intensive overtone to her historical, political discourse on Ireland. Ronia's lips—in their natural state—are beautifully swollen, succulent morsels of flesh that harmonize with and seemingly caress each syllable pronounced. They move in soft waves, motions of energy that coat everything she says with a pleasing, enriching, palatable air. Alan notices delicate strands of web-like, almost microscopic veins that start at the apex horizontal line of her upper lip and trail off into multifarious directions, curves, and angles underneath the rose-colored diaphanous skin that protects both lips. The perfectly curved outline seems to mirror the sensual curves of a woman's naked profile—reclined.

Alan savors the tangy, spicy vegetable juice with its piquant splash of vodka. He can feel it clearing his sinuses and bathing his taste buds in saucy, sentient tomato Russian bliss. "Sir, would you care for another one?" a tall, thin waiter who looks like Jeremy Irons asks. "No thanks, I'm doing fine," replies Alan. Alan looks out the window and becomes momentarily transfixed by the enormous cascading wake that is cut across the water from the impact of the bow of the ship. Whitecaps become blue and blue becomes whitecaps. "Alan, do you see that man seated behind you?" Ronia whispers. "He's the one with the bushy, curly beard. I wonder if that's natural or if he gets it permmed." Alan turns around to see a corpulent, ivory-complected gentleman with a long, curly snow white beard who appears to be in passionate conversation with an affable, portly fellow who looks like it might be his brother or cousin. The bearded man's face is buxom, slightly ruddy, and cherub-like, almost a living embodiment of old St. Nick. Alan overhears the two men engaged in a heated debate about the infamous, long-standing conflicts between Protestants and Catholics in Ireland. The voices resound:

"When the English granted land and planted settlers, the Protestant Reformation was effectively imposed upon traditionally Roman Catholic Ireland. We've been fighting the fuckers ever since," quips the amusingly coifed man to his companion. The companion replies: "The IRA begins their campaign in the 1920s to try to force the northern countries to join the Free State. The IRA—in representing the Catholic community's better interests—understandably evolved the Sinn Fein to do battle. Catholics and Protestants have been fighting ever since."

Alan detects accents indicative of Australia, although the two men look very Irish. He contemplates the interesting but disturbing paradox that the men's conversation limns out: specifically, the oddity that Christians have never really been able to get along with one another despite the altruistic, loving ideals to which Christians supposedly aspire. "Ronia, why do you think it is that within a monotheistic belief system— that idealizes precepts such as 'love thy neighbor' and 'be kind to others'—there can be so much strife, discord, and even bloodshed?" "I dunno, Alan. It's all very strange. I suppose when you've got a confluence of political interests that are inextricably bound up with firmly enmeshed but disparate religious views, there is a potentially highly combustible, problematic scenario. No one wants someone else pushing political or religious restraints on them. That's why you Americans had to get away from it all." "But it strikes me as extremely odd that in places like Israel or Ireland, heavily religious and monotheistic places, people cannot agree on the edicts that underlie the core of their very religions. It is hypocritical to say that one loves in the name of God and then kills in the name of that same god. I understand that there are great social/political issues that seem to go beyond religion, but if religion is purported to be the quintessential basis of life for certain peoples, why do those same people participate in violence that outweighs any violence in other, arguably less religious countries? It's fucked up." "I know, it's fucked up," she replies, with a very quizzical look that says basically there are things that happen that unfortunately defy logic and rationality.

"Ronia, what does the book say spurs the Irish economy?" "Let's see. It explains that Ireland's economy is primarily based on agriculture. Industrialization has been pursued and manufacturing is becoming increasingly more important. One issue that seems germane is that, according to this book, the Irish economy became especially dependent on the British market when the island was divided in 1922 into the Irish Free State, or the Republic of Ireland, which remains part of the United Kingdom. The economy of the republic was cut off from most of the industry including mainstays such as linen and ship building." "Oh, I see. It's the same old story. Money, religion, and politics all intertwine into a helix of confusion and chaos—a vortex from which any remedy or intelligent discourse is rarely, if ever realized." He grabs the waiter and orders two more drinks. When the waiter returns, they down the drinks fairly quickly, lean their heads back and begin to nap.

Several hours elapse before they awaken to discover—when looking out the window—the first sight of land on the other side of the North Channel. An announcement over the intercom informs them that they will be docking at Whitehead, which is near Belfast. Alan orders two cups of coffee and then begins gathering their bags. Approaching the mystical island of Ireland sends shivers up their spines.

A gentle mist hovers welcomingly over the bay as the barge navigates a narrow canal and drifts past several fishermen's piers before being docked. Alan and Ronia wait in line to exit as the crewmen systematically wave and say goodbye to each departing passenger. When they are off the boat, they will take a cab into Belfast, explore the area by foot, and then rent a car for the rest of the adventure into Ireland. A light cool breeze brushes past them as they descend the plank onto the dock and then promptly hail a cab.

"Sir, please take us to Belfast, if you will," Alan tells the driver. They hop into the car and enjoy a nice, scenic drive through verdant hillsides and winding, well-paved highways which lead to Belfast, the city with dense blocks of nineteenth century brown, bricked, wood-roofed homes. They pass textile manufacturing plants and ship building and repair warehouses. Military jeeps ride on the same streets as miniature Japanese and European economy cars.

The driver pulls over in front of a cybercafe adjacent to what appears to be a late 17th century church. A protruding steeple peers through towering oaks and reveals a stalwart, decorative cross at its apex. The facade of the church is gray and an imposing but beautiful Celtic cross—ornate in its structure and design—hangs over the entranceway like a Gothic stone guardian. Various expressions of cherubic children are carved images in groups of three—on three separate panels on the lower rung of the cross—while at the top, an isolated group of cupids dances gingerly hand-in-hand upon a spiraling, geometrically intricate mandala. Within the mandala is a skyward display of stars, planets, suns, and moons: all strung together by celestial strands or cords, comparable to lights on a Christmas tree. A singular, smaller cross is situated in the middle. Alan and Ronia get out of the cab and begin to walk on the sidewalk and step into the cybercafe that holds over its entrance an unfurled red and white banner which reads: "Voices From The Edge": A Surrealist's perspective of darkness within light and lightness within dark; by John Bryant. The name of the cafe, written in bold black letters is: "The Cosmic Delight."

They enter a large, darkened main room which serves as restaurant seating and bar. Covering all the walls are sundry paintings by this John Bryant, who seems to be the man in the corner of the room, seated at a table signing posters and talking about his work. Alan and Ronia sit down at a table, and begin to look around at the interesting paintings on the walls. Strategically arranged Gothic candle holders with illuminated yellow light bulbs project light upon every painting. Each painting depicts a particular state of agony or despair—conceptualized through the image of a man's face in particularly revealing countenance. The face, an ethereal, apparitional white glow of form, contorts into an agonizing scowl in one painting. In another, the look of torturous, dreadful fear bespeaks a countenance mired in the bowels of hell.

Alan scans the room until his eyes land on the creator of these bizarrely interesting works. With long, sinewy black hair that seems to reach his lower back and a grisly goatee with alternate strands and bristles of black and brown, the artist sits motionless, except for his moving arm that is signing autographs. He wears a long black coat and feather-lined black cowboy hat. Periodically, he puts on a pair of sunglasses, as if it is somehow too bright in this cave of a bar. Striking silver earrings in the shape of a skull and crossbones dangle from his ears. Despite the macabre appearance, the man smiles effusively when certain things are said to him.

Alan and Ronia order food and drinks before Alan notices behind the bar a wide array of liquor that is stacked in neat, orderly rows that seem twenty feet long. Fluorescent lights of many colors emanate from the backs of the bottles, where a large gold-framed mirror hangs majestically and creates the illusion of another room. Around the edge of the inner frame is a collection of photos and postcards—the photos, shots of partying patrons and the postcards, representations of places all over the world. A television hangs in the upper left-hand corner of the bar. Alan notices something interesting when he walks up to pick up some matches: a constantly moving scroll that sits underneath the glass bar top and provides drinkers a stimulating array of abstract art by sundry local artists. To Alan, the paper used for the scroll appears to be a tan-stained imitation parchment or rice paper. On the paper, there are geometrically swirling designs which look to be a psychedelicists' surreal interpretation of Chinese script: the *Tao Te Ching* after about eight beers, if you will.

"Alan, Alan Agrippa," Alan remarks as he introduces himself to the artist, John Bryant. Mr. Bryant shakes hands with him and asks Alan if he enjoys the work. "Well, it's definitely intriguing. I'd have to say it's certainly riveting to gaze at, which, in art, is saying a hell of a lot. Anything that evokes such a strong reaction is worth a closer look. By the way, where do you get your inspiration?" The avant artist runs his fingers roughly through his hair and darts his eyes toward one particularly haunting image of a devil prancing through the cortex of one of the heads. "I guess I get my inspiration from analyzing the powerful and often disturbing forces that operate through men's minds. I take the darker (he pronounces darker as if he is parodying society's use of the term) sides of my nature and society's nature and recapitulate onto canvas what I feel. I also like toying with the ideas of "evil" (same parodying, as before) and enjoy exploring any terrain that is infused with great emotion of one sort or another."

It is undeniable. The man speaks with an assurance and eloquence, that not only belie his hard-core appearance, but actually convincingly encourage the listener to give the works a more thorough review. Alan notices the man is wearing a silver cross on the end of a lengthy chain that dangles loosely upon his chest. Alan looks over at Ronia and observes that the food is arriving. "I'm 'bout to go eat, but perhaps we'll talk more before we have to leave."

"That would be great," the gentleman replies. Alan goes back to his table and begins to eat.

"Alan, what did the artist have to say?" Ronia implores anxiously. "He basically gave me a brief overview of his creative process. Whether the guy worships Satan or not is beyond me. He speaks rather persuasively that his desire is to capture a certain force in the world and somehow conceptualize and realize it on canvas. Very pleasant, articulate individual actually." "Wow, how bizarre. And to think we are adjacent to a church! The irony is killing me."

Alan smiles and sips his wine. He ponders the dichotomies of religion in their interplay of so-called "forces" of good and evil. He wonders if there really is a "good" side and "evil" side that are polar opposites or if they are simply mutually inclusive halves to a singular whole. Surely, death and destruction are "evil." Peace and love seem "good." What fascinates Alan is that certain individuals who appear to revel in "evil" actually turn out to be thoughtful, conscientious humanists who promote "good." The rock band, Black Sabbath, is an example. While growing up, Alan had perceived Black Sabbath as somehow in cahoots with the devil. However—on second look—one can see that Black Sabbath actually spoke cynically and disparagingly of the atrocities that man commits, such as in war. War Pigs was a perfect example. Often the donning of the customs of one's enemy is the most effective way of overcoming one's enemy. "The food is good, right?" Alan asks.

"Yes, it is great." When they are close to finishing their meal, John Bryant comes up to the table. Alan introduces him to Ronia. "So guys, how are you doing over here?" "Just fine," Ronia responds with an intonation a bit jumbled from being slightly spooked. "I just wanted to ask you," she begins... "As an artist, are you ever confronted with the expectation or demand to create a medium that enhances and uplifts according to certain sensibilities or are you quite satisfied putting out what makes you happy and leaving the spectator to discover what they want?"

Alan pulls back a chair and motions for John to sit. "I am in a state when I am creating my art that is a primordial, impulsive instinct that I feel in retrospect dictates to me what it is I need to say and how I am going to say it. It seems to go beyond conscious review or effort if you will." He continues: "I relinquish control over the creation of the work." What ordinarily would have seemed trite and clichéd to Alan comes across sincere and warm as John Bryant speaks. This man, whom Alan perceives as being quite angry at the world, has found a way to express himself in a manner that seems to have an appreciative audience. Psychosis and pure existential dread are certainly not everyone's cup of tea for art; but to some it is exemplary of reality—symbolic of the seedier, more morose elements to life. To revel in the darkness on one hand seems a perpetuation of it. In another sense the acceptance of and deliberate exploration into and out of darkness seems transcendence beyond it. The transubstantiation of darkness to light means for some immersing themselves into the monster where time, space, order, and reason are all relative and Newton's laws are simply local ordinances. From front row seats, one can effectively surmise the situation, delineate its coordinates, and methodically challenge and expose its contents. To know pain is to experience it. To feel loss is to be lost to it. To understand horror is to live it. At least this is how Alan is reasoning it.

Ronia points to a painting beside her that encapsulates the prototype face with bloodied eyes, pale blue cheeks, and the jaws tightly clenched on the blade of a dagger. Behind the face and high above is a sensual depiction of two planets converged in a seeming act of coitus: merging, melting orbs curved and intertwined like human bodies. Beneath the painting is a name card with the words "Cosmic Tantric." "What is this one all about, Mr. Bryant?" Ronia queries innocently. The artist lights a cigarette and replies, "That is my work on the notion of tantrism combined with the theory of the Big Bang. I took the idea of tantrism—that basically sex can be a means toward union with God—the hieros gamos is the divine intercourse, the original orgasm that spawned the whole fucking world, man." "I get it now. The planets are fucking. Pretty cool," Ronia responds demurely. The artist continues: "I believe that woman is representative of the creative force that sets the whole thing in motion. She is a goddess, in a sense representing one who lets down her hair in order to create the world. Please look at that one over there." John points to a midnight blue painting over next to the jukebox. The face has long curly hair that rolls out into branches of colorful planets which bob like Christmas tree ornaments. "That one is called, 'Objective Inflective.'"

"If woman represents that which is positive, or creative, then why does she have a scowl on her face," Alan posits. The artist responds sternly but patiently: "My friend, that is because the goddess is equal part disease and war. Within tantrism, some acts of sex are conducted in cemeteries. Did you know?" A long strand of hair has fallen in front of John's right eye, thus increasing his mysterious look. "The woman in a sense becomes a force of dissolution," Ronia chimes in, continuing: "According to Mircea Eliade, the man experiences the same profundity of emotion while gazing at his naked woman as he does with the revelation of cosmic mystery." "That's it exactly," enthusiastically concurs the artist, adding: "Now you have it!" Those are the last words spoken by the artist-philosopher before leaving the table. Alan and Ronia had complimented him on his work and said goodbye.

As he walks away, his long black hair reaches the dangling chain that hangs from his belt. A pantheon of tattoos seems to lie under his shirt, for when he gets up, his collar drops low and reveals color that stretches at least as high as his lower neck. Alan is thinking two things: Friedrich Nietzsche and Harley Davidson.

Alan and Ronia depart the cafe and walk outside with their bags in hand. They stroll on a sidewalk that winds its way in front of stores, churches, and homes that seem simultaneously haunting and charming. Ireland, itself, seems to Alan to possess a tranquillity and a nervousness that—strangely coexistent—are omnipresent. "Alan, that man is a trip. His works were not exactly light fare."

"No, I'd say his works are not to be shown in any kindergarten class too soon."

"Shall we find a place to stay?" "Sure!"

CHAPTER 22

Alan leads her to an information station, where they find out about a bed and breakfast on the outside of town. Alan and Ronia rent a car and follow the directions to a quaint, Victorian chalet that has a flourishing garden and a lawn with vibrant pines. Much to Ronia's pleasure, the inn is run by a French couple in their upper thirties, Mr. and Mrs. Postel. Speaking mellifluously in her native tongue, Ronia makes arrangements for the room. They carry their bags to a second floor room with a spacious, overstuffed bed, paisley curtains, and a pleasant view of a pastoral brook behind the home. "They're preparing tea downstairs and seem quite pleased that I speak French. Can we go down and talk with them a bit?"

"Sure," Alan replies. "First thing's first, though." Alan leans and kisses her on the cheek. She blushes. After descending the stairs, they enter the dining room and sit down at the table with Mr. and Mrs. Postel. The couple is a studious, attractive looking pair with short brown hair and pale, lucid skin. As a courtesy to Alan, they speak mainly in English, occasionally slipping into French with aphorisms and recognizable quips like: bonsoir, bon vivant, Le Juif Errant, Francais-Anglais, joie de vivre.

On the center of the table sits a colorful, intricately painted vase; finely painted vines and leaves in burgundy, lavender, and hot red spin and interweave themselves upward into a radiant helix upon an ivory background. Seven long-stemmed pink roses blossom forth from the vase in reaching, turning, peering, and roaring beauty for the humans' aesthetic and olfactory pleasure.

Mrs. Postel pours everyone a cup of tea. Small wedges of lemon and lime line the plates while a jar of honey beckons with a spoon. "So, Alan, what brings you to this part of the world?" Mr. Postel asks. "Well, I've always wanted to visit the United Kingdom and found myself with the opportunity to do it. So, here I am." "What do you think, so far?" "I enjoy it very much," Alan replies, then takes a sip of tea. "The people have been immensely friendly and interesting. The places we've been thus far have been beautiful. I'm highly impressed." "Alan has varied interests," Ronia offers. "He has a keen interest in mysticism and philosophy. Obviously, Europe is rich in these areas."

A bright smile overtakes Mr. Postel's face. "Mysticism and philosophy, I see," he says. "You might find what I'm about to tell you pretty interesting," Mr. Postel beams, as he looks in the direction of his wife. "I am actually the descendant of Guillaume Postel, a notable mystic from the 1500s." Alan races his memory banks and has a glimmer of remembrance of seeing this name. "Please go on, Mr. Postel. I would like to hear more about this," Alan requests pedantically. "Well, Guillaume Postel was born near Auranches, which is in the Normandy region of northwestern France." Alan glances at Ronia to see if she recognizes the name, which she does.

"Guillaume Postel learned Greek, Hebrew, and Arabic. A Jewish doctor gave him a copy of the Cabala. Among other things, he was appointed Professor of Mathematics and Oriental Languages at the College Royal." "Honey, tell them about Joanna," Mrs. Postel implores. "Okay, I was getting to it," Mr. Postel retorts playfully. "Guillaume felt that it was his calling to unite the three religions of the Book in his *DeOrbis Terrae Concordia,* which was in 1544. He traveled to Rome to try to persuade Ignatius Loyola of some of his findings or theories. He was promptly placed in prison. When he was released..."

Mr. Postel pauses to light a cigarette and offers one to anyone who wants it. "When he was released, he translated a book of the Cabala, Bahir. While working as an almoner at the San Giovanni hospital in Venice, he served as confessor to a 50 year-old illiterate cook named Joanna. He grew to believe that she was the 'sacred Mother of the world' and believed that she would reconcile Eve's fall from grace, the anima, and would lift up the animus. His soul told him that Joanna would be the female Messiah. Needless to say, the Inquisition did not look on this behavior lightly. They basically declared him to be mad, or insane."

"Can I ask?" Alan interrupts. "How did the public consider Postel?" "Well, Postel took up teaching, which he had done before. His lectures were quite popular to the point that people lined up in droves to see him speak. He published *Merveilleuses Victories des femmes du Nouveau Monde* in 1553. In this publication, he espoused his conviction in the Gilgul, a Cabalist term for a reincarnated soul. Some found this interesting. To others, it simply distanced him again. Many followers such as, Guy Le Feure De La Borderie, and Jacques Gaffarel, went on to create highly controversial works." "Wow, that's interesting," Alan replies, adding: "His interest in universal agreement among religions seems bold and lofty. I can see the controversy he must have conjured." Ronia speaks up:

"Alan and I were earlier discussing the role of the mystic or artist in delving the inner reaches of darkness or controversy in order to mine or extract a higher knowledge or to reveal a hidden truth. What your infinitely great grandfather seems to have done is similar. He boldly explored the unknown or the off-limits and returned with esoteric knowledge that the establishment was not happy with."

Mrs. Postel had been relatively quiet until this point. She decides to break her silence: "I think that what you've hit on is the process of ritual. Ritualization involves the revealing of a rite or archetype. The mystic identifies with those precious elements revealed to him and plays with a reality that is mythological. The activating of myths or the activating of ritual is a process that enables the mystic to discover that which is..."

"Invisible!" Mr. Postel interjects. "Yes, invisible," Mrs. Postel concurs.

Alan stands up and begins to walk across the room. He stops at a painting on the wall next to a bookcase. The painting depicts the face of a lion staring in a semi-drugged, almost introspective glare with large, beady orange eyes and piercing black pupils. Its nose and whiskers protrude prominently and its ears are furry and erect. Its head is covered with brown spots. A chill prances up and down Alan's spine. In silence, Alan ponders the unusual coincidence of encountering this intriguing couple. Synchronicity and coincidence are all around. "How are you doing sweetie?" Ronia whispers as she places her hand on the back of his neck.

"Fine, how are you?" "Good. Do you want to go out soon?" "Yeah, that would be good." A family is arriving at the time Alan and Ronia step out.

Driving to the neighborhood of Queen's University—which was Mrs. Postel's former employer—Alan and Ronia decide to pull over and walk around the campus, which houses buildings devoted to theology, agriculture, and education. They tour Belfast College of Technology and Parliament House. Earlier in the day, it had been sunny, with only sporadic fluffy white clouds. Now, it is becoming overcast, with an influx of gray and charcoal clouds that float in almost ominously, triggering light sprays of mist and rain. Roaming Belfast begins to cause Alan a certain degree of malaise.

Army tanks traverse crossroads on streets, the same streets played on by kids who are kicking inflatable balls around. Women hang their family clothes out to dry on a line connected to brick walls stained with gun powder. Thunder begins to roar in the distance as Alan and Ronia walk alongside postered and spray-painted walls filled with British propaganda and IRA retorts. Catholic–Irish tension hangs in the air like a dense, combustible rain cloud. They wither away a good part of the day in another coffee shop where they mournfully discuss among themselves the planet's difficulty in maintaining peace. They will probably leave Belfast the next day.

When they arrive back at the house, the steady rain has subsided and left a glistening layer of moisture that twinkles as the sun's last rays bid the day goodbye. The relative placid nature on the outskirts of the city is—as it is with most cities, but particularly this one—a welcome respite from the industry and stress of the city. Alan knows that objectively it may be unwarranted, but subjectively, the entire time he is in Belfast he feels he might be shot or bombed. "Probably that's how tourists from Europe feel in Los Angeles or New York," he reassures himself. They let themselves into their room and fall asleep quickly.

This night, Alan dreams of winter in Belfast, with smokestacks hurling funnels of smoke high up into rain clouds. It appears to be around the time of World War II and Belfast shipyards are constructing merchant ships and aircraft carriers for battle. American troops are training to do battle in Europe. Alan is seated next to a soldier who is philosophizing about the war. He offers Alan a cigarette and begins to speak: "You know, Satan's reared his ugly head and the tear gas and bullet shells are evidence that he exists. Look around you my friend. Nostradamus had a point. Hitler's the fucking devil." Soon, a monolithic cloud that the soldiers refer to as "angel of destruction" or "angel of deception" spreads out across the entire sky and begins to rain a downpour of bullets and bombs. It is 1941 and German raids are attacking the city. Alan begins to hear the shrill of terrified children when he suddenly awakens.

He is in a cold sweat as Ronia lies peacefully beside him. He gets up and retrieves a glass of water before pacing the room briefly. He grabs a pack of cigarettes and his lighter and then goes outside for a smoke. Crickets and mosquitoes are in busy overtime. Fortunately, so are lightning bugs—fireflies—who flutter and flicker a wondrous light show. A luminescent three-quarter moon showers the backyard and nearby stream with additional light. Alan pulls up a lawn chair, lights a cigarette, and sits back to enjoy a more idyllic show than the one in his dreams. As he inhales the rich tobacco smoke, he watches as the fireflies perform their amazing display. He begins to contemplate the various effects that watching fireflies must have on the human brain. His memory banks scan images of the thalamus—that tiny, bean-like structure in the middle of the brain. He ponders the corpus callosum with its serpent-like coil that curves in elegant cortical repose around layers of gray matter. A dendritic, neural symphony of energy must be mirroring the light display before him, he theorizes.

"Excuse me, young man, but what's going on?" comes a voice from the night. Who should it be, but Mr. Postel? "Hello, Mr. Postel. I hope I didn't wake you. It's got to be 2 or 3 in the morning." "No, you didn't wake me. I've been getting up a lot, lately. I don't know if you've noticed our garage over there." He points to their garage. "My wife's been very busy lately on a project in addition to us running this house. She's a documentarian, as in filmmaker. She and her crew have been interviewing IRA members and British politicians to put together a film which captures the conflict and all its sides. That's a major reason for why we're here." "Do you want a cigarette?" Alan asks. "Sure." Alan hands him a cigarette and the lighter.

"So, what is your take on this? How did things get so complicated here?" Alan asks. "It's strange. The Boundary Commission began work in 1924 to separate Northern Ireland and the Irish Free State. The commission made recommendations for only slight changes. Catholics continued to be pissed that the North has not joined the Free State. Catholics and Protestants cast aspersions at one another, among other things. Protestants believed that Catholics were disputative and divisive by keeping their community apart. Catholics have complained about being discriminated against in politics. Here's the real grabber, though. Catholics experienced alienation in so far as the ruling Unionist Party, affiliated with the Orange Order—of course a Protestant organization— was the ruling part of government dedicated in their relationship with Great Britain, and virulently anti-Catholic." "It is odd how religion intertwines with politics so inextricably and how Christianity can be so monumentally self-paradoxical," Alan pontificates. "It is odd, indeed." The two men exchange a few stories and then call it a night at about 4:00 a.m.

Ronia and Alan awaken to the smell of sizzling bacon and aromatically cinnamon brewing coffee. They descend the stairs and sit at the table with the entire group: Mr. and Mrs. Postel and the other family, a lively, charming couple and two kids from South Africa. Over breakfast, Alan speaks privately to Ronia about their next destination. He has loose plans for driving through rural Ireland but realizes that the Moksha Revellers concert is happening in a matter of days. They decide to head south along the eastern Irish coast and down into the Dublin area. Based on the map, it would take a couple of days of leisurely driving to get to the racetrack, where the show is going to happen.

They say their good-byes and begin the drive that takes them through Lisburn, Portadown, Newry, and Lowth before they stop at a small town called Dunany Point, which overlooks the majestic Irish Sea. Their first stop is a pay phone with which Ronia makes two calls, to England and France. She explains to Mary and Jim what is going on and she calls her office to handle some work issues. She then phones home and talks to her family briefly, promising them that she will write. Alan calls America and chats with his parents, informing them of his tentative travel plans and that he is having a wonderful time.

Alan hangs up the phone and grabs their book on Ireland. He begins to read silently while Ronia sits back and takes in the view. He scans through sections on topics such as: "Patterns Of Living," which, among other things, colorfully describes bands of gypsies called tinkers, who travel in trailers and tents on roadsides. In the Labor section, a notable bit of trivia describes a man by the name of, James Larkin, who declared: "a divine mission to preach discontent," in order to inform about the deplorable conditions of low wages and poor housing in the early twentieth century. In other sections, Alan reads about social welfare issues such as the fact that welfare benefits in the Irish republic fall short of those provided in the north by the United Kingdom. Alan learns that education is compulsory and free-of-charge for children through age fifteen.

With Ronia behind the wheel, they get back in the car and drive a little longer to the thrill of curvaceous verdant hills that slope along jagged promontories jutting over the cerulean sea. It is entrancing and Alan feels that they must stop again very soon in order to spend more time soaking up the view. She selects a spot on a grassy section of a promontory that is laden with heather and ferns and juts out in a monstrous precipice. They climb out of the car to the welcome, comforting sounds of soaring seagulls that frolic madly over crashing waves. Giant wafts of mist billow from the surf and drift into varietal sheets of white that paint wavy designs through the air. Alan feels the cool rush of wind that only the ocean can produce. He takes Ronia by the hand and they stroll to within about ten feet of the edge of the cliff. He holds her in his arms and begins to kiss her shoulder and neck. As the sturdy winds begin to tousle her hair, Alan presses his lips against hers and tastes the sweet taste of ambrosia. Running his hands along the sides of her waist, he gently presses his body against hers and in this soft, warm touch feels he is tasting a hint of blissful, paradisiacal immortality. Anthropomorphic

God might not have been looking down on them, but at this moment, Alan feels truly blessed.

Knowing that no other human is within miles of them—but not really caring too much if anyone is—he gently kneels her back upon the grass while caressing and kissing her all over. As they both kneel to their knees, he strokes the back of her head and with a firm but sensitive kiss guides her back to the ground like a beautifully wilting, voluptuous rose ritually laid upon silk. Softly unbuttoning her shirt, he slowly runs the tips of his fingers along her heaving, pulsating chest that begins to tingle with goose bumps and lightly tinge with sweat. (The flesh of his lips reunites with the flesh of her neck like two counterparts of soul once made material returning angelically to incorporeal sanctity—primordial spirit.)

With gently laid, sporadically but methodically placed kisses, like a connoisseur he feasts upon sinewy strands of her neck. Barely sonorous whimpers give way theatrically to cries and moans of undiluted ecstasy as he cradles her with one arm. With his other hand he positions their bodies. Erogenous waves of synchronicity and heavenly copulative repose mirror the turgid, rejuvenating Irish Sea beneath them. They plunge willingly into folds of flesh like seagulls catapulting themselves into ocean with utter, reckless abandon.

As the sound of gargantuan waves crashing into boulders echoes from far below, a reverberation penetrates the cliffs as the two lovers plummet into their own oceanic, orgasmic depths. Rapture—at least for the moment—is elevating lust to a higher ideal. They fall upon the grass and instantly transfix upon the clouds and light above. The great vault of earth becomes their mesmerization and ancient, mythological ruminations sweep them into idyllic slumber. They rent a cabin by the sea and spend the rest of the afternoon sipping Cabernet and talking metaphysics.

The next day, they are awakened to generous rays of sunlight that spill upon the sheets of the bed. Hypnotic, swishing, rustling sounds of waves emerge from below. Alan and Ronia are looking forward to Dublin. Before leaving their cabin, Alan carries his backpack over to a wooden desk that sits facing a rectangular window overlooking the ocean. He flips on the light, removes his book on mysticism, and quickly turns to the bookmarked page, which he reads aloud:

"Theravada Buddhism is solely concerned with the individual striving for Nirvana and it underestimates the role of the Bodhisattva: Whereas Mahayana Buddhism is concerned with the individual helping mankind in striving toward Nirvana, so therefore praises the Bodhisattva for his spiritual altruism. It is easy to see parallels between an accomplished, widely praised piot in the East and the degenerated and often incarcerated 'schizophrenic mute,' in the West. What differences—if any—exist between these types of individuals separated by culture and why does the Orient praise what the Occident abhors? Many capitalists would say that the development of a rational consciousness—which is capable of productivity, precludes any desirability for a 'spiritual awareness'; and that given our economic and material superiority over the East, we have succeeded in being more prosperous. But which is a more valid criterion for 'prosperity,' a material wealth or a spiritual wealth?"

"I can see we're off to a usual spiritualistic note this morning," Ronia remarks. "Well, the author brings up an interesting point. The dichotomy between capitalistic production and spiritual progression is obviously an important issue," he responds. "Alan, look!" Ronia points to a regal-looking red bird that has just flown up on the outside window sill. It is a majestic cardinal that flutters its wings and peers into the cabin as if it is checking in on the humans. Its brilliant design and coloring are an awesome representation of nature. Alan and Ronia perceive it as a fortuitous sign of things to come.

They load up the car, place the key in the mailbox—as instructed—and begin the scenic drive along the coast toward Dublin. The day is sunny and fairly clear. Spectacular scenery of the Irish coast soon leads them to O'Connell Street, which merges into Westmoreland and then Grafton. As they cross over River Liffey, they pass artistic enclaves, hip cafes, and gourmet restaurants. Passing through Meeting House Square, they observe an amphitheater, a food market, and a boardwalk area where people are playing backgammon and chess. There is a multimedia center that seems to coalesce innovative online activities with art events. What is readily evident to Alan and Ronia is that Dublin is another quintessential mergence of metropolitan sophistication and old-world charm.

Impeccably dressed Europeans with Cappuccinos in hand stroll the winding cobblestone streets while discussing movies, politics, philosophy, and religion. Students and artists with Bohemian flair fill the cyber-cafes with youthful energy and progressive zeal, eagerly rhapsodizing about the latest film or painting project. Musicians' vans line the fronts of the clubs as bands prepare for their weekend shows. Long-haired, tie-dye-shirted rockers carry guitar and bass cases in as diligent roadies follow with amplifiers and cords. Alan and Ronia simply drive around town with the windows open and try to familiarize themselves with where everything is.

They drive past Trinity College—home to the illuminated manuscript, *The Book Of Kells,* and then pass by the station of local icon, Molly Malone. In Merrion Square—former home to Oscar Wilde and William Butler Yeats—Alan and Ronia take notice of the spacious Georgian doorways of many of the buildings. It mentions something in the Ireland book about the doorways being designed to accommodate ladies hoop skirts. Ronia reads out loud from the book: "Doors are painted different colors so residents could find their way home after drinking at the pub." With the windows down, they are both captivated by a piquant odor which turns out to be drifting from the local Guinness Brewery. This brief tour through town provides a taste of the diversity and spirit alive in Dublin.

After passing over a hill near St. Stephen's Green, they arbitrarily choose a charming, oak-built inn that, from a patio, possesses a regal view of Dublin Castle. Checking in at rather pricey rates, they find the way to their room, a spacious, fashionably decorated suite with large bay windows overlooking a cobblestone street dotted with the occasional vending cart and quaint little shops selling bouquets of flowers. On the inside of the room hang various paintings by the artist Guggi. For what they paid, the quality of the room seems fair.

After unpacking the bags, they grab the backpack and are on their way. "Alan, the room is wonderful. Hardwood floors, pastel colors, and big fluffy comforters are essentials. I love it!" Ronia exclaims, as they descend upon the sidewalk. "I'm glad. It is pretty nice. It seems that Dublin takes pride in their hotels. From what I read in the book and from what we've seen, they are more luxurious than modest." "You're right." "The town seems carefully planned and preserved, but not in a way that would seem contrived but in a relaxed, comfortable way."

They walk toward Dublin Castle and notice several leaflets posted on a towering light post. Upon closer inspection and much to their delight, it reads: "Party For The People: An Intergenerational, International Love-Fest featuring Smokes On Dopes, Starphase, The Trashcan Picassos, Galactica, and The Moksha Revellers." The date listed for the concert is the following day and directions are provided on the leaflet that they tear off. "How's that for timing?" Alan muses. "Perfect," she replies, smiling as she takes him by the hand and they glide to the castle. "Would you please grab that Irish book and in the index find some reference to Dublin Castle; I'd like to know a little about it?" Alan requests. "Sure."

Ronia scans the pages and begins to read: "The Irish disliked Charles's abusive rule. Rory O'Moore and Phelin O'Neill led an Irish rebellion. They were joined by the Catholic Englishry of the Pale who were vexed at the Protestant authorities in Dublin Castle." "It goes on to discuss the Cromwellian Period." "Does it talk about Oliver Cromwell's Puritan army?" "Yes. It discusses their imprisonment of Charles I."

When they arrive at the castle, they look up at its fortified antique stone and hauntingly beautiful medieval design. They sit back on the grass and allow themselves to be transported back to a time of intrigue, warfare, and romance—when the fate of all of Ireland hinged upon the horrifically violent ebbs and flows of power. The arresting beauty of this mystical land stands in stark opposition to its unbridled, tumultuous history. What is now an emerging pinnacle of culture had once upon a medieval time been a place where the glimmering sword had executed a stream of bloodshed across the verdant landscape. Pristine fair maidens had surely waited in the darkened but candlelit corridors of castles such as this, while bribery, corruption, propaganda, and greed reared their ugly heads and fought to rule the land. As they recline on a large rock with a view of the entrance to the castle, Alan grabs his original book on mysticism and begins to read:

"For a western mind to grapple with this question is a formidable task. For a brain that's been conditioned from the very first day of its life to seek pleasure in material comforts and crave more and more stimulation, the idea of even considering this alternate perspective—of attempting to become ascetic—is almost oxymoronic. There are those who believe that it is possible to strike some balance between spiritual cognizance and material progress—that one can actually integrate 'otherworldliness' into his mundane existence without having to escape into oblivion. There once was an interesting story about the author Joseph Campbell traveling to India and observing a spiritual guru attempting to educate his followers on the path toward enlightenment, but seemingly to no avail. They were insisting on understanding what must be the only correct path—one of pure asceticism—denying the so-called illusory world of the senses. Joseph Campbell asked the guru: 'If Brahma is the ultimate and only reality, isn't all of this (everything around them) Brahma?' The guru answered, 'Exactly, that's what I've been trying to tell them all along.'"

Alan closes the book and sets it back into the bag. Ronia has closed her eyes and the shadow of a branch now covers her cheek. She rests her head on Alan's lap as he whispers to her:

"Brahma winked and bestowed upon earth the everything incarnated in one fragile, beautiful woman: that is you." She smiles and leans up as he tilts his head down, her lips meeting his in a caressing touch that makes them both melt inside.

"Brahma. It's an interesting concept," she mutters, and continues: "How bizarre that Muslims say 'Allah' and Christians say 'God.' If one is a monotheist, then why should it matter that others refer to the concept of god with different terms? If one is a polytheist, it would make sense because he would be offended that some favor one god over all the others. To a Christian or a Muslim or even a Jew, it should just be a case of simple semantics." "I hear what you're saying," Alan replies. "One problem is that Hindus are polytheists in the sense of varying manifestations or gods. A lot of Christians certainly do not like that." He stands up on the rock and lifts Ronia up. They begin to circle the castle while talking more.

"Ronia, I have been dreading and avoiding the imminence of this conversation but I guess we have to discuss it at some point. When do you have to leave to go back to London?" She pauses and contemplates her answer as they step along a dirt path: "I want to enjoy Dublin with you and then travel for at least a few days through Ireland—if that's alright with you. Then I think I'll have to return sometime within the upcoming weeks." Her answer—sincere and straightforward—leaves Alan forlorn. Something within had allowed him to perpetuate the hope-filled delusion that she would renounce her academic career and travel with him perpetually, or at least until they settled down somewhere they like. His deepest interests are for her to be happy and fulfill the pursuance of those things in life that she truly wants. Selfishly, Alan's desire to simply be with her often has taken precedence over all other thoughts and considerations. Alan despises this aspect of his thinking and behavior. He knows that he loves her and feels that, without her, his soul would be irreparably ruptured or crushed.

Silently, they walk through a clearing of trees that leads to Grafton Street. Hand-in-hand, they move at a methodical but casual pace that allows both bodies to move in unison. He takes notice—as he has often done—of the delicate, graceful manner in which Ronia walks, that seems more representative of a serene mythical nymph than a clambering human. It is partly in her transcendence of an otherwise normal human activity that Ronia shines in a brilliance that is aesthetically addictive. To be in the company of such an angelic creature makes him feel, in essence, as much part of that ethereal realm. Her departure would surely bring sorrow from the absence of this feeling as from the absence of her. He resigns himself to placing his concern out-of-mind, for he wants them both to enjoy the following day as much as possible.

From Grafton Street, they proceed to Westmoreland in front of Trinity College. Alan is continually impressed by the well-kept buildings and streets that seem to rise to the challenge of modernity and innovation while preserving the quality of antiquity. They notice a lot of friendly commotion coming from a coffee shop called, Cyberium.

CHAPTER 23

They step up to a large arch of a doorway which opens up to a spacious, PC-friendly environment that houses several modernistic tables and chairs in bright yellows and blues. Science fiction paraphernalia lines the walls. They sit down at a table adjacent to two plaques on the wall that commemorate Buckminster Fuller and Arthur C. Clarke. Alan and Ronia order two espressos and begin to look around and listen to groups of young hipsters discussing the forthcoming concert. "The show is going to be brilliant," says one. "Galactica is coming all the way from Germany," says another. "The pot will flow freely," cheers an eccentric Anglo lad in a Jamaican beret.

At a large circular table directly behind Alan, there are six or seven students with books scattered around and feet propped up on the edge of the table. A bespectacled, studious-looking young woman with chestnut colored hair pulled back in a ponytail and a vocal Cockney accent opens a large picture book to a bookmarked page. She lays the book open and Alan looks closely to see a photograph of a magic pentacle.

He listens as the students speak loudly: "The pentacle is known as the key of Solomon or the secret of secrets. It is located in a special 17th century manuscript in Paris," the young woman announces to the group, continuing: "The magician believes that his world is inhabited by spirits that he has the power to control." A young man with tousled, medium length brown hair and a wrinkled Bauhaus t-shirt speaks up: "I believe, love, that the magician aligns the invisible with his will. He incorporates cosmic energies into his operations and works in accord with the spirits, like he does."

The kid points in the direction of Alan, which makes Alan shudder. It turns out the kid is pointing to a photo high up on the wall above Alan's head. The photo is of Emanuel Swedenborg, famed mystic and mathematician. "Swedenborg claimed to have received messages from angels. He put himself in a breathless state that allowed him to have certain visions," remarks the young woman. She passes the photo of the pentacle around to everyone at the table. With interested, focused eyes, each person looks at the picture and passes it around. Alan leans back in his chair in order to see the picture of Swedenborg. Underneath the photo is a caption which reads: "Of Heaven And Its Marvels And Of Hell According To What Has Been Heard And Seen."

One of the girls at the table begins to sketch the image of the pentacle on a black piece of paper. As she traces its circular and square arrangements, she begins to speak: "The initiate into the world of magic experiences a sort of death to the world, a descent into darkness." "From this darkness emerges one who is a microcosm in the image of the macrocosmic universe," says another. "Jung's individuation parallels this—I believe," speaks the guy with the beret as he passes by their table on his way to replenish his tea. Alan and Ronia smile at each other with a knowing glance which reveals an amusement at the sense of intrigue and exploration displayed by the Irish students.

"Alan, these youngsters sound like they know their stuff. What do you think?" Ronia whispers. "You're right," Alan replies. "They are erudite and open-minded. I hope American kids are keeping up." "Alan, it's funny how Dublin seems to morphically resonate, in terms of us encountering these people who are obviously discussing the mystic path—that which you have been talking about all along. All of heaven seems to conspire to remind you of the way." "That's the way I like it," Alan responds playfully, arrogantly.

Ronia rises and walks to the counter to get them two waters. When she returns, she is sucking on a lemon wedge that she has placed in her mouth; eroticism abounds. As she removes the wedge from her moist lips, he leans and kisses her, quickly tasting remnants of sour lemon mixed with the nectar of her saliva. "Tomorrow's going to be a lot of fun," Alan remarks. "Yes it is," she replies, energetically. "You'll get to see your buddy, Peter. I know he'll be glad to see you, the great white Rasta—extraordinaire." "I like that: the great white Rasta—extraordinaire." "Come on, let's go!"

She grabs his hand as he drops off money and they scramble out into the sunny street. A horse drawn carriage with a newlywed couple on board trots by. Eclectic, ethnically diverse people fill the streets as late afternoon reaches Dublin. American tourists are always fairly easy to pick out. Often portly and ever confused, they wear an array of logo-imprinted t-shirts advertising everything from the Dallas Cowboys to Kermit the Frog. As Alan gazes at buxom tourists of apparent Irish and English descent, who have come to see their ancestors' homeland, he wonders if migration to America has been such a good thing. The land of opportunity has left its indelible imprints on the dress and physical condition of its most devout enthusiasts. It's not that Alan doesn't see native Irish who are in less-than-exceptional fashion or physical condition. It's just that the American appearance—if we can generalize—has an idiosyncratic banality, commercialism, and superficiality all its own. Beyond dress and physical condition, Alan sees an exuberance and *joie de vivre,* an apparent basic goodness that warms his heart and makes him glad to be a part of the human race. Everyone walks around with their own concerns—their own ideas and perspectives for viewing the world. Each has his own particular expression and countenance and his own particular way of walking that reveals something unique about the individual.

Alan has always found Asians to be beautiful people. Their olive skin and slightly slanted eyes in congruence with high, well-defined cheekbones make them mysteriously beautiful. During this afternoon in Dublin, he watches as a few Asian families—probably Chinese—stroll along the sidewalk. One woman—with delicate symmetrical features—walks with a certain softness as she pushes a baby in a stroller while two other small children scamper beside them. The woman has medium-length dark hair and soothing, dark, hazelnut eyes. As she walks, her hips shift balletically as her loose-fitting white sun dress gently sways with each movement. Her eyebrows are perfect, delicate arches that yield pleasantly to an efflorescent smile. The space that descends from her dress is a shapely *objet d'art* worthy of further study. Her shoulders tilt slightly backward as she walks and her round buttocks firmly but gingerly bob, leaving at least one onlooker breathless in aesthetic arrest. An average looking jewelry-adorned woman walks beside her and serves as attendant to the children. Alan marvels at that special beauty a woman exudes after childbirth: a mature, evolved sexuality unfettered by the anxious, awkwardly virginal look of women younger and inexperienced.

"Hey look over here," Ronia exclaims while pointing to a shop. She leads him by the hand toward a doll shop that is amusingly designed like a gingerbread house. Beyond the storefront window, deep inside the store, sits a voluminous display of dolls: different types representing ethnicity and dress as sundry as the people on the street. "Alan, let's go in!" Ronia expresses, with childlike exuberance. "Alan, look at this one over here." She points to a male doll of a British soldier in a regal-looking, heavily medaled navy blue uniform and distinguished matching hat. A well-trodden, creaking but solid wood floor responds sensitively to each step they take while perusing several shelves filled with dolls. High up above the shelves—on a special stand, sits a ballerina doll in an arabesque pose. Next to her stands a rugby player. One section of the store is devoted to pretty, lavishly adorned Victorian girls with curly hair and straight hair, long dresses and short dresses. One has the countenance of a wink and a playful grin and is carrying a parasol. Alan watches with great amusement as Ronia gleefully roams the aisles and peruses the shelves like an aficionado.

She finally makes her way to a section of mythical, elf-like dolls that sit on a display with an interesting arrangement of gazing balls and crystals that the dolls lean on or hold in playful poses. There are dolls that resemble stereotypical leprechauns with floppy green hats and pointed felt slippers. One looks like Tinker Bell with a magical, sparkling wand.

Ronia pores over this section as if it is one of her favorites. She lingers for several minutes while Alan wanders around. He decides to wait for her by the entrance on a wooden bench next to a fountain. A few minutes after Alan sits down, Ronia sashays up to him with a smile on her face and a look that says she is ready to go. As they step out onto the sidewalk, Alan asks her, "Do you want to get some ice cream? I see a place a couple of doors down."

"Sure, that would be great," she replies. They walk a couple of doors down and step inside an ice cream parlor called, "The Divine Dairy Delight." Promptly, they order a scoop of vanilla and a scoop of chocolate; both in cones. "Ronia, if you'll wait right here, I'll be back in a minute. I've got to do something real quick," he remarks, after they have sat down at a table by the window.

He rushes out of the store and walks back to the doll store. He opens the door and excitedly walks back to the stand with the fairies and elves. He carefully but quickly decides on a mythical being in pink that looks like an amalgamation of a fairy, joker, and elf. It has a sly, quizzical expression and slightly bent, relaxed limbs. It is very cute and has an almost human baby look about it that makes it slightly more accessible than some of the gnomish-looking ones. He picks it up and carries it to the counter. After paying for it, he has the clerk put a bow around its head.

Alan carries the little tike in his arms, almost cradling it, and rushes back to the ice cream shop. Quickly stepping up to the table, he smiles and presents the doll to Ronia. "I got this little something for you. I thought you'd like it." Ronia sets her spoon down and accepts the gift. "Alan, this is so sweet." She leans over and gives him an enthusiastic, loving hug. "Alan, I love it. It is so precious." As she pronounces the word, "precious," in her distinguished French accent, Alan treasures the sound, like some ambrosiac morsel. "I'm glad you like it. I saw you looking at them and knew that you had to have one." "You are so sweet," she gushes as he leans and kisses her on her forehead. She sets the doll upon the table and it seems to watch them as they eat their ice cream.

When they finish, Alan places the doll in the backpack and he leads Ronia on a leisurely stroll along River Liffey. On a bridge near Westmoreland Street, they watch as ducks scoot along the shore collecting pieces of bread that tourists have dropped. Alan and Ronia stand on the bridge as the sun gently acquiesces to dusk and a light balmy wind brushes through Dublin. Trees along the river sway gently, their leaves rustling in a way that is soothing to the ears and the eyes.

Alan takes Ronia by the hand and they stroll east along a walkway that runs parallel to the river. Joggers, bikers, and other pedestrians sporadically pass by. "Alan, what do you think you'll do when you have finished your traveling? I mean, do you think you will go back to America, or will you consider staying in Europe?"

"Well, for one thing, I hope to never 'finish traveling.' I wish to travel all of my life but I understand what you're asking. When I settle down next, I'm not really sure where it will be." Alan picks up a rock and skips it across the water. "The trip so far for me has been enriching and enlightening, not to mention incredibly fun. Meeting you and spending time with you has lifted my soul to heights far above the clouds. I never expected to meet someone and fall in…" Alan almost completes the phrase "in love" but he stops himself by inserting "into a state of rapture with."

"I'm sort of taking one day at a time and I'm not really sure where I am going to end up. What about you? When you finish school, will you end up teaching in London or Paris or will you go on some great anthropological adventure somewhere?" "Well, I'd like to have the security of a nicely paid position but also the thrill of adventure and exploration that exotic travel affords. There's also the invaluable added benefit of furthering my knowledge and expertise doing field studies. That could take me just about anywhere."

"Alan, will you kiss me?" He smiles, wraps his arms around her and happily complies. As he softly kisses her mouth, he begins to feel tears trickling down his cheek. Ronia's eyes become moisture-filled orbs that overwhelm her delicate lashes and rain salty drops down her face and Alan's neck.

As Alan feels moisture on his lower eyelids, he momentarily cannot determine if they are her tears; they might be his. "Darling, what is the matter? Why are you crying?" he asks. "I just love you so much," she utters through a whimper and a sniffle. "I want to hold on to this moment for as long as I can and treasure this joy that I'm afraid life will never duplicate." As she speaks, her body becomes almost limp as she leans into him and he holds her with his arms full around her; her body is now a soft, willowing, almost lifeless form.

Running his hands along her back and alongside her ribs, he feels the warmth and gentle curves of her body, that feel like nothing else. Within his mind, he tries to conjure energy for her and somehow telekinetically send it to her or transpose it. He wishes that somehow through holding her he can imbue her with a strength that will allow her to endure any emotional strife or hardship. As a passenger on an airplane attempts through careful concentration to achieve a successful takeoff and landing—but knows deep down inside that all the wishing in the world may have no effect whatsoever on what ultimately happens—Alan wishes for Ronia's peace of mind with every chord of psychic energy he can harness.

They depart for the hotel via cab. The car glides along the smoothly paved roads which lead to the hotel. They hold hands and gaze out the windows at any passing scenery they can catch before dark. Alan requests that the driver stop. They pull over at a pay phone in front of a Japanese restaurant about a block from the hotel. He picks up the phone and calls to get information about the concert.

After directions are confirmed and it is determined that the Moksha Revellers are on at 4, Alan takes Ronia's hand and walks with her up to their room. Upon entering, Ronia goes into the bathroom to start getting ready for dinner. Alan reaches for the original book on mysticism and flips to the bookmarked page.

With the book turned open in hand, he stacks two pillows against the headboard of the bed, leans against them, and begins to read: "In Evelyn Underhill's, *Mysticism,* she contrasts mysticism and hysteria (an obsolescent term) by saying, 'So too both mysticism and hysteria have to do with the domination of consciousness by one fixed and intense idea or intuition, which rules the life and is able to produce amazing physical and psychical results. The mono-ideism of the mystic is rational, whilst that of the hysteric patient is invariably irrational.' She proceeds to argue for the hope of the mystic reaching a much higher and adaptive level of existence than the so-called normal individual by stating: 'The exalted personality of the mystic—his self-discipline, his heroic acceptance of labour and suffering, and his inflexible will rises to a higher term than normal power of mind over body which all possess. Also the contemplative state—like the hypnotic state in a healthy person seems to enhance life by throwing open deeper levels of personality. The self then drinks at a fountain which is fed by the Universal Life. Often, says St. Teresa, even the sick come forth from ecstasy healthy and with new strength; for something great is then given to the soul.'"

Alan hears the shower running as he continues to read beyond the quotes of Underhill: "One is reminded of the fictional character Hans Castorp in the book *Magic Mountain*; who progressed through a radical transformation of consciousness and ideals while enduring a supposed lung disease in a Swiss sanatorium. Through weeks and months of exposure to the Swiss climate and scenery, prolonged conversations with mystically-inclined intellectuals, and the ill health itself, Hans Castorp emerges an enlightened and concerned man, mirroring the mystical individualism of his humanist pedagogue, Herr Settembrini. Thomas Mann speaks through one of his characters: 'Had not the normal, since time was, lived on the achievements of the abnormal? Men consciously and voluntarily descended into desire and madness in search of knowledge, which acquired by fanaticism, would lead back to health; after the possession and use of it had ceased to be conditioned by that heroic and abnormal act of sacrifice. That was the true death on the cross, the true Atonement.'"

Alan takes a deep breath after reading the concluding quote of Mann. Alan reads one more line in the book before setting it down: "Again, we are forced to consider the proverbial line between genius and insanity, of which so many historical and fictional motifs have dealt." Alan closes his eyes so as to concentrate on his thoughts. With auditory prowess, he tunes in to the interesting, comforting sounds of Ronia getting ready in the bathroom.

With cerebral prowess, he begins to imagine writing a novel that deals with his travels in the United Kingdom and the provocative notion that this chapter has just spurred. This idea—that one must delve within to become enlightened—begins to have for Alan not merely objective, intellectual merit, but actually a tangible, meaningful realization in the form of personal experience. Alan has, after all, been on a quest. Call it visionary. Call it surreal. Call it whatever. He has participated in a concentrated, focused attempt to understand that which is so difficult to grasp—the nature of the universe, itself. Through a process of self-exploration and geographical exploration of some of the countries of his origin, he has become increasingly more adept at understanding the essence and nature of life—of the universe. Visceral, cognitive diving into an exploratory awareness of the universe within and the universe without has raised his levels of perception and understanding to incredible heights. He feels alive.

Alan thinks back to his state of mind when he began his trip: to the world he had known and all its limitations and hopes. He had been melancholic, confused, and a little distraught. Any meaning that life had to offer had to be actively procured. It was not going to jump out and grab him. He had set off to learn a little bit and experience a little bit. When he started, he was not really sure where he was going or where he would end up. Rather humorously, he had once wondered if the world would become his oyster, or his half shell. He really didn't know. All that he knew was that he needed to enrich his life with understanding and experience.

The idea of sitting down one day and writing about what he discovered seems a meaningful way of imparting to others and exemplifying through example what he has learned; in a sense giving back after receiving so much. In allowing others to benefit from his personal quest, he feels that this will complete the "DNA project" he felt he was fulfilling.

At this moment—on a mild, tranquil evening in Dublin with an exotic, alluring woman in the room with him—he senses something that he had not known before, something that is simultaneously purposeful and exciting: a sense of direction. He would compile notes and memories of thoughts and ideas that he had experienced during his travels and synthesize them into a novel that would entertain and stimulate others; it seems to him to be a worthwhile avocation. In part autobiographical, part historical, and part neurological, his book would catapult the knowledge of mysticism and the magic of esoteric understanding into the public mind—titillating and enriching. It would encourage others to think for themselves and question authority while opening minds to the novel idea that life is to be enjoyed in a capacity that respects other life and encourages them to be optimistic about the whole process, to enjoy each and every moment, as if it is a precious fragment or memento of eternity—of immortality.

He can feel a change within him that not only is as strong as love and synonymous with love, but something that encompasses love. It is a sort of calling to navigate his nervous system in the most interesting and expanding ways possible: to increase his brain power; to expand his knowledge while undergoing a profound neurological, metaphysical, and spiritual change.

It has become noticeable to him that he has learned to relish the rich, chaotically unpredictable patterns of life; to embrace life. He has grown comfortable traveling in foreign places while experiencing transpersonal states of mind. The infinite levels and dimensions of experience would never fully be realized, but to have made the journey is worthwhile in itself.

He watches as Ronia steps out of the bathroom in her underwear—a pure carnal desire that man surely holds dear. The esoteric intellectual pursuits surely have theirs.

For Alan, the goal of happiness is to find congruence among the multitudinous pleasures in life while serving and helping others. As he thinks back to the social service work performed dutifully by the priest in the food line, he decides that he will convey this message in his book. There is a place for intellectual advancement and Alan will encourage this in his book. There is a place for unbridled, sensual delight and Alan will encourage this in his book. *A Bible For Hedonistic and Altruistic Intellectuals,* comes to mind as a title but it sounds too didactic. *Akashic Divinorum,* comes to mind but it sounds too esoteric. *How to Fuck Friends and Influence The Laws of The Universe,* comes to mind but it sounds too comical and plagiaristic. He decides he will wait until later and hopefully the laws of Moses, Buddha, Mohammad, Jesus, Aristotle, Algebra, Calculus, Magic, Bob Hope, Jackie Gleason, Quantum Mechanics, and Felix the Cat will all come together into a unified thrust of energy from which the appropriate title will miraculously emerge.

"Alan, what do you want for dinner?" "Ummm, pizza sounds good. I dunno. Maybe we'll do Thai." Ronia—still in just her underwear—strolls near the bed and Alan reaches out, wraps his hand around her waist, and pulls her slowly astride his lap. He begins to massage her lower back as he continues on his ideas for a book. Her long, slender body—in its ivory tone and silky, elegant skin—has rounded, slim, and perfectly well-defined curves that not only satisfy aesthetically, but surprisingly provide energetic stimulus for intellectual ideas. Maybe it is the increase of hormonal activity that gives rise to a turbo-kick for the intellect. Alan's mind continues to race along corridors and avenues of a sundry sort. "Alan, what are you thinking about? You seem so deep in thought," Ronia remarks, as she undulates until her body is on its side, parallel, but not on top of Alan's. "I am thinking about the evolution of the mystical mindset. I am considering the interesting pursuit of a higher, more divine state than man is usually operating at. Everything we've been reading in this book on mysticism seems to point out the ideal of the mystically enlightened state. There seems to be something to be said for a diligent, assiduous, and sometimes arduous undertaking toward achieving or reaching this rumored state. Through meditation, exercise, concentration, special breathing, and certain drugs, man seems capable of pushing himself toward a wise, rational, lucid, and refreshed state of mind. I feel like I'm playing the role of the Bodhisattva vouchsafing to you the secrets of the other side, when you may be closer than me."

Ronia runs her fingers through her hair and smiles effusively. "I'll gladly play the role of student to you, my guru and lover, and my friend!" she playfully, self-effacingly quips. In a relaxed, insouciant manner, Alan continues: "Let us define the borders of consciousness and learn to expand them into the further reaches until man is a savvy humanist who is operating at an accelerated, mystically enlightened pace," Alan victoriously announces in a tongue-in-cheek pedantic style.

Ronia crosses the room and starts a pot of coffee. Her svelte, creamy arms outstretch and extend in balletic, muscular repose; the sinewy, well-defined biceps and triceps serving as crowning achievement of DNA's exceptional abilities to evolve not only what is sufficiently functional but also devastatingly beautiful. Strength and beauty have wonderfully coalesced in this creature who had been born in the approximate middle of the twentieth century.

Alan marvels at her as he has done so many times. Unlike other times, today he is lingering in his stare; because he does not know for certain what the future will bring. The number of moments that remain between them might be limited, so he treasures this evening like it is his last.

As she begins to dress, she responds to him. "The concept of consciousness evolving into an enlightened, mystically attuned entity is something which very well may be the hallmark of high culture. Within the arts, sports, fashion, and science, great strides have been made—exemplifying the ingenuity of man. We know so very little about the hundred something billion neurons that interconnect in the human brain. As there are exponential leaps in advancement of technologies like computers, perhaps there is now an even greater reason to find a center or focus that pins the core of man to a goal or ideal in terms of the state of his mind. A firm basis in a focused, advanced, mystical mind just very well may be the sort of foundation man needs to withstand and peaceably ride the waves of progress."

She pours herself a cup of coffee and asks Alan if he wants one. "Sure, I'll get it in a minute, though. Thanks." "So, Alan…" she begins, after sipping the coffee, which has aromatically filled the room. "I concur with these views and I think the history of anthropology—among other things—confirms it; that as organisms on the surface of this strange orb hurtling through a solar system among billions, we are constantly striving to advance ourselves in all capacities. If the very foundation of what it means to be human is consciousness, then it is within consciousness that at least some of the major advances must take place."

Alan smiles and nods in agreement. He then gets up and walks over to his backpack, removes a cigar, and then steps to the window, where he sits in the sill to have a smoke. As the waves of nicotine bliss wash over his brain, he begins to articulate out loud: "I'm going to have to write a book—a metaphysical diatribe, if you will—not preachy or dogmatic, but something hopefully educational; something that opens minds to the infinite possibilities of brain change—of brain evolution; something that shares with others the joy we have found in expanding mental awareness in the contexts of travel, sex, love, and concentrated but spontaneous explorations of knowledge; knowledge of the inner worlds of physiology and the outer worlds of geography; a compendium of the adventures of evolutionary agents that set out in a spirit of joy and fun, and along the way learn a thing or two."

Alan quickly extinguishes the cigar and goes to the bathroom to get ready. He showers, shaves, and gets dresses. "Are you ready for dinner?" he asks her. "Yeah, where do you want to go?" "I don't know. Maybe we'll just go out and figure that one out. We'll find a place. I'm sure." "Okay."

CHAPTER 24

They lock the door and head down to the street. After walking a couple of blocks, they stumble upon an Indian restaurant that has an ornate red and gold sequined cloth-covered awning and a sign above it which reads, "The Palace Of India." They enter and are seated at a dimly lit circular table in the corner that is surrounded by rich, colorful tapestries that display various incarnations of Hindu gods in breathtaking, splendorous natural landscapes.

They order a variety of Tandoori meats and vegetables with white rice. The restaurant, quiet and elegant, exudes a soft glow from candlelight. It is half-full and has an exceptionally attentive, colorfully adorned waitstaff. Ronia and Alan order some hot tea to have before dinner.

Ronia reaches into the backpack and pulls out the original book on mysticism. She finds where Alan had left off and begins to read in a volume discernible to mainly the two of them: "It is interesting to ponder the multifaceted experiences of the 'illumination of the self' or the 'divine communion.' The 'awakening of consciousness,' or 'realization of the absolute,' are just a couple of the expressions used to denote the mystical experience. We hear of increased visual acuity, enhancement of auditory signals, and the intuitive understanding of the interconnectedness of nature with organism, and foreground with background. God is experienced as a circle whose center is nowhere and whose circumference is everywhere. Early initiates of Dionysus, an early Greek mystery cult, sung the following verses by Plato:

O blessed he in all wise, Who hath drunk the Living
Foundation, Whose life no folly staineth
And whose soul is near to God; Whose sins are lifted
pall-wise As he worships on the Mountain."

We can trace an interest in mysticism at least as far back as the early Greek philosophers, extending up until the Age of Scientific Reason and stretching far beyond into the twentieth century." Ronia stops reading.

Their food arrives and they begin to eat. As they both eat the food and contemplate the esoteric message, their senses become heightened as a result of the spices in the food merging with the equally pungent thoughts they have recently entertained. Alan has ordered a bottle of white wine with dinner. As they toast to epicurean bliss, their minds buzz with a delectable, savory energy that makes them feel in harmony with physics. "The Tao of Fine Living," is a title that comes to Alan's mind.

Ronia is captivating in a loose-fitting black dress with her nipples slightly erect. Her alert, vivacious stance accords with their stimulated, titillated pallets left obviously aroused and heavily induced to hunger by the scrumptious, savory foods before them. Underneath the table, Alan gently strokes one of Ronia's feet which is temptingly wrapped in a web-like black leather slip-on that is Gothically fetishistic. Despite himself, Alan becomes throbbingly erect. When they finish dinner, he pays the bill and quickly leads Ronia out of the restaurant and back toward the hotel.

As they scurry along the nighttime cobblestone path, a stream of moonlight guides them along as if to portend in accompaniment and harmony with the infinite twinkling stars that Alan and Ronia will soon be making love. The moon—in its charmingly luminescent glow and through a simple act of anthropomorphizing—grants to them the wondrous, cosmic approval to reap an interstellar, phantasmagorical orgasm out of the night. It seems only seconds before they are naked and in bed under the sheets.

Alan pulls back one of the curtains slightly to allow the moonlight to catch up to them as he gently maneuvers himself within the soft, warm crevice of her thighs. As he draws closer into ecstatic union with her and begins to run his fingers through her silky strands of hair, undulating cries and moans of pleasure fill the room and escape surreptitiously into the night. Silence and sleep follow as the moon endures in its glow.

Morning arrives with rain showers that drop pitter-patteringly sonorous pellets on the roof and against the window panes. Alan awakens first. She lies peacefully with her beautiful naked back partially covered with the sheet. He kisses her back where the shoulder blade meets the spine in fluid form and then lays the left side of his face against it and feels the timelessly soft, smooth skin. She begins to yawn and slowly awaken. "Good morning, sweetie," she speaks and then hugs him. "Good morning, little angel," he replies. He slowly climbs out of bed and begins to get ready as she stretches her arms and gradually reunites with her senses. She exudes a smile that only sex can bring and it pleases Alan to see this.

When they are both ready, they go downstairs and have breakfast, which consists of toast and butter, coffee, orange juice, eggs over easy, hashbrowns, and fresh tomatoes. From the dining table, one can catch sporadic streams of sunlight breaking through charcoal gray clouds in the sky before pouring through lush oak and pine branches across the street.

As the waves of vitamin C, caffeine, and protein invigorate our two travelers, they watch with great anticipation as the night's storms have gradually and gently segued into what turns out to be a pleasantly mildly windy day. Incessant overcast skies share their canopy with the sun in careful intermissions, offering the audience a variety of natural splendor to harmonize like music. "The concert's going to be so much fun," Ronia exclaims. "Yes, it is. I guess we can kill time until it starts," Alan responds. "I'm anxious to go outside." "So am I." They excuse themselves from breakfast, leave a tip, and head out to the street.

Stepping out on the wet cobblestone proves palatable. The leather from the soles of their shoes hugs the stone, while muscles and tendons of their legs stretch and strain for the first time today. Their lungs open up to the refreshing Irish air left slightly damp and cool from the rain. Heading in the direction of the river, Ronia and Alan simply walk together and talk: "This idea that I've hit upon recently..." Alan begins: "that of summating or articulating the ineffable—the mystical—is something that I'd like to do in the foremost as a book, but at the same time it could be done as a movie." "Wait, watch out!" Ronia exclaims, as she points to a large puddle that Alan almost steps in, but quickly evades.

After being happily diverted, he continues: "The concept is to demonstrate through a time, place, and specific characters that life is something that is filled with intrigue, mystery, and importance regardless of who you are or what you do. It is the idea that being alive on the surface of this planet has given humans—for whatever reason—a consciousness that is not only self-reflective, but capable of reaching out into vast, disparate spheres to contemplate and conceptualize the most bizarre, seemingly inexplicable things. One does not need to dive full speed ahead into beliefs in ESP, clairvoyance, and telekinesis—or even UFOs and other conspiracy theories—to tap into a stimulating sense of transcendence. The very fact that we are conscious and use our cortex to think is absolutely awesome. The idea is to push ourselves to understand and experience the multitudinous phenomena out there and, as a result, become more compassionate, thoughtful, and enlightened—everything that makes up the hallmark of being human."

Ronia smiles at Alan's exuberance and charisma. "I think what you're talking about is something that people would like to hear. It's amazing how much people can be affected by a powerful, enlightened message, especially when it is demonstrative of the road to greater understanding and fulfillment. You could give them a sense of the humanist, or the mystic, who shuffles off the shackles of ignorance and restraint and moves up to a higher level of knowledge. To show others what that path is all about would give them hope and God knows that hope is something that we need more of."

Alan leans and kisses her. It brings him immense joy that she supports his endeavor. He continues: "To have traveled to a different part of the world and learned a little more about the parameters of the soul is something that would be a shame not to share with others. To share it with others seems the logical rapprochement or fulfillment of me being here." Alan seems to have found a reason or justification for his travels that moves beyond entertainment or education for its own sake.

"My uncle would have wanted this. I am sure." Ronia detects that in thinking about his uncle, a certain sadness befalls his mind. She thinks about how individuals are affected and spurred to do certain things or make significant changes when someone close to them dies. Out of death comes a renewed interest in pursuing things that perhaps one has not previously considered and been somehow restrained from trying. During this moment—while listening to Alan—Ronia decides that life is something that humans may never be able to explain but through furthering understanding and actions could be transubstantiated into something remarkable—something of value. Seeing this metamorphosis in Alan propels her to consider what occupational and avocational paths she might take for herself. Simultaneously, she is compelled to consider her deepest feelings for Alan and where life is going to take them in terms of their relationship. She knows that she loves him and her commitment and attachment to him grow increasingly with each new experience they have. He had shown her not only a new way of experiencing the world but a new way to experience something within her that had always been there, yet never fully realized—the capacity to truly love. With every chord and fiber of her being she had evolved a passionate, unbridled, hopelessly long-standing love for him.

Prior to meeting Alan, Ronia had been involved in relationships based on a somewhat emotionally detached, intellectual basis that allowed her to share common interests on the subjects of the day. There had been relationships based on a more impulsive, a sort of dog-like trance toward the physical—a sort of lust, devoid of anything other than somatic pleasure.

What she finds is going on in her feelings toward Alan is the strangest, most wonderful coalescence of intellectual, spiritual, and physical interest that ties neural bonds and strands in the most delectable, satisfyingly interweaving locks. This makes the thought of being without him seem painful, existentially dreadful. She feels her personal universe intertwined with his in a portentous, divinely dictated helix that she is fearful to disrupt; for she has given herself freely to him.

In opening up intimate feelings and thoughts which she had once thought impossible, Alan has shown her a respect, love, and care in return—which make her thankful and comfortable with giving herself to another. She smiles and watches as he gazes around at his surroundings with a wonder, a refreshed, nascent perspective of pleasantly unrefined, unrestrained glee reminiscent of a boy. It is this sense of youthfulness that she feels Alan would preserve his entire life; it would in equal parts foster itself in others and this is why she would continue to love him. She is attracted to the man in him but also drawn to him for this "rejuvenalized" spirit that makes each moment precious and sanctified. Each day that he awakens lucidly to a new experience in turn imbues her with a playful, excited perspective that not only allows her to see the world through his eyes but, also, to undergo a change within herself that makes the world seem experientially new. The mysticism that Alan has spoken of has infected her like a sweet nectar that nourishes her soul and expands her horizons into vistas beyond other worlds. Gently sliding her fingers between his, she lightly grips and then squeezes his hand.

She feels her pulse race as she gazes out over a verdant hillside on the edge of town. In the distance flies a flock of ducks in an almost perfect "V" formation through the now almost sunny sky. Their symmetrical shape and synchronous, fluid flight are breathtaking. Cumulous shadows momentarily pass over the ground, blanketing the valley with a contrast of light and shadow. This underscores the myriad topographical and geographical features that infinitely complicate the land of Ireland. It is at this moment—as she stands with Alan by her side and she looks out over a paradisiacal view—that her sense of self peacefully withdraws from its microcosmic structure and becomes seemingly suspended with the hovering clouds. Her normal sense of self—that which she understood to be the heavily conditioned, constricted set of patterns and reflexes largely formed by early imprints and involuntary, half-conscious responses—suddenly withdraws behind the curtains of perception. As she gazes out over the valley, her awareness stretches and expands to encompass not details within her neatly circumscribed pattern of self, but the vast entire pattern all around her. Foreground recedes into background. Subject converges with object. An awareness develops, one that bespeaks the fact that Ronia, Alan, the clouds, the valley, the sun, and the graceful balletic flock of birds are all vibrations or incantations of an energy or field of consciousness that is the everything. Fear segues into solace. Hopelessness and worry slip off the gargantuan precipice into the absolute and become eclipsed by a warmth and consolation that reveal some higher meaning. Within Ronia's mind, she considers whether or not there was something or someone that had set the entire process in motion, or if the concept of an original initiator is simply an imposition—a fabrication on the part of the human brain to explain the unexplainable and create a creator.

Ronia puts her thoughts into words: "Perhaps all of this—everything around us—is something that has always been and forever shall be. Perhaps there was never any beginning and will never be an end—simply varieties of life and form emerge, play their games, and then dissolve into the absolute, the everything."

"Well, again, we seem to be swimming in pretty heady waters. No mundane conversation here!" Alan responds. "Ha, ha, ha," Ronia chuckles.

"Alan, I guess what I'm trying to convey is that through the course of being with you and exploring the mystical ideas, I feel I have come to a realization, not just an abstraction or intellectual conception, but a deep, resoundingly pervasive realization that what mystics have been professing for thousands of years is consistent with rational, discursive Western thought. In anthropology, we study the origins and details of the cultural development of man. We study the idiosyncrasies and vagaries that make men and women tick. Here, let me see the backpack, please."

She reaches into the bag and pulls out the original book on mysticism. As they sit back on a rock that juts prominently over a vivid picture of the valley, she begins to read:

"In the book, *The Masks of God,* Joseph Campbell traces the history of mythology back to the neolithic beginnings around c. 4000 B.C. through the Mycenean Age c. 1405–1100 B.C., delineates the disparate philosophies, and explains the original rupture that separated the two. Campbell describes that in the neolithic village stage of development and dispersal, the goddess Earth was the focal figure of all mythology and worship and was perceived as the mother and nourisher of life as well as receiver of the dead for rebirth. He suggests that in the temples of the first of the higher civilizations (Sumer, c. 3500–2350) the Great Goddess of highest concern was 'a metaphysical symbol: the arch personification of the power of Space, Time, and Matter, within whose bound all beings arise and die: the substance of their bodies, configurator of their lives and thoughts, and receiver of their dead.'"

Ronia sets the book down and exclaims, "So what we're talking about is a shift in consciousness about to take place; one that moves from a now mostly forgotten sense of harmony and mysticism toward a more divided, Cartesian duality, something that at least portends or suggests Des Cartes, who would come on the scene later." She reads on:

"So the focus for these early mythologies had been on this all-pervading feminine essence that serves as the ground of all being, synonymous with the unconscious and the 'absolute.' The *Tao Te Ching* describes the Valley Spirit which never dies:

It is named the Mysterious Female
And the Doorway of the Mysterious Female
Is the base from which Heaven and Earth Sprang
It is there within us all the while.

Campbell writes, 'The aim of the earlier mythology had been to support a state of indifference to the modalities of time and identification with the inhabiting non-dual mystery of all being. However, between the Bronze Age (c. 1250 B.C. in the Levant) a drastic philosophical change occurs due to the emergence of nomadic, patriarchal tribes whose traditions are reflected in the Old and New Testaments as well as in the myths of Greece.'"

"So, Ronia," Alan interrupts. "What you're saying, or what the book is saying, is that there was once a closer perspective toward the mystical union or communion of life on this planet but that as tumultuous changes cut across the landscape, so did there occur seismic shifts in human thought?" "Precisely," she responds, continuing: "Now, we are not implying that there were not beneficial changes taking place in human consciousness. Obviously, the development of tools and other acts of ingenuity were coming into play. The implications are that some of the major changes were within religion, in terms of how individuals perceived the cosmos, including the idea of a central Creator or god." He reads on:

"The distinctions between typically Oriental religions and Occidental religions are easily understood when recognizing that with the intrusion of a rationalistic, domineering, patriarchal people, what is suppressed or wiped out is the more matriarchal, natural, or instinctual side of human thought. Campbell's belief concerns the Semites, who as ranging nomads in the Syro-Arabian deserts herded sheep and goats and mastered the camel, and the Hellenic-Aryans who grazed herds of cattle and mastered the horse in the broad plains of Europe and South Russia. He speaks of the new mythology as being, 'to foster action in the field of time, where the subject and object are indeed two, separate and not the same—as A is not B, as death is not life, virtue is not vice, and the slayer is not the slain.'"

As Ronia shuts the book and rests her voice, Alan beams in the knowledge that at a minimum, Ronia's pursuit of anthropology would take on new, interesting dimensions. He envisions her scanning and recording data from the hikes at Petroglyph park in New Mexico; studying the bizarre configurations and images depicting the rich mythology of native American Indians.

"Ronia, it's interesting. What you're reading about seems to tie in with Terence McKenna's notion that psychedelic plants were pivotal in propelling man into evolutionary leaps of awareness as the brain developed through millennia. Certainly, there are archaeological facts to support this claim." "You're right. I think what is interesting to ponder is the multifarious ways in which the brain consolidates its stereotypically 'left hemisphere' and 'right hemisphere' functions. In regard to the anthropomorphic male god, well that's straight out of a Freudian textbook on the Super Ego." "You said it, not me," Alan quips as he feigns cowering underneath a lightning bolt or a pissed off god.

"Whatever the nature of God is, I'm glad he—I mean she, or it— brought you to me," Alan adds. Ronia laughs and puts her arm around him. "Do you want to get some lunch?" he asks. "Yeah, that would be great," she replies. They walk in the direction of the hotel with plans of getting the car after lunch and heading to the concert. After walking relatively aimlessly for about a half mile, they discover a Thai restaurant called, "Bonzai." They enter the restaurant and saunter back to a table against a wall that showcases a stunning collection of black and white photos depicting everything from various black and white shots of the

Manhattan skyline to sundry expressions on the faces of ethnically diverse people in metropolitan cities all over the world.

Alan orders two Thai iced teas and requests that the waiter give them a couple of minutes to peruse the menu. Ronia pulls the bangs from her face and sits upright in her chair: "Alan, what is interesting about life is that our consciousness happens upon this planet without any apparent choice on our parts. We are aware of our existences and we know that our awareness is but one fragment in a rich, diverse, seemingly random tapestry or landscape that encompasses other forms of life seemingly less aware than we are but vital, living organisms, nevertheless. When we are in the presence of a cat—for instance—we share in a similar process of life in that we breathe the same air and require sustenance in the forms of food and water. Yet we sense that the cognitive capacities are of a wholly non-reflective nature, or at least a very different form than that which we possess. But the playfulness and love that we share with a precious little thing like a cat are something that reveal a graceful, elegant communication among life; this bespeaks a sophisticated energy that moves all life."

Alan watches as she punctuates her sentence by gracefully stirring with her straw the thin layer of cream at the top of the tea. She then lifts the straw to her mouth and gently licks the tip of it with her tongue. "Sweetie, I understand what you mean," he replies.

After sipping from his drink and ordering red fish curry—Ronia orders garlic vegetables—he continues: "The essence of living seems to be the participation of one life with other lives in a pattern or symbiosis that is somehow meaningful. Whether it is the love between family members or the attraction of two lovers, or even the companionship of a human with a pet—like a cat—the purpose and the meaning seem to derive from the interaction, the communion of kindred spirits or souls, if you will. To take it a step further, we really have no choice but to become conscious creators of meaning in a way that parallels an artist creating or performing her art. Meaning and significance for us all seem to lie in the direction of the energy we expend toward whatever endeavors seem to turn us on. In other words, we must actively create destinies and proactively participate in the process of living." "Life throws us into the ring and it is up to us to fight the rounds, right?" she paraphrases. "Yes, precisely," he answers. "Sir, would you like red curry or green?" the waiter asks.

"Red, please," Alan retorts. "Didn't I tell him already? So, anyway. My take is that, yes, it is strange that we are here. Yes, it is something that we may never be able to explain. So what are we going to do about it? I think that pursuing philosophical questions in the context of a healthy, humanistic, delightfully pleasure-seeking capacity is a great place to start. Finding ways of feeling good about the world and figuring out about the world are tasks that we all must undertake. Intellectual tools and resources must be harnessed and implemented to handle the enormous challenge of living. Let's face it. We all go through fucked-up periods where we say, "What the fuck is happening?" "Why is it happening?"

"Will it ever end?" "Will it get better?" "What in the fuck does destiny hold in store?" "When we go through these questions, it is a part of being human. Now, assuming that human consciousness isn't just some annoying little mutated aberration of the developing cortex—assuming that human consciousness is something desirable and accepted—then what is one to do but defer to those departments of knowledge and logic that we have built in our skulls and try to interact with others in our environment as happily and productively as possible? *Cogito ergo sum!*" The waiter delivers the entrees and the two culinary connoisseurs indulge in a sentient and gustatory carnival of spices that piquantly bathe their taste buds in moist, titillating flavor and zest. Sweating profusely and moaning ecstatically, they give praise to Allah for all things good, namely flavorfully biting, spicy ambrosia from Thailand.

When they finish lunch, they begin to drive to a place beyond the sun where a long, tortuous highway winds east along pine-strewn hills and spacious valleys toward a large amphitheater nestled on a grassy plateau. Upon this site, one can see out over a vista dotted mainly by a bustling crowd of concert-goers and a bevy of booths, hawking everything from hemp wear to beads, jewelry, and cyber wear. Barren hills and moorland indicative of the less verdant regions of Ireland provoke within Alan images of the southwestern United States. The spacious, haunting serenity of the rustic, natural scenery bristles today with a youthful energy and radiance of music enthusiasts from all over Ireland and probably a little bit beyond.

Alan and Ronia follow a long stream of traffic, which leads to a general parking area where hundreds of cars park in multitudinous positions. Scantily-clad concert goers barrel out of their vehicles with packs of beer and various things to smoke; they open up their trunks and doors to remove lawn chairs and coolers for a huge, communal parking lot fiesta. Partly overcast, grayish skies hang overhead as throbbing drum-n-bass and jungle rhythms emanate frenetically from jam boxes sitting in opened trunks. A light breeze refreshes the crowd as small pockets of partiers gather outside and within the complex to kindle a spirit of pre-concert jubilant, happy revelry. Alan and Ronia stroll through the crowd wondering where and when they might see their friend, Peter. As they wind through, Alan draws much amusement from the rich, diverse Irish vernacular dialects that are spoken.

"Aye, Johnnie. I'm going to call mi' band, 'Reality Shifting Frontier,' and then I'll kick arse on the bass," speaks a short teen lad with his head shaved in three bold stripes and an oversized bomber jacket around his shoulders, cut-off shorts, and dusty combat boots. "I'm fuckin' seeing things like I never seen 'em," effuses another.

As Alan and Ronia approach the entrance to the venue, Alan quickly notices through the perimeter fence trailers set up behind the stage, with an additional fence separating the backstage area from the general admission. The trailers are obviously set up for the musicians and Alan hopes to locate Peter somewhere in this vicinity.

After passing through the entrance and approaching the backstage area, Alan and Ronia initiate conversation with a rather forlorn, bemused security guard. Alan speaks first: "Excuse me, sir. There is a member of one of the bands playing today. His name is Peter Lesh. The name of the band is the Moksha Revellers. I was wondering if you could perhaps inform him or one of his people that his friend Alan is here to see him." The security guard, a bristly-faced portly man with a devilish sneer, stares into Alan's face piercingly in a manner that suggests to Alan that his request creates a major inconvenience. "Hold on just a minute," the guard responds, before looking around until he spots a casually dressed roadie with a walkie-talkie. "Hey, Jim," the guard calls out. The roadie removes his headphones and approaches. "Yeah, what's up mate?"

"This guy says he knows Peter, the reggae dude. What d'ya think?" The roadie turns on his walkie-talkie, covers the mouthpiece, and asks for Alan's name. "Alan, Alan Agrippa," Alan responds. "Hello, Ron. This is Jim. I gotta guy here who says he's friends with Peter. His name is Alan Agrippa. Okay, I'll hold." Alan can hear the first band taking the stage. He cannot tell which one, but it sounds like a cross between Afro and Celtic centered tunes. "Alright, I'll send him back," the roadie remarks.

"Okay, come with me kiddos." The security guard pulls back the gate and allows Alan and Ronia to enter, whereupon the roadie immediately wraps backstage cards around their necks and begins to lead them through a labyrinth of trailers and tents and up to the foyer of a tin building that looks like an airport hangar. They ascend a flight of steps and enter a spacious room resembling a market hall. The room is filled with roadies, press people, caterers, film crews, and privileged young adoring fans; are all moving briskly in various directions with either jobs to do or people to meet.

The roadie leads Alan and Ronia to the far side of the room toward the corner that has an open bar and several picnic tables lined up. They are filled with fashionably adorned men and women who smoke and drink up a storm. Alan peruses the faces and quickly spots Peter, who sports lengthy dreadlocks, a colorful Mexican poncho, and lightly yellow tinted sunglasses. Peter looks up, spots Alan immediately, and rushes up to him, quickly throwing his arms around him in a bear hug. "Alan, I can't believe it, mon. What a surprise! I am glad to see you, mon. Ronia, come here. You look fabulous, girl." Peter kisses her European style, on both cheeks. "What's been going on? How's life treating you?" Alan asks him. "Oh, terrific. A record company has been knocking on our door. The tour is going great. The government is leavin' us alone. Things couldn't be better. I'm havin' the time of my life. What can I get you to drink, Alan?" "A vodka o.j." "Ronia?" "A vodka o.j. Hey Peter, you can stay here and talk to Alan. I'll get the drinks. Do you want anything?" "No thanks, I've got my beer right here. Tell them to put it on my tab, dear."

Ronia goes to get the drinks. "So you guys are playing well? How's it playing with those other bands? Is that pretty cool?" "Yeah, it's alright. There's a sense of community here, a very good vibe. It's a mixture of music that I think is good for the people. Tell me, Alan. How are your travels going?" "They're going well. Ronia and I have been through England, Scotland, and Ireland. I feel like a part of me belongs to this glorious land they call the United Kingdom. It really is majestic." "You are right. It is a magical place. Alan, I'd like you to meet Sophie."

While they had been talking, a slender tan blonde with a beautifully exposed, pierced navel and sculpted stomach—a midriff rainbow striped top complements provocatively tattered blue jeans—has slithered up and wrapped her arm around Peter's waist. "It's nice to meet you, Sophie," Alan extends his hand to shake hers. She smiles coquettishly and reaches for her drink. Peter continues as Ronia arrives with the drinks: "I think you might recognize the members of my band."

Alan and Ronia glance around the table and say hello to everyone. "Alan, we are going to tour America after this. Our manager has us playing smaller venues like clubs and bars from Berkeley, California to Manhattan, New York. The American scene is happenin'. I think we might even integrate some tribal dance into the package to give em' a special treat." "I think that would probably work great. Your sound is eclectic enough to branch off into different directions. I can't wait to hear you guys today." Alan beams.

"Ronia, this is Sophie. Sophie, Ronia," Peter introduces them. "Peter, your idea for music is like the quantum physicist's goal of exposing the diversity within unity," Ronia proposes. Peter smiles and adds, "And the unity within diversity!" "Which reminds me," he goes on. "Mr. Alan, have you come up with a plan to educate the masses about the world as we know it?" Alan chuckles. "Actually, I am planning on writing a novel which will hopefully entertain and educate along the lines of seeing things as they truly are, or at least point people in the right direction." "Will you give me an autographed copy when it is finished?" Peter asks. "Sure," Alan replies.

A studious-looking publicist rushes up with a clipboard and urgently informs Peter: "Mr. Lesh, the interview with Starstride magazine is in ten minutes. It will be in the Phoenix boardroom." "Alright, thanks kindly," Peter answers. "Boardroom; sounds pretty corporate," Alan quips. "Ha, ha, ha. I know. Perhaps I should slip into my pinstripe suit and tell them to hold my calls," Peter jokes. "I'll bring you the copy of investments strategies, immediately, Mr. Jenkins," Ronia adds. "And I'll make coffee while the stocks skyrocket!" Sophie chimes in. Peter chuckles with a loving, Jamaican warmth and power which immediately reveal his island-blessed vocal prowess: a deep, molasses infused, guttural intonation and rhythmic, elegant beat of cadence.

"Alan, wait a minute." Peter prances around to the other side of the table where a brown leather bag sits. He reaches into the bag, removes some items, and returns while Sophie looks on, gleefully. Peter takes a swig from his beer, pulls some dread strands from his face, and begins to speak: "Alan and Ronia. I've got to go here in a minute but I hope you enjoy the show. It ain't U2 but it's what I do. I want you to have these things.

He reaches out and hands them two t-shirts and a CD. Ronia unfurls one of the shirts which reveals a fluorescent, colorful, amalgamated image of sun and moon. A surreptitious smile peers from the celestial, androgynous orb as streaks of sunray and moonglow protrude on the exterior into a circular string of sentences which reads: "Into the infinity. Beneath the deepest seas. Beyond the horizons. A message of hope, love, and music of the cosmos from The Moksha Revellers; World Tour into the Eternal Now." The CD box contains the same sun/moon image. For some reason, Alan opens the CD case and discovers nestled between the lyric sheets and the plastic a thick, luscious joint. "Oh man. How can I repay you? This is so generous," Alan effuses. "Don't mention it, mon. I just want a signed copy of the book. That's all." "It's a deal," Alan responds. Alan confirms a number at the band's management in order to stay apprised of Peter's future whereabouts. "Au revoir, Ronia," Peter calls out. "Au revoir," Ronia replies. An entourage quickly escorts Peter away as he exclaims, "I hope you enjoy the show!"

CHAPTER 25
CONCLUSION

Alan and Ronia retreat to the door and depart with a proud glow to the lawn; as if by being allowed to go backstage, they had truly received providential privilege. The band on stage plays a synthesized-based modernistic upbeat version of The Beatles' "Norwegian Wood," as Alan and Ronia search for a perfect spot to see the show. They settle on a spot three-fourths of the way back that provides them a clear view of the stage and the breathtaking Irish sky in the background. While the bands playing preliminarily to Moksha Revellers run through an eclectic blend of original and cover tunes spanning the spectrum of hip hop, techno, and ambient, Alan and Ronia recline back on the grass and decide to smoke a little grass—the hallucinatory sort. Before they light the joint, Alan reaches into his backpack and grabs his original book. He picks up where they had left off, reading softly for only their ears:

"Although the future of mysticism at this time seemed inauspicious, we will find that a resilient interest in returning to the naturally spontaneous mystical state would continue throughout the centuries and sporadically arise in the most uncommon circles. Before ceasing our discussion of the major emergence of a new philosophy of action and power from the philosophy of nature and harmony, it is important to consider the significance of Zoroaster in radically transforming the mother-goddess motif toward a more pragmatic and dogmatic system. Campbell writes, 'In the orient of India no attempt was ever made to bring into play in the religious field any principle of fundamental world reform or renovation. The cosmic order of eons, ever cycling in a mighty round of ineluctably returning ages from eternity, through eternity—would never, by any act of man, be changed from its majestic way.' Beginning with the development of scientific thinking in ancient Greece and culminating in the onset of Aryan domination over the religions, a struggle began and would continue between the two opposing doctrines, the yin and the yang, if you will." "Alan, look," Ronia interrupts. The lead singer of an acid-jazz-sounding band begins to climb the light scaffolding above one of the huge amplifiers; this incites the crowd to sing along if they know the lyrics. "Do you want me to stop?" Alan asks. "Is this stuff kind of dry?" "No, please continue," Ronia responds. "Your voice is pleasant with the music accompanying it." "Alright, here I go."

"During the Persian period between 539 and 531 B.C., Zoroaster created a view of the world as being corrupt by accident and in need of reform by human action. Unlike the traditional mystical view, Zoroaster's religion sought ultimate being and truth through active engagement with the environment, not renunciation or passive acceptance. Whereas traditional views in religion had placed emphasis on the unity of all things and a primary communal importance for man, a change was occurring paralleled by early Christianity and Greek thought, one which would instill more importance in man as a rational, independent being, entirely self-sufficient with a conscious self or ego. This change would foreshadow the later industrialization of the West and the apparent dearth of mysticism to follow. Will you read for a little bit? We're actually almost finished with the book."

Alan hands the book to her. "Okay, here I go!" she announces playfully: "We would consistently find that at every turn both sociologically and psychologically toward duality, men's inevitable ruptures and errors would be unified and rectified through the mystic way. Whereas most of the world's religions mandated idiosyncratic conformance to a prescribed set of sociopolitical and legal constraints, mysticism allowed man to experience the universal wonder that every nervous system embodies and is capable of receiving and exuding independent of any orthodox guidelines. This non-dualistic perspective would strive toward finding that particular congruence between 'godliness' and 'worldliness' which would enable an individual to function appropriately within his society yet transcendently. In Campbell's terminology: 'to abide in phenomenality, as a material, social phenomenon,' while maintaining a heightened sense of God's omnipresence and realization that every object is an individual manifestation of the absolute, is truly the way of mysticism."

Ronia sets the book down and then leans to kiss Alan. They both gaze out over the masses of tie-dyed shirts, cutoffs, and tattoos. Hordes of people gather to celebrate the communal, ritualistic spectacle of a modern day concert festival. It is a celebration of life and the spirit and energy of the show that fill Alan and Ronia with excitement.

Alan observes a rich diversity of ethnicities, ages, and styles of fashion among the crowd. A lively group of blacks ranging in age from their latter twenties to early thirties dances enthusiastically with colorful African berets and flowing robes. Adjacent to them stands a group of shirtless white teenage boys with baggy jeans and various tattoos on their arms and backs; they are alternately slam-dancing in tune with throbbing percussion that echoes throughout the quadrants of the park.

There are hippies, yuppies, conservatives, liberals, young, old, wasted, sober, physically fit, and comfortably portly. Young, beautiful women in their lower twenties with midriff exposed, toned flesh, and hips swaying gently to the music, glide elegantly, hand-in-hand with boyfriends—adolescently complex, angst-ridden but optimistic athletic types with troubled expressions behind acne dotted faces that occasionally break free into smiles that glory in the comforting, uniting tunes. Optimistic, educated and trans-global in their musical tastes, these are children and adults of the new millennium. Alan senses a community of creative, ambitious, open-minded individuals who would implement change and set innovative trends, which would reverberate the planet.

As an energetic, gyrating cyclone of centrifugal dancing undulates, pulsates, and swirls into a vortex of grooves about thirty feet in front of them, Alan opens the CD container and removes the joint. Plump, firm, and delicately wrapped on the ends, this innocuous-looking—palatable to the touch—marijuana cigarette harks of realms beyond the ordinary senses, where fairies prance; humans are joined in mystical, compassionate union, and the heavens above rain tears of joyful, starry dust that sprinkles the planet with titillating, optimistic, quantum-sparkling pleasure crystals.

Alan lifts the silky, alabaster paper tendril to his mouth, carefully lights the opposite end, and smoothly but resolutely inhales the rich, fresh smoke until it subsumes and deeply caresses every microscopic pore within his mouth. He then hands it to Ronia, who promptly places it between her lips and proceeds—with eyes closed and her head leaning against Alan's lap—to smoke it.

Within minutes, he begins to experience a visual clarity and an almost indefinable, shimmering quality to the sunlight as reflected from the sundry pieces of chrome, metal, and steel on the stage equipment in the distance. He picks up the mystical book, and as a techno act takes the stage and commences to deliver a stunning, captivating display of psychotropic lights and sound, he begins to read: "The LSD experience is interestingly ambivalent in that during one episode an individual may realize his own vast cosmological importance and be elated; another experience may bring profound existential anxiety and even horror-filled moments may befall him. When Alan Watts interpreted the basic myth of Hinduism as being, 'that the world is God playing hide and seek with himself,' does this metaphor serve for some as a source of inspiration and affirmation while for others it presents an immediate terror at the prospect of eternal reincarnation and endless monotony? Perhaps the line of demarcation between the mystic and psychotic lies at the point where the individuals are given the same message and forced to either assimilate and adapt to this new information optimistically or reject it and withdraw into a protective shell of mental oblivion. John Lilly, M.D., once hypothesized that a psychotic may allow himself to slip into the 'schizophrenic state' in order to punish family and friends by forcing them to care for his physical existence. While realizing that so-called mental illness couldn't possibly always presuppose volition, there may nevertheless be a hint of truth to Lilly's hypothesis. The LSD experience is commonly articulated as the immediate realization that 'all is one—an absolute.' How one chooses or is capable of dealing with this newfound knowledge—albeit profound—may be the fundamental issue at hand. Of course, there are predisposing psychological factors that affect different outcomes for different individuals. Different levels of philosophical and emotional development must dictate different reactions to the LSD or mystic experience. Psychoanalytically, the concepts of ego development and object relations probably have their play as well, but when anyone reaches out and receives that very first message, maybe we would all do well to follow in Watts' shoes and 'hang up the phone.' Listening to an eternal empty cosmic dial tone would not be the most colorful route to wire one's existence." Alan closes the book and sets it into his bag.

"Wow, that's some pretty trippy stuff!" Ronia exclaims. "Yeah, it's pretty interesting," Alan concurs. Ronia keeps her eyes closed and her mind focused on the pure, undiluted, undifferentiated glory of neural stimulation in her head. Alan has extinguished the joint so as to conserve it for the entire show. Delectable layers upon layers of techno stimulatory aural nuances bathe their eardrums with spacey, transcendent harmonies that are perfectly conducive to the drug. Visually, Alan remains hypnotically entranced by a certain ethereal glow that pervades in soft pastel hues his entire perceptual field. Bright colors systematically refract as through a prism as thoughts begin to percolate in his mind. "Alan, how do you feel? It's simply beatific, is it not?" "Yes, it is sweetie." He leans his lips to her forehead and kisses it.

The techno band finishes their set, roadies begin to disassemble their equipment and Moksha Revellers' staff begins to bring out their equipment. A huge curtain is pulled in front of the stage. It is a large mural of Bob Marley's face in perfectly paradisiacal pot-happy countenance as he holds a joint within a cloud of smoke. The crowd disperses for refreshment breaks as they do between sets.

Alan begins to view this show as a crowning climax—an apex to his trip—being not just the particular vacation from his mind he is currently taking, but the journey upon which he had embarked from the United States and had taken him throughout the United Kingdom. He synthesizes a summary, a sort of synopsis that seems to encapsulate much of what he has read, seen, and experienced along the way. He takes out a pen and his pad of paper and begins to write down some of these thoughts, as the olfactory touch of cloves permeates the air:

"We are all God playing hide and seek with himself," he repeats the phrase that is attributed to Alan Watts. Alan continues to write down thoughts from his own mind: "If life on this planet is simply God donning and then shedding different masks, which are our faces, and the world is a grand stage inhabited by Shakespeare's 'players,' then perhaps when one appears to be 'losing a grip,' or 'out of touch with reality,' he is simply 'forgetting his lines' or 'missing his stage cue.' Albeit this particular production seems to be of grave complexity and importance, requiring all one's faculties to maintain performance continuity. Nevertheless, it is highly entertaining if you think about it. The brain is capable of providing a vast array of pleasure for the organism to experience. Within this skull, there lie profound realms and potentialities which, when properly stimulated, give rise to sundry sensations varying in intensity, quality, and duration. The physician calls it neurology and the mystic calls it illumination. The esthete simply revels in it while the monk forbids recognition of its existence, or at least prescribes a recommended dosage."

Alan notices voluminous billows of smoke that must be rising from dried ice behind the curtains. The lights above the stage appear to be in their last stage of being tested, as streams of blue, red and yellow beam sporadically. The roadies have left the stage as the background music traverses a slightly muffled, rhythmic bass line.

The diaphanous curtain reveals reds that protrude from the eyes of Bob Marley and through the mural in a generation of lifelike ambience to the icon of reggae. Alan continues to write: "As sentient beings, our nervous systems are hooked to environmental stimuli in a relationship which is by its very nature reciprocal. Try not to breathe. It cannot be done. The biggest shock to an over-inflated ego is the realization that one is not even in control of a simple respiratory function. The oxygen we inhale that propels our bodily systems willy-nilly we have the desire is a product existing out of specific environmental conditions. Neurologically, light, sound, and touch are constantly creating synapses (neural connections) in our brains—the nature of which we only have the vaguest clue. Of course, although we can exert some control over what comes into the perceptual faculties, most of the time our brains are being affected automatically and in ways that we are simply unaware. The beauty comes in openly and we happily realize our lack of control and simply allow ourselves to openly and actively participate in the interactive, biophysical adventures constantly happening. Juxtapose a photograph of the spherical layers surrounding the Earth's atmosphere to an ultrasound visual of the amniotic layers of a pregnant mother's womb. The process and structure of the tiny embryonic organism being protected from harmful effects strangely mirrors the process and structure of the cosmic organism planet Earth being protected from equally harmful effects. The developing human organism—within its spherical pregnant realm—symbolizes the developing planet within its stratospherical cosmic realm."

Alan sets the pen down and listens with great anticipation as the Moksha Revellers band is introduced and kicks off the show with a pulsating, rocking number called, "Revamp The Planet." Fluorescent green streaks of laser shoot out from either side of the stage and collide into a vortex around Peter's head. Peter's dreadlocks flop playfully, wildly around his head as he swoons and sways to jubilant reggae rhythms. Glowing, captivating light is reflected majestically off the vibrantly sweaty forehead and cheeks of Peter's face. The mural encapsulating Bob Marley is now strewn across the back of the stage as smoke trickles up from beyond the rafters and a spectrum of light prances multifariously throughout the instruments on the stage.

A spiritual, technical symphony is in full swing; Alan considers it an apex not only for himself and his travels but an apex that is somehow for all the world. That this blue planet has evolved such a spectacle seems truly amazing. Alan is not sure what tomorrow will bring.

Ronia sits up and relights the joint. After inhaling, she passes it to Alan and he assiduously inhales with a sense of pleasure and concentration unparalleled. With the tip of his forefinger, Alan gently strokes the soft curve of Ronia's cheek. She smiles and tells him that she loves him with all the divinity she can harness and all of the emotion a human can possess.

As the crowd around them suddenly stands in an uproar of cheers, Alan gazes into Ronia's crystalline, cerulean eyes and discovers that the world is sublime. He does not know where they will travel the next week nor for what period of time he will be with her. He only knows that he is thankful that he has lived to feel this moment in all its splendor.

As the band continues to play, Alan takes another puff and soon reaches a more magnified euphoric realm where colors can be tasted and sounds touched; his logical, linear mind is equally at work as it begins to contemplate the writing of his book. In the midst of the chaotic, massive gathering, a solemn, beautiful stillness arises through indefinable osmosis.

He sets the pen to paper and begins to write: "A fiery red streak shoots out across the late afternoon sky, leaving a tracer trail of alternately fibrillating and soothing retinal images. The images give way to undeniably rapturous, euphoric sensations that systematically penetrate every cell, permeate every muscle, and catapult normal waking consciousness into seemingly perpetual reverie—oneiromantic ocular orgasms, if you will."

Alan pauses and thinks of how the postscript should read. He continues to write: "I am Alan Agrippa and the journey I have taken has been a sort of Secare Mysterorum: an intersection of mysteries, or the mysterious travels. I'm not sure about the Latin, but the term seems to convey the experience I have had. It encapsulates within two words the sense of having explored interior and exterior geographies and a refreshed, spiritually alive return. I would encourage each and every one of you to find your own Secare Mysterorum and discover worlds of infinite possibility in your time on this planet. I hope you have enjoyed a vicarious journey through my eyes. For the book you hold in front of you—the book you have just read—is a document of my journey..."

"I am Alan Agrippa, wishing you all the best."

"I am Alan Agrippa..."

ABOUT THE AUTHOR

Brian Wallace is a freelance writer who lives in the Dallas area. Although writing is his full-time pursuit, he has a background in psychology and social work and has taught individuals with developmental disabilities and has run social work programs.

Although he misses the California coast, he enjoys being close to his family, particularly his grandparents and his nephews, Alejandro and Carlos.

Brian enjoys reading and was immensely influenced by writers/thinkers such as: Aldous Huxley, Alan Watts, Thomas Mann, Joseph Campbell, Hermann Hesse, Umberto Eco, Thomas Pynchon and Timothy Leary.

Music is his second great love and, if you give him a minute, he will tell you how cool are Peter Murphy, The The, Bryan Ferry, David Bowie, The Cure, Depeche Mode, Dead Can Dance, Cobalt 60, and C-Tec.

Travel is way up there. With Cherie, his compatriot in the game of life, Brian has enjoyed travels to: Scotland, England, Switzerland, Greece, Hawaii, Costa Rica and throughout the U.S. He enthusiastically recommends travel **in any state of mind**.

Brian can be reached by email at:

wallacebcm@hotmail.com (or) wallacebcm@davidbowie.com.